Sex and other bits

Ghosts and raw emotions

Sex and other bits

Ghosts and raw emotions

Fabiola Piedad Maria Alicia Reynales de Berry

This is a work of fiction. Characters, institutions, organizations, mentioned in this novel are a product of the author's vision and any resemblance to dead or alive individuals or existing entities is purely coincidental.

ISBN 978-0-9924911-0-9

By the author

Franc – life through feline eyes

Contents

Pretty little girl

It was a typical humid day, the sky was cloudy and grey. I was four years old.

My mother, grandmother Nena, auntie Tuni and great-grandmother were on their way to visit great-grandfather's grave. I had asked to be taken to visit his grave on many occasions but they always said: 'no, you are too young'.

On this particular day they said: 'yes, you may come along'.

I carried the flowers. There was a sense of expectation from my part since it was the first time I was allowed to visit great-grandfather's resting place. That place sounded very special. I thought so because of the way they talked.

I expected to see flowers everywhere, I imagined the place was like a garden, but when we arrived at the cemetery everything was silent and didn't look as I thought it would. It was a quiet and vast space with many rectangular stones that seemed to stand pointing to the sky with their sharp straight edge. There were also rectangular spaces marked on the ground with a perimeter small wall, sometimes the wall was made of just bricks on their side held with cement, others had big shiny stone blocks which covered the ground, some had vases with fresh flowers, others with old wilted ones and some spaces didn't have anything but long yellow grass in need of water.

What a strange place I thought, it also felt creepy. All of a sudden as we walked in between the grave rows which formed a path, I felt several extended hands about to touch me.

I heard deep in my head almost as if someone or several persons said: 'lovely little girl'.

I also felt the energy of whispers in my ear. Where were they? I couldn't see anybody but I felt their presence.

We started to walk along the path towards the grave, and by the time we found it my hands were sweaty and the flowers were beginning to wilt; all those people around me looking at me trying to touch me; old people, young people and children as well, my heartbeat became faster and my mouth was dry. I clung to mother's leg. Auntie Tuni and grandmothers cleaned, washed and filled the vase with water. I had the honour of placing the flowers in the vase.

After all the cleaning was done they began to say strange prayers which I hadn't heard before. Some of the prayers' words were terrifying. There was a particular one about the dead coming out of their graves on the resurrection day. My imagination saw all those dead bodies getting up and pushing the stone slabs in front of me. We left and as we walked towards the exit, all those people extended their arms to touch me. I felt a cold sensation around me in the tropical warm late afternoon. This was the first time I experienced what some people call a gift, the gift of being able to feel the spirits of the deceased and to be able to communicate with them.

I didn't say anything about those people who tried to touch me. Did they try to touch mother and grandmothers as well? I didn't ask because I thought it happened to everybody.

We lived in a beautiful colonial home of a classical style perhaps built during the early 1900's. It had an elaborated and imposing façade, the narrow tall windows were adorned with señorita wrought iron bars, those bars made with a generous swirl at the bottom; from the street the passerby saw a large solid timber, panel door painted light aqua green, distressed finish and an ornate façade painted light green colour as well. There was no garden, the house was built where the footpath finished, and when the main door opened, it revealed a wide and long corridor with another door at the end, that type of door is called a portón. As the portón opened it took the viewer into a square shaped, tiled courtyard which had tessellated tiles of varied colours laid in an array of complicated Moorish patterns.

The timber columns which supported the roof had ornate bases painted creamy colour, and the roof extended into part of the courtyard to form a cool interior space, the verandah. This space was decorated with large wicker chairs, and small tables. All the furniture pieces were placed on the shady side, and large terracotta pots with coffee plants were placed in the centre of the courtyard. The coffee plants' luxurious, shiny foliage and the red berries gave the area a cool, relaxed, and inviting appearance. The bright coloured berries seemed to complement the simplicity of the space.

The house layout presented two living rooms facing the courtyard, dining room and the main bedroom. The second courtyard was austere but full of light; here, the guest room, a couple of bathrooms, ironing room and kitchen. More timber columns framed another smaller verandah, behind it there were more rooms, those rooms faced a very large backyard with fruit trees, an old big maple tree and a variety of plants which were the living quarters of Mabel the tortoise, Pepe the Amazon monkey, Ramona and Ramón the hen and rooster; there were also a couple of big and fat ducks which for some particular reason didn't have names.

Since the death of my father, mother and the four of us shared our uncle and auntie's house. Papi and Tuni contributed not only to a privileged childhood but also gave us unconditional love and affection. Included in the family unit were also my great-grandmother and grandmother who visited us quite often. We looked forward to their visits because of the many activities that occurred during that period.

Grandmother's arrival was always a real treat because apart from the pleasure to see her, she always brought a little animal as well as sweets characteristic of the region where she came from. I remember those little parcels wrapped with banana leaf, sweet and with a delicate flavour; white and gluey because they were made with rice and milk. She also used to bring a crunchy type of bread, a bit salty and cheesy which melted in the mouth. We loved to eat the bread with hot chocolate.

From time to time grandmother brought a teenage country girl to help with the normal chores of running a household. The girls grandmother brought with her were always very shy and we used to imitate their speech. These girls stayed with us until grandmother's next visit when they returned to their homes.

Our great-grandmother sometimes arrived with grandmother as well and they remained at home for several weeks; during this time grandmother was very strict with our upbringing and fairly critical of aunty Tuni's soft and generous approach to our sensitivities and tastes.

The household became quite busy as well; relatives who knew of their visit would come to see them. The relatives often arrived for morning coffee, called media mañana, or for afternoon coffee. On Sundays, lunch lasted several hours. All those relatives who had seen us perhaps six months before invariably made the comment that we had grown up quite a lot and that was the reason they felt old.

There were also parties from time to time and a large number of guests once they had afternoon coffee started to dance to the Latin rhythms of cha-cha-cha, rumba, samba, bolero and mambo. We used to escape the zealous eyes of the nanny to watch the grownups kiss, cuddle and dance. In general the ladies seemed to be fairly rotund and displayed bright red lips which left a mark on the cheeks every time they kissed someone.

Sunday lunch was an important affair, therefore preparations started on Saturday morning with the trip to the markets to buy fresh produce. It was the custom that auntie Tuni and the kitchen maid discussed all the details, and with typical waving of arms and the crescendo in their voices each approved or disapproved an ingredient.

La Señora always selected the right ingredients and also arranged an appetizing menu for the guests to enjoy the following day. El plato fuerte or main course was organized with the finesse and precision of major surgery; herbs and spices aside, the quantity of food allocated per guest and the additional portions in case someone asked for seconds; when everything was agreed, all the ingredients were placed with care in the pot to marinate with the selected meat or poultry to blend with the flavours until the next day, Sunday.

El plato de entrada or entrée and el dulce or dessert demanded the same attentive detail, and until an agreement was reached, and finally when Tuni was happy with the ingredients selection, the work to prepare the entrées and the desserts began to take place. The sweets were mouth-watering. I remember very well el dulce de natas. Complicated and time consuming; I had to wait for a long time before I could lick the pot and the wooden spoon. The milk was placed on the stove with the sugar and cloves and a cinnamon stick was added.

The contents took an eternity to reduce under the gentle heat, and every time it reduced, the thick coating from the top was removed and placed into a porcelain container until the original amount of milk dried out. The preparations for this sweet started fairly early in the morning and were completed in the afternoon. By that time, I probably must've driven everybody insane asking how long before I could lick the pot, and after I licked the pot, I always felt sick because of the richness of the concoction didn't agree with my stomach.

Guests arrived for lunch between 1am and 2pm and everybody talked and waved their arms at the same time, we giggled a lot and imitated them like if we were in a play, and as the children started to arrive we all ran like chickens that had been left out of a box. The nannies and mothers tried to retain control but it was total chaos and in the end everybody gave up.

Great care was taken with every detail. The table was extended to fit twelve people; delicate scented flowers were beautifully arranged in the middle of the table, handmade white linen table cloth and serviettes were used; those items had been embroidered by the convent nuns.

The white and translucent porcelain plates had ornate flower design and a gold trim line on the edge; the position of the cutlery and glasses was measured with a template to make sure everything had been placed on the table correctly. The coffee began to brew early in the morning, and the fresh aroma of bread permeated the air. The service girls were dressed in soft blue and pink uniforms they also wore aprons with lace on the edge of their pockets and collars. Water, Señora? The girl would ask politely.

The children were seated just outside the dining room in the courtyard around a large round table; our mothers relaxed and trusted our respective nannies to keep a vigilant eye on us.

Around 4pm and after many cups of coffee, homemade biscuits and more cakes everybody was ready for some sort of late siesta. Some guests tried to stay awake and conquer the afternoon with juicy gossip and more coffee, others rocking on the wicker chairs had difficulties controlling their heavy eyelids until the heat forced them to close giving into cat naps; many guests just flopped on the chairs like sleepy butterflies who avoided the afternoon heat, others we noticed locked the bedroom door and disappeared for a while.

The absence of a refreshing breeze combined with the warm heat of the sun and the golden colour of the light suspended most activities, perhaps.

The only people working during that time were the maids who collected empty plates, carried jugs filled with aromatic coffee and cool lemonade. The maids never seemed to get tired. The maids never complained or showed dissatisfaction with their long working hours. They were there to serve the patrons and to attend to our needs. Most of the maids had been with the family since before I was born and although we were their family, in a way an invisible barrier kept everybody in their place. However, we loved them and they treated us with affection.

We often went to lunch at Papi's unmarried sisters. Papi's unmarried sisters were: Rosa Tulia, Mercedes, Barbarita; Stella, the youngest, was the only one who had found a husband. Barbarita sometimes invited her boyfriend as well. We used to ask mother why Barbarita had a boyfriend when she was so old. She responded: 'just be quiet'.

His eyebrows were bushy and the hairs stood up like the bristles on a brush, he had big hairy ears and both ears were full of cotton wool which gave the appearance that it grew from inside the ear. Since Stella was the only one married, her husband Luis Alonso and their three children were always there as well. Alonso was the oldest, Fabiola, was a bit older than me, and Stellita the youngest who was probably six years old.

Papi's sisters lived in a spacious old colonial house in an area which was called the old city centre. Most of the houses in this area looked like they had been built during the late 1800's;

the white painted façades were adorned with small balconies with timber balustrades and the occasional wrought iron railing; those houses didn't have a garden, the footpath terminated against the high walls of each property and the only entry was the oversized main timber door with the big door knocker and the cloister window.

Papi's sisters' house had many doors which were closed most of the time, this was in a strong contrast to our house which was filled with light and had a large garden. Their house didn't have a garden; instead it had a bare courtyard where not a single weed was able to pop the head through the cracks in the cement, and they didn't have pot plants either; probably they had an aversion to anything green.

All the rooms except the kitchen were lined with dark timber panels which stopped short of the ceiling, and muslin curtains covered the tall narrow windows. The fabric dropped on the floor like a long skirt and on the sides of the window a heavy dark material was supported with a golden plait to a hook.

The whole house had dark and shiny creaking timber floors, and the rooms were full of oversized dark antique timber furniture. Those oversized pieces gave the house a gloomy morbid feeling.

Papi's sisters, for some strange reason were absolutely noise intolerant, a characteristic which didn't seem to affect Alonso, Fabiola and Stellita who were accustomed to whisper all the time and accepted this strange habit as if it was a normal part of life.

It was a bizarre situation for us and it was really weird that we had to whisper.

During those visits we had to be extremely quiet. We talked softly, our laughter was converted into a series of muted giggles and we walked on our tip toes to keep the floor boards silent. This dull ambience contributed to the development of a morbid game we called 'spot the ghost'. Spotting the ghost kept us very quiet. Immediately as we arrived, all those ghostly figures appeared to become part of our lunch, and we saw shadows and movement behind the curtains which wasn't the wind because all the windows were locked firmly.

There were many ghosts in that old house; all of us felt their presence and that made my sister Alicia unsettled. As soon as the game started Alonso and I were able to describe the gender, age as well as the main characteristics of the individuals we felt around us. However, we never saw anybody like a normal person; all those figures looked like translucent water colours on a painting. Many times we felt a strong presence in the room, sometimes it felt like a cool breeze that passed by in front of our face. Alonso used to get carried away asking questions such as where they have come from, heaven, limbo or hell.

Sometimes we did feel scared. Often, when we were ready to leave we left the spirits hovering around as we found them. We normally returned home before dusk because Papi was reluctant to drive in the dark.

We went to bed and invariably had difficulty falling asleep, and at times we felt as if someone had followed us, and we had to leave the bedroom light on all night. Alicia used to cry a lot and in general we were very unsettled. Mother wasn't at all relaxed during those lunches either. Mother always said that there was something creepy at that place. She was unsettled by the enormous portrait of Papi's father which was hung in the main hallway, and as one entered the house his imposing figure seemed to scrutinize the visitor with a severe gaze.

He wore an army uniform with lots of medals on his lapel as well as a sword by the side, his face showed the fashion of the time when the portrait was painted, a stiff moustache with upturned ends which gave the appearance that the end of the whiskers were glued to the side of his nose.

We never told our mother about the game we played; she would have been horrified because she was afraid of the dark. We did talk about it to Deyanira, our nanny. She believed that it was bad to do those things because it showed lack of respect to the spirits that were floating around trapped on this earth. She couldn't explain what it meant.

Those lunches unsettled all of us and it took several days after our visit to Papi's sisters for Alicia to stop crying and I felt very nervous. Sometimes I would wake up during the night hearing steps in the corridor outside our bedroom as well as in the courtyard, and to the sound of someone's voice close to my ear.

We didn't engage ourselves in this game when Alonso and his sisters came to visit us, on those occasions we were free to run and play. We were very different to them; we listened to music, we were able to dance classic dances as well as popular ones, we played happy games, and we had animals in the garden which made them feel scared.

They were strange and creepy and in a way quite boring; they talked without articulating their mouth, almost as if the words squeezed out through the corner of their lips, and saliva accumulated on the side of the lips. We mentioned this to mother but she said to be quiet to avoid offending Papi.

Alonso loved our ping pong table top, he being the oldest was an accomplished player, and the game didn't stop until he won each game and we girls were terribly bored as well as exhausted. We only enjoyed their company for a short period of time, but after a while we used to feel bored and in a way it was good when they left. However, when their parents indicated they were ready to leave, they begged for some extra minutes with us.

The game we played at Papi's sisters during our visits had developed a sense of fear in me because of the things I was able to experience. I'd become more aware of something which was difficult to understand.

Sometimes I sensed a presence and a shadow similar to the ones at Papi's sisters, I felt it was odd to ask questions about it, and in addition I didn't know what to ask.

Papi and Tuni occupied the main bedroom just in front of the main courtyard; it was a large room with dim light, a little cool since the sun rays in a very shy manner only penetrated half the space because of the verandah. I felt an unusual and in-explainable element of fear each time I entered or passed in front of this room. Fairly often I experienced a fast heartbeat, goose bumps on the arms and the back of the neck. I also felt cold air around me, a sensation which wrapped my body not unlike when one walks into a large spider web.

The feeling surfaced many times until one day I discovered the cause of my fear; there was a tall, slim man standing in a corner of the room, he was peaceful and didn't want to cause any harm he said. He was there for some inexplicable reason.

He didn't move, always stood in the same corner facing the window. As I passed in front of this room I had the urge to look towards that corner. I stopped and looked in with the expectation the man made himself visible to me. He looked like those translucent water colour figures I had seen at Papi's sisters; he didn't move his lips but I understood what he said and as the years passed by I even felt his presence while Tuni and Papi were in their bedroom.

Papi had a chest infection and it was recommended that he remained in bed because the rainy season had arrived. It was easy for the chest infection to develop into something more serious due to the weakness left in his lungs, after he contracted tuberculosis at a younger age. Papi was truly pampered by auntie Tuni and by all of us as well. We all loved him dearly and since we knew him to be susceptible to severe chest infections, we were his nurses. We must've driven him crazy with our attentions.

We wanted to play games, we brought our dolls, read him stories until he fell asleep and while he tried to read the newspaper we sat quietly by the bed side and read the comic section.

It was probably around 10.30am when I brought warm milk and honey instead of coffee. Papi was reading one of his large books. The large book was English history which he had become interested in since he had coordinated the railway construction project with the English engineers, who he had great admiration for and often talked about. It was a change from his normal reading material which I loved and I used to ask him to read it to me because I found it fascinating. Pliny the Younger stories were his favourites, and I couldn't comprehend how a person could've written all that so many centuries ago and the paper didn't deteriorate.

I sat on the edge of a very high bed and began to talk to Papi when all of a sudden I felt the man's presence. The man as usual stood in the corner looking at us.

His presence really agitated me and I decided to tell Papi about it. Neither Tuni nor Papi had ever seen or felt anything; I described the man to Papi. He is tall with dark skin.

'What is he wearing? Papi wanted to know'.

'He is wearing khaki pants and khaki shirt with pockets on the front, his hair is straight brushed back, the hair is shiny and looks greasy; his skin is smooth, doesn't have a moustache and his nose is like a hook'.

'That type of nose is called an aquiline nose'. Then Papi asked if I knew what this man wanted, or whether he had said anything.

'He makes me feel scared'.

'Concentrate' Papi said. 'Perhaps someone needs help or something that Is affecting their peace has to be known, and that is the reason he is making himself known to you, because you have that special gift of perception, you feel things that other people aren't aware of. Does he have a name? Where does he come from?'

'He knows you'. He worked with you and the English engineers and he has a message. 'He is worried about the counterfeit notes he left at his house'.

'At the time everybody seemed to know about it', Papi said. But that was long time ago, why to try to make contact now?

Papi didn't say anything else, and from that day the man appeared again from time to time, until his presence appeared less frequently and eventually he was no longer there.

A secluded life

Several years of private tuition had made me eager to go to school. Mother's belief that private tuition provided a superior education was often discussed with Papi and Tuni, but mother always found powerful reasons to prove her case against the standard school system.

The nearest primary school was situated a couple of blocks away from our house; I used to stand by the window to wait for the girls to pass by on the way to their homes, during the midday recess as well as in the afternoon when they returned home. During the three years of my private tuition friendships developed with a couple of girls who passed by the window every day. The girls used to express their curiosity by asking many questions, perhaps the girls felt sorry for the lonely little girl by the window.

Señorita Pola, our tutor, was very rigid and boring; she had received her Education Diploma the previous year, before we started with our private tuition, and therefore the reason mother engaged her to be our tutor. Señorita Pola was interested in pursuing a career outside the standard school system, and she was, according to mother, the perfect person to carry out our primary education, but in her pursuit for a superior academic education, mother appeared to have forgotten the social impact isolation may bring to children.

It took a considerable effort from my part to convince mother that going to school was a good idea. Papi and Tuni tried their best to reason with mother; they often expressed concern about 'la niña' being lonely and very naughty due to the lack of interaction with other children.

I had also developed the unusual pattern of hiding when unfamiliar people arrived home. Perhaps the contact with other children in a school environment would be beneficial for her development; after that debacle my first school day finally arrived and with it a brand new uniform, new books and a new leather school bag which made the day very special. Miss Pola's job had been carried out very well. She had provided me with a solid academic standard, which made the transition to school effortless, although, it was already near the end of the third year first semester.

It was difficult for me to get used to the school routine as well as a new environment; because of the previous isolation I was very shy and didn't like the large groups the teacher formed to do certain tasks. I clearly preferred to work on my own and I was able to communicate well while there were few girls in the group, finding it quite difficult when I had to deal with larger groups. I felt I wanted to disappear.

The new academic year started. I had passed to fourth class and in addition to the standard curriculum I was enrolled in flamenco dance, piano and painting. School life was absolutely wonderful and in spite of my shyness I wanted to be the best in everything I did.

General vaccination day arrived without any warning, and at about 10am we were asked to leave the classrooms in an orderly manner and wait until called.

We heard cries and screams coming from the infirmary, the vaccination programme had started and soon it was my turn.

It didn't hurt, it felt hot. I went home for the mid-day recess feeling hot and unwell. By the time nanny Deyanira took my hand I felt as if I was going to collapse; she noticed how hot I was, and as soon as we arrived home she helped me to get into bed and called mother.

'Señora, la niña is not feeling well and she feels very hot!' I rested my aching and pulsating head on the pillow, and almost immediately I began to hear the sound of a ping pong ball, as well as steps which started from the top end of the courtyard, and followed the corridor towards my bedroom door. The ball was collected to be released once more in front of my bedroom; the sound of the ping pong ball as well as the steps became softer as the ball reached the top of the courtyard. I also heard my name called close to my ear.

La niña is hallucinating! Everybody said.

I was very sick in bed for the rest of the week, the leg where the vaccine had been applied looked like an enormous salami, the skin so red and hot, it appeared as if a fire had been lit under it; I couldn't lift the head off the pillow because of severe dizziness, and also the headache was intense, it felt as if my head was splitting in the middle, and every time I ate something, it came out faster than I could swallow, my lips were burnt and the skin cracked. I lost focus therefore everything was blurry and when I opened my eyes the room spun around me like a carousel in an amusement park.

Doctor Aureliano, said my condition was a severe allergic reaction to the vaccine and there wasn't much that could be done about it. The high temperature I experienced somehow diminished towards the end of the week and my health improved greatly. I was able to lift my head off the pillow, but fainted every time I tried to stand up. The strange thing was that I could still hear the ping pong ball and footsteps coming and going along the corridor.

I told Deyanira that I could hear the sound of a moving ping pong ball and the footsteps every time I began to fall asleep, but while I was awake the sound was stationary in front of the bedroom door.

She said: 'Niña, you were very ill and you still are'. At times we all prayed for your soul because it appeared that you almost died, you looked like a rag doll and lost consciousness many times; we knew you were alive because we could see you chest moving just so slightly. Doctor Aureliano could do nothing. He looked desperate on several occasions. Nobody slept and for the entire week someone sat by your side day and night checking that you were breathing. You felt so hot and delirious we didn't stop putting cold towels on your forehead, the towels were straight from the fridge.

'The high temperature gave you bad dreams, Niña'.

I continued to wake up many times during the night to the sound of a ping pong ball running up and down the length of the corridor, and after a while it stopped allowing me to fall asleep.

On my return to school after a couple of weeks I found out that many girls had been ill after the vaccine, but nobody seemed to have suffered the intense allergic reaction I had experienced. The health officer and the teachers were concerned about the severity of the vaccine reaction, and there was speculation that it could have been a bad batch.

It was the second day after my return to school when shortly before lunch time I saw Papi outside Señora Niní's office, the head Mistress. Soon after, Señora Niní entered my classroom and asked me to follow her. I walked alongside her towards where Papi was waiting for me.

Papi held my hand tenderly but as usual didn't say much. I didn't stop talking about all the things we did at school that morning. My stories had not yet finished by the time we arrived home and we found Tuni crying, mother looking sad; both were wearing an anguished look and a general feeling of tragedy was evident.

Mother said: 'Alonso died this morning'

The school vaccination programme was a normal school procedure, as it was a regular visit to the dentist, as well as the x rays. Alonso's school had the vaccination programme that morning, and although Alonso communicated to the health worker that he was allergic to some medications, nobody believed him. He also said that he thought he had been immunized recently but he couldn't tell the type of vaccine received.

'Alonso suggested to the health worker to call his father'.

The health worker conferred with the teacher in charge of his class but the teacher didn't believe his story; with nobody to confirm or deny his statement, teacher and health worker decided to proceed with the inoculation. Within thirty minutes Alonso had difficulties breathing and a doctor was called. Finally, contact was made with his father who left his office immediately. Unfortunately Alonso died before his father reached school.

That morning at around 10.30am Mercedes, Alonso's aunt interrupted her sewing work for morning coffee. The coffee as usual was brought to the drawing room, the tray was placed on the coffee table and Mercedes relocated to the armchair placed by the large window that faced her sister's garden.

As Mercedes lifted her head and looked towards the house across the garden, she saw when Alonso dropped his school bag and waved to her indicating he was coming across.

She acknowledged his gesture and thought that it was an unusual hour of the day for Alonso to return home. She waited for him. The sound of footsteps from the stairs and hallway were clear; after a couple of minutes she called his name, and since there was no reply, Mercedes stood up and decided to investigate. Alonso liked to play games and tricks.

Mercedes went to talk to the maid who was in the kitchen and asked her if she had seen Alonso. The maid confirmed she had seen Alonso walking across the garden. He greeted her with a brief 'hello' as soon as he entered the house, and continued to walk along the corridor straight to the drawing room.

Mercedes was perplexed and telephoned Stella to find out if Alonso had been at home. There wasn't a reasonable explanation, so Stella called the office to talk to her husband.

She was informed that he had left the office in a hurry without saying anything.

Stella and Mercedes decided to contact the school to find out if there was a problem with Alonso. However, nobody was able to give them an exact explanation, all they heard was that Alonso had become ill after the vaccination, but they were certain that he was being treated and everything would be fine. They couldn't tell whether Alonso's father was on his way. Their answers were confusing and unclear.

Luis Alonso finally returned home with the grim news of Alonso's death and immediately telephoned Papi; after Papi talked with Luis Alonso he decided to pick me up from school.

We children didn't attend the funeral, only Papi, Tuni and mother.

I have vivid memories of the days that followed Alonso's death. Our house felt extremely quiet, there was gloom, and for me, the sound of the ping pong ball every night running along the corridor didn't stop, it continued for a long while. I was getting used to it because I knew it was Alonso playing a trick on me.

On the anniversary of Alonso's death a service at the church was followed by lunch at Papi's sisters' house. Lunch was served in the courtyard perhaps to dissipate the sadness of the occasion and to take advantage of a mild sunny day. As it was the custom we children sat at the round table and nobody sat on the spot Alonso used to sit. The ambience was sombre.

A morbid gloomy silence was interrupted only by the light clicking sound of the cutlery and glasses.

The dessert was served, and as I raised the spoon I looked towards the dining room tall window. There, behind the muslin curtain was Alonso; a translucent water colour figure like the ghosts we had seen before. He had joined them and he was making signs with his hands inviting me to come over to the window. I felt very scared. On this occasion we didn't play spot the ghost, we remained on the terrace and played some card game. After this event we never went back to Papi's sisters.

Papi's sisters continued to live at the old colonial house, however after a couple of years following Alonso's death, the house was sold and soon it was demolished to make room for a large apartment complex. Tuni made the comment one day that for a long time after Alonso's death, everybody seemed to hear his footsteps and there were other strange things which happened around them, like lights being turned on during the night and day, and when they got up to turn the light off, the switch wasn't turned on, a cold breeze passed by often as they sat while they carried on with their normal life, his constant presence as they entered a room was felt.

Those series of events contributed to a very distressing time for everybody around the house, and after having lived in that house since they were little girls, more or less half a century, they couldn't be in peace anymore, and although it was a hard decision to make, the sale of the house was impossible to avoid.

We also lost contact with Fabiola and Stella. As we grew up we saw less and less of them although we did see Papi's sisters from time to time. They used to visit us. However, Alonso was never mentioned again. The absurdity of it all was, that on every occasion Papi's sisters came to our house Alonso was there with them, and I could see him poking his tongue at everybody, and making fun of whoever was around.

It was mortifying to see him; I did tell Papi that although nobody talked about Alonso he was there and it was creepy. I don't know if he believed me or whether he told Tuni and mother. Papi's sisters' visits were less frequent after that. The ping pong ball came back from time to time, and I wasn't delirious.

Life as I had known it was going to change dramatically for me and with that change a lot of things would be forgotten.

First sex lesson

The last year of primary school ended and a boarding school to continue my education was selected, it was located in a town a couple of hours from home. I wasn't at all concerned because the event looked distant from the holiday we were about to enjoy.

I was more interested in the new guests who were to arrive soon. They lived in another city and were long-time friends of Papi, Tuni as well as grandmother.

The family consisted of the mother Anita, the father Isidoro, sixteen years old boy called Yesid, Isidorito, and Anna about thirteen years old.

The family finally arrived with a nanny and mountains of luggage. Isidoro, the father was fairly tall, dark olive skin and a great big moustache similar to the ones the actors exhibited on the Mexican movie posters, it curled downwards at the ends making him look as if he had stepped out of a movie set.

The mother, Anita was a short, pale and a rotund lady, light coloured hair fixed in a bun; her very small teeth from time to time moved forward when she appeared to be absent minded.

Lucia the nanny, a tall girl with honey coloured hair. She was very different from our sweet and gentle nanny Deyanira.

Lucia was loud and bossy, she elbowed and pushed the boys and the three of them were always playing rough. Lucia and Yesid talked in a sort of code language and they laughed a lot. The topic of their conversations we hardly ever understood. When we asked questions they made fun of us and said that they couldn't tell because we wouldn't be able to understand. Isidorito, was a little subdued and a bit insipid; their sister Anna was very quiet. Initially we thought she couldn't talk.

Anna looked exactly like her mother, very pale, rounded body with fat legs and incredibly big boobs for her age. Even her brothers used to make fun of her looks and called her 'big tits', which was cruel. Probably that was the reason she didn't talk.

Lucia and Yesid organized all our games after dinner; it was always hiding and seeking. It was real fun except that it used to take a long time to find Lucia and Yesid.

One particular evening dinner was served in the courtyard, it was a lovely balmy night, the smell of banana and mango floated in the air, while the sun disappeared in the horizon the moon began to rise looking like a big tangerine balloon. The table was cleared and we all got ready for the hide and seek game. It was my turn to search for the ones hiding and I began to count to 100 before beginning the search.

I had to count loudly and in between each number I had to say the number plus half before the next number. Everybody was found except Lucia and Yesid, but nobody took any notice of that because I was the one counting. I finally decided to look for them in the backyard where Pepe the monkey and the other animals were kept.

I walked with caution to avoid making noise. I looked everywhere for them, and almost on my way out from the backyard I decided to look into the hen's house which mother called the hen's hotel, because she thought Papi had built the hen's pen with too much space and luxury. Timber boards from ground level to about a metre high to the first shelf, and a ramp with narrow pieces of timber across, as well as small compartments for Ramona and the other hens to lay eggs in privacy. As I looked into the hen's house floor Yesid was on top of Lucia his bum moving up and down and they were making strange noises. 'What are you doing?' I asked.

They looked surprised, sweaty and flustered; their heavy breathing was as if they had been running. 'Get lost' they told me. Yesid stopped moving his bum but stayed on top of Lucia, her legs were spread open and her skirt lifted. I just stood there.

Composing themselves quickly, they said: 'We were doing some sort of special type of exercise; I could exercise as well if I didn't tell anybody about it, and they laughed'.

Somehow I didn't believe they told me the truth, it had to be something else.

The following day they talked in an irritating code, they whispered all the time in each other's ear; they looked at me and laughed. It annoyed me not to be able to know their secret, and from that day I began to pay a lot more attention while they talked, but couldn't understand anything.

I'd begun to like Yesid, and I was experiencing the first symptoms of jealousy. Yesid had grown taller; he was a very beautiful boy, golden skin, black hair, dark eyes with long curly lashes and a contagious laughter, when he laughed his beautiful super white teeth showed all their perfection.

Our relationship changed temporarily, and I felt angry. Since they didn't want to tell me their secret, I was going to avoid playing this game.

This frosty situation only lasted a couple of days until Yesid and Lucia asked me if I knew the meaning of the word coitus. I said no, but I would look in the dictionary and they laughed loudly as I went to look for it.

'Coitus': Technical term for sexual intercourse. From Latin: a uniting, from coire to meet, from ire to go. How strange, the dictionary didn't explain what the word was at all, and it didn't mention either it was the name of a particular form of exercise. Then I looked at the word intercourse, the meaning given was: 'communicating or interchange between individuals'.

It was very confusing indeed. Unable to understand the obscure meaning provided by the dictionary, and with the book in my hand, I went back to them and asked for an explanation; again they laughed and made fun of me as they said I couldn't even read properly and refused to tell me.

Lucia, after letting out a loud belly laugh finally walked out of the room.

Yesid whispered in my ear that coitus was the name given to the act of putting a chocolate bar in the woman's parts; with a big grin offered to show me how it was done and reassured me it felt really and truly fantastic. Better than anything else I had ever tasted, but I couldn't tell anybody if he showed me. 'Tell me when you want me to show you'. He smiled.

This subject was confusing and difficult to understand, therefore, I didn't bother about it anymore.

Our games continued, Lucia perhaps more cautious. I didn't catch them again doing their exercises. Yesid became fairly affectionate towards me, sometimes he would jump from behind a door kissed and embraced me; then we started a kiss and tickle game, our brothers and sisters tickled but Yesid and I kissed more frequently.

I didn't know that was love, but I wanted to be near Yesid all the time. His mother sometimes made strange remarks I didn't know the meaning of. There was an occasion when we had been kissing passionately, and Yesid arms were wrapped around me when his mother walked into the room; she took Isidoro's belt, lifted her arm and belted Yesid with a strong force over his legs.

I was sitting behind the sofa when Anita and Tuni entered the drawing room while they talked about Lucia, the nanny, and some sort of suspicion Anita had. Anita continued telling Tuni that with teenage boys it was incredibly difficult to keep any sort of domestic assistance. She had the feeling that something was going on between Lucia and Yesid. She hadn't caught them yet, but it was just a matter of time before she did, like it happened with the other one.

'What happened with the other one?' Tuni asked.

Anita continued, oh that girl was absolutely fabulous; she was gentle, I liked her like one of the family until I found out that not only she was giving it to papa Isidoro, but to Yesid as well.

She used to leave the door open for whoever was ready to enter her rooms; as a matter of fact papa Isidoro was the one who found Yesid giving her oral. Since I was ignorant of what was going on, I obviously didn't understand why papa Isidoro insisted on getting rid of her.

The day I found out that continuous sex encounters had been going on under my nose for months I really hit the roof. I went to play bridge and returned earlier than usual, didn't make any noise, took my shoes off and quietly walked the length of the corridor towards the maid's quarters and there he was. Yesid had entered her room, she was totally naked on the bed, her legs spread as wide as possible ready for it as she told him, I hesitated for a second, meanwhile I heard her moans and when I pushed the door open Yesid had his head deep into her crutch, he was also naked. As I opened the door, of course she jumped and tried to cover herself. When I told her to get her belongings ready to leave, she tried to upset me more by confessing that el Señor Isidoro had also benefited from her and she, therefore was entitled and wanted some sort of compensation before she left.

I was so angry with myself that these things had been occurring under my nose for months; all I wanted at that moment was for her to disappear, but before her departure, I, in a rage demanded that she told me everything, and when all that had started.

'Are you sure Señora?'

'Yes, I am positive!' I said full of fury.

'The first person was Señor Isidoro, it was really an accident because I was expecting el joven Yesid. I had agreed to leave the door ajar for him. I had a shower, dried myself and absolutely naked I stood in front of the mirror when Señor Isidoro walked into the room. I tried to cover myself but he said my body was too beautiful to hide and put his hand into my crutch; because it felt good I let him run his fingers all over the inside and when he had a big one I ate it there and then. He composed himself and left after asking me not to say anything and that on the following pay packet I would be rewarded'.

'Later that night el joven Yesid appeared in my room and as agreed we did it, of course I didn't tell him that his father had eaten me first. The encounters continued with Señor Isidoro, to be honest I didn't expect it, but I allowed it because I really liked what he did and I was learning new things which I could teach to el joven Yesid; I tried to satisfy them both; my pay packet increased and everybody was really happy, consequently I didn't think there was anything wrong with it because whatever we did it was always satisfying'.

I gave her all the money I had in my wallet and she left.

That night I could've ripped papa Isidoro's instrument, but as usual his fingers began to do their job, and in the process excited me, and since he is always so good in bed, and the dexterity of his member is so exquisite, everything returned to normal in a matter of seconds.

Deyanira entered the room and asked Tuni about the children's dinner menu; Anita and Tuni left the drawing room and I was more confused than ever; tried to find the meaning of crutch which didn't make sense with letting the fingers run inside. I was dying to ask Yesid about it and finally the opportunity to talk to him presented itself.

We sat for dinner and as usual he was next to me. 'What is the crutch and how do the fingers walk into it?' I asked. He let his hand under the table and touched me. Nothing else was said.

The school holidays came to an end, Yesid and his family returned to their home, and for me it was time to go to boarding school.

Two men arrived one morning with bails of wool and large needles to manufacture the mattress I was to take to school; specially made with pure merino wool, not those cheap ones made of cotton which were available at the furniture store. This was the last item to be marked with all my names; four given names and two surnames were written in black ink on each item. It was Sunday afternoon when Papi, Tuni, mother and I arrived at boarding school. A large timber gate painted grass green in front of us; the colour had lost its vibrancy a long time before. An ordinary, ugly three storey, pale yellow brick building with small timber windows, it was not the gracious colonial structure surrounded by trees, flowers and a fountain in the middle as the photo on the prospectus cover.

I felt such apprehension and fear, my stomach knotted and I felt sick, with a faint voice I said: 'please do not leave me here, take me home'. The doorbell was pressed and a small door within the gate opened, a nun dressed in black wearing a white, very tight head cover, which hid her hair and ears and on top of it another black veil, very pale and wrinkly face with a sour look. 'Is she the new girl?' She asked.

We entered a cool, dimly lit corridor with highly polished, mint green terrazzo floor and two large timber pews along the walls; a T shaped corridor, one end revealed a large glass panel door which looked like it never opened, and the short end of the corridor had a heavy, brown timber door, which had a cloister window covered with thin metal bars that formed a cage on one side, on the other side the opening was covered with a flap held by a clip to keep it closed. It was surreal; it seemed like a bad dream. We had to follow the nun to a small office to fill out some forms and for mother to sign the admission papers. Papi and Tuni looked concerned and mother looked worried. The nun proceeded to give several instructions about where to place the luggage and explained the unloading system. I just stood there as if I was paralysed and didn't know what to do. My belongings unloaded and after the admission forms were completed, the nun said it was time to say goodbye and to acquaint myself with the school surrounds. In a sharp tone of voice she said: 'Let's go!'

I turned to Papi, Tuni and mother, who stood there with some hesitation not knowing what to do; they looked as distraught as I felt. 'I don't want to stay here' I said in a faint voice. 'I want to go home'. A flood of tears poured down my cheeks, soon the tears became loud sobs, and the fear of being left in this horrible place filled my mind with a kind of panic I hadn't felt ever before.

There was no choice but to follow the nun along a green polished terrazzo corridor; several rooms on the left and an enormous concrete patio on the right with a flag pole in the middle. A large, ugly space with no trees no flowers, not even a weed popping its head through a crack could be seen. The sandstone wall of the chapel, tall and imposing, curved towards the end of the patio, it separated the big patio from another space; everything was so daunting and enormous for a little girl that until then had never been alone or separated from the family.

A large covered verandah connected this building with the chapel, and at the end of the verandah on the left a wide staircase to the first floor; several classrooms on one side of the building, the other side with an open verandah. It took a while before we arrived at another wide staircase.

The second staircase terminated on the second floor, the dormitories. Light, mint green terrazzo floors everywhere, the corridor, the dormitories the staircases; on either side of the corridor enormous rooms with many rows of beds along the windows, rows of beds in the middle and against the corridor's wall.

Groups of girls were chatting in an animated way, others sat on their own crying, and their red noses indicated that they like me had been crying for a while. Some girls looked at all this with bewilderment and with panic painted on their faces just the same I felt. Rolled mattresses were placed on the floor, piles of luggage and from time to time the loud scream when someone found a friend. I just stood there not knowing what to do until a short nun who moved rapidly and twirled around as if she had wheels under the sole of her shoes, asked my name and then she pointed out my allocated bed where the merino wool mattress and the rest of my luggage were on a pile.

Next to my belongings on the other bed, was a girl who seemed as lost as I was; she was small and skinny, medium length dark straight hair, cut in a bob and a fringe, very bushy brows joined in the middle over her nose.

'I am Yvonne' she said. 'I am the youngest and only girl from a large family'. Her parents had decided she needed a proper education because with eleven older brothers her manners imitated the masculine side of the family.

She mentioned that her parents lived far away in another city. Her guardian brought her to school, and he was the person who was going to look after her needs from here on. While she talked I stopped crying, but I couldn't say anything about myself, my life at home was very different and I did not behave in a masculine manner.

The nun instructed me to carry on making the bed and to begin to put my belongings away. I rolled out the merino wool mattress; it was thick and heavy, it also spilled on the sides of the narrow metal framed bed, like a fat person's bum overflows over the side of a narrow chair, it certainly looked very different from the ones bought at the shop.

To me it looked soft and welcoming, thick enough not to feel the metal springs of the narrow bed. I liked it. It was different from all the other mattresses. When the bed was made it looked round on the edges, not square like the other beds. The next task was to fit all my belongings including the shoe polish bag into a bedside table which had one drawer at the top, and a tiny little door underneath. Not a lot fitted into that confined space, so I left the rest in my suitcase under the bed.

At the sound of a bell nuns appeared from everywhere in the same way ants come out from their nests before the rain; they clapped their hands and with stern voices ordered everybody to proceed to the corridor to form a neat and orderly line, and to wait there for further instructions.

We walked to the corridor and stood there waiting for a while until a loud speaker announced it was 6pm. It was the beginning of the absolute silence. For me it was as they spoke in a foreign language because I didn't know what an absolute silence was. Not knowing what was going on, it was a moment of distraction from my anxieties. First, the sharp sound of a whistle followed by several nuns clapping their hands in unison to direct us to the chapel; the clapping of hands was the way to communicate during absolute silence, I learnt later, however it was a shock introduction to a really bizarre practice.

It was Sunday and therefore it was necessary to attend Mass complete with long sermons, hymns and prayers, the absolute silence was going to last until 7am the next day the voice said. We followed in an orderly line until we were ordered to sit on long pews; each place had a book with black cover, the pages printed on translucent paper which was full of pencil and biro marks, some drawings and remarks which probably the nuns had never seen.

Following Mass and keeping with the absolute silence we were directed to the dining room; we had to wait again in a line until directed to the place assigned for each person to sit during meal times. We finally made it to the dormitories; it was around 9pm.

My bed was made but the suitcase still to be unpacked; there was no room available for most of the personal effects. Some small pieces fitted in the very small bedside table, but aprons, the uniform and bed sheets were an impossibility to fit in. Shoes, shoe polish, etc were all pushed into the lower section of the bedside table but the door didn't close.

I pushed everything else under the bed, changed into my pyjamas and jumped under the blankets and with me the saddest feeling of loneliness and abandonment.

The nun in charge of our dormitory rushed to my bed pulled my arm out and made me kneel, we still had to say the last evening prayer. 'Do we have to say more prayers? We prayed a lot while in the chapel. God must be tired of listening to all this', I said. The nun gave me a dirty look and with sign gestures indicated to stop talking. Finally the lights were turned off and I put myself to sleep trying to suffocate the loud sobs under the blanket; it appeared that we had just fallen asleep when we awoke from a deep sleep with a loud ring while it was still dark; again the nun clapped her hands and urged everybody to get up.

My eyes incredibly heavy and dry didn't want to open; all those awful fluorescent lights were turned on to shine over our faces like elements of torture. We got dressed and half asleep marched along cold, light green terrazzo corridors, and after several flights of stairs we finally arrived at the chapel where all lights were turned on. Strong smell of incense, many candles on the altar, and nuns seated alongside the building perimeter walls. Some loud organ music began to fill the chapel, and we had to stand up.

The priest entered while the organ music continued to play and then we sat on those cold hard timber pews. The priest began to talk about the return from holidays and the sins that might have been committed while being idle. He continued to talk for a long time until the sound of his voice became more distant. I was awoken from a cat nap to the sound of bells and the sound of people walking along the isles on the way to the altar to receive communion.

This chapel episode stretched for hours until we were finally ready to leave. I was almost on the verge of collapse because I hadn't eaten since I'd left home the day before.

The Mass service completed, we proceeded to the patio with the flag pole in the middle, and in silence and always standing in a line, until the nuns directed everybody where to stand before we began to walk towards the dining rooms.

The absolute silence reached its end for the day but not knowing anybody I remained silent. I stood there forming a line mesmerized by the austere, ugly surroundings and the loud chatter of those girls who were acquainted with the way of life.

We once again arrived at the dining room which was rectangular, had two sets of dark heavy timber doors in the centre; it was a room without windows, and it faced another concrete courtyard. A set of long tables ran parallel to each side of the long walls and followed the shape of the room. The tables were covered with white heavy textured linen tablecloth. The centre of the table had a jug of water and ten plates along each side; on each plate a little, pale, sickly looking orange, and a minuscule bread roll.

Several maids placed simultaneously two metal jugs on each table, one jug with coffee, the other with chocolate, the aromas filled the room. As the contents of one of the jugs filled the first cup a brown coloured liquid stained the white table cloth, the stain looked as if a chocolate tablet was dipped in water for a second or two to provide the liquid with colour; the other jug had coffee. The coffee served had the appearance of a street drain after heavy rain. Following this meagre breakfast the nun in charge said that before leaving the dining room she would inspect the tables to check on the cleanness of the table cloth. She would grade the tables according to how clean the table cloth was because that was a clear indication of the social class we belonged to.

We sat there waiting for the inspection, the nun arrived at each table, and as she inspected the table cloths she began to say that some girls were like raw livers, and therefore during the following sitting, which would be lunch, the tables would be re-arranged for the girls of the same social class to sit together, and not to have to endure the bad manners and roughness of the lower class individuals. It sounded bad and we left with our heads low and with great concern about being placed as a lower class. We also wondered what it was to be a raw liver, whatever it meant.

We assembled again within the confine of the concrete patio with the flag pole in the middle; the bell rang indicating it was time to proceed to the classrooms which were located on the first floor. The nun in charge of each group signaled her group to follow. My classroom was located on the side of the concrete patio with the flag pole in the middle. It was fortunate to be given a seat by the window because I could see the sky and the sun shone over my desk. The nun in charge gave instructions, and our lessons started. It was only 9.00am.

I felt as if I hadn't gone to bed for several days; sleepy, tired and missing home so terribly it was difficult to cope with such a different world. The following days passed by ever so slowly; the loneliness seemed to be overwhelming. I couldn't understand why I ended up at this place and my heartache was an impossible emotion to describe.

I often thought about Pepe, the monkey who I loved so much; I wondered whether he was suffering because of my absence as much as I was suffering this separation from everything that was dear to me. I thought about Chispas the little Spanish terrier that used to sit with me while I did my primary school homework. I believed the years of private tuition were lonely because I didn't have other girls to talk and play with, here I was surrounded by hundreds of girls, but there was a terrible loneliness everywhere.

A different world

The first month passed by, it was a lonely and sad time indeed. It was difficult to eat horrid food and sometimes we found white maggots in the soup, at other times several groups experienced food poisoning, and in addition we had the fear of being called raw livers. Anybody who spilled food on the table, a diminutive speck of food which stained the table cloth, condemned the person to stand up in the middle of the dining room as punishment for possessing bad social skills and belonging to a low social class.

The person, according to the nun, had to be humiliated in order to improve the manners, and to help mould the individual to achieve a better social status.

There was a particular menu we called poison menu because without fail it created midnight havoc, and during the wee hours the whole group made the trip to the bathroom. The feared menu consisted of rice, two slices of salami and a cooked mango, this concoction was served at least once a week and although we felt hungry many of us ignored the food to avoid being sick.

The other casualty in our simple life was hygiene; we were unable to shower every day because the ratio of shower cubicles was inadequate for the number of boarding girls. In a way it was fortunate since only few showers had hot water connected to them. The water's origin was the melted snow of the cordillera, as the melted snow entered the flow of the river, and made its way to the water reservoir the icy water was so incredibly cold that when each droplet fell on the head, it felt like a sharp needle was perforating the skull. It was also mandatory to wear a garment made out of cotton which covered the entire body while we showered. This was necessary in case the nun opened the door, so the garment acted as a curtain between our naked body and the nun's voyeurism. What did she have to open the shower door for?

Visits were permitted the first Sunday of the month; the visit took place on the ground floor salon near the main entry. There were three rooms allocated for these visits and nobody was allowed to leave school. The Sunday visit finally arrived! As soon as the loud speaker called my name, I ran as fast as possible towards the visitor's room. Papi, Tuni, and mother were waiting for me by the door. My eyes were filled with tears, the anxiety grabbed my throat so tight I was unable to speak, and the deep distress converted the tears into loud sobs, the suffering and loneliness I had experienced had overwhelmed me. I cried inconsolably, there was so much to tell but the profound emotion didn't allow any sentences to be formed.

The sadness of it all took over and didn't allow me to put a month of loneliness and grief together for them to understand that life was truly awful.

Mother decided to talk to the nun in charge while Papi, and Tuni tried to ease and soothe my pain, but the intensity of my distress was aggravated by their attention. I was only able to say: 'please take me home'. The bell rang and the visit finished.

Papi,Tuni and mother who had just arrived had to leave. The sign on the big timber door indicated that the visit time was in between 10am and 4.30pm. The sign on the timber door did not specify that visits were interrupted for prayer and lunch at 12 o'clock sharp.

Papi, Tuni, and mother obeyed the order and without any objection began to say goodbye, they kissed and embraced me. I stood there as they started to walk towards the door, my faint pleads became screams muffled by tears and loud sobs. They turned around and cuddled me once again.

Papi said 'I would get used to it'.

Pain like a blade cut through my heart, the agony of being left behind was too much to bear; I stood there totally paralysed and overwhelmed with strong feelings of loneliness and abandonment.

I didn't move, I just cried. I wasn't the only one who had felt that way. Several girls pleaded with their parents to take them home. The tense ambience of this room was saturated with tears, and a cloud of despair wrapped the chairs and the individuals sitting on them.

Several parents had arrived just before noon and to their surprise the visit had been terminated. Somebody's father said to the nun who roamed the room: 'I brought my child to have a good academic education; I wasn't told you run these premises like a prison'.

He took his daughter's hand, walked towards the gate, pushed it open and they left. The room fell silent all of a sudden, and the sound of his deep self-assured voice stopped my tears.

I felt happy that someone had left. Several girls left school that afternoon; unfortunately I wasn't one of them.

I pushed open the heavy timber door which led to the big patio with the flag pole in the middle; many girls had formed groups, and they were getting ready to proceed to their respective lunch rooms to leave the parcels their parents had brought them. Parents had brought biscuits and other goodies which were shared at the dining table.

The rest of the day moved so very slowly. I sat behind a desk in a large, cold study room, the blue of the sky seemed so far away and I had a terrible headache. Rows and rows of desks, the desks had girls sitting behind them, their minds lost in space and their eyes staring into infinity, at the same time a record player filled the room with the melodious sounds of Beethoven pastoral symphony.

I rested my head on the desk and closed my eyes, then began to listen to the crescendo sound that created the storm, and fell asleep while the storm began to dissipate allowing the sun to shine again.

I was familiar with classical music, mother as a student of the conservatoire of music, had taken me to orchestra and opera rehearsals many times. The familiarity with some classical music seemed to calm me down temporarily. It was quite fortunate that classical music was introduced on Sunday afternoons by Sister Federica. She was slim, from time to time strands of blond hair accidentally popped out of her uncomfortably tight white headdress; her light almost translucent grey eyes looked distant and sad, she was in charge of the physical education programme as well as Sunday study time.

We thought Sister Federica was peculiar because every time we had physical education classes, we marched most of the time to the sound of military tunes, and we had to extend our leg forward exactly the same way German soldiers marched on the movies. We gave her the nickname Adolfo.

Despite these peculiarities I liked her because she brought music into our dreary life, but most girls disliked her choice of music; they found classical music to be dull and unappealing, they would have preferred to listen to popular music instead. I loved her choices, one of my favourites was Vivaldi's four seasons, Chopin piano concertos and classical Spanish guitar; those sounds really transported me home, and for me, there was one thing at least I was familiar with, and that created a temporary tranquillity within my disturbed self.

Another month passed by, still felt depressed and I often remembered Papi when he said 'I would get used to it'.

Those words didn't bring me comfort, instead I felt more depressed, lonely and abandoned, it was difficult to focus my attention during classes, I felt more like a flower dying of thirst.

Sunday visit arrived. Papi and Tuni visited me without mother, I begged them to take me home with them; Papi calmed me down with his kind, loving words; he reassured me that he would discuss it with mother, and quite possibly an alternative school would be found.

By the time Papi and Tuni left, I was still sad and in tears, but I knew for sure that Papi and Tuni would do their outmost to discuss my loneliness and unhappiness with mother, and this time I had the opportunity to let them know how I felt. I believed they would find a solution, and therefore, I would wait another month with the great hope that I would go home.

Three months had passed by; Yvonne who was older seemed to be more resilient and mature than me. She had become a good friend. She was kind, but I doubted whether she really understood how lonely I felt, because to me, she appeared to be more like a boy and I didn't think she had the same upbringing I had. She was very unrefined, the way she ate her food reminded me of the workers that from time to time arrived home to carry out some repairs; Yvonne had an unusual way of eating bread, instead of tearing little pieces she put the whole piece of bread in her mouth and tore it with her canines.

I had grown with so much attention, pampering, and refinement and Yvonne lacked refinement. Even at that early age I noticed the difference. Inez, the other friend showed great generosity towards me, she shared the parcel contents her parents sent every week. Inez was a sweet gentle girl, dark soft skin like the colour of caramel, shiny hair and a very pretty face. These girls were as lonely as I was, but they were strong and had assimilated well. They didn't receive many visits because their respective families resided in distant cities. Yvonne and Inez appeared wise, didn't cry as often as I did. Both girls were the youngest children from large families; Yvonne had eleven brothers and her parents were fairly elderly, Inez had six brothers and sisters. I wondered sometimes whether this fact made all the difference in adapting to the boarding school system.

I was the oldest child. My life until then had been lived in a silk cocoon environment. I had the same nanny since birth. Deyanira. She helped me get dressed, my uniform was always pressed and ready. She combed my very long and abundant hair, prepared my breakfast, and when I was ready to go to school delivered me to Papi, who very patiently walked with me every day to the school gate. At breakfast Deyanira extended her hand pretending to read a menu which offered everything I fancied, and then as I chose from her imaginary menu, breakfast was served. During primary school days Deyanira waited for me at the gate during the midday recess as well as at 3pm when classes finished in the afternoon, and then I returned home to Papi and Tuni's warm, unconditional love and attention, as well as mother who always had been affectionate and motherly in spite of her youth.

Chispas, the Spanish terrier greeted me at the door waving her tail, after saying hello to everybody the first priority was to run to the backyard holding a piece of cake in my hand to share it with Pepe, the monkey and Chispas. I sat close to his tree house, he sat on my shoulder, his little arms around my neck and Chispas sat near my feet. The three of us shared the cake. Pepe removed small crumbs from my face and my skirt then he groomed me; parted my hair and ran his fine fingers through it. We had a tremendous bond; when Pepe arrived home from the Amazon forest, he was in a little cage his capturers had put him in, perhaps he was hungry the morning of his arrival at our house, and I gave him a piece of fruit. He took the fruit and in the process bit my finger, his bite drew blood and I cried; it didn't matter to me that he bit me, I gave him another piece of fruit and then he put his little hand through the wires and touched my face.

All that warmth and affection I had grown up, my animals, the large garden with the many trees and plants, everything so remote from the new environment. The absence of all those comforts made me suffer.

I was at this boarding school, away from home and everything that provided a sense of belonging. I had never felt loneliness, abandonment, and isolation as I was experiencing here; these feelings until then I didn't know existed.

I couldn't make my bed to look square like the others because I had a merino wool handmade mattress; my long abundant hair was a nightmare, it was impossible to comb the knots out of it. My uniform was without doubt wrinkled, and the pleats were marked on the wrong spot since it was difficult to hold the heavy mattress while the pleats were adjusted. Yvonne and Inez helped me make the bed, the thick heavy merino wool mattress made them laugh; it always looked bulky, voluptuous and different, as it was saying on my behalf: 'I do not belong here'.

We had been allocated a fixed desk position in the class room. A day girl sat at the desk behind me, a tall girl, kind and gentle. Her name has disappeared from my memory. During class one day she said that she could help to unknot my hair, so I gave her my big comb which I think was hardly used. She began in a gentle way the daunting task of removing three months of accumulated knots. While she combed my hair I thought of Deyanira, and everything else I missed from home; I allowed my imagination to run free and in a magic moment I was transported home. I could see Papi and Tuni having morning coffee, mother running around as she always did, Pepe under the shade of the maple tree and Chispas the Spanish terrier stretched in front of Pepe, the ducks foraging for worms under a carpet of dead leaves, and I could almost smell the trees. Reality awakened my mind, I felt tightness in my chest and my heart began to ache, those tears that until then had silently run down my cheeks turned in a torrent of uncontrollable sobs.

The nun was terribly annoyed by the disruption, and accused the girl who was combing my hair of disturbing the class, and sent her out of the classroom. The nun then demanded of me to stop the nonsense, otherwise I would have to stand on the concrete patio with the flag pole in the middle for everybody to see how ridiculous my behaviour was.

The days just passed, one after the other. Every day was the same, the only difference was that some days were cloudy and other days were sunny. Easter arrived and we had to remain at school. We were about to experience three days of absolute silence, fasting, and chapel services during the day and night, and we could only read religious books until Easter Sunday. During this period of silence I thought about escaping as another girl had done few weeks before. Nobody knew how she managed it. There was a rumour about a window at street level near the theatre. If I could find that window which was low enough to the ground I would be able to jump to freedom.

It was Good Friday. The chapel service finished at 5pm and everybody was directed towards the main patio, while the nun wasn't watching, I managed to hide behind a wall until I considered it was safe to proceed to the stairs that ended on the third floor, where more dormitories were located. This new part of the building had been built inside the walls of the old colonial building. The old monastery was built on the perimeter of the land with courtyards in the centre, vegetable gardens, flower beds and beautiful big trees which obviously had been removed to allow the extension of the new building, which included the theatre and another concrete patio. We knew this because there were old photos scattered around the corridors walls.

On the dormitories level there was a wide verandah and half way below the verandah floor, the tiled roof of the theatre. This roof extended to meet another verandah where there were doors to the upper level of the theatre storage rooms.

The toilets below had small square windows not too high from the street level, and those windows didn't have bars or any other type of security. Engrossed in thought while calculating where to land and how to jump onto the roof below, I experienced a cold, uncomfortable sensation around me, it was as if someone standing next to me had opened a window and a cold gust of wind touched me.

I turned around expecting to see somebody, but no one was there. Again I tried to figure out how to jump on the roof below when I felt as if someone was about to touch my shoulder. I turned my head to look, but no one was there. I began to climb on top of the wide railing, one foot on it with the other ready to come up when the nun who was in charge of the choir appeared. Sister Barbarita was her name, an older nun who taught chemistry and physics.

'What are you doing girl?' She asked calmly with a stern voice. She put her arm around me, and asked my name and the reason for being there, when all the other girls had gathered in the main patio. I began to cry. I told her how terribly lonely it was without my parents and sisters. I missed my animals, the garden, the trees, and the dance and piano classes. She was kind, and when I mentioned the dance and piano classes, she said that I could join the choir if I liked music. She asked many questions; I mentioned the things I disliked the most, then with her arm around my shoulder she suggested that we walk down to where the other girls were. While we walked she said that where I was standing a girl had a terrible accident which was the cause of her death; she had intended to jump onto that roof perhaps with the idea of escaping the school walls.

We began to walk towards the main patio where everybody was standing in an orderly line ready to proceed to the dining rooms. Sister Barbarita approached the nun in charge of my group and left.

I joined the choir and Sister Barbarita made a memorable introduction. She said to the other girls that I was a great asset, because of my good musical ear, and that I could play the piano as well as dance. I thought it was a kind introduction. There was choir practice twice a week; Sister Barbarita made the effort to talk to me every time, but I couldn't understand why she always called me Sophia.

The choir group was invited to visit other schools from time to time; schools which belonged to different religious orders, and we could appreciate the tremendous difference. No other religious order was as strict as our school nuns. We appreciated those fantastic outings because we mixed with other girls, had good lunch or afternoon tea with cakes and biscuits. As a bonus for good behaviour Sister Barbarita and her assistant, the Sister who played the piano, allowed us the freedom to walk within the perimeter of the school outside the school walls. I looked forward to the choir practice, it broke the monotony and in the process a good relationship developed with Sister Barbarita, who was a different nun from the rest.

June, and the time to go home on holidays arrived! Five long months had passed since I left home. As the days drew closer to the holiday release, the sunsets did not arrive fast enough to allow a new sun rise to begin a new day. Time stood still until the day to leave for our holiday finally arrived. My name was one of the first names to be called on the loud speaker. I ran to the gate and there she was, Mamá Nena, my grandmother waiting to take me home. It was wonderful.

'As soon as we arrive home I would tell mother I don't want to return to this horrible place! What do you think grandmamma?'

We arrived home after two long hours, everybody was expecting me. Mother, Papi, Tuni, but my sisters who had almost forgotten about me looked at me with curiosity and said:

'Nené you look different. Are you the same Nené who used to live here?'

Everything felt and looked very strange to me, and my sisters looked at me with certain bemusement, touched me as if I wasn't the same person they knew. Deyanira, the nanny was gone. Mother said 'Deyanira left because she wanted to get married'.

Several days after my arrival there was a strong and loud argument; Papi, Tuni, Mamá Nena, and mother disagreed with something so vigorously it affected the normal calm of the household, with loud voices and shutting of doors.

After the loud voices dissipated, grandmother made the comment that Papi and Tuni were upset because mother had begun a relationship with a man they didn't approve of. However, without having met the gentleman in question, it was her opinion, that the best option was to allow mother to make her own decision. Mamá Nena indicated that I was too young to understand these complexities, and in spite of my persistent questions, she didn't offer more information. She said 'shouting and getting angry will not resolve anything'.

I asked myself why every time there was a storm certain events occurred; those events which appeared to arrive with the thunder and the lightning had the capacity to change the course of life, so when mother asked me to get ready because we were going out to the theatre to see a play, I thought it was strange.

'But it is raining' I said. Mother insisted I had to go with her; the absence of any interest from my part was no deterrent. We arrived at the theatre and were greeted by an old man, well dressed in a dark suit and coat; he had been waiting for mother, I noticed his false teeth. He shook my hand and offered me a box of chocolates.

Was this the man Papi and Tuni so strongly disapproved of? His name was Maximiliano, he was mother's friend. He had light grey eyes, black hair, and greasy, olive skin complexion, possibly he had been a handsome man in his youth, but he looked pretty old to be mother's future husband.

There was something I didn't like about him. 'I am always like that; I like or dislike a person instantly'. There was no obvious reason to dislike him, it was an immediate reaction. Perhaps his dismissive manner or it could've been the fact that obviously he didn't want me to be there. I was an imposition he didn't expect, and he had to control his displeasure towards me. He hadn't met grandmother and my other sisters.

The rest of the holidays continued to be quite uneventful, no parties, not many people visited and we didn't go places. There was tension and unfriendliness between Papi, Tuni and mother. Mother was difficult to approach, she was always angry, she didn't want to listen to my grievances about school, and as far as she was concerned, I was attending a prestigious school and that was the end of it.

Mamá Nena indeed tried to persuade mother to find an alternative school closer to home, her refusal was even more heart breaking for me when I discovered my sister Fena had been matriculated at a sister school 30 minutes away from home, while I found myself getting ready to return as a border, just three weeks after I had arrived home for holidays.

A week after my 11th birthday and the holidays over, Mamá Nena took me back to school. It didn't matter how much I cried and pleaded not to be taken back, nobody listened.

Just sex

The house, the life left behind had become part of a happy past, the happiness of my childhood was gone and the future disintegration of my family life had just begun. We left home and I returned to boarding school, as we left I felt that I had lost everything; ahead of me, six more months away from home.

We arrived at the school gate, this time I didn't have many tears, I was overwhelmed by sadness of a different kind; it felt as if I wasn't going back home ever again. It felt as if I had been totally abandoned and that nobody cared, not even Mamá Nena was able to help me anymore, she kissed me and left. I was sure she was sad as well.

The new school semester was not much different from the last, the loneliness; the feeling of abandonment and the sense of despair were still present. I was able to control my tears but my heart still ached. Yvonne, Inez and the other girls were happy to see me back and showed their affection.

It was Sunday late afternoon and before dinner we went to Mass, it was the norm to go to Mass to make sure everybody fulfilled the obligation to hear Mass on Sunday, and in that way avoid a sin.

Monday morning, we went to Mass because it was Monday and like so, it continued for the rest of the week and the rest of the days I spent in that institution.

We were told during the service that everybody had to confess the sins committed while on holidays. The classes started, and after the second morning lesson ten girls at a time were sent to confess. The chaplain had a purple cloth in front of the confessional and the side panel doors were open, it was my turn to confess the holiday sins, I knelt and said that I didn't have anything to say. The priest after asking my age proceeded to enquire whether I had contact with boys and wanted to know about the sort of games we played.

He asked if I had played a game called little house; boys lay on top of the girls doing movements with their erect member, he also asked if I had ever seen an erect penis.

I said I didn't understand what he was talking about. He continued to ask questions about my awareness in relation to the things parents did in the bedroom, whether I had seen or heard anything. You are eleven years old he said, and a lot of girls do certain things with boys when they are your age; surely if you played with boys during the holidays you must have done something of that nature. By then I realized he was breathing heavily and his questions were boring me, without saying anything at all I stood up and left.

As soon as I left the confessional a thought entered my mind; was the priest talking about something related to Yesid moving his bum up and down while Lucia was lying on her back, with her legs spread, the skirt lifted, while making strange moaning noises the evening I found them on the chicken pen floor? Or was he talking about the oral, whatever that was, while Yesid had his head buried in the nanny's crutch when Anita opened the bedroom door?

They said they were doing special type of exercises and if I didn't say anything they would let me do it as well; but another day Yesid said it was a bar of chocolate not an erect penis as the priest had said, and what about the fingers walking in the crutch?

We had two new girls in our class, Maria del Pilar and her sister Remedios. Their parents, older brother and younger sister had arrived from Spain recently; the family lived in town so the nuns accepted the girls as day students. Maria del Pilar possessed an animated and friendly personality, Pilar and I shared a double desk, and as we commenced to talk, soon we found out that we shared many things in common like, music, dance, painting and most of all reading. She also had an inquisitive and curious mind.

It was a warm sunny morning, while we walked towards the concrete patio for morning break, she started to sing a

Sevillana song accompanied with clapping of her palms and I started dancing. From this day every morning she sang and I danced on our way to the main patio for morning recess; sometimes as she sang Sevillana verses we both danced to the vibrant happy rhythm, while the other girls enjoyed the performance. As our friendship developed we talked about many subjects, things we didn't understand she normally found an answer in the encyclopaedia at home. Another day after confession we discussed the priest's type of questions, I said frankly that I didn't know what a penis or an erect member was, but I wondered whether this had anything to do with Yesid and the nanny when I found them in the hen's pen.

Pilar said she was well versed on those matters because she had seen her sister Remedios and her brother doing it while their mother had gone shopping. She was aware that her brother visited Remedios's bedroom early in the morning while it was still dark, the bed motion and the panting had awoken her many times, but she was unable to figure out the nature of his visits until the day Remedios stayed home because she was sick.

Pilar returned home from school a bit earlier as her mother had instructed her; the house was quiet and Remedios didn't respond when she called, as she walked along the corridor she heard some panting coming from Alfredo's bedroom, it was the same she had heard many mornings around dawn, this time it was a bit noisier and animated with grunting. She walked slowly without making any noise and then saw Remedios and Alfredo naked, Remedios was on the bed with pillows under her back, while Alfredo was standing, Remedios had her legs wrapped around Alfredo's waist, while his hands were rubbing her genitals, and he was taking his penis in and out of the orifice; they were breathing heavily and after a while of doing that Remedios removed the pillows and Alfredo moved on top of her, Remedios rested her feet on the floor while Alfredo began to move his bum faster and faster until after a big sigh, they stopped, but he remained on top of her for a while.

She stood there in silence watching everything until they stopped, and then saw Alfredo remove his penis from Remedios, it had some liquid attached to it which looked white like glue. Pilar thought the whole thing looked pretty exciting because of their wriggling and sighing as they did it and Alfredo said: 'It was really good this time Remi, did you enjoy it?'

'Yes' she said. 'We should do it like this more often'.

The last issue of one of the monthly magazines her father received had good graphic drawings of a flaccid and an erect penis, the article had also information about the sex subject, Pilar informed me. Pilar brought the magazine the next day and we hid it carefully within the other books while looking for an opportunity to read it; the perfect time arrived when the religious instruction class started, the nun was a nice old lady who wore thick rimmed glasses, extremely long sighted and she also had a fairly calm nature, she never seemed to mind what we did during her class, sometimes there was a riot and she still kept on talking about the church as well as Jesus.

The sex subject wasn't an easy topic to understand as I'd thought; I looked at the drawings many times, I read the apparently clear and scientifically informative article, and yet I couldn't comprehend how these things supposed to work. Where do men put it all? How does it double the size, was my thought. The article mentioned average length, diameter of a flaccid and an erect member, as well as the sperm quantity and quality for the reproduction purpose; nothing was mentioned about doing it because it felt good, while Pilar's experience and my experience of having seen the act suggested that people do it for fun and pleasure. It was too complicated!

Boarding school was beginning to change my personality. I'd become more talkative, and a little more extroverted with a touch of mischief, perhaps it was Pilar's personality and the ability to communicate that brought a ray of light into a monotonous routine. Popular music was banned, radios were confiscated, and the only music available was a narrow repertoire of classical music which included Beethoven pastoral symphony, Chopin concertos and polonaises, and some baroque chamber music which we listened to during study time on Sundays.

The concept of a real library was totally misunderstood since the only books available to us were of a religious nature, as well as some Spanish classics, and Dante's Divine Comedy, but not a great deal of local or lighter content books. Books and magazines brought into the school were confiscated.

We couldn't write or receive letters except from our parents, and the letters were open and read before being passed to the person concerned; the use of the telephone was not permitted, a phone call was only allowed in cases of emergency which were assessed by the Mother Superior.

To mention a masculine name who wasn't a parent or brother was unthinkable, because males were a source of suffering to women. Men, including husbands, did terrible things to their wives according to the general information supplied by the nuns. We normally asked the nun who mentioned those terrible things: 'What terrible things? How do you know? Please tell us'. However, nobody offered a logical explanation and consequently, we're kept guessing about those terrible things.

I thought maybe men do what Alfredo was doing to Remedios and the nuns thought that to be horrible, perhaps the nuns had done it, and that was the reason they became nuns because they didn't like doing it. However, Pilar said it was a bit disturbing to watch because it was difficult to assess whether it was pleasurable or painful, by the movements and the heavy breathing, it appeared quite enjoyable.

The male genre was evil, and under no circumstances socializing with those creatures or talking about them was allowed, curiously enough the nuns did talk to some fathers, especially the ones who donated money for school projects, and of course the chaplain could do no wrong.

Once my mind was diverted from those sex issues, it returned to the awareness of my situation. There was no green space, no trees, no grass, and no flowers; luckily some sparrows graced the courtyard while picking some crumbs. Concrete floors, concrete floors everywhere.

Oh how much I hated all of it!

The choir was invited to participate in a religious festival of schools that belonged to the same religious order. The older girls said that this was a type of competition among choirs and was part of the normal schedule every year. The performance normally took place at a larger school; school chaplains and nuns from the participating schools selected the best choir.

On the first day of the festival we left school fairly early after a quick breakfast; as the bus began to climb the narrow road, the sun's rays perforated the mist allowing the majesty of the Andes peaks to float above it. Around every bend the nuns increased the volume of their prayers as if God had gone around the next bend and couldn't hear them; the tight bends on the road gave the impression that the bus had one wheel floating on air, and as the mist lifted, we could see the depth of the precipice.

The precipice showed many scattered crosses, some close to the edge of the road, others deep down the side of the mountain; as the land dropped further and further from the road, the remains of some vehicles that perhaps had gone too fast around the bends while God was looking the other way, rested silently, hanging precariously from the strong branches that didn't break when the bus fell down the edge. Some vehicles looked fresh as if the incident had just happened the day before, others had been eaten by rust and their colours faded under the mist. Some cars were upside down with the wheels looking at the sky, the skid marks had made dents on the vegetation like a pair of ferocious teeth devouring everything in their path.

The bus continued its descent into a wide green valley still covered by thick mist, in the distance the silhouette of a large building began to appear, and as we approached the property an avenue of mature trees stood elegantly, inside the enormous wrought iron gate which had been opened to allow the passing of vehicles to the main area. The ground under the trees was covered with masses of small white flowers that looked like bells.

Sister Barbarita insisted that everybody had to present the best behaviour; she also informed us that boys had been invited, but it didn't mean that we could socialize with them at any time. Nobody paid attention to her last words, because as soon as she finished her sentence everybody's eyes began to search for boys standing around the premises.

We entered a fairly large courtyard and in the middle of it a square fountain; on the perimeter a verandah framed with arches like a convent, and boys everywhere. The big girls were instantly impressed and began to giggle; they arranged their hair and began to search for the handsome one, or the one they had met on previous occasions.

The nuns very quickly and in an orderly manner pushed the girl's group to the theatre and after the usual introductions the festival began. Our group, was the last to be called during the morning session, we walked to the stage climbed on the platform, tall girls at the back, small ones at the front. We finished our performance and returned to our seats until it was announced we were going to the dining room for lunch recess.

Segregated groups of boys and girls stood everywhere, as if some sort of infectious disease had infected both sexes and nobody could talk to each other for fear of contamination. I was standing with the girls from my school when I heard a loud voice calling: 'Nené I didn't know you were here'

I turned my head around, Yesid was walking towards me, his arms extended and before I could say anything, he lifted me off the ground and planted a big kiss on my cheek. 'I am so glad to see you! From now on, we will keep in touch, I may even visit you. Your Papi has agreed to be my guardian while I attend the final years at boarding school, I might even spend some weekends at your house' he said.

'I never go home for the weekend, I am in a prison and the visits take place behind bars'.

He took my arm gently and led me away from the group of girls, and then he whispered in my ear: 'Did you ever find out?'

I knew precisely what he was talking about. 'Yes, I did'.

'Well, Nené we will do it during the holidays' he said with a wicked smile. I looked at him, not knowing what to say. I thought it was funny.

He held me tightly against his chest and kissed me once more while my feet were still dangling above the ground; he said: 'I loved you from the first moment I saw you Nené, you are the prettiest girl anybody could find. Can I give you a true kiss, or do you think the nun will send the arm guards to take you to solitary confinement? Goodbye in case your nuns don't allow us to talk again'.

His kiss lingered on my skin and I felt an intense pleasure and delight. I didn't want him to move away.

He was taller, more handsome and more mischievous than I recalled; that beautiful smile together with the sound of his wicked laughter were forever imprinted in my memory. I returned to my group, my heartbeat racing and the sensation that my feet didn't make contact with the ground. My heart and head full of affection, warmth and desire, I just wanted to be near him and feel his kisses.

The girls bombarded me with all sort of questions about the handsome boy, and Sister Barbarita reprimanded me for allowing him to kiss me. They all talked but their voices sounded distant, and all I felt was the warm embrace and his kiss.

The performances continued, we sang for a second time and someone won the event. It wasn't possible to see Yesid again, but the effect of his embrace and kisses was long lasting. He was imprinted in my memory and I thought of him a million times. From that day onwards he was my last thought before I fell asleep.

Unbearable unhappiness

The second term was well underway and my grades were poor. The family visits didn't happen with enough frequency to relieve the loneliness and sadness that had taken control of my soul; somehow I had a tremendous feeling of rejection.

I was certain that Papi and Tuni loved me, but during the holidays I began to feel that mother didn't want me near, and during school visits when she arrived on her own she was also very critical of me for one thing or another. It was my general appearance or my hair was untidy, my academic performance wasn't good enough, my uniform looked creased, my finger nails were too long. Not once she asked me how I felt.

At meal times we listened to stories sometimes read by the nun in charge or one of the older girls. At the time the story of the rich sultan was read. The sultan during one of his hunting expeditions into the forest caught a beautiful bird which displayed iridescent feathers of many beautiful colours. He placed the bird in a golden cage he had made specially, and hung his cage in the best room the palace had, but the bird never sang its harmonious song again, didn't eat and the feathers began to lose their lustre. The sultan ordered his loyal servants to bring fruits from the jungle, exactly from the place where the bird was found. The servants brought the fruit and took it to the bird on shiny, gold trays, but the bird didn't eat at all. One day the window was left open and another bird landed on the window sill, while it sang and conversed with the caged bird, the caged bird understood the message. 'In order to live he had to die'.

The following day the bird was found lifeless on the floor of the golden cage. I felt like that caged bird; my cage was made of concrete and ugly yellow bricks and I didn't know how to die. If I could only escape the prison I was in!

It was visit time again and with great expectations I waited for my name to be called, but lunch time arrived and my name hadn't been called, after the lunch recess the visit time extended to 4.30pm but this Sunday the loud speaker didn't call my name. My heart ached, I couldn't eat and my eyes didn't have enough tears by the time we went to bed.

The days which followed that Sunday immersed me into a deep sadness and depression. It was difficult to function and to execute normal tasks was a big burden. The desire to eat left my body, and I used to wake up during the night with a terrifying fear of being left there totally alone and abandoned. I even thought that if I could escape, maybe nobody would be there for me. The feeling of being abandoned was so overwhelming it devoured each second of my day.

Some nights I woke up with the very real sensation that a person was standing close to my bed, other nights I felt as if someone was sitting at the end of the bed looking at me and that person wanted to talk. One night I awoke when I heard close to my ear my name being called in a whisper. I opened my eyes expecting to see someone next to me.

My fear was so intense that I felt compelled to walk to the sister's bed enclosure to tell her how frightened I was, but she sent me away annoyed that I had interrupted her sleep.

I was thirsty and decided to leave the dormitory to fetch a glass of water; as I walked out of the dormitory the strong sensation of being followed closely made the hair at the back of my neck stand up and my pulse rise. I found myself gripped by the agonizing fear of something unknown. I turned my head around thinking that the nun had followed me; it was only the darkness of the night out there. As I bent down to drink water from the basin tap, an invisible presence stood beside me and I felt that presence was about to touch me. I ran back to the dormitory as fast as possible. I jumped into my bed then tried to wake up Yvonne but she didn't respond.

I curled into a tiny ball under the blankets, trembling and in a lather of sweat, I remained awake until the bell rang, it was time to get up. That morning during Mass Sister Barbarita asked me to join the choir; I followed her to the chapel's mezzanine without saying a word. She asked me to wait for her after the service. Sister wanted to find out what was wrong with me, she said I looked pale and withdrawn. I didn't feel like talking and I didn't feel like being there either. I said: 'All my heart desires is to go home'. The abundant tears came from the heart and I cried inconsolably.

Sister Barbarita held my hand and tried to calm me down with the type of words nuns use, adding prayer to everything with the hope that God listens, and the problem disappears by magic. I managed to say: 'Nobody visited me on Sunday. Maybe I have been left here and nobody wants me', finally Sister Barbarita was silent and left me alone.

Another Sunday arrived and as usual we were in the big study room, while the record player offered the sounds of Chopin piano concertos. My head rested on the desk while my heart listened to the wonderful melodies; I loved the tranquillity classical music provided, and at a very early age when mother used to take me to the conservatoire of music for rehearsals, I used to close my eyes to let the melodies invade my body, sometimes I felt the sound in my chest and at other times the sounds just took possession of my being, and now in my present situation when I listened to this music I was free of pain.

The nun in charge tapped my shoulder and instructed me to follow her outside the study. Closing the study door behind, she said with a sombre voice that somebody was waiting for me at the visitor's room. 'Please, go down' she instructed.

I went back to the study, packed my things and went downstairs to the visitor's room where mother was waiting for me. She said I was allowed to go home because Tuni was sick. Mother was silent during the trip and she appeared preoccupied as well as remote. As we approached home she told me to be quiet and not to run.

At home there was no sign of my sisters. Papi greeted us with a worried face and walked in a hurry with long steps while he lifted his heels off the ground. Papi took my hand as we entered Tuni's bedroom.

She was in bed, her head resting on many pillows, her olive skin had taken a pale translucent shade, and her curly hair was brushed back; she also spoke with difficulty, and extended her arm to touch me, I noticed the chipped enamel on her otherwise perfectly manicured finger nails. Tuni had suffered a thrombosis during the middle of the week prior to my Sunday visit; her left side was partially paralysed, her speech and eyesight affected and there was a time when the expectation for her survival was very low. Somehow she did pull through during the night; it was precisely the night I heard the whisper in my ear calling my name. I left the room shortly because Tuni was tired.

Out of the blue mother asked me about school. An unexpected opportunity to tell her about the awful food, the lack of a garden, and all that concrete which I found so depressing, because it even prevented the pleasure to see birds or hear them sing. I don't recall seeing a single bird in the courtyards, perhaps the occasional sparrow from time to time. She did listen for a while, then she said there was no choice but to stay there until the final year of high school; she also added that there was a great possibility she would marry Maximiliano the following year.

My return to school was marked with a mixture of terribly confused feelings, and a sense that an imminent change in my life had begun to take shape; I was only a little girl and big people made big decisions whether it suited me or not. I knew for sure that something was vastly different at home and after the trip to visit Tuni, I had no more visits for a long time. I thought Tuni was very sick and perhaps this was the reason nobody visited me.

The loud speaker called my name, it was around 2.30 pm. with my eyes filled with tears I didn't run this time to the visitor's room, I walked slowly listening to my broken heart; at this hour the rooms were fairly crowded and there wasn't sufficient space available to sit or have a little privacy, two or three nuns usually paced up and down interrupting family conversations with unnecessary chatter.

I knocked on the door and identified myself, the door opened, and the nun told me that my older brother was waiting for me in the small room. I negotiated my way through the narrow and crowded corridor; the small room was crowded as well. There, standing by the window was Yesid. He kissed me and embraced me affectionately, as he held my hand he said that the nun had questioned him, and she was the one who said: 'Are you here to visit your sister? Good lad'.

We talked about school, laughed at the entire system and at all the silly things that went on; compared notes on the horrible food and the lack of freedom at my school. Yesid was more fortunate than I was, his boarding school had a more liberal approach; they enjoyed time out every Sunday from 10am to 6pm. During the week they watched television for a couple of hours and on Friday night, movies were shown in the school theatre. Everybody had access to telephones during recess hour, their calls weren't monitored, and the call length depended on the amount of money they had.

The library offered a diverse variety of books and current magazines, the sport curriculum included a range of sports like rowing, fencing, tennis and many more activities. I listened to all this with amazement. I interrupted often saying, 'Are you serious? My boarding school is like a prison or more along the lines of a medieval cloister'.

Yesid mentioned that his parents had invited us to spend the next Christmas holidays at their hacienda. The nearest town was 1 hour from the house, but there was plenty to do around the property, like horse riding, swimming in the stream of clear water, we could go into town for the open air movies, also he and I could discover many more things. At this moment his cheeky grin was followed by laughter. I knew I loved him.

The bell rang, and I thanked him for the visit. He embraced me tightly and I felt something hard below his waist, maybe it was his wallet. I wished that moment to last longer; we kissed and he said: 'I will come to visit you again one day'.

I opened the timber door and in a trance walked towards the big concrete patio. Yesid had just found a permanent corner in my heart and mind; I savoured every word he said, felt his goodbye kiss on my cheek, his warm tight embrace which aroused a desire to be with him, to touch him and to feel his kisses. He occupied my thoughts for the rest of the afternoon, and he was my last thought before I fell asleep. The family visit lost its importance, I had a new love.

November arrived and with it the preparation for the end of year exams, and we would go home during the second week in December, I tried hard to improve my academic performance, studied with diligence and dedication, hence just managed to pass to second year of high school.

That glorious day when we would go home finally arrived. After early Mass and breakfast we congregated in the main theatre for the medal and prize presentation programme, which started mid-morning. Some parents perhaps eager to collect their daughters arrived early; we saw them as we entered the theatre.

The clock hands moved ever so slowly, they appeared glued to its face as my watchful eyes checked them so often. Most of the girls left soon after the presentation programme finished and I found myself alone; I realized the nuns had gone to their dining room, and I was the only girl sitting alone on the chapel's external edge, which faced the concrete patio. I was hungry, I was sad, I was lonely.

Mother finally arrived to pick me up at around 3 o'clock, and all she said was that she forgot about the time I was supposed to go home, I felt resentful and angry. Mother asked about my academic performance and she also asked if I had received any medals.

The answered was no. She then proceeded to chastise me about the lack of academic performance and she continued blabbing on, but I didn't listen; a terrible feeling in my gut that mother didn't want me home was very real this time, as a matter of fact the first time I recalled this thought was on the way home at the end of the last semester.

Mother was very hard on me for not having good academic marks, which was unfair since those months of boarding school were so traumatic; she was also reluctant to accept my feelings of loneliness and the fact that I really felt abandoned, in addition that constant praying, the horrid cold showers, and disgusting food. Deafening silence followed the duration of the trip home. After two hours of almost absolute silence between mother and me, it was delightful to arrive home to Papi and Tuni who lovingly welcomed me.

I cried and complained to them about the many hours I had waited to be picked up, I told them I was the only girl left at school but there was no reply. There was something not quite right at home, Papi and Tuni were addressed by mother in an angry tone of voice, the strain on the relationship and the tension I had noticed during the last visit had increased.

The last time I was home, I felt like a stranger among my sisters and this time there was no difference; they had grown as much as I had grown physically, but the mental barrier was wider than the physical barrier, I had changed dramatically and didn't enjoy their simple games anymore, I felt totally out of place as if I didn't belong there at all. It was such a horrible feeling. I had seen my sisters twice during the last eleven months. Three weeks during June holidays and a couple of days at the time of Tuni's illness. I had ceased to exist for them, obviously I was only remembered when they saw me. I was asked many times, 'are you the same Nené who used to live here? You look different'

I had changed physically and intellectually. I had grown up, and I was reserved and quiet, more aware of the events which developed around me, my form of speech had also changed, and I didn't like to play the simple games we used to play before I left.

The lovely mother I knew before my departure to boarding school had vanished; instead I found an unhappy angry person who showed a great deal of displeasure at everything I did or said.

She noticed I folded each item of clothing and neatly placed it on the chair, as I changed into my pyjamas before I went to bed. I was still a little girl, but a profound change had taken place within me. I began to question everything, and I disagreed with mother on many issues; she gave orders to do this or that, but I found everything so petty and silly. I missed the interesting conversations I had with Pilar. The desire to play with my sisters as we used to play before boarding school had disappeared; I enjoyed solitude and preferred reading.

Papi had a good library, as an engineer his books were varied and interesting, the French revolution and Napoleon battles, as well as the Russian revolution and a fairly large book of medical journals, also there were many books about trains and geographic maps of distant places where railroads had been built, together with photographs of places and people. Papi didn't receive monthly magazines which discussed the sex issue; not a hope to find sex information during my incursions into his library.

There were many intense arguments between Papi, Tuni and mother. Life was dreary. I was terribly unhappy at school and although I was home, somehow I didn't fit in anymore. In a way I was happy to be with the family, but the amount of change that had taken place, made it extremely difficult to get accustomed to the new environment in a short period of time.

I phoned Pilar, I told her how bored I was. Her holidays on the contrary had been good, her father had rented a hacienda, the house reminded her mother of the Spanish houses and everybody was happy. Friends arrived from Spain and with so many people around there was no room for nostalgia about their country of origin.

Remedios and Alfredo still had sex almost every morning, she said it was easy to understand why they liked to do it; now that she knew all about it, she thought it was a fantastic pasttime, however, she was concerned about the fact that her parents could find out and then there would be some sort of trouble. 'It was incest'. On the other hand she said, 'if you don't practice with somebody you feel comfortable with, how can you possibly learn about those things that nobody talks about?'

While life at Pilar's home continued on its course, for me some days appeared to return to the normality of the life I was familiar with before boarding school, the usual tension somehow moved aside for us to enjoy moments as we always had enjoyed them, with great harmony and love. From this time my life was divided into two sections; life before boarding school and life after boarding school.

Papi and Tuni sat on the wicker chairs enjoying the shade of the verandah while they waited for las onces to be served.

Onces, refers to morning coffee which is served at around 11am. It takes the name from once which is the Spanish word for eleven. Exquisite, warm little crisp cheese cakes on a silver tray, la cafetera full of coffee and the fresh aroma of Arabica grain filled the air; we loved to sit on our little chairs listening to Papi stories about the days when he was a boy growing up in the capital, and the method of transport from their house to the farm where they bought honey and milk; apparently the only way to get around was on horseback, and some mornings the entire ground was covered with ice, and as far as the eye could see the grass had a picturesque white gloss, while the fog enveloped the landscape.

He also had his favourite stories reminiscing about the time when he was the local team, head engineer during the railway construction. The most fascinating story was about the time when Papi, with the British engineer Mr. Bircher, the surveyor and some men walked into the jungle, instructed the crew of workers to clear a large area of vines and other plants. Unexpectedly they had to leave the site soon after it was cleared. The tropical rainy season started earlier than anticipated. A couple of months later once the rainy season came to an end, the group returned, and to their surprise they found that thick vines and a large variety of plants had grown back, and the entire area was covered with a fresh green mantle as if it had never been disturbed.

We used to say 'please, please Papi tell us the story about the vine that grew and grew'. The jungle grew faster every time the story was told, bits were added and the story re-constructed. Gigantic leaves with a mind of their own, capable of climbing unassisted up the legs of a beast or human that stood still for too long; the curly tip of the leaves rapidly twisted and wrapped around the body until it was completely covered, as if by magic the body disappeared under the weight of the leaves. At this time we all shouted: Stop! Stop! Then we laughed.

Our onces was interrupted with loud voices coming from the main courtyard; we stopped to listen and soon realized that Mamá Nena had just arrived, we rushed to the entry door where grandmother stood in the middle of a circle formed by baskets, boxes and luggage, as usual she had brought a little animal, a turkey this time, which we immediately gave the name of señor turkey. Grandmother with her arms wide open attempted to embrace all of us at the same time, and standing next to her, Rosa a cousin, who everybody called Rosita.

Rosita arrived to stay with mother until our return in the New Year. Rosita was tall, gentle and beautiful; she wore a white blouse, a long flowing skirt of brilliant colours and lots of crinolines under, they were called polleras, her skirt usually had flower prints. Her short and curly hair was brushed back behind her ears, she moved in a fluid and elegant manner, the swing of her hips pushed her skirt in a rhythmical side to side motion.

She only wore black flat shoes, a ballerina style of shoe. Rosita was rather conscious of her height; she also walked with her chin tilted up which gave her an air of haughtiness.

She kept her shoulders absolutely straight. Her cheeks were pink. Her name complimented her appearance perfectly. Her skin was pale and delicate, and her manner was gentle. She did look like a rose.

Rosita lived in a small town with her parents. She had decided to stay with her parents instead of continuing her studies, because she claimed not to have the brain for books, and from the age of sixteen she stopped her academic education; instead she learnt to cook and to sew, activities which provided her with a reasonably good income.

Her parents had a hacienda and running through the property a creek which was used to irrigate the many fruit trees which provided her with enough fruit to make conserves and cakes. She used to make wedding dresses and in some occasions Rosita organized the entire catering for weddings and other special gatherings. She was more or less mother's age, but she hadn't married yet.

We saw Rosita frequently. Mamá Nena had brought her home several times in the past. Sometimes she had stayed for several months, mother and Rosita were fairly close, and they used to laugh a lot. Unfortunately, unbeknown to us this would be the last time we would see her, tragedy wasn't far away.

Love or Sex

Papi, Tuni, Mamá Nena and the four of us left home as the sun began to rise. We finally arrived at the hacienda after several wee stops and many more stops, when Fena looking as green as a frog, proceeded to empty the contents of her frail stomach.

Anita, the boys and the entire household were waiting for us with refreshing cool glasses of lime juice, and naranjada with big chunks of ice. It was the first time we had been at their house, a large house painted white with an ample courtyard full of light; an enormous tree in the middle with brilliant light green, heart shaped, glossy leaves, which danced to the rhythm of the breeze allowing the sun to form patterns on the floor. Yesid stood there, taller more handsome than the last time I saw him. I felt the flapping of thousand butterflies wanting to escape from inside my chest, and the burning desire to be embraced, and to experience once more the kiss I had tasted, when he thought the nun would've sent the arm guards to place me in solitary confinement. We managed a shy and quiet hello.

Anita asked Yesid to show us the house, and we followed him. Several bedrooms, living and library rooms around the main courtyard; an open corridor entered a second courtyard with an al fresco dining area, in between a beautiful tropical garden on both sides. In the middle of the space a large, solid, timber table surrounded by equally solid, oversized, timber framed chairs, the back and the seat of the chairs were covered with cow hide, which kept the hairs as the cows had them while they grazed the nearby pastures. Mother would have considered those chairs unrefined and confronting. I thought it was like a testimony to all the brown, white, yellow, black cows that had lived in the area. We continued the inspection; Yesid and I managed to touch hands.

At the rear of the house, the maid quarters were separated from the main house by lush, tropical gardens and fruit trees. At a short distance from the house large mango trees, paw paws, custard apples, oranges, and lemons. The smell of fruit filled the air with that typical sweet aroma of the tropics, and stunningly beautiful, colourful birds pecked on the ripe fruit.

Further away from the property, the stables and a large shed where many bags of grain and cotton where stored, the shed had a dry and sweet dusty smell. As we walked into the shed, my sisters and Yesid's siblings scattered behind the piles of bags, that moment created the perfect opportunity for a kiss. A small wish had been granted but it was not enough, this time that burning kiss wasn't planted on my cheek it was the second real kiss and it felt as if something else was needed to fulfil the moment.

As we started walking out of the shed, I remembered all the things Pilar had told me about her sister and brother, and for the first time, I felt I'd like to do that too.

We followed the path under the fruit trees, until the land began to drop gently towards a stream of clear water, which ran along the extent of the property. To our surprise the water was very cold. The melting snow from the cordillera was the source of the freezing cold, sweet tasting water, refreshing as if nature had mixed its own formula of enriched flavours.

We returned to the house, it was already 6 o'clock, and it was getting dark. We started to unpack and familiarize ourselves with the layout of the rooms. The bedrooms were spacious and full of light, the walls were painted white, and the floor was covered with highly polished terracotta floor tiles, which reflected the light almost like a mirror.

We were told that dinner was normally served around 6.30 pm. The reason was, that Isidoro the head of the family, usually left home before sunrise, and after a long day in the fields he liked to eat early to be able to enjoy some time with the family before going to bed. Yesid re-organized the table placing, so we sat next to each other. During dinner while everybody was talking he turned to me and softly said that he loved me, adding that he thought about me quite often since the school visit. My heart expanded rapidly, thousand excited butterflies flapped their wings in my belly, our eyes met and we smiled to each other.

The house had been built in the valley at the foot of the cordillera, so the climate was hot and dry during the day and a refreshing, early evening breeze was a welcome change to the heat, but as the breeze died, hungry, annoying mosquitoes arrived fast and ready to bite every bit of exposed flesh. The mosquitoes drove all of us insane, the next day we were full of pink, itchy blotches from head to toe, and Mamá Nena as usual with prompt remedies alleviated the terrible itch; the swollen, pink bites disappeared fairly soon, but the remedy left on us a smell similar to an old lady's wardrobe.

The next day workers arrived with piles of cow dung and piled it near the open areas where we would be sitting for dinner and later for games. As dusk arrived the piles of cow dung were lit and as if by magic the mosquitoes disappeared and left us in peace. Mamá Nena rubbed our legs and arms with a very effective potion as well.

Time passed very quickly. We went horse riding, Yesid invariably by my side; when it was a bit too hot to play outdoors we went swimming in the icy cold stream, we stayed in the water until all our fingers and toes turned wrinkled and purple. The boys climbed the mango trees to search for succulent ripe fruit, other times green mangoes were picked and the acid, light coloured flesh was sprinkled with salt. Sometimes we ate too many mangoes, and the lips and tongue became red.

The boys had a large pole with a hook attached to one end which helped to bring the ripe paw paws down, when the fruit fell and burst open it showed deep orange flesh and glossy seeds. We pretended to be birds, and flat on our bellies took bites from the ripe paw paw's flesh without using our hands. Our faces were smothered with fruit and that was a good excuse to begin the water fights. Armed with water pistols the battle lasted until everybody was drenched and finally we were told to get ready for dinner or lunch. We walked under the canopy of the open forest, picking small fruit from banana trees that had escaped the rigours of the plantations. We walked long distances until fences indicated the property boundary had been reached. Sometimes we went into town to the open air cinema, which showed the latest Mexican movies according to the posters.

An agreement between el señor alcalde and the church párroco didn't allow love scenes and kisses to be part of the screening, so the theatre manager obliged and every kiss was cut out of the reel. However, there was plenty of serious kissing in every dark corner of the theatre, and when the passions became too hot, loud whistles crossed the air.

Christmas was a great event. Fireworks were organized for the employees and many presents were placed at the nativity base. A big party to celebrate Christmas was part of the family tradition, and a large number of people were invited. Preparations for the asado commenced early on Christmas eve; an area of ground not far from the house was covered with big logs, the round metal stakes pierced the earth anticipating the arrival of the poor beast's carcass, which had been slaughtered that morning; soon the fire was lit, the coals burnt slowly until they provided an even heat and it was then when large pieces of meat were fixed to the stakes.

Soon after dusk the musician's platform quickly filled up with men dressed in white and they also wore white straw hats. They carried guitars, accordions, maracas and timbales. As night fell and the stars began to fill the sky, guests made their way towards the garden to form an animated, happy crowd, who talked and waved their hands in unison to the sounds of merengues, rumbas and mambos, sensuous melodies more inebriating than the large sangria glasses on the silver trays.

We ran and screamed, while disorderly teenagers took advantage of the crowd and the night's darkness to experience the first twinges of passion. Yesid asked me to follow him; after some minutes that felt like hours, I walked towards the shed where the cotton and grain bales were stored; I felt nervous, however, the invitation was somehow expected and I followed him. At that moment I wanted to feel his kisses and embrace.

The shed was dark, the dusty smell was stronger than during the day, and the dust particles danced and shimmered like pretty little diamonds responding to the brilliant evening light that managed to penetrate through the narrow openings in the walls. Once we became accustomed to the darkness, and the distance in between our faces diminished, we walked behind a large pile of cotton bales and kissed passionately, the skin became so sensitive so receptive to the touch, it was strange. Yesid caressed my legs, his hands and kisses felt hot, hotter than the midday sun, and I felt his hardness against my body for the second time.

All of a sudden I said: 'I know what you and Lucia were doing that night when we played hide and seek'.

'Do you do that when you love somebody? Did you love Lucia?'

'No', he said. 'Lucia needed to have sex and I was there to learn from her everything I could'.

We walked out of the shed sat under the moon light and Yesid became gentle and a bit subdued; he kissed me again, held my hand, and then proceeded to tell me all the things he knew about sex and the best way to do it. He asked me about my knowledge of sex and how I had learnt about it. I told him what Pilar had described so vividly.

He said: 'that is incest'. Then he added that sex can be done whether you love someone or not, it's done for pleasure or need; you have to be completely naked to be able to truly enjoy it, that is true, but if you love someone, sometimes it is difficult to do it because it would be considered disrespectful.

I didn't understand. 'Even more confusing was the fact that he said he couldn't do it to me because he loved me'. 'I love you too', I said.

We returned to the shed. I rested on a soft bale and his body rested over me, we were fully clothed, we kissed with tremendous passion and I felt the energy of his embrace surround me; he moved with desperation until something happened then he stopped and said: 'Nené, we can't do this. It's wrong, and I will be in great trouble if someone finds out'. 'I want to do it to feel what Pilar described'.

'Nené: you are just a little girl, you are only eleven years and six months old; you are a child, a precocious little girl who has found out too much too soon'. I have to go to the house to get changed before anybody finds out that we are here.

I walked slowly out of the shed and joined the happy crowd dancing to the sounds of a merengue. Nobody seemed to have noticed our absence.

Some days later Mamá Nena took me with her to the town's markets; I walked away from Mamá Nena to inspect other sections of the market where the basket weavers and cloth merchants had their stalls. While walking and looking with fascination at the variety of goods, I met a girl from boarding school; we didn't attend the same class but we were friendly to each other; I didn't know she lived in this part of the country.

I informed her that we were staying at Yesid parent's hacienda for the duration of the holiday, and when I told her, she insisted I had to go to her house for the afternoon; she would come with her brother to pick me up after the midday siesta the next day.

Lila arrived with her brother at around 3pm as agreed; we drove directly to her house which was on the town outskirts, it wasn't an imposing hacienda, it was a large house with the bluest swimming pool.

The maid offered us cakes and fresh fruit juice, and we sat on the wicker chairs under the cool cover of a wide veranda, which was filled with ferns and many plants that had spotty leaves with all sort of colour variations. The glossy, spotty leaves gave the impression they were painted with a brush, it was an exuberant, beautiful garden. She said her mother loved to look after the plants and the girl who looked after the house was her helper.

We talked about school, likes dislikes and so forth; she wouldn't return to school due to the loneliness she had experienced, and the distance didn't allow her parents to visit regularly, therefore, she had been enrolled at the nun's school which was just three hours from where they lived; it didn't have the same prestige and quality of the boarding school we attended, but she could return home every Friday afternoon and stay home until Monday morning; the nuns would allow her to catch the bus if her parents weren't able to bring her home.

As we talked, I realized how sad my situation was, and also that my return to boarding school was impossible to avoid. That feeling filled me with an immediate deep sorrow.

The sun had begun to set when I called the hacienda to ask if someone could pick me up. Yesid answered the phone, he said, that everybody had gone to an asado and that they were returning home late. Anita had asked him to remain at home in case I called. He was coming to pick me up and take me to the gathering where the rest of the family was.

Lila and I continued our conversation until it was interrupted by the sound of car brakes on the loose surface. A ball of dust followed and then Yesid stepped out of the car, he must've driven at a tremendous speed, because it felt like just 10 minutes from the time I finished talking to him to the time he arrived.

He took me home instead of following Anita's orders to take me to the asado where everybody was. I didn't mind it. The house was deserted except for the maids who were preparing the next day baking; we had a glass of lemonade and sat on the hammocks, which were permanently fixed to the courtyard columns. Yesid took a hammock directly opposite mine, but shortly after he moved to my hammock and we began to kiss. The kisses became more passionate, and he realized that the buttons on my blouse left gaps in between because they were placed too far apart. Yesid found this amusing. He lifted the edge of the fabric and as he inspected my budding bosom said: 'Nené your tits look like mosquito bites'. He then ran his hand under my blouse and touched my boobs while we kissed; a tingling sensation from head to toe made me aware of every pore on my body, it was a lovely feeling.

We continued to kiss, his hand moving up and down to my belly button, he pushed his body against mine, I could feel something hard.

'Do you still want to do it?' He asked.

'Yes, I think it will be interesting and exciting' I said.

'You are just eleven years old Nené'.

'No, I am eleven years and six months old. Is there an age limit when you could do those things?' As a matter of fact the priest who I had to confess my sins said, that a lot of girls do things with boys and their erect member at my age, and he wanted to know if I had done anything with boys.

'Not really' Yesid said. 'I am going to be eighteen, soon after I finish high school, and I started doing it at the age of fourteen, shortly after Lucia arrived at our house'.

'That isn't true! I heard that you were giving her oral; whatever that means to the other nanny'.

'Who told you that?'

I told him that I heard it while I sat behind the sofa during the holidays. Anita said that even papa Isidoro was doing it with the nanny. So in reality you started having sex at the age of twelve. 'See, only six months older than my age'.

'How did you start with Lucia?'

'Well, I touched Lucia's breast accidentally; I apologized but she didn't believe it was accidental; she smiled at me and said it didn't matter and added that I could do it again if I wished. Come to my bedroom tonight I will leave the door unlocked, be very quiet so nobody can hear you. I arrived at her bedroom and she was waiting for me'.

'What did happen?'

'Nené, you ask too many questions'.

Lucia was naked under her dressing gown and she asked if I had done it before, I told her that I had read about it, and my older brother Fabio had said a couple of things to me. 'I may be able to teach you many things, but you must keep it quiet otherwise there would be trouble'. She began asking me if I had seen a naked woman and whether I wanted to see her before we did anything, of course I wanted to see her, was my response.

She opened her dressing gown, spread her legs to show me everything and suggested that I could touch any part of her body; I began to touch her breasts, she put a nipple into my mouth and then she took my hand and moved it to her stomach and below, with her hand over mine she moved it to her sexual organs and moved it up and down, by then I was ready to do anything else she had asked me to; she began to take my pyjamas off and started stroking my back as well as my organ while she guided it with her hand towards her crutch, she rubbed herself with the tip, then I followed her instructions and it went in, she told me to move slowly and she put pressure on my back when she wanted me to stop to avoid an early ejaculation. It was very rewarding.

I couldn't keep away from her bedroom, and had sex almost every night during the time Lucia was our nanny. Mum didn't suspect anything and dad was always too busy to think about it.

Lucia left after the holiday we spent at your house, mum said that she left because we had grown up and she preferred to look after younger children

Anyway, mum said that I have to take you to the asado, she will be mad at me if we don't show up, and the old maid will tell her that we arrived early enough. He composed himself, I fixed my pony tail and we left. On our way we stopped many times to kiss and cuddle; we finally arrived and nobody said anything. He tried to distance himself to avoid any questions from Anita or Mamá Nena.

Did anybody notice the effervescent passion developing between us? Nobody seemed to have paid attention, except one of the older maids, who from time to time warned Yesid to be careful and mind his actions, and not to get into trouble.

The days that followed were unusual, Yesid and I became very close, we continued to play with our brothers and sisters, but we were consumed with the desire to be close to each other. We caressed, held hands and he placed his hand under my skirt and touched my leg while we sat during meal times, other times he stood so close to me it was impossible not to feel his breathing as it became deeper.

We often resumed our encounters in the shed, but it was increasingly difficult to do it without attracting some sort of suspicion. When we managed to escape, and finally entered the shed we kissed with such passion and hunger that in reality we needed to have sex, but the fear of being caught always stopped Yesid, and all that was left of those passionate moments was the memory of an unfulfilled desire.

Behind the cotton bales we kissed and brought our bodies as close as possible. On one occasion I asked Yesid to show me how he was made, for me to understand how his organ changed from normal to erect. He laughed and said 'NO. That is indecent'

I did touch him over his pants at the beginning, and as his erection developed, I left my hand on it to experience the process. It felt strange.

It was like he had a live animal under his pants.

I couldn't understand how it worked, but that day we decided we were going to do it; the problem was to find the moment when we could be alone, and with so many people around, it was a difficult task.

Yesid appeared behind me when nobody was looking; he put his arms around me and squeezed me tightly, he pressed his body against mine. Our encounters in the shed had to be carefully arranged to avoid suspicion from our siblings or anybody else.

Late at night while everybody was asleep, he arrived at the bedroom window. He put his hand through the bars and touched my head; I used to get up to find his lips in between the wrought iron bars. If I had fallen asleep and didn't respond when he touched my head, he ran his hand under my pyjama top and stroked my mosquito bite boobs. I opened my eyes and felt his warm hand caressing me. I couldn't sleep after that.

Isidoro offered to send some horses, so we could go for a ride up into the hills near the base of the mountains; everybody was enthusiastic about it, but the next day when the horses arrived, everybody had changed their minds except Mamá Nena who with Yesid and I decided to go. We left early to avoid the hottest part of the day, I had a lovely little pony with great temperament, Mamá Nena had a beautiful palomino horse and Yesid had a great big black horse. By midday we arrived at the foot of the mountain, we had our picnic and while we had lunch, Mamá Nena casually said: 'Yesid, do you love Nené?'

He was speechless, his face lit like a light bulb, he didn't know what to say and after some moments of hesitation, he finally responded to Mamá Nena in a totally unexpected way.

'I will marry Nené when I grow up'. However, Mamá Nena's question made me very nervous.

Mamá Nena continued, 'loving Nené is easy, she is beautiful, she is my first granddaughter and therefore I consider her to be my treasure. You must look after her when I am not around. You will never hurt her or allow anybody to hurt her, and if you marry her when you grow up you will make sure to make her happy'. Mamá Nena didn't say anything else. That was enough. Yesid understood what she meant.

We were very guarded after that day, perhaps she observed us when we didn't realize she was doing it. Perhaps her age allowed her to grasp the feelings and emotions we had just begun to experience. Our behaviour changed from that day, we felt Mamá Nena watched us from the distance. It was difficult to conceal the passion we both felt, children are not supposed to experience feelings of that sort.

Yesid and I went to the matinee movie; while at the movies Lila appeared with her brother and once again invited us to her house for lunch. Yesid called his mother, after Anita conferred with Mamá Nena, they gave us permission to go to Lila's house with the condition we had to return home before dusk.

On our return to the hacienda, the house was empty. It was Sunday and the maids had the day off, we didn't know where everybody was, we thought they had forgotten about us. Initially we listened to the radio while sitting on the hammocks and after some moments started to play rough. The music became monotonous so we went to Yesid's room to select other music; we selected the music and began to listen to it, danced a little, then embraced and ended up against the wall kissing and feeling our bodies immersed into a great passion; he let his hands under my blouse, caressed my torso, and I too moved my hands under his shirt, his skin was hot and sweaty, the energy and the suppressed desire stronger than any will power could control, then we moved to his bed possessed by the desire to be closer and continued to kiss, we laid next to each other, his body tightly held next to mine, everything else didn't matter; we didn't hear anything or anybody calling. A loud voice right on top of us shouted: 'Yesid, what do you think you are doing?' It was Anita.

How long had she been there? She was furious, had a tight look on her face and while she talked her eyes had an incandescent colour. She hit Yesid with her bare hands.

Anita instructed us to compose ourselves and to follow her. We were going to join the rest of the family at their friends' place; she combed my hair and punched Yesid on the arm as we left.

Anita said 'she wouldn't mention this incident to anybody, but if she found out that we had continued this nonsense, she would talk to papa Isidoro. Also, starting from tomorrow you will get up early and go with your father to work in the field'. She said to Yesid.

Isidoro, Yesid's father was a burly tall man with a handsome face, we hardly saw him except when all of us sat at the dinner table. After dinner that evening Isidoro called Yesid to his office. The next day Yesid was absent during breakfast, but I was afraid to ask where he was, the kitchen maid said that el joven Yesid had gone early in the morning with el patrón to help with the harvest.

Fabio, Yesid's brother arrived for a brief recess from his army duties. The first night Fabio was home, he took Yesid with him to town, and every night of his vacation as well. After a week of town excursions, Yesid's behaviour changed; he no longer looked at me with the intensity of previous days, he blew me kisses, but it wasn't the same. I often wondered what happened since Fabio arrived; after Fabio left to re-join the army, there were only a few days left before we returned home.

Does unhappiness have another name?

The return trip took us across the cordillera, the beauty of the landscape was breathtaking, we could see the peaks of the Andes with their permanent snow cover; the mountains that appeared to be so close were 3.000 metres above sea level. There was great abundance and variety of vegetation, plants with gigantic shiny leaves, and the perfume of tropical fruit mixed with the tempered air; we passed coffee plantations on the lower slopes of the cordillera, the terrain looked slippery and the plants had glossy leaves with red berries. Papi said it was almost harvest time and soon there would be men and women with baskets attached to their backs to be filled with the ripe beans. As the altitude continued to increase, there was mist and light rain, and all of a sudden the temperature dropped dramatically.

We stopped in front of a waterfall so high on top of the mountain that the water looked like fairy floss, and on its way down the water made a great splash accompanied with a mighty roaring sound. After we had travelled for several hours on bendy narrow roads, which gave the impression that only one car could fit at any time, the tall mountains on one side, the precipice on the other, we finally started the descent from the cordillera leaving behind the mist and the cold air.

The change in temperature made us sick, even my stomach couldn't take it anymore, but there wasn't any space on the side of the road to stop; during the few occasions when the road opened up, Papi stopped the car and everybody stepped out to enjoy the fresh mountain air.

The smell of banana filled the air, banana trees along both sides of the road and stalls displaying several varieties of fruit tempting the passersby. We stopped to buy some very small bananas not bigger than a couple of centimetres long and two centimetres diameter, silky smooth freckled skin, their golden flesh sweet and aromatic. Big bananas with dark brown skin, under the dark skin the flesh colour was like the colours of the sun set.

We were tired, it was a long journey. Almost near the end of a narrow winding road that went across the mountains, the terrain opened up to show luscious flat valleys and emerald green grass dotted with cows. Two more hours and we would be home. We arrived home late in the afternoon, it had been raining and the air was cool, mother was pleased to see us, but she was cold towards Papi and Tuni.

The following day after our arrival, the books for the second year of high school were delivered; they looked interesting and I loved their crisp appearance. Mother said that I had to cover them with plastic, and my name had to be clearly written on the label. I began to feel a knot in my throat, but mother wasn't sympathetic to my complaints, she was determined that I would complete the entire high school years at the same school, however, I was also equally determined to find a way out of it.

Fena had been matriculated at a sister school located just 30 minutes away from home, it had been arranged that Papi would take her to school in the morning and pick her up in the afternoon until she got used to the bus journey. It was hard to accept that my sister stayed at home, while I had to go back to the boarding school prison.

I asked so many times: 'why? What is the difference between Fena and me? Can I try at least for a couple of weeks?'

My questions didn't hear a response and that silence made me very angry. It was unfair and unjust; Mamá Nena tried hard to help me. I just couldn't understand the inequality of the decision.

The day I had to return to boarding school arrived, and with it my throat closed so tightly it was difficult to eat, and I developed sore throat, stomach cramps, and nausea. When mother said it was time to leave, I felt ill. During times like this my refuge was to run to the backyard were Pepe the monkey was, I cuddled him and cried. He ran his little fingers down my cheeks and tasted my tears, he made some sounds and put his arms around my face, he sat on my shoulders as he used to do when his protection was required, so mother couldn't come close to me. This time he began with loud screams, he showed off his sharp teeth and jumped in front to protect me, but it didn't last long, I had to obey mother's call. She was getting impatient. I cuddled Pepe and told him I was coming back soon. I cried all the way to school and mother was extremely annoyed. I didn't talk at all during the journey.

We arrived at school, the gate opened; I walked inside and disappeared in the crowd.

Yvonne was there with Inez as well as many girls from the previous year, and also many new faces that looked anxious and bewildered not knowing what to expect. It was fairly late and the horrid absolute silence was about to begin. This time I enjoyed the silence, I didn't feel like telling anybody how I felt. Mother didn't want me home, it was a sad reality.

I loathed that awful absolute silence previously; however, it offered me comfort this time. Engrossed in my-self pity I was more in tune with other events that occurred around me. At this time last year among the sadness and confusion I experienced, I also felt other people around me, those invisible people that hovered as if they wanted to talk and tell their stories as well. Girls of various ages; some of them cried while they meandered among the crowd.

Was I going mad? Or was this like the man I used to see standing in the corner of Papi and Tuni's bedroom?'

This time it was clearer, there were girls, nuns and some other people I couldn't identify; it appeared to be people who had passed through the place. After going to the chapel for late Mass, we had dinner and following a short break retired to the dormitories, another prayer and to bed. The lights were turned off and we commenced the routine which some of us were familiar with. I had a sensation like we were watched by people walking in between the corridor formed by the line of beds, it was unnerving. At times I took the courage to lift the blankets off my face to see who was there. The next day I asked Yvonne whether she had felt anything unusual the night before.

She said 'It was spooky'.

Yvonne and I ended up in the same dormitory we shared the previous year, this time we quickly relocated the mattresses and selected beds by the window. My idea was that perhaps I could leave the blinds open to look at the stars. The next day we were placed into squadrons in accordance to our age and then directed to the classrooms. My classroom was dark and dingy with timber panels half way up the walls, this room never saw the sunshine and the nun in charge of the second year was an old, unfriendly and ugly nun.

Sister Irene introduced herself. She seemed to rejoice any available opportunity to humiliate and belittle every girl in the classroom without exception. Her assistant, Sister Emilia, was the opposite. Sister Emilia would be our new English teacher, her family lived in an English speaking country for long periods of time and after her family returned to South America she had decided to enter the convent. This was her first teaching assignment. She didn't look like a nun. She was softly spoken and quite refined.

The first week of classes was a real struggle, in addition to my loneliness and all the other emotions, we had to face Sister Irene's obnoxious disposition. Unfortunately we had Sister Irene for accountancy, typing, shorthand and religious education. Sister Irene managed to make all those subjects so deadly boring we used to fall asleep during her classes, so inadvertently we gave her the opportunity to abuse all of us. She intimidated, and took Sunday visits away.

By the end of the first month the entire class failed several of the subjects Sister Irene taught; the apathy and lethargy during her classes made this classroom darker than it was, and at times not even the ceiling lights appeared to produce enough brightness to illuminate the cavernous room.

I had escaped her vicious tongue until the day she asked me a question while I was thinking about Yesid. My mind was truly away, I was resting in that hammock with his hand under my blouse, I felt his touch and his warm kisses. I didn't hear Sister Irene's question, consequently, there was no possibility of giving her the required answer.

She unleashed her tongue, taking this opportunity to humiliate, belittle and make fun of me in front of the entire class; I stood silently without responding to her insults. I waited for morning recess to see Mother Superior; I knocked on her rooms' door and in the most humble way asked if it was possible to talk to her about a problem I had. I told the nun who opened the door that I would be very brief. The initial response from the nun in charge was that I hadn't made an appointment to talk to Mother Superior.

'But it's urgent' I said. She looked at me and said: 'very well'.

I not only told what Sister Irene had said to me, I also made Mother Superior aware of the constant verbal abuse to other girls and the impossibility to even begin to like any of the subjects she taught because of her obnoxious manner, and that her presence made that classroom darker than it really was; with candour I admitted that the only way to make time elapse while we had to listen to Sister Irene was to think about happy times.

Never in my wildest thoughts would I have guessed the impact of my action. We didn't have any more classes with Sister Irene that day.

The following day all of a sudden Mother Superior walked into our classroom during the second lesson. A couple of girls had already been humiliated, and someone was crying. Mother Superior excused herself as she entered the classroom, and said to Sister Irene to ignore her presence and carry on with the lesson. We all looked at each other with curiosity, Mother Superior listened to Sister Irene who appeared nervous and hesitant; however, while Mother Superior was in the classroom the verbal abuse was omitted when someone didn't have the correct answer.

I didn't tell anybody that I had spoken to Mother Superior. My greatest fear was that perhaps my life would take a turn for the worse since Sister Irene was in charge of the class; after that day Sister Irene continued to be absolutely boring, but she didn't abuse and humiliate us in the same manner she had done previously. She totally ignored me, never asked me any questions, and my tests were just marked with no comments. From that moment I decided I was going to win by not allowing her to give me bad marks.

This was for me, the beginning of the realization that I had something extra within myself and I would overcome the situation, and as I began to obtain good marks on all Sister's Irene subjects, the rest of my academic performance started to improve; the lonely days continued to be lonely, but this simple incident brought the desire to learn and I enjoyed the process.

It was Easter already; everything the same as the previous year, endless praying. Two and half months and June holidays would bring the time to go home. Did I want to go home? I thought about it many times and couldn't find an answer to my question. I longed to be home with Papi and Tuni, but mother had become angry all the time, and in many occasions she was very critical of me for the simplest of reasons.

I wasn't able to understand what happened at home. I didn't enjoy school, but I'd begun to enjoy learning. Papi and Tuni visited me a couple of times independently of mother; during the visits they didn't tell me much when I asked questions. They always referred to Maximiliano as that awful man your mother is seeing, but nothing else was said. I don't recall any events up to June when it was time to go home. Mamá Nena arrived very early to pick me up, one of the first girls to be called. I was happy to see her and even happier that I didn't have to wait until the afternoon as the previous year. We arrived home and the tension was palpable. As usual I ran to the backyard to see Pepe the monkey, but he was gone; his little house was still there under the big tree, with my eyes full of tears I asked where he was. I was told he had been sold because he had become very naughty since my departure.

My heart really ached. Pepe had been with us since I was eight years old; he was another member of the family who I loved dearly. How could he be sold? How could anybody sell a member of the family? This was the beginning of a sad holiday indeed, I had lost my beloved pet, my mother's constant arguments with Papi and Tuni had become very heated. Mamá Nena tried to be the arbitrator but doors were shut, and long silences were more frequent. During this time mother used to tell us to agree with her, and to dismiss Papi and Tuni's point of view because they were old and decrepit with an archaic way of thinking.

On the other hand Papi and Tuni said it was a disgrace mother was paying attention to that awful man Maximiliano.

I was absolutely torn inside. The sadness of not having Pepe around was overwhelming, I used to go to the backyard where his little house still stood under the tree and I cried; I felt an intense pain in my chest, my grief was intense, and in addition my happy home didn't exist anymore. Four weeks had passed by and my birthday happened to fall the day before I had to leave home. Tuni made a cake and I had some presents, but nothing could bring happiness back.

I don't remember who took me back to boarding school the following day; everything is an amalgam of emotions melting and merging into each other like the colours on the artist's pallet. Sad events and I was really sad.

I arrived once more to my prison, six more months and it will be Christmas. The ugliness and harshness within those walls reflected my other life, my happy home life which slowly had begun to disappear; my beloved pet monkey gone and my sisters didn't recognize me anymore. I used to ask myself: 'does unhappiness have another name?'

That period of time exist in the unhappy memories drawer only; those events were captured into a heavy mist that lasted for a long time.

I took refuge in my studies and therefore I excelled in most subjects, I became practical and well organized as well as very determined to get out of there. As I was to call it, the prison for the body and soul, but where would I go?

I didn't know whether Papi and Tuni would be there on my return, all the certainties in my life were disappearing slowly in front of my eyes.

The study hours were fairly long; we had a brief recess after the class finished in the afternoon around 4 o'clock. Then at about 5pm we were confined to the study until 7.30pm and at the sound of the bell we began the exodus to the dining rooms.

That dreadful absolute silence commenced then, and it was only interrupted by a short break at the end of dinner; shortly after that we formed groups according to the squadron arrangement, and in silence went to the chapel for the evening prayer, from the chapel we went to the dormitories.

We polished our shoes, cleaned our teeth, another prayer and the lights were turned off at around 9.30pm. It was a boring routine. No opportunity to play or talk to our friends.

Radios weren't permitted, not even a small radio with its own ear piece was allowed. Some girls owned little portable radios which were passed around and we listened to music under the bed covers. Anybody caught with a radio had detention on Sunday.

We frequently asked the friendly nuns to explain the problem with a radio and why we couldn't listen to music. We argued that in fact we weren't nuns, and wouldn't become nuns either, so having a simple radio couldn't affect us in any way. The response was that we had to follow the rules. The rules are unfair was our reply.

I was told to stand outside the classroom as punishment for talking without permission; while I stood in the long and wide corridor with shiny, green terrazzo floor something called my attention; there was a very large metal box recessed into the wall, the box had two doors with a little metal lever through a loop, I gently pulled the door open and found those white ceramic pieces with wires, after touching one it made a short buzzing noise that sounded interesting, so I pulled several ceramic pieces, put them in my pocket and forgot about them until late that day when the pieces were discarded into the rubbish bin.

That night we had to do our homework using a candle light. I didn't connect the little ceramic pieces with the blackout, and of course nobody suspected that someone had done it, because the town's electricity supply was unreliable.

Visits from home were infrequent. A girl told me on a certain Sunday that my grandparents had just arrived, so I asked permission to leave the study and went downstairs. At the door the nun said that they had just left because mother had given instructions that nobody apart from her was allowed to visit me. I couldn't believe what the nun said was true. Maybe it was a mistake.

How could it happen? I ran to the first floor near the theatre, the bathrooms little windows which faced the street would allow me to see them as they passed by. As soon as I saw them my screams called their attention. They said it was a cross to bear and that it was going to pass; for me it couldn't get any worse. 'All these problems were Maximiliano's fault', they said. 'He was a horrible man who had brought disgrace to the family'. They left promptly to prevent further problems.

I found the theatre store room unlocked; walked in, sat under the racks of dusty costumes and other theatrical gadgets. No tears this time. It was anger, hate towards the nuns, mother and everything that caused my unhappiness. What could I do? I was powerless and my life was getting worse by the moment. I sat there for a long time, my back against the wall, I was absorbed in many thoughts; finally I closed my eyes and I remembered my life the way it used to be, then the tears began to roll. I was powerless and dependant. In spite of my sorrow there was nothing I could do. I must have been there for a couple of hours immersed in my sad emotions.

A stern voice woke me up. 'Girl what are you doing here? Go back to your duties'. It was horrible Sister Irene. I hated that nun! Her blotchy skin looked patchy like some type of creepy crawly that just surfaced from under a rock. She pulled my arm, and continued to lash warnings about detention after classes, and the loss of my visit. She asked questions, which I didn't answer. She demanded answers, which I didn't give.

Weeks passed by before I had a visit. My name was called, and I arrived at the visitor's room but mother wasn't there, I asked the nun in charge that perhaps my name had been called by mistake because mother wasn't there. The nun said there was a lady who had asked for me; she instructed me to have a look in the small room, she was probably there. Mother had sent a distant cousin of hers. A person called, Bertha, she was a distant relative who we seldom saw. I remembered that after the few occasions when we saw her, mother was always very critical of Bertha and the terrible way she brought up her children who were wild, bad mannered and invariably got into trouble with mother on every occasion they visited us.

Bertha recognized me and called my name as I was about to leave the room. Her visit was short, there wasn't a great deal to say anyway, and she appeared to be in a hurry. She was doing mother a favour.

I was puzzled! Papi and Tuni weren't allowed to visit me for whatever reason, mother didn't visit me; yet she sent a person who meant nothing to me to pretend that someone cared for me. I didn't know whether Papi and Tuni would be there on my return.

All the certainties in my life were disappearing slowly in front of my eyes. Mamá Nena visited me on one occasion; my questions were not answered, the conversation changed when I asked about what was going on, and why Papi and Tuni weren't allowed to visit me.

Mamá Nena didn't seem to be aware that Bertha had been sent to visit me, she was surprised; after Mamá Nena's visit I decided that I would not come any more to the visitor's room regardless of who came to visit me. I would wait until it was time to return home for the next holidays; that was if someone turned up to pick me up.

It was the end of the school year, time to go home. Again it was mid-afternoon, and I was the only girl left at school. It was 3pm and I was sitting on the chapel's ledge when I saw Bertha push open the big, brown timber door. Apparently the reception was unattended and she walked onto the big concrete patio where I was. She was surprised to see me alone, and she asked where everybody was.

'Everybody has gone home because their parents want the girls to be home with them', was my reply.

She began to justify mother's behaviour and whatever was happening in my family, I didn't bother to listen because it didn't make any sense to me. Finally we arrived home, which wasn't home. It was a different house, ordinary and dull. We entered a dark ugly corridor which opened into a courtyard devoid of light. Maximiliano was there and to my great surprise I had a new brother. He was very pretty, big blond boy with beautiful brown eyes. I loved him from the moment I saw him. 'Was he the cause of my troubles?'

I returned home for the Christmas holidays but it wasn't home for me. Soon I realized that Papi and Tuni were taboo subjects. Mother became furious just hearing anything about them, we couldn't even talk to them on the phone; we weren't allowed to visit them either. Fena and I were absolutely heartbroken, so we decided to develop ways to escape to see them.

We invented outings with friends who didn't exist and didn't have a phone, in this way we couldn't be contacted. We rehearsed every word and everything to avoid being caught. We invented a complex deception and avoidance mechanism which enabled us to visit Papi and Tuni. They lived about one hour from our new place of residence. We lied to mother to be able to spend some time with them, and while we saw them time appeared so brief. We cried every time we had to say goodbye and we left them with tears in their eyes. It was a difficult situation for them as well as for us. It was cruel. The pain we experienced was intense, and to try to minimize the agony of the separation, Papi and Tuni always made us think and look forward to the next visit, which we tried to organize as soon as there was an opportunity.

Meanwhile, a tremendous dislike towards Maximiliano was evident, and we blamed him for the separation from Papi and Tuni, as well as the obstacles that appeared all of a sudden and prevented us from seeing them. We thought that our mother couldn't be so cruel, because she knew that Papi and Tuni represented in our life. It had to be Maximiliano!

My resentment towards mother increased by the day, she had changed beyond recognition, she was always angry and critical of everything we did or said, the maids were dismissed from their normal duties and mother gave them other tasks in order to make us clean, cook and look after our young brother. It was tough to start with, but I discovered the rewards of cooking; for me it wasn't a form of punishment, on the contrary it was quite enjoyable, but I never said anything because I had the feeling that it would've been taken away from me.

Maximiliano had the ability to upset us with his dismissive manner and acid comments; he was insensitive and made fun of us with a type of sarcasm that we loathed; he also criticized us at every possible opportunity. In turn we used our wit to make fun of him behind his back. His eating habits were appalling, so we began to imitate him during mealtimes.

We slurped the soup, bit the bread instead of tearing it in small pieces, filled our mouth to excess so our cheeks inflated like cushions and talked with the mouth full of food. The other thing we did when fruit was served was to bite it instead of cutting it, we stabbed the fruit with the fork and held it up in the air close to our face and bit off great chunks. Mother had a predicament on her hands if she corrected us she had to correct him; therefore for us it was comical. Fena had a tremendous way with it.

A very unsettling situation began to develop with mother's consent; Maximiliano had decided to chaperone us when we were invited to afternoon parties, the parties were the typical gathering of twelve year old girls and boys usually at the house of one of Fena's friends; since Fena was a day student she was able to associate with the girls during the holidays while my friends lived in distant cities.

The parties were usually chaperoned by a group of mothers who also got together for afternoon coffee, while the children danced to the latest hit songs; Maximiliano didn't talk to the mothers since he was the only man, and obstinately decided that he had to either dance with us or with the other girls. We were repulsed and embarrassed by it; the situation was so disgusting that we started to avoid parties. We avoided afternoon party invitations as a way to resolve the problem with Maximiliano.

We organized with the girls to have afternoon cake making instead, which always became a party when their brothers and their friends turned up to taste the cakes. We organized small gatherings which we absolutely enjoyed, and we finally got rid of Maximiliano.

We had the last and the loudest laugh when we plotted to make Maximiliano feel embarrassed; we asked permission to go to an afternoon party when it was only a gathering of a couple of girls, who intended to learn how to make a chocolate cake with one of the mothers. As usual he got dressed and merrily took us to the party perhaps thinking that it would be the usual arrangement; we arrived and everybody was in the kitchen around the mother who was teaching how to mix the ingredients. There he was, that stupid man all dressed up and perfumed. The mother offered him an apron and invited him to mix the ingredients. We all laughed.

Those gatherings didn't happen often either, mother had the theory that girls should not be allowed to go out too frequently. I was in a prison during the scholastic year and during my holiday, home had become another prison. The reality of the situation was incomprehensible to us during those early years.

Our life was divided into work at home as some form of punishment for something we didn't know we had done, and prohibitions left, right, and centre of everything. There were so many things that we weren't allowed to do, that there is an empty space when I try to remember the things we were allowed to do; perhaps the occasional shopping outing on a Saturday afternoon, a matinee movie once in a blue moon, because mother decided that she didn't like the movies, and that was enough reason to prevent us from going to the cinema.

It became quite difficult to escape to see Papi and Tuni, and we believed that Maximiliano and mother planned it that way. Boredom continued to be the guideline during our holidays, and our main preoccupation was to gather a moment to see Papi and Tuni before Christmas, but we couldn't.

The first Christmas we spent at this place was one of the most miserable and depressing occasions we experienced. We spent Christmas alone that is just the four of us, our new brother, mother and Maximiliano, even the maids decided to leave.

Dinner was served and since the presents had been placed at the base of the nativity decoration, mother decided that we could open the presents after dinner. The only present Fena asked for, was a great shiny red apple. I asked Fena why a great big apple. Her reply was that she thought it could be an enchanted apple, and then she could ask for a wish. She received a beautiful, red shiny apple, so big it didn't look real.

Maximiliano took a look at the beautiful, red apple, and asked Fena if he could have a bite, Fena extended her hand and gave Maximiliano the apple, and as he took a bite, mother jumped out of the chair and began to scream.

We witnessed the most incredible argument. Among the many insults and names they called each other, the most memorable one was when Maximiliano called mother a hyena, as the argument continued on, we left the table and went to bed.

We went to our bedroom and wept in silence, we cried not because of the horrible argument; we cried because our life was so miserable, and there wasn't any relief in sight to our terrible unhappiness. We were still dressed when we dropped on the bed and cried until we went to sleep. The next day nobody said a word, we avoided sitting at the table for breakfast.

The rest of the week was weird and upsetting; we didn't talk to mother or Maximiliano at all. All I remember is how quiet and lifeless we were. I don't recall exactly what happened. Maximiliano organized fireworks for New Year and everything was well prepared on the terrace for a midnight display. Dinner was served at around 9pm. and during dinner Maximiliano as well as mother tried to make us feel enthusiastic about the fireworks; we were too depressed and feared another argument after a week of tension. We kept silent at all times. As soon as dinner was finished we left the table.

I took a bottle of brandy to our bedroom and proceeded to drink some of the contents straight from the bottle, and so did Fena. In a matter of minutes we were in another world. I remember being so dizzy it was impossible to stand up.

We heard the calls to go to the terrace to watch the beautiful lights, but we just laughed uncontrollably making fun of Maximiliano and mother. We continued drinking brandy until we reached the red line mark on the bottle's label, by then we began to feel sick. Maximiliano and mother weren't aware of our condition and sent cousin Ye to talk to us, but he realized the futility of it all and left us alone.

We heard screams sometime later, and shortly afterwards, Maximiliano entered our bedroom to inform us that mother had burnt a hand and that we should come to help, but we couldn't stand up. We continued to laugh until we began to throw up, right there on the bedroom floor.

The next day suffering a horrendous hangover, we faced Maximiliano's criticism and sarcasm for the lack of interest in family matters. I still laugh as I remember Fena's response to Maximiliano when he finished his reprimands. 'You a Señor so perfect, so dignified, and so elegant, but I still do not like you'. He unable to respond walked away. We looked at each other and laughed uncontrollably behind his back.

Since this confrontation he seldom spoke to us or made any other sarcastic comments about what we did or said. He ignored us completely and we liked it that way. We knew there was no other choice but to put up with him, and as long as he didn't interfere we avoided confrontations with him; mother was a different matter, she had become really nasty, in many occasions we couldn't even listen to music; when we read the Sunday's newspaper comics she said we were wasting our time.

It was a very tense existence, from time to time we would go to picnics where mother wanted to play the happy family like in the movies, but it didn't work. It always ended in a disaster. We thought that the picnics were organized to keep us away from Papi and Tuni, and everything Maximiliano and mother did, we converted into a plot to prevent us from having any contact with Papi and Tuni.

Our cousin Ye arrived to live with us at the beginning of the year, he was about to start the final year of chemical engineering. Papi and Tuni had given him some assistance during his previous university years, but for some reason he had decided to take mother's side and she had offered him accommodation.

The acceptance of her offer was a terrible mistake, and this decision would make his life very difficult within a very short period of time. He didn't know Maximiliano's real self or mother's true character.

We had already seen the changes in our lives and we did warn him, but cousin Ye wasn't aware of the reality of our situation. His visits were sporadic and brief; not enough time was spent with us to allow him to see what was truly happening. Perhaps cousin Ye thought that whatever we said, it was the typical twisted and mad interpretation of crazy teenagers.

We grew up with Ye, he loved us, his little sisters as he used to call us, and we loved him; sometimes he introduced us to his university friends, he also took us to the movies and we found in him an ally to our parties, and a relief from the ghastly intrusion Maximiliano presented. He used to take us to our parties and left us there, because he said those parties were full of sardines and the big sisters weren't there most of the time; he returned at a sensible hour to pick us up and we were all happy.

The fondest memories I have of Ye, are the numerous stories about his many love affairs; it was riveting to listen to the drama. Ye, a handsome man, loved music and reading and as a member of the communist party, he received a monthly magazine directly from Moscow. The magazine had lots of pictures and long articles about Fidel Castro, the possible fall of the oligarchy in Latin America, and how the masses would punish the bourgeoisie when they took control through a systematic uprising.

'What sort of punishment? Aren't we bourgeois?' I used to ask.

I enjoyed enormously the discussions I had with Ye about the communist party, what was offered to the masses and consequently their freedom from the bourgeoisie. He normally explained the meaning of complicated topics and at the end he used to say: 'It's all bull shit'.

I went back to boarding school. This time, Ye took me back. Ye said, he would visit me if mother wasn't able to make it with the condition I introduced him to some spunky chicks. It was a fair compromise and I agreed.

This was the third year of boarding school. I was determined it was going to be the last. Since my arrival at school, I began to disrupt everything I could possible include in my agenda of disruption. I disconnected the power, this time the ceramic fuses were left in their sockets, I just moved them far enough to avoid contact with the board and therefore created a blackout. I also lit fires here and there in the back rooms.

I believed my fire lighting techniques were safe because the whole building was made of brick and concrete, and I made sure there wasn't too much timber around, like desks or chairs.

On several occasions I spread the contents of a shoe polish box under the nun's bed sheets, poured water on another nun's bed, put pins under the sheets, and threw bed side tables through the windows just missing the electric cables.

I was totally detached from the havoc I created, and therefore behaved as it was someone else who carried out the deeds; never made any comment to anybody, didn't have any conscious guilt. While I plotted the next move, I still kept my studies under control and I did well in every subject.

My academic improvement was helped by the fact than Pilar and I had a competition to be number one.

The first Sunday visit arrived and I was delighted to find cousin Ye waiting for me. He was wearing white jeans and a black shirt; some girls joined the conversation and flirted with him. He visited me a couple of times and his popularity increased on each occasion, some girls began to ask me whether my cousin was coming to visit me. The visits stopped all of a sudden, and absolutely nobody visited me. It was time to go home for the mid-year holidays. It crossed my mind that perhaps I was going to spend my holidays at school.

To my great surprise my name was called early the day we departed for holidays, it was grandmother waiting for me and we went home. It would be another miserable holiday. Mother was truly unbearable; she was pregnant, and the condition gave her an excuse to become agonizingly painful. We couldn't listen to the radio, we couldn't watch television, we couldn't go to the movies; it was impossible to invite someone for an afternoon because the sound of our voices irritated her. The arguments between mother and Maximiliano were endless; even the sound of our laughter bothered her and gave her the opportunity to tell us off. Mother exploded at the most insignificant of things, everything and everybody displeased her.

My disagreements with mother increased, and the more she criticized me the more antagonistic I became. The other casualty of this family situation was cousin Ye. Mother and

Maximiliano had stopped providing meals for him, I realized that meals for him had stopped during the first of my cooking punishments, I was told not to leave dinner for Ye.

Having been told that a person in the family was not going to have his meal obviously took me by surprise. I asked why and mother's response was: 'Just because that's the way it is'. I couldn't believe what I had just heard. Was there a need to be so cruel and mean? What had he done? It didn't matter what I was told, I decided that every time I cooked, his dinner was hidden and I left little messages for him describing where he could find his meal, also I left part of my dinner on other occasions.

Cousin Ye didn't have any money; Papi and Tuni weren't helping him anymore since he had moved in with mother; his father a bit of a bastard who hadn't been interested in facing his parental duties while cousin Ye was younger, didn't show any interest at a crucial time when his help was pivotal to his future; his mother couldn't afford the expense of his university final year, and it was difficult for him to find a job, because of his lecture crazy time schedule.

Maximiliano and mother began to ignore cousin Ye when he was around; they didn't speak a word to him, they were mean. The manner in which he was treated was beyond my understanding. In my view, Ye didn't do anything wrong, how could he? He left early in the morning and returned at around 10pm. I went back to school and often thought of him.

Stick or a dick?

My days at boarding school were different; although my mischievous ways continued I became fairly reserved, never told anybody about my home situation. Not even Pilar was aware of my troubles. I began to believe that nobody was able to help me, and that I had to resolve everything myself, but I didn't know how. Yvonne from time to time used to comment on how naughty I was, and sometimes she had to bear some punishment just for being next to me.

At the beginning of the term, a week after the return to school from the holidays a retreat was organized for girls over thirteen. It really suited me this time to be quiet, there wasn't anything good for me to say. We were encouraged to examine our thoughts and actions, to go to confession and to have talks with the nuns and the priest running the retreat. We were given self-improvement books that although of a religious nature, contained interesting topics.

We had to talk to the priest, my appointment arrived, but I didn't have anything to say apart from my family situation and I wasn't prepared to go into it. I began to say that there was nothing for me to tell because my holidays were very boring. He then proceeded to talk about Jesus, the saints and all the marvellous things achieved by the church, and how we were responsible for spreading the true religion. When he said that, I asked him to explain how he knew it was the true religion, he mumbled something incomprehensible and I left.

The retreat continued to give me the opportunity to read as many books as possible, the most interesting passage I found in one of those religious books was, how through the power of God it is possible to achieve everything. It said, "Ask and it shall be given". I thought it was an interesting concept, however, I didn't believe for a moment that I had to involve a particular God to achieve my goals, and I began to think about the things I wanted to achieve in my life; every night before I fell asleep I thought about the life I would like to live when I grew up, not in a question form but as an affirmation and a belief. I saw myself far away from where I was, I would be surrounded by nature, not far from the sea, and great harmony and beauty would be around me. Perhaps this was my way to bring a bit of tranquillity and balance into an otherwise unsettled life, and with this new way of thinking I developed a positive and optimistic outlook, and I began to expand the idea that it didn't matter how bad it appeared to be, it would be better tomorrow and since everything happened for a reason I would be able to understand it later.

I was only thirteen years old, and by this time I had already made decisions which would determine the path I would follow for the rest of my life; I had already decided that I didn't like religion at all, I didn't feel guilty of sins of any sort, and I didn't think prayers forwarded to someone up in the sky sitting on a cloud would take anybody anywhere, because everything had to be resolved within if an external solution had to be found.

All that talk about saints and their ways of punishing themselves was emphasized by the nuns on a regular basis, and some sort of self-inflicted suffering in silence was the preferred option, followed by flagellation and self-torture, which had achieved sainthood for many of those individuals. That type of behaviour was considered to be a wonderful example of a Christian mind and should be followed to achieve eternal life.

I also realized that my love for nature and the animal world brought true happiness to my being. The affection I had for Pepe, the Amazon monkey, and the heartache I experienced after his departure highlighted the incredible communication and love animals give unconditionally. I felt that Pepe taught me to understand his feelings and fears.

Pepe made me think that without animals and the joy that nature brings into one's life there was emptiness. I used to discuss those issues with Pilar, she agreed on everything except the importance I placed on animals and nature; she thought people were more important. Oh Pilar I used to say, 'I could live without people, but I do not wish to live in a barren environment like the one we live here, without animals and so devoid of the natural world; I would rather die young than live a life without a bird's song or a flower's perfume'. Every time I expressed those feelings she was silent.

The rest of the year continued in an uneventful way, towards the end of the year the Sunday visits instead of being once a month were increased to once a fortnight, which didn't make any difference since nobody visited me. There was a slight change in our routine as well, some Saturdays we were taken for a walk around town, sometimes we went to the highest hill which housed an old church, and other buildings that looked like at some point nuns or priests had inhabited those dwellings. Other times the walk headed to the town outskirts where there was a bakery. A couple of kilometres from the bakery we could smell delicious fresh bread. The bakery produced traditional old style bread, several types of small cheese bread and cakes to accompany coffee; the cheese bread was made with corn flour and fresh cheese. It was a real treat.

We talked, walked and looked around the gardens; park benches were scattered under trees, we sat to admire the lovely flower beds, and enjoy the fresh bread as well as the aroma that permeated the air. A short walk from the bakery brought us into the main road which was the main access to the town centre; at this point we had to form lines of three girls and began to walk in silence towards the school. The road was narrow with views to the paddocks, and a few houses in the distance; old big willows and eucalyptus trees were scattered on each side of the embankment which often was higher than the road; the grass grew taller on the outer ring of the tree canopies, and from time to time on a sunny afternoon we could see some individuals enjoying the sun's warmth.

We looked forward to the bakery outing, it was a very popular place, and sometimes we met day girls who invited us to indulge in more than one cheese bread. This was a walk that provided an outlet for the girls who rarely left school because their parents lived far away, or a girl like me, although my family lived relatively close to school didn't receive visits. But as it happens sometimes, things are destroyed by external circumstances beyond anybody's control, and our enjoyable walk was spoiled forever.

We left school earlier than usual, it was a warm sunny day, and as we began to walk towards the town outskirts, along the narrow road we saw a short man wearing a poncho, which was the typical garment of country workers. He looked at us as many people used to, because it was a rarity to see the posh convent girls walking in silence towards any part of town.

We went to the bakery, spent some time there, and on our return we saw the same man leaning on the high side of the embankment. The grass was long and the man seemed to disappear in it.

The leading nun walked past, and the man took his hat off and said hello, as the rest of the girls walked in front of him, the man lifted his poncho to expose something that came out of his pants, it was purple and long, it rather looked like a thick stick; other men were also by the side of the road and began to say things we didn't understand. As the first man exposed himself, he encouraged others to imitate him.

They said: 'we can fuck you all front and back' and then they made backward and forward movements while their hands touched their bulging, exposed parts. Ahead of those men was another man, and as he held his stick, he rubbed it furiously until white stuff began to pour out of it.

The nun leading the group didn't have a clue of what was happening, while the nun at the back was telling everybody not to look, but of course we did the opposite; by the time we arrived at school we had been told to say probably a thousand Ave Maria Mother of God.

I told Pilar on Monday morning about Saturday's events; she was going to bring a drawing of it, which she did, but I couldn't understand how a man could keep in his pants something big like that. She said the white stuff was sperm. We discussed it at length and finally after a lot of explaining from Pilar, I understood. It was easy for her because she had seen it all, I also mentioned to Pilar that I had touched Yesid's over his pants and that the thing moved like an animal under covers. She burst out laughing until she cried. Apart from the conversation with Pilar this incident was forgotten, it didn't seem to have any relevance except that our walks to the bakery didn't happen again.

The nuns involved in the incident never talked about it, they didn't explain anything, and nobody knew how to ask questions either

It was a relief to see the end of the academic year, but it was difficult to feel enthusiastic about going home. It was evident that there was not a great deal of difference between boarding school and home.

Living with the family had become another type of nightmare. While I was lonely at school, I had good friends and I was a popular girl among the other students who didn't mind the fact that I was extremely naughty, and caused them a lot of problems if they happened to be in my vicinity when the nuns distributed some punishment for being unruly; at home I was lonely in a different way, there was no joy, and seldom we laughed, there was no intelligent conversation, and mother made life really unpleasant for those who didn't agree with her.

Fena had grown accustomed to the life of arguments and in a way she had adapted to it, while for me it was very different; although I was unhappy at school, school was peaceful; there were no arguments, and the punishment of standing in the corridor or next to the flag pole didn't have a long lasting effect on me anymore.

Mamá Nena arrived to pick me up after the presentation ceremony, and on the way home she mentioned that we had a new brother who was born in October. As soon as we arrived home mother asked if I had any prizes or medals. The reality of the situation was that nobody had visited me since I had returned to school. That didn't seem to matter. Some stupid medals had more importance than how I felt. I hadn't seen anybody for such a long period of time.

I hadn't seen mother or anybody else since June and all she was interested in was a couple of lousy medals. I did have a couple of medals and a book, but I didn't mention it. I wanted to see her reaction. Mother proceeded to chastise me; Maximiliano obviously agreed with her and had to add some acid comments of his own. However, they didn't get any answers from me.

Fena failed her second year of high school; of course it was kept quiet while my inquisition was taking place. 'Don't let them bother you' Mamá Nena said.

Mamá Nena remained with us for a couple of weeks and that made a lot of difference to me. She cooked, we baked bread, went shopping, and made dresses; she offered the girl in charge of the kitchen ways to improve her cooking skills. I paid a great deal of attention to Mamá Nena's tips and advice to Elsi. I often said to Mamá Nena that everything she cooked always tasted delicious, followed with the comment that when mother cooked it was invariably not very good. Mamá Nena's response was: 'Believe it or not love is a very important ingredient in cooking, as important as salt, pepper or any other condiment. Your mother doesn't cook with love and that is the reason the food she prepares doesn't taste good'.

Mamá Nena had brought Elsi from the country; her parents' had decided to send her to work in the city as a domestic employee, she was intelligent, neat and tidy with a lovely round face. Mamá Nena suggested I should teach her to read and write during my holidays.

I absolutely loved the idea and began with great enthusiasm to gather my early childhood books; ripped the pages from the old exercise books and used the clean pages for her homework. Every afternoon after 3 o'clock when she completed her tasks I commenced the lessons. It was so lovely! I also taught her geography, a bit of history, arithmetic as well as drawing. I lent her my colour pencils and my primary school text books. On those occasions when my punishment relieved Elsi of her kitchen chores, I still started the lessons at 3pm. Soon she began to read and as she progressed I decided to cut segments out of the Sunday newspaper comic section.

The day she was able to read without running her finger under the line, she threw her arms around me and with tears in hers eyes said that I had given her the most beautiful present she had ever received, and she was never going to forget me.

Mamá Nena often took me shopping with her and on some occasions I accompanied her to visit old friends, and on the way to their place, she took the opportunity to tell me stories related to the people we would visit. I guess she felt comfortable and didn't mind my constant and indiscrete questions, and without failure she explained situations I didn't understand.

Grandmother said: 'let's go, we are going to visit Hilda today. We must be on time because she booked our visit and we have many things to talk about'. This time you will not find other children around because we are going to the convent where Hilda lives.

'Why does she live in a convent?'

'That is a long story', grandmother said. I will start telling you from the very beginning, however when we arrive at Hilda's convent you mustn't ask any questions and whatever I am going to tell you today, it's a story like many others and you will keep quiet.

Hilda belongs to a very wealthy family, we have been good friends since school days and we spent most of our holidays together until Hilda had her problems. Our families used to be fairly close; Mamá was a good friend of Hilda's mother, but once Hilda had her problems, Mamá never spoke to her again, not because Mamá didn't want to talk to her, but it was Hilda's mother who never wanted to communicate with Mamá again.

It all began when we were invited at one of those parties that used to last for several days; Hilda's parents' hacienda was in close proximity to ours but it took the entire day to travel; what I mean is that we had to leave fairly early in the morning before sunrise, and we normally arrived late in the afternoon at sunset. The horses were ready to take us and we left early with Mamá and some of the servant girls; Papá followed up after he made sure that the luggage was properly loaded and the rest of the servants had clear instructions until our return.

By the time we arrived many other people had already arrived, and we joined them for some cool drinks before proceeding to our accommodation quarters; there were some new people who just had entered the circle of friends, among them a banker who had arrived from Spain, his wife and two sons, one son absolutely handsome and debonair; tall and slim, light coloured eyes with a hint of amber, long eyelashes and a truly charismatic personality.

He had finished his secondary school and with certainty he would return to Spain to further his studies. Most of us were fascinated by his incredible beauty, and many guests made the comment that he was almost better looking that most of the girls present at the gathering.

It was a fantastic party, there were musicians, the food was exquisite and we just had a tremendous time playing games and singing songs, what we didn't know was that Hilda was smitten by this boy. We returned home and for a long time talked about one of the best parties we had been to in many years.

I saw Hilda with the same frequency I had seen her throughout our friendship; our friendship didn't change, however, Hilda told me that the boy had written some letters and they were returning during the Christmas holidays. Hilda often mentioned that she fantasized about him and was looking forward to his future visit; what she forgot to tell me was that the boy, his name was Alejandro, had visited her several times after the party and that his visits were carried out in her bedroom.

Hilda was definitely in love with Alejandro, and she raved and ranted about him nonstop until the day she let it slip, and accidentally mentioned that he had visited her bedroom several times already. They had sex without penetration almost since the day they met. Grandmother couldn't understand how they managed to carry out their affair without anybody noticing it.

'What do you mean grandmother?'

'It is a little difficult to explain, but it is a type of sex where there is no risk of falling pregnant because the sperm does not have a chance of impregnating the egg'.

'What egg? Do women have eggs like the hens?'

'Yes, in a way'. I will gather some drawings from a medical book and show you how everything is formed and how it works.

Let me continue with the story. Hilda asked permission to visit us and her parents agreed, but Papá and Mamá didn't know that she was coming to stay with us; it was all a front to be able to elope with Alejandro. She worked it all out and at the last minute she told me about her plans. Hilda put me in a difficult situation because of the great friendship and affection we both had for each other. I struggled whether to tell or not to tell; I couldn't sleep and I became a bundle of nerves since I knew about the day she was going to elope. I prayed that someone would find out, and in that way I would be relieved of the burden on my conscience.

Alejandro's secret visits continued until they were ready to elope; the urge to have sex was stronger than anything else and they began to have sex with penetration, which meant the possibility of getting pregnant; someone had told Hilda that if she inserted an aspirin prior to the sexual act that would kill the sperm, and she wouldn't have to worry about an unwanted pregnancy. The aspirin trick must have worked because the sex encounters continued for a long time, and nobody seemed suspicious of their liaison until the day they supposed to elope.

Alejandro visited her and as usual they had their sex, and agreed on their departure time and day. The day arrived and Alejandro didn't turn up. She waited in vain, and then became desperate and hysterical; out of frustration or something else she confided in one of the maids, who immediately informed her mother. Too late, the upheaval had already started. Initially nobody suspected about the sex encounters, and the annoyance towards her was more related to her undisciplined ways. As it was the custom during those times, the girl was locked in her room until the parents decided about the course of action.

Hilda was confined to her room; she was under constant supervision, the door and window were locked, there was no chance of escaping or communicating with Alejandro; weeks passed by and she began to feel the effects of an early pregnancy, but not knowing what it was, she didn't disclose her discomfort until she couldn't hide the symptoms anymore.

The physician was called and the worst fears were confirmed, she was pregnant, she told her parents who the father was, and consequently her parents contacted their new friends who already aware of the problem had dispatched Alejandro abroad and he was on his way to Spain.

The only alternative left was to send her to a convent until the child was born, give the child for adoption and then decide her future. A convent was contacted and since her parents had a great deal of wealth, it appeared that the convent not only agreed to take her for the duration of her pregnancy but to keep her after the adoption.

A large sum of money was negotiated and Hilda started her new life in a convent as an unwilling nun. She found ways of communicating with me and I always received her letters, but I couldn't answer them, and I couldn't visit her either because everybody firmly believed that I was an accomplice. Perhaps, if I had talked I would have rescued her from the events that took place; it is impossible to foresee how a situation is going to evolve, and for me to disclose what she had entrusted me with was a form of betrayal.

A child was born, a boy, she called him Alex, of course.

She knew who had adopted him immediately after the birth. She only saw him briefly. Hilda believed that after the birth of her child she would be free to leave the convent, but she was unaware of the decisions her parents had made on her behalf, and the nuns didn't release her either.

Initially I felt so incredibly sorry for her. Her letters were full of anguish and unhappiness; however, after a while Hilda appeared to have accepted her life.

Hilda turned twenty one and thought that being a grown up woman, she was able to make decisions about her life, but it wasn't to be; her father died shortly before her birthday, and her inheritance was left to the convent, which meant that if she left the monastic life, she was alone in the world without any finances to support her. The convent financial rules were not negotiable; either she remained with the order and the order would look after her or nothing else. Afraid of a life without money Hilda made the decision to continue her monastic life, and accepted the consequences of her previous actions. She gave in to the pleasures of the flesh and she had to pay for her sin.

It was only possible to visit her after several years; I arrived at the convent and identified myself as a member of her family, since nobody had visited during those years, I said I was her sister. I waited in the small room which was full of religious objects on the walls, it was austere but serene, and when the door opened a rotund woman with pink cheeks, dressed in black, and with her hair covered, appeared in front of me. We embraced and couldn't stop the torrent of tears, after a long pause we began to talk.

She had accepted her life, and that acceptance had given her a tremendous serenity. I talked about my life, I had married and I was expecting your mother. After that visit many more visits followed, I could write to Hilda and she answered my letters.

She always kept me informed of her convent life, if she had been transferred somewhere else, she would let me know and that is why we are going to visit her today. She was transferred recently and it is a great opportunity to see her. Just keep quiet, do not stare, and do not ask any questions; if she asks something reply in a simple manner.

We arrived at the convent and the nun directed us to a small room full of light, the room had a curved window with a ledge and on the ledge some colourful, embroidered cushions; grandmother sat on a chair and I sat on the cushions, fairly soon Hilda entered the room. Grandmother and Hilda embraced and then she introduced me once more; apparently Hilda had met me when I was three years old. They talked and laughed and after a short while Hilda invited us to visit the rose garden where she was involved with the upkeep; grandmother and Hilda walked and talked while I looked around and smelled the roses, I do not recall anything else. We left after some cakes and lemonade; on the way home grandmother made an interesting remark.

'Before you intend to have sex, always ask yourself: what can happen after sex?'

We arrived home and I forgot about Hilda's story in the same way I forgot all the other stories; grandmother spent some more days with us and then she left.

A large number of boxes that had remained unopened since we moved to the house were finally unpacked and the contents placed on the shelves. The books belonged to Maximiliano, the books looked old and well used. Among the many authors were Dante, Cervantes, which I knew about and new ones I began to discover; some of them very interesting like Ernst Hemingway, Françoise Sagan, Simone de Beauvoir, Kafka, Jean-Paul Sartre, and some poetry by Pablo Neruda among others.

I used to escape to the terrace and climbed the slippery roof with a book until I read several of them. 'The Sun also rises', 'Bonjour Tristesse', and 'Nausea' I had great delight reading those books; so enlightening, although more often than not, I had to read the same paragraph several times to comprehend the meaning of those words; like when I read 'Nausea' and 'Bonjour Tristesse'. In many occasions after my chores were carried out, I disappeared for a couple of hours. I could hear mother calling, but I knew that if I responded my reading moments would've finished, instead I continued to read until my bum got tired of sitting on the hard slippery surface.

My place of solace was the roof; I climbed the roof just on the other side of the terrace where hidden by the ridge of the tiles nobody could see me. After a while and when the calls stopped I found the appropriate moment to enter the house, and sat somewhere quietly until someone found me. Nobody seemed to understand that I had changed profoundly; mother didn't acknowledge that the distance from home, and the lack of visits had created a great rift in between me and the rest of the family.

I had become a little person who had my own thoughts, and although I was only thirteen years old my mind had been opened to different views. I did enjoy solitude, silence, and most of all I loved to read. I disliked enormously all that noise, chatter and the impossibility to just be myself; I was a real stranger among the so called family, and I didn't belong there anymore.

I was foolish enough to ask Fena if she had read the books on the shelves; I didn't think she was very intelligent because she had failed the second year of high school, but the degree of her stupidity left me flabbergasted; I also realized she was sly and secretive, also behaved like a spy. After I mentioned the books to Fena, everything from the shelves disappeared.

I asked mother about the books, her response was that since I had such a dirty mind, she didn't have any other option but to get rid of them. I told mother that she wasn't any different from the 15th century Spanish Inquisition, and to complete her duty she should burn me at the stake with the neighbour's black pussycat.

She slapped me across the face leaving her hand printed on my cheek; the colour on my cheek changed from red, purple, green, to the final yellow, until all the colours disappeared by the end of the week. By then I was more attentive to Fena's behaviour, she seemed closer to mother and used to agree with her most of the time, when I was critical of mother and the way our life had turned out, mother used to make comments about it later and subsequently, I blamed Fena for losing the books.

There was a newspaper column which gave advice on family issues, so I made the decision to write asking for help and advice in relation to the situation we were living. I wasn't aware that mother searched every drawer and read every piece of paper she found. I started to write the letter, first I began to explain the basic problem, which for us was the brutal separation from Papi and Tuni, then the awful life we were living through the arguments, the lack of balance in our lives, and the many restrictions which we considered to be unfair.

I folded the pages and placed them in the drawer to finish later. I also made the comment to Fena that our life wasn't normal; I continued to say that when we went to a friend's place, the mother was kind and treated the girls with love, they talked in an amiable manner and the mother listened to them without criticism.

Mother found my unfinished letter. She belittled me more than usual, she proceeded to tell me that I had a horrible character, a repulsive personality, I was going to encounter many difficulties interacting with people and absolutely everybody would dislike me, I had to change. I had to stop the insatiable appetite for reading immoral books, and that a deprived mind like mine would only bring suffering throughout my life. To sum it all up I was a libertine, like the worst of them I would probably end up in prison.

I calmly said: 'those books aren't mine, tell Maximiliano how deprived he is for having brought the books to this house. I think if I had a father you wouldn't dare to treat me like this'. Well, I had just recovered from my purple cheek and I received another one. The more my cheek became purple the more I disliked mother.

I still continued to disappear to my place of solace, the roof, on several occasions even mother arrived looking for me; I kept quiet and avoided being seen.

To make matters worse Fena didn't have any difficulties going to parties or getting new dresses, but I did. Everything I asked for, mother disagreed with and denied. I couldn't go anywhere I couldn't buy anything, I received punishment for one thing or another on a regular basis, as well as constant and bitter criticism.

People sometimes made positive remarks about my physical appearance or provided good comments somehow related to me; mother invariably responded with a negative remark about me, completely ignoring the other person's positive words. She proceeded to tell how wonderful Fena was, her great qualities, her good nature and good character, adding without failure that my difficult personality caused many problems and that she had to punish me frequently for my rebellious and libertine behaviour.

To spice up the negative part of my personality, mother also informed the listener that I had a twisted mind ready to read any filth that was put in front of me. The person who made the initial comment was left speechless and changed the conversation to another topic when I was around.

Those incidents widened the rift between mother, Fena and I, every day almost without failure, an argument developed and after the argument there was punishment. It was a vicious cycle which didn't show a possible end.

The last time Fena and I planned to go to a matinee was as disappointing as on many other occasions. We saved the money, did all the chores during the week, the day we asked permission to go, mother refused because she had changed her mind. I said that wasn't enough reason for a denial. Mother said she didn't like the movies. I told her that was her problem not ours. We liked the movies, we had saved the money, and we had done everything she had requested.

Fena turned to me and said, 'I was really horrible for not accepting that mummy changed her mind that day'.

The relationship I had with Fena terminated there and then. Mother was probably happy she had achieved what she intended. I was finally out, and had no support whatsoever from Fena and it suited her. I would go to school in a couple of days anyway, I would disappear into the obscurity of my prison, I would be behind bars for the next six months, whatever feelings or thoughts I had they were all irrelevant.

I hadn't noticed until then the relationship between my other sisters, Alicia and Nohora. There was something weird and odd about it. Although their ages were nine and six there was so much dislike and animosity towards each other; they never played together as we had done when we were little girls, they hardly spoke to each other; and they went to school independently of each other, and fought constantly. Mother was more lenient towards Alicia because she was the youngest and blamed Nohora for everything that happened in between them. Nohora resented mother, and took her frustration and perhaps perceived rejection on Alicia. The absence from the family unit helped me to be more aware of the change and destruction that occurred within.

Nohora liked to look after my brothers, she played with them, prepared their bottles, changed nappies and she truly enjoyed it. It was surreal. She was like a surrogate mother.

Cousin Ye was the only person I had left to talk to. He continued to live under the same roof, although, experiencing incredibly hard circumstances. Maximiliano and mother had used every method within their reach to torment him; they took his mattress to begin with, then his bed, he had to sleep on the floor; for no apparent reason his room was emptied of all furniture and then he had to move to the ironing room, where wicker baskets and a large ironing table occupied most of the space. He spread his blankets on the floor and used them as a mattress while he covered himself with the dressing gown. He discussed his future with me; it didn't look good because he had unfortunately failed two subjects.

He had to find a job and accommodation; it was a shame because it was his last semester. 'Ye, I hate them! When I grow up, I will go away as far as possible from them, I will go to the furthest corner of the globe, where the ocean is vast, the continents are far apart, and I will escape their mean and callous nature. Somewhere so far away that for them it would be like trying to reach the moon'.

Ye never said anything bad against Maximiliano or mother. His only comment was that when you encounter people like them, their narrow minded and vindictive characteristics make it quite difficult to reason. Messing up my hair he used to say: 'life will be better for all of us in the near future, Maximiliano and your mother think they have the upper hand, but life will show them that they will be the biggest losers, believe me'.

He finished his sentence and I was overwhelmed with a deep sense of sadness and an immense sense of emptiness, not because everything had been moved away from the room, but because I felt death around us as we talked. 'Do you feel anything strange?' I asked Ye. 'I feel as if someone died here and that person is trying to say something about emptiness and the meaning of it'.

I saw a coffin in the middle of the room, big candles on large silver candle holders on each corner of the casket, timber chairs against two walls. A man died in this room, there was nobody to pay him respect, I said to Ye, and I left the room without saying anything else. Each time I passed that room the initial image was very vivid, one day I felt a change of temperature around me; that was scary! As I felt the cold air around me I realized the coffin and chairs had been moved to the adjacent room; other people walked those rooms, a woman wearing a blue apron with large pockets, her hair tied at the back; she seemed to argue and dragged her feet, she wore slippers instead of shoes. There was also a man with straight long hair. I started to wake up during the night. I felt someone standing by the bedroom door, that person wanted to talk to me because he had a complaint of some sort.

It was terrifying. I couldn't say anything otherwise they would have sent me to a sanatorium for the insane.

Holidays with grandmother

Mamá Nena arrived early January. I told her everything about Maximiliano and mother's manner towards cousin Ye. I also told her about the way I was treated and the favouritism towards Fena. She had a discussion with mother and within the next two days Mamá Nena and I left to spend the rest of my holidays with her. I met many relatives; we went horse riding and participated in functions to raise funds for the new church.

A world famous magician who resided in town suggested that I do the fire dance, so Mamá Nena and I went to his house where he had many trunks full of glittery items and costumes. The trunks were covered in black leather and had colourful stickers from many European cities; the stickers reminded him of many of his travels and performances abroad. He also had on the table a crystal ball covered with black silk; I was very intrigued by it and began to ask questions.

Mamá Nena was concerned about my questions but the magician didn't mind answering them. He said that all that belonged to another life which he wanted to forget, although it had been successful and it had given him great satisfaction.

The magician's name was Vargas, he'd been famous practicing magic as well as foretelling the future, but he no longer read fortunes because he knew his life had reached its end, and wanted to dedicate his time to contemplation and good deeds.

At a later time we went back to Vargas's house to select the items for the intended performance, Vargas had taken many pieces out of the suitcases, and had spread the costumes all over the furniture; Mamá Nena chose the costumes that best suited me.

Vargas looked at me, and without warning said: "You are a pretty girl and you possess a rare gift; you are already aware of it, this gift will become more evident as you grow older. You have an old soul that has lived many lives, and your destiny will take you to a far away land, a language unknown to you at present will be spoken as well as your mother tongue. Along the course of your life you will encounter many people who, jealous of you beauty will make your life difficult; probably you've already found them. Let them go. Walk away. Don't pay any attention to their hurtful words. Don't let others undermine your wonderful self with words that tell you that you must change to suit them. Your external beauty is just the reflection of your inner self, and your silence makes people nervous because they sense something that can't be explained. Things will be different, but it will take many years for the appropriate change to arrive'.

At that point Mamá Nena requested Vargas to stop; 'perhaps his predictions would make me nervous' she said.

'Please Mamá Nena, I want to know more'.

We collected the costumes and the music; it was time to begin a rehearsal wearing those strange outfits. The garments looked very oriental, meaning Middle Eastern. Lots of shiny beads were sewn into the fabric, golden frills and round golden coin type of sequins which made a clicking sound as I moved.

I wrote meticulously what Vargas said to me. I kept that crinkled piece of paper for many years until the pencil letters almost faded away and the paper tore on the fold line; I also memorized every word he said.

The return home after three carefree weeks was hard. I implored Mamá Nena to keep me with her and not to let me go back to boarding school. Obviously she couldn't possibly take care of me. We stayed at Anita and Isidoro's hacienda for a couple of days, Yesid was there, it was lovely to see him. He was about to start his second year of university and Papi continued to be his guardian.

I had almost forgotten my home problems when Yesid mentioned how upset Papi and Tuni were after the breakup of the relationship with mother. He apparently, had tried to visit me during the period when mother vetoed all visits; having been discouraged, didn't try again. He also wrote to me, but I never received his letters. Once again he said that he loved me, and tenderly kissed me while nobody was looking.

In the evening, after dinner we sat in a distant corner of the verandah always under the watchful eyes of his mother and Mamá Nena, we played monopoly, we held hands and from time to time he made me aware of his love for me. The night before we departed while we sat on the verandah he lifted his head to look at a moonless dark sky, the space was filled with pulsating stars. Then said: 'Nené, look at the darkness of the night, when you see so many stars think of me'. He wrapped his arms around my shoulders, it was a tender moment mixed with a little sadness.

During the trip home, grandmother knew how to question me about Yesid. I confessed that I liked him, but didn't say how much. We also talked about the home problems and my dislocated life. I don't like school, yet when I am home it is really horrible; I don't fit in. My life is boring and mother has become difficult and angry, she also punishes me for the smallest of things. She says that I am a horrible person and everybody dislikes me, I think she is the horrible one, I said.

She listened and suggested that perhaps it would be better if she took me with her during the holidays.

We arrived home, a gloomy, unhappy household. Cousin Ye had left. Maximiliano stood with his hands in his pockets watching us as we carried the luggage.

There were a couple of days available to organize everything before my return to school, barely enough time to prepare books and all other items, luckily this time Mamá Nena was there to help me. While my sister's books had been organized, I struggled to collect whatever was necessary for my school year. Mother didn't show any interest in what I needed, my sisters had used some of my school garments, some items were missing and other items were dirty.

On my return to school I found out that the visit time had been changed once again. Parents or guardians were able to collect the girls every Sunday from 9am and return by 5pm or alternatively arrange transport with someone else.

Mother signed the square that I was to be collected every Sunday, I wasn't allowed to catch public transport and I couldn't go with anybody else either. I knew this was a sentence to confine me to school most of the time, as well as to prevent me from seeing Papi and Tuni.

Part of my holiday had been good, unlike other times I was able to tell about the events of the two weeks I spent with Mamá Nena. It was the beginning of the fourth year of high school and the fourth year of my internment, as I used to call my time at boarding school.

We had a new Mother Superior, a nun who had been sent from Europe where the religious order had originated and had its headquarters. She was more progressive than the previous Mother Superior, and many things changed with her appointment. Numerous new nuns had arrived and some others had been relocated to other schools, however, Sister Barbarita and horrible Sister Irene were still among us.

The new academic year was different from the previous years; there were forms to be signed by the girls who wished to terminate school by the end of the scholastic year. Those girls formed a different group; they learnt new subjects and dropped other subjects like philosophy, languages, history and physics. The thought of leaving school with an intermediate certificate was very tempting; my biggest fear was what to do at the end of the year if I signed the paper. The new subjects were of no interest to me; that was one of the reasons I continued my studies. The love of philosophy, the arts in general and literature gave me the courage to continue.

Since the new Mother Superior was more liberal than the previous one, we were allowed to go for walks again, perhaps everybody had forgotten about the men, their sticks or dicks and whatever they had said about fucking every one of us.

Plays were performed more frequently, movies were shown on Saturday afternoon, some activities like singing and classical dancing were encouraged, art books began to appear on the bookshelves as well as biographies of saints that belonged to their order. Other schools were invited for debating, of course only girls were allowed.

I found myself a bit more settled after the good rest I had with Mamá Nena, and for the first time in four years I had good memories; the unpleasantness of the family home seemed far away.

My studies began well. New and interesting subjects formed part of the curriculum and I didn't disrupt life with the same vigour. We started with the same routine of previous years, confess the sins committed during the holidays, the same questions, the same prayers, but there was a new chaplain; young and so incredibly handsome, nobody was forced to confess, everybody wanted to tell him the sins committed during the holidays. To stop the rush to confession we had to talk to the nun in charge of the squadron, and we had to discuss with her our personal problems and the gravity of the sins, for her to allocate the time with the handsome chaplain.

My feeling was that the nuns wanted to poke their noses into our personal life to find those little extra snippets of information. How could I talk about my life, nobody would believe if I told all those things that were happening around me. The nun asked many questions but I avoided the answers, I didn't particularly want to confess any invented sins. My problems couldn't be resolved by discussing those issues with anybody, and I didn't want their pity either. My sad situation would be resolved either by escaping the school grounds or waiting until school finished. The nun frustrated by my silence, sent me to see the handsome chaplain for a talk and to take the opportunity to free my soul.

I was nervous because I had such pressure from the nun to talk about myself. I told him that I didn't have any sins because my life during the holidays was very boring. The new, handsome chaplain was great. He had a good sense of humour, didn't pry into my life, and didn't ask obnoxious questions like the previous one. He asked about my age and said, that I shouldn't have any worries at all. Looking at me intensely he made the comment that I was a very beautiful girl with a face that looked like a renaissance painting, probably like a Botticelli, you must hear that very often, he added.

'Only strangers and my grandmother say that'. I responded.

'Don't you think you are beautiful?' With a grin he said, 'I had lips to be kissed and told me to go and not to worry about anything because I had beauty on my side'.

The nun wanted to know what the chaplain had said. I informed her that he'd said, 'I didn't have a thing to worry about'.

First Sunday arrived, and as I thought nobody turned up to collect me, it wasn't too disappointing because in a way it was expected; girls who lived in distant places remained at school, but this time we were allowed to go for a walk into town with a nun who brought us ice cream.

The biggest disappointment for me was that Pilar and her family had gone back to Spain; I missed her terribly. Yvonne, Inez and the other girls returned, but my intellectual friend had gone.

The new academic year was fairly interesting; the only blotch was a new nun from a city south of the country; according to her, that city was gentile and elegant and it was a real pity she had been transferred to this place which lacked so much class. This nun was a carbon copy of Sister Irene from the second year, with the addition that she firmly believed she belonged to a social class above ours; but it was all in her mind because the poor woman was as ordinary as they come; she thought her social standing was improved by osmosis, since she had associated with some rich families, through the students who frequented the gentile southern city school.

Sister Ignazia had a horrendous disposition. She belittled and humiliated everybody who crossed her path; she was bitter and twisted beyond belief. We also noticed her ugliness, she looked more like an ugly man, and she had whiskers on the top lip.

She possessed a masculine mannerism and she looked at us with a strange intensity and scrutiny that was a bit unsettling; Sister Ignazia made some of us stand up and said that pretty girls shouldn't have difficulties being intelligent and showing it; however, ugly girls should learn to behave in an intelligent manner, improve and refine their social skills to take the emphasis from the lack of physical attributes.

'You ugly girls are like raw livers'. Oh no! Not another expert in raw liver!

I studied hard and with great diligence; my assignments were neater, cleaner, and tidier than any previous work. I did it to avoid humiliation. Sister Ignazia divided the class into two groups, the intelligent ones and the raw livers, as she used to call them. Among the intelligent ones were two hopeless, pretty girls who had been her pupils at the gentile, elegant southern city.

We were in constant fear of being humiliated, the abuse that poured out of her mouth made everybody tremble. Talking to Yvonne about Sister Ignazia I mentioned that on several occasions she had a strange look, and the manner in which she licked her lips when staring at someone was disturbing.

Yvonne said: 'Nah, she is harmless, but I am sure she likes pretty girls like you and I don't think she will give you any trouble. My brothers say of women like her, that they are born with balls in-between their legs as well as tits, and that makes them rather confused'.

The new academic year also brought a horrendous flu epidemic; some girls were confined to bed for two or more weeks. The flu was a very nasty one and everyday more and more girls were affected; while the classrooms were nearly empty during the day, the dormitories were getting more crowded than the classrooms. With so many girls afflicted with the virus the largest dormitories began to fill rapidly.

I was one of the last girls to catch the flu which brought deep congestion, chest pain, high temperature, sore throat, and a horrible cough that lasted for weeks. It appeared to be a severe type of whooping cough.

The infirmary nun brought sugary Eucalyptus tea as well as big pots of hot water with eucalyptus leaves and placed them in several areas of the dormitory to alleviate the congestion. The nun and her assistant visited us several times a day to check the temperature, and relocate girls who were in worse condition to other dormitories.

The worst affected girls developed swollen lips with big blisters around them and violent fits of cough. However, no doctor was called, the nuns wanted to resolve the epidemic by them-selves and with God's help. Instead of calling for medical assistance, the chaplain was called on Sunday to bless the dormitory with holy water and incense.

All meals were brought to the dormitory, the doors were locked and we had to ask for the doors to be opened to go to the bathroom. As we felt better the confinement was very boring, but we had to remain locked up until the contagious stage passed; some girls had suffered a relapse and had to be brought back.

It wasn't Sunday but the chaplain arrived with his incense and holy water, unfortunately he wasn't the handsome one, he was a temporary replacement. He was old, had a type of nose that looked like a fig, and his teeth were stained yellow. He began to walk in between the rows of beds, he asked questions here and there while the infirmary nun was present; when the nun's attention was called elsewhere, he moved closer to the side of the bed.

He finally arrived at my bed, after a short hello I felt his hand under the blanket, I tried to move away, by then his fingers were touching my stomach and quickly moved in between my legs, while he continued asking questions giving the impression that everything was normal. I tried to move away but his fingers followed my body until a violent fit of cough saved me from his intrusion and he left me alone, then he proceeded to molest someone else. His walk in between the beds and in between the girl's legs continued until one of the nuns returned to the dormitory. After he left we started talking, some girls didn't say anything initially, and after the first girl broke the silence, everybody began to recall the experience. Most girls had been touched in between the legs.

The old priest visited the dormitory on other occasions bringing his incense and holy water with him; the nuns were present most of the time and followed him as he moved from bed to bed. During one of his walks, even with one of the junior nuns present, he managed to put his hand under the blanket of one of the older girls. She must have said something to the nun in charge, and in turn the nun passed the complaint to the Mother Superior.

The Mother Superior arrived at the dormitory to make clear that those nasty rumours didn't spread. 'Rumours and vicious gossip, she said, are like chicken feathers spread to the wind'.

Our health improved and we returned to normality; during the following week we learnt that the girl who passed the information about the chaplain had been sent home, and her parents had to remove her from school. Apparently a prestigious school couldn't afford to house girls with such vivid and blasphemous imagination.

Time passed by, soon Easter came and went and I hadn't gone home once; finally on a Sunday at around 2 o'clock I was called. I found mother waiting for me rather annoyed that she had to come to collect me. I begged her to allow Papi and Tuni to pick me up, but she refused. I could catch the bus and I would be home by 11am. She also refused.

The weekly routine gave stability and a firm base to my life, but Sundays really agitated me. I was never sure what was going to happen, whether I would go home or stayed at school.

I envied the girls who left early in the morning and returned at the latest possible time, and they enjoyed the day with their parents and friends.

On every occasion I went home I found unhappiness, arguments and the day was invariably very boring. We didn't go anywhere, mother argued from the moment she picked me up until she brought me back. I was such an inconvenience in their life. Maximiliano was irritating and he was always ready to criticize me using his stupid, acid sarcasm. There was tension among my sisters; even Elsi the maid, began to talk about her discontent.

I arrived at the conclusion that it was better for me to stay at school, I had good art books to read, I could take them with me to the study; we also had some good biographies which although of a religious nature were interesting. The art books were mainly of Spanish or Italian origin, but we had moved from the dark ages into the renaissance and that change brought some tranquillity.

We listened to music; the repertoire had increased, and included mainly baroque operas by Italian composers, as well as some folkloric music from different parts of the planet. The Saturday walks continued, sometimes we climbed steep hills and walked along the meadows and the many beautiful areas the region had to offer. On other occasions we carried colour pencils and a sketch book to paint the landscape.

I started to ask myself whether the effort to go home was worth it, the incessant arguments, the constant criticism I was exposed to; either I was a libertine with a filthy mind, or my mannerisms appeared to show an aristocratic style, which made mother feel that I believed to be of a better class than the rest of the family.

Was that place I called home, my home?

It must have been May already; I knew it was Mamá Nena because the call happened at 9am sharp. We went home, and as happy as I was to see her, my thoughts were vague and uninterested; she talked most of the time and tried her hardest to engage my attention with her stories. The best part was when she said I would spend the next holidays with her; the thought revived me a little. I was in a morose mood. Mamá Nena tried to cheer me up. She said that I could have new dresses made for the June holidays. She took my measurements and I told her about the fabric colours I wished to have. She assured me that rain or hail I was going to spend the three weeks of June with her, she would pick me up, and we would leave the very next day, and not to say anything for the time being.

That Sunday during lunch I learnt that the family had a holiday after Easter and that they forgot to pick me up. They only remembered when they arrived at the hacienda which was located around eight hours from the capital; of course it was too late. They talked about the funny times they had and about all the things they had done. I sat there in silence, and in absolute detachment. Maximiliano took my brothers to the park after lunch and I sat to watch television.

I heard when Mamá Nena said to mother to show at least some interest instead of giving so much criticism; she also said to mother that she was putting all her attention on the wrong one. I realized they had been talking about me when mother responded that she found it too difficult.

Mamá Nena brought me back to school with the promise that she would return to pick me up in June, and asked me not to worry if nobody visited me, it was probably better for me to remain at school. Grandmother noticed how mature and sophisticated I was and she understood that home wasn't the place for me. 'Home has too many unpleasant distractions and negatives for you my darling granddaughter. I wish I could be of more help, but financially I can't afford it'.

I was fortunate to enjoy my academic studies and time passed quickly as we learnt new subjects; learning was easy, and therefore, I managed to obtain good marks. I enjoyed the learning process. I was able to write all my assignments quite fast; therefore I had time to engage in painting with charcoal and aquarelle. No time was left to carry out all those disrupting activities as in previous years, because I was happily occupied with my artistic pursuits. My charcoal and aquarelle paintings were popular as a souvenir at the end of the semester, and I always gave them away to whoever asked for them.

Mamá Nena was correct. Nobody came to pick me up until she arrived the day we left for the June holidays. We arrived home with the knowledge that we wouldn't stay long, but grandmother requested that I didn't mention anything about the holidays.

The usual events at home just passed in front of me and I didn't take notice of anything. Just two days after my arrival from school Mamá Nena said that she couldn't stand the cold humid weather, it would be a good idea to start moving soon, and she was going to take me with her. The day we left Maximiliano's chauffeur drove us to the station.

The trip was very interesting indeed. Long tunnels crossed the mountain from one side to the other, and the approach to the tunnel was normally announced by a long, deep beep.

Small stations, some were beautiful colonial buildings, with flower pots and a small ticket window facing the tracks; other stations were rundown, discoloured timber buildings with metal roofs; instead of columns, the awning was held with a couple of skinny timber posts that looked as if the timber could collapse with a slight breeze.

The train climbed up the cordillera very slowly, at times reversing to gain sufficient force to climb the hurdle nature had presented, and from time to time people stood by the side of the tracks to watch the train pass, they often waved their arms, and with a smile said: 'adios'.

The train stopped to collect new passengers, and several vendors took the opportunity to offer their goods, women held on their heads trays full of fried bananas, potatoes, and tapioca. On their trays also an assortment of items wrapped in banana and corn leaves, as well as cheese bread and a fantastic variety of fruits. Mamá Nena only bought fruit that hadn't been cut for fear of catching some stomach upset, which was very common with this type of goods.

Grandmother talked to people who sat on adjacent seats and she sang opera arias in her beautiful, soft soprano voice. People offered compliments and said that her voice sounded like a bird's song. She also told everybody her travel companion was her favourite and most beautiful granddaughter; introduced me to strangers, and at the end of a long trip, everything had taken the appearance of a wonderful, great adventure. Mamá Nena enjoyed my company and I loved to be with her.

Our first stop was at Anita and Isidoro's hacienda, they had sent one of the workers to pick us up at the station and Anita was waiting for us at home. We had a shower and quickly got ready for the asado, which had been organized as a welcome gesture. Friends and relatives arrived; many relatives appeared when I was with Mamá Nena, and the introductions seemed endless.

Yesid hadn't arrived yet for the holiday. Anita believed that boy was having too much fun and she was preoccupied about his studies. On June 29th we would return to the hacienda for the celebration of the region's patron saint, San Pedro. Friends and relatives had accepted the invitation to celebrate San Pedro's feast as well as Isidoro's birthday.

The following day we continued our trip. We were staying for the duration of the holiday, at Stella and José Louis's house. They had four children, Raul and Amparo my age more or less, Stellita and Magali. Stella's mother and sister lived in the same town some blocks away from them. José Louis had arrived from Spain as a young man, in exile from General Franco's civil war. He was much older that Stella, he was jolly and happy with a touch of grumpiness as a contradiction to his good nature; I had met them on previous occasions, but this was the first time we were guests at their house.

There were parties and lunches organized to collect funds for the new church. I didn't understand why a new church had to be built, I thought the old colonial church built in the late 1700 was characteristic of those little churches scattered all over the Spanish colonies; the building was painted white inside and out, and had great architectural character, it wasn't falling down or showed cracks on the walls like many buildings of that époque.

José Luis said, 'everything had to follow the lunatic idea someone had'.

During my spare time I painted water colours for a raffle; having learnt a new style of painting I was keen to try the new technique. I'd discovered Picasso and the cubist period, and I wanted to imitate the great masters. The nun in charge of the art class had started a new technique using geometry to draw flowers, buildings and animals; we used very soft water colours to fill the spaces formed by the lines the compass had marked; the result was a delicate mixture of colours and geometrical shapes that represented the object in a totally different light.

People looked at the water colours and asked what the painting represented, José Luis encouraged them to buy the little water colours, and suggested that perhaps one day I would be famous like Picasso, and they not only had helped to build the new church, but they would have something from a famous artist.

The holidays passed by so incredibly fast, it was time to pack. Before we returned home we would spend a couple of days at Anita and Isidoro, also we had a party to attend to. Yesid didn't arrive for his father's birthday, I was terribly disappointed. Fabio his older brother was there, a fairly handsome man. Mamá Nena said that when mother and Fabio were in their teens the families used to spend a great deal of time socializing.

Fabio hadn't shown any academic interest; instead his preferred option was to join the National Armed Forces' Infantry. He looked very much like Isidoro. He was tall, strong, had a great sense of humour, deep commanding voice, and a moustache which dropped on the sides of the mouth imitating Pancho Villa' style, the Mexican patriot.

Fabio approached me after lunch and began to talk; he asked many questions among them my age. 'I will be fourteen tomorrow' I responded. 'Nobody talked about your birthday' he said, otherwise I would have bought you a present.

People began to arrive at the party, the music played until the animated and noisy crowd was interrupted some time later to offer a toast to Isidoro. A large cake with many candles was brought to the table and next to it a smaller one with fourteen candles, which was for me. Anita called me to blow the candles out. She mentioned that Fabio had approached her early that afternoon to see if it was possible to make a cake for me since my birthday was the following day. How sweet I thought. That was indeed a thoughtful and kind gesture. Even Mamá Nena complimented him for his quick thinking.

We spent two more days at the hacienda; Fabio organized some gorgeous looking horses for Mamá Nena and me, I was given a young docile mare of a copper colour with white spots on her forehead. We spent a glorious day riding up and down small hills looking at the plantations. Fabio had also organized food to be ready as we arrived at a certain destination, and his father's employees were always attentive to our needs. We returned home for a well earned rest as the sun was beginning to set.

The next day we went to pick wild plums. The trees had a wide base with some branches close to the ground, very easy to sit on them and pick ripe, juicy plums with the unfortunate effect that the stomach couldn't cope with so much fruit, and the first symptoms of indigestion became apparent before lunch. Mamá Nena asked for some bicarbonate, she mixed a little of it with warm water, made me drink it; in 20 minutes I was like new again.

The hammocks were ready under large trees. We had a rest to avoid the mid-day sun and after the siesta we began the return home. We had to leave the luggage ready that night because the train departed around 6 o'clock the following morning. The return trip was subdued. Feeling sad I asked Mamá Nena if it was possible for me to live with her. It caught her by surprise.

She smiled and said: 'Why?'

I haven't told you everything about school. Nobody makes any effort to pick me up during the days we are allowed to go home. Papi and Tuni can't visit me, if they were allowed to see me, that would change life a great deal, and I would be able to go home with them, and then I wouldn't be so lonely.

On my return home from school I can't go anywhere, not even to a movie because mother says she doesn't like the movies and Fena takes sides with her to make me feel bad. Fena is a real brown nose crawler.

I don't have new shoes when I return from boarding school, and I have to wear the same moccasins I wear at school; most of my dresses don't fit me or my sisters have used everything and it's a real struggle to buy something, mother claims she never has the time to go to the shops, and when she does, she buys precisely the colours I detest, like brown and grass green. Tuni and Papi bought some items of clothing for me, and mother in a rage confiscated those items with the excuse of how dare they!

I spend some days with you and although I leave all the uniforms and the rest of school items in my wardrobe, on my return I find that everything had been removed and used, so my school items are no longer there when I need them.

I am constantly punished for one thing or another, Elsi is relieved of her duties fairly often and I am sent to the kitchen to cook for so many people and nobody helps me. I am not allowed to read, the books I was reading disappeared. To steal a moment of solace I have to escape to the roof and hide there.

I don't know what is worse, to be at school or to come home. 'Are you sure my father died when I was small? Is mother my real mother or did she pick me up from somewhere and that is the reason she hates me?' I asked.

She listened and then said that nobody hated me. I am aware that on your return from school, you live in a truly unhappy household. Your mother has been very unhappy for a long while because she has many problems with Maximiliano. He turned out to be a womanizer and your mother found out soon after they married, he also drinks to excess, and those actions create a lot of friction in their marriage.

Oh I said. 'That was what Papi and Tuni used to say at the beginning of all this misery'.

Maximiliano buys beautiful dresses for her but she doesn't want to go anywhere or do anything, he always complains that mother doesn't want to go to the dinners and parties he is invited to. Mother always finds an excuse not to go, and Maximiliano goes to the parties alone, arrives home really late, he is usually drank, goes to bed, and the next day from the moment he wakes up, we have to listen to continuous arguments. All I hear on my return from school is constant altercations between Maximilliano and mother, and an endless criticism of me.

I don't understand the reason for him to stop us along the corridor to ask questions; if we stop to talk to him and respond to his questions, mother usually turns it into an argument; therefore, we can't talk to him for fear of arguments.

The house we live in is awful, dark, has no trees, no real garden, the courtyards are all tiled; the house is full of ghosts everywhere. At school I have friends and I can talk to them. At home I can't express my thoughts because whatever I say is frowned upon either by Maximiliano or mother. Mamá Nena said: 'I will see what I can do'.

We arrived home late in the afternoon; I had less than a week to prepare my school items. The next day with Mamá Nena's help I began to collect what I needed for school. I was able to show Mamá Nena the reality of what I had said previously.

Everything had been removed from its place and had been used. I couldn't understand why this was the case, because there was absolutely no need to use my things. It was almost a deliberate attempt to sabotage everything I needed, and it was the same when I returned home.

I heard Mamá Nena when she asked mother for an explanation about the treatment given to me. I moved away before mother answered. I knew there was no justifiable answer. The following day Mamá Nena and I bought everything I needed. She wrote my name on all the labels with black china ink and then helped me sew them on each item. With the list of books and other requirements in our hands we went to the shops and purchased everything that was on the list. We returned home marked everything and packed, it was time to go back to boarding school.

Mamá Nena took me to school and promised she would take me with her during the following holidays. Her intention was to pick me up from school; we would spend a couple of days at home and then leave before Christmas, but not to say a word about it. It was the second time that my return to school was peaceful and full of hope for a better semester. I hadn't seen Papi and Tuni since early June, and I decided to send them a letter to let them know that my holidays with Mamá Nena had been very happy, and I informed them that if they tried once more to visit me, perhaps the nuns would let them see me, because many things had changed around the visits. Mother, if she came to visit me always arrived late, so to avoid a clash it would be a good idea to visit me early in the morning.

The following Sunday my name was called to the visitor's room and my heart jumped with joy when I saw Papi and Tuni. How much I loved them, and how hard it had been since all that mess had begun.

Papi's hair looked almost white he was so distinguished and refined. Tuni had aged. She cried as soon as she saw me, and for the first time we sat without fear of being late or I having to rush back home.

'We have to co-ordinate these visits carefully because we want to avoid you further punishment', Papi said wisely.

It was difficult to know when mother would visit me. Equally difficult to guess whether she would collect me on the days we were allowed to go home. The conclusion we arrived at, was that they would always come early at 9am and they would come to see me once a month to be safe. I was happy, a little was better than nothing at all.

During the visit I told them the same things that had been discussed with Mamá Nena, and casually I asked the same question about my father's death, and whether I was an orphan somehow left in a basket, and mother picked me up, because it was very strange that I didn't fit into the family unit, and she appeared to dislike me intensely. My feeling was that I didn't count at all. It appeared to be that anything related to me was a burden, a duty that somehow had to be fulfilled, and as a consequence there was no interest. On the other hand the constant criticism of me was hard to take, and I was tired to be told continuously that I was the worst in the world.

Tuni said once more that it was a very difficult cross to bear, and in her opinion under the present circumstances there was no solution to the problem. The best I could do was to excel in my studies, then, I would have freedom to do and be whatever I decided.

I did well academically, but apparently I had become very chatty, and was punished frequently for talking at the wrong time. Sister Barbarita had her way and involved me with the theatre group as well as the chorus practice; the theatre practice was a good outlet. In addition we were taken to other schools for the performances and it was fun. Life was better at school and I'd certainly forgotten about my so called home. The family appeared to exist in a remote way, like a distant point in the vast universe. I rarely thought about them; mother and the rest had become irrelevant. I just wanted to grow up as quickly as possible.

Mother came to visit but said that she couldn't take me home. I didn't care anymore. One of the nuns arrived to talk to mother and complained about me being too talkative, but she added I was a very good student. 'The lack of discipline is a negative factor that has to be addressed seriously'; she said and patted me on the head. This comment was transformed into sufficient ammunition for mother to commence her usual criticism of me.

My hair was untidy, the uniform did not look clean, my shoes weren't polished well enough, my manners were appalling, and my nails were long. Mother carried on with the usual tirade; everybody was going to hate me because I was a horrible person; the fact that I had a libertine mind prepared to read filth would contribute to the great unhappiness I would encounter throughout my life. She added: It was such a shame indeed my character was not more like Fena's. She possesses such wonderful qualities and in addition she is beautiful.

'Have you finished?' I asked her. I turned my back and left her standing there; I began to walk towards the exit door which opened onto the concrete patio with the flagpole in the middle. I pushed the heavy door open and left the room. I disliked her immensely. I wished I didn't have to see her again.

I entered the patio feeling confused and agitated. Nobody was there to communicate my feelings to, and to express how I felt; I was alone with my thoughts and emotions.

I continued to walk towards the chapel's wall, the sun rays made the stone walls pale and creamy, looked for a spot on the ledge where the sun was shining. I sat with my back against the wall, closed my eyes to allow the sun rays to warm my face.

I was alone. Papi and Tuni as well as Mamá Nena loved me, but there was nothing they could do for me. Many feelings crowded my mind as well as a deep sense of hopelessness mixed with feelings of anger and despair. The situation made me feel terribly lonely. I was fourteen years and a couple of months old. Not much I could do at this stage of my life. Sadness took a back seat. I was angry at the world for being so unfair. I didn't deserve what I was going through. Then, I thought about the recent holiday spent with Mamá Nena, life was different and nobody hated me.

I sat there until the sun disappeared beyond the ugly tall building which in a way I saw as a reflection of my ugly unhappy life; by then the sun rays had restored my energy and I was fit to return to the study. As I walked in, the sound of one of Chopin's polonaises filled the room. I sat down, rested my head on the desk and fell asleep.

The bell rung, it was time for a short recess before we proceeded to the dining room.

A profound change had begun to evolve within myself and I started to question everything, beginning with the religious education I had received until then. I refused to confess with the claim that I didn't have any sins. Every time we had to confess it was a battle with the nun to make her understand that I didn't have anything to say. Often I was forced to go to the chapel and the nun stood by my side until I knelt at the confessionary. Invariably I told the chaplain that I didn't have much to say, he always said: 'when you are ready come back'.

During religious education I had the opportunity to ask the questions that perhaps everybody wanted to ask, and didn't have the courage to put across, because of the fear of being called a heretic. I also began to answer back if I considered the punishment to be unfair.

I lost many visits which I didn't care because nobody visited me anyway. I had detention more often than not. I began to throw more items out of the windows, and created more blackouts in spite of the lock attached to the meter box. I turned off the water mains; initially the town supply was blamed until someone discovered that something else was the cause of these mishaps. The most perplexing thing was that I never told anybody; it was the same as on previous occasions, I calmly carried out all these deeds and nobody found me out, or had the slightest suspicion it was me. I sat with the rest of the girls to do my homework with a candle light.

Sex as it is

It was the middle of the week when we heard loud sobs coming from the corridor. A tall girl dressed in black passed in front of our classroom on the way towards the big girls' classroom. She was a new girl who just started boarding school.

Why would anybody want to change school at the end of August? Anyway, she was introduced as Clara.

Her appearance was strange. Her hair was a deep tint of black cut in a sharp bob and a fringe, her eyebrows almost non-existent; she had wide black pencil lines on the upper and lower eyelids and blood red lips. She wore a super short tight black skirt and a fluffy tight pullover with silver buttons.

She cried all afternoon, and during the evening meal she looked even worse because her eyes were swollen, and the nuns had ordered her to remove all traces of makeup.

We were intensely curious to find out the reasons for her late arrival. It transpired that she had been attending one of those free schools where pupils didn't wear uniforms, selected the academic subjects they would like to carry out during the scholastic year, never did homework and left school after lunch.

She was allocated to Yvonne's classroom, and at morning recess we all talked about Clara and how weird she looked with no eyebrows. Clara had quickly found girls compatible and interested in her. She had a sunny disposition and a good personality.

The following week Clara, all of a sudden arrived in our classroom; she had been demoted because she wasn't able to cope with the advanced curriculum of the class above. Clara struggled with every subject, and to our amazement, Sister Ignazia didn't call her a raw liver. Sister Ignazia said to Clara that she was really hopeless, but it wasn't her fault. 'See girls,

Clara attended an inferior school, and although her parents paid a substantial amount of money for her education, those modern systems don't work'.

Sister Ignazia continued to help Clara and assigned a girl to help her with each subject.

Clara didn't appear to make any effort to understand the subjects within the curriculum and she didn't do her home work either; she always copied from the other girls without understanding what she copied. She was absent minded, and of course the boarding school system was too much for her to cope with.

I was appointed to help her with geometry and philosophy, but we laughed most of the time, and she was really funny. I faced the problem that the rest of my homework was left incomplete for lack of time. At the beginning the nuns were lenient when I explained the reason for not having the home work completed, but I began to fall behind, and didn't like it.

I had to do well first and then I would help Clara. I decided that during the first hour I would do all my homework and during the second hour I would help her. It worked very well, because I didn't have time to be mischievous, and that spared me a lot of trouble. As I began to help Clara, we first talked about things in general as well as the reason for her to be at boarding school, when she was accustomed to so much freedom.

Clara was really hopeless, her memory didn't retain anything, it was like a sieve and it was difficult for her to understand simple things. She always wanted to talk about boys and the things she did with them, one afternoon she said: 'shit, I really need a man today'. I can't take it anymore! 'I am dying to feel a man inside me'.

'Why do you need a man inside you?' I asked

'Don't you know anything about life?' She responded.

'What does a man inside you have to do with life?'

'Because that's all about life; not being able to screw and enjoy the pleasure of it, is a real pain'.

'What type of pain, something that hurts? Where does it hurt? Does it hurt because of the screw?'

'No, no, you fool'

'Why are you here at this time of the year when the academic year is almost finished?'

Clara started to tell me that she had been brought to boarding school because her father had found her in the boot of his car.

'What were you doing in the boot of a car?'

'I was having sex, we were naked from the waist down and his dick was inside me, we were about to come, he was moving furiously'; shit, I get horny just thinking about it.

'I didn't know you can have sex in the boot of a car' I said. 'Where were you coming to?'

'I will make it easy for you to learn, but you must tell me everything you know about sex'. I told Clara, that if I tried to summarize it all without too many words for her to remember, perhaps she could understand things better and at least pass the tests. It was a good exercise for me as well, so the next day we began a new method for her to learn and for me to begin to hear all there was to know about the virtues of sex.

'Haven't you had sex yet?' Clara asked.

'Not yet. I am only fourteen years old, and it's a difficult subject to understand; it's rather confusing'.

'There is nothing to be confused about', she said. 'It's simple, you just open your legs and the boy you are with puts it in'.

'What happens after they put it in?'

'Oh it feels really good and you don't want to stop, but if it finishes too quickly it can be done time and time again'.

'How do you know when you are going to do it?'

'Let's say, you are at a party or with some boys somewhere and someone looks at you; you check if he has a hard on, if he has one, you smile and look at his face first and then direct your eyes to the area under the belt, look at him again and smile. He then moves next to you and asks if you wish to go somewhere else. Depending on where you are at that moment you say, we may go inside the house or to the car'.

To be permanently ready for sex it is better not to wear underpants when you go to a party, so all you have to do is lift your skirt or unzip your jeans and you are ready. It also arouses you not to wear anything under the garments. The very moment you tell them that you aren't wearing underpants it sends them crazy!

'Can you do it with anybody?'

'Sure, why not?' Sex is very enjoyable; the longest I have been without sex since I first had it, is these two weeks.

'I thought you did it when you love someone', I said meekly.

'No girl. You do it when you want it, who you want it with, anytime, anywhere, whether you love them or not, it's all about pleasure'.

The manner in which Clara explained sex sounded simple, and maybe, I had it all wrong and that was the reason for my confusion.

We continued with our lesson, but my mind didn't want to function academically, I was totally confused, and I began to think about Yesid the day Anita found us on the bed; the kisses were very hot and the embrace brought our bodies so close, perhaps if Anita hadn't arrived we would've had sex that day because the emotions were like a wild, out of control, powerful desire.

Clara still needed a man the next day and the day after, but the weekend arrived and she went home to try her luck.

To avoid the feeling of abandonment I joined the group of girls whose parents lived far away and didn't have regular visits. On Sunday after lunch the group was taken to different places like the bakery, or other walks around town. It was relaxing to go outside the school walls.

Clara returned to school on Monday morning; the rule was that everybody had to return by 5pm on Sunday. How did she manage to do it?

Her parents took her to a party, and apparently, forgot to bring her to school. The situation was perfect for Clara, who managed to arrange for someone to visit her room, and therefore was able to have sex many times during the night. She said 'she felt raw'.

'How can you have sex many times?'

'The more you have sex the more you want to do it'.

'What do you mean you feel raw?'

Clara laughed loudly and said: 'You will find out one day, and when you do, you will remember what I've just told you'.

'How long does the raw feeling lasts? Does it hurt when is raw? What happens next week if your parents suspect you're going to have sex, and then you can't have it?'

'The raw feeling only lasts a day and that is why you need more sex'. 'That won't happen, everything has been arranged', Clara said very sure of herself.

Once more I had a bed by the window, I could see the moon and sometimes I opened the blinds to let the moon light illuminate my face. I used to close my eyes and fly away to distant places I'd never seen; there was a beautiful forest dotted with flowers, big trees, and the sun shone through the branches forming shiny patterns on the grass which looked like gemstones, I could feel happy and content. How long before I could fulfil my dream?

After a while all my thoughts returned to Clara and the information she had provided. It didn't seem real.

Clara and her sex talk brought a distraction from the dullness of life, and I wasn't sure whether she was telling the truth; somehow the new information coincided with Pilar's description, as well as the excitement I felt when Yesid embraced and kissed me.

It was October, Clara didn't show any improvement at all, and I was getting tired of the sex talk because it was also affecting my studies. We had to prepare for exams and oral tests, and it was impossible to try to help someone who didn't have any academic interest.

The sex talk had saturated me, I felt confused and I didn't want to hear any more about it.

However, there was a crazy incident on the way to the chemistry lab; as we passed in front of an empty classroom Clara suggested we open a window to see the outside world.

It was absolutely forbidden, but in view that nobody was there, we reached the leaver, opened the window, and we saw a delivery truck parked just below. The man was unloading trays full of potato chips and Coca-Cola bottles' on a trolley.

Clara whispered: 'Hey throw us some chips'.

The delivery man looked up and said: 'Yes, if you show me your tits. You pretty girl, show me your tits too'.

Clara looked at me a bit hesitant and said: 'what the heck, let's show the poor man some upper class tits'. She took her jumper off and began to unbutton her shirt, come on girl, you too. Show him your tits. I just stood there.

Clara opened her shirt and threw her ample bosom over the window sill, the man seemed to be content with her boobs, and threw two bags of chips; see I told Clara, your boobs are big enough for both of us, and I didn't have to show him my mosquito bite boobs.

Clara with great impulsiveness said: 'He may have a large dick, and the man isn't too ugly, he is young. Wait for me here, I'll see if I can get in the van with him'.

She rushed out of the classroom and went downstairs; perhaps nobody was at the receiving dock because I saw her entering the van and the man followed her. She stayed there for some moments. The man walked out and had a look around; then he looked back towards the van and made a gesture for her to come out. She stepped out of the van quickly and returned to the classroom.

'What did you do?' I asked

'There was nobody down there and I asked the man if he wanted a bit of fun so he obliged; not bad he had a big dick which functioned quite well for the occasion'.

'What did you do to make him ready?'

'I just lifted my skirt and bent back, and at the same time opened my legs to show my anatomy; that was all'.

Clara had her eyes on the handsome chaplain. She decided to make an appointment to talk to him about the sins of the flesh as she called them. The chaplain received his visitors in a little room beside the chapel, he normally took his meals there too; there was a desk, a small divan and an armchair. A large crucifix was fixed above his desk, and a statue of the Virgin Mary stood near the doorway.

The door was always closed and nobody went there without previous arrangement. Sometimes there was a sign attached to the door asking not to disturb.

Clara arranged her appointment at a time when we were confined to our study and the nuns had evening prayers. She perked herself up, and hurried along the corridor towards the chaplain's room.

She returned to the study as we were ready to proceed to the dining room, she must have spent 45 minutes with the chaplain. After dinner on our way to the chapel she caught up with me and whispered: 'I will tell you tomorrow'.

I thought, probably she had sex with the chaplain because she always needed a man. During recess the next day I asked her how many Ave Maria Mother of God, she had to say to find God's forgiveness. She laughed and started to tell me the minutiae details of her confession.

I began telling him that I like sex very much and don't think it's bad at all because everybody does it. The important thing was to keep it secret, and as long as nobody knows you are doing it, it is ok otherwise parents get the knickers in a knot just because you are doing what they have been doing for a while.

She continued. I also told the chaplain that very often I feel the need to have a man. At this point I looked at him and smiled, then looked down the buttons of his cassock and saw his hardness beginning to appear. I looked at him again and smiled. He put his hand in his pocket, walked away and re-arranged himself. Then, turned to me and said: 'Clara this is a serious matter, you have to control those impulses and when a thought of that nature enters your mind, say a prayer. A prayer will help you to overcome the desire, because to consummate the desire is a sin'.

I stood against the wall under the crucifix, spread my legs and lifted my skirt to show him my parts; with my fingers I opened the skin for him to see the deliciously pink, wet skin inside and said: 'I need a man right now, and nothing overrides that need'.

Touch me I am wet already; then I moved forward and I took his hand, brought it under my skirt and made him touch me. See, I am telling the truth. I held his hand and moved it up and down until I felt his fingers penetrating me; he touched me in the most sensual way. No other man has done that to me.

I came up quickly and felt that sticky stuff running down my legs. It was great; I think he was excited as well.

Then, I suggested we move against the wall which he did after he made sure the door was locked and had the sign do not disturb. He proceeded to unbutton my shirt, had a bite at my boobs, lifted my skirt and penetrated me with the biggest, stiffest dick I have ever seen.

'Are you serious? Are you telling me the truth? What did he do afterwards?'

He composed himself and said: 'Please, Clara you must try not to do this again' and then wiped his hand with his handkerchief'.

'Didn't you like it?'

Then he said: 'Clara, please recite a couple of Ave Maria Mother of God, and ask for forgiveness'.

'I had a good sleep last night', Clara added.

The bell rang, and in silence we formed a line ready to proceed to the classroom.

Clara continued her visits to the chaplain's room at least once a week; she didn't make appointments through the nun anymore, and didn't tell anybody what she was doing. I was the only one aware of her whereabouts. On her return from the visits she always described in minutiae detail the event which had taken place just minutes before; sometimes she said she could smell his sperm on her; that made her even hornier and she felt like having more sex.

On the way to the study Clara said she had a plan, tell sister if she asks for me that I was suffering one of those terrible migraines, and I had to go to the infirmary to ask for an analgesic.

Clara returned to the study, she was a bit sweaty and flustered. She described this particular sex session with the chaplain in vivid detail.

'Well what happened? What was your plan?'

I decided to see the chaplain; I locked the door and as I entered his rooms he said: 'oh, it's you Clara. What may I do for you today?' 'I am desperate' I said, and without any further words I leaned on his desk leaving my feet on the ground, lifted my skirt and began to masturbate. I think he was perplexed for a couple of seconds, but soon he reacted as I expected. He let his hands touch me and without any hesitation his member was inside me instantly, and he continued to move his hands on my genitals. I've never experienced anything like that, torrents of liquid came out and the pleasure was indescribable. I didn't want him to stop, please don't stop, I said several times; when he finished I tried to get up but my legs were wobbly, and all my inside was on fire.

I was speechless. Such vivid descriptions of how the sex sessions happened. I had better get used to the following sex exploits with the chaplain, because Clara's story telling even began to excite me. In an interesting way, most of the times the chaplain was eagerly waiting for her arrival, and in many occasions he was ready with an erection in full swing, it was a matter of finding a suitable position for their interlude.

She would rest her body on the desk, lift her skirt and he penetrated her instantly as soon as she arrived, it lasted longer than with the boys she normally did it with; other times he would be sitting on his chair with an unbuttoned cassock and as she arrived he would open the garment like a curtain to reveal the full extension of his member. She sat on him while he penetrated her and at the same time he filled his mouth with her breasts.

'He even gave me oral sex and I also gave it to him' she said.

'What do you mean oral sex?'

'I don't know how to explain that to you; it's done with the tongue and after he did it, he penetrated me. It drives me crazy'.

No wonder she couldn't learn anything. This was heavy stuff!

The day he gave me oral sex Clara continued, I entered his room locked the door and sat on the back of the divan, I stretched myself along the head rest with my legs opened, one leg on the floor and one on the divan's seat. I lifted my skirt put my hand on my genitals, opened up, and showed him all my anatomy, I also told him how good it felt when he touched a particular area. He then lowered his head and bit me gently. It was heaven while he began to move his tongue and continued to bite me. I searched for his dick and began to pull it; at the same time pleaded with him to fuck me, which he did until I almost collapsed with pleasure.

'What is to fuck?'

Gosh girl! What is the matter with you? 'Fuck is a simple word which means you are penetrated with a dick'. 'You are so innocent, if you died you'd go straight to heaven without the knowledge and taste of carnal pleasure'. How can you be so innocent?

Oh I said. That was what the men who stood along the road shouted when they were rubbing their dicks in front of us. They said they wanted to fuck us all, front and back while the white stuff poured out of their dicks.

'How do you do it in the back?

Oh, Clara said. 'I personally don't like it, because it hurts and shit comes out'.

'What do you mean?'

You are really innocent! So innocent!

'They push their dick up your asses'.

The best is to have sex the normal way Clara said. There are many positions to try, some better than others. The most important thing is to have an orgasm, because if you don't, you have to keep going until it all comes out, otherwise the pleasure is incomplete. She explained all the details and her reasons for doing it

I love to spread my legs, and let them see all my private parts, with my hands I open everything and show them all that pink, moist flesh ready to be used. That moment of exposure brings me a great deal of pleasure, and in general makes them salivate, and helps them to get stiffer with greater speed.

I like that he takes my boobs into his mouth and he bites them gently, and since I don't wear a bra, men usually love to bury the head in my boobs. I love to be absolutely naked. It gives me a great feeling of freedom.

The best I could do when I see the chaplain is to wear nothing under the uniform. It was terrific to lift my skirt and be able to expose everything, or to open my blouse and let my boobs jump out and be ready for him. Is there anything else you would like to know?

'Aren't you scared to be caught? What about if a nun knocks at the door when you are doing it? Don't you feel embarrassed when you lift your skirt to show all your bits? When did you start having sex?'

Clara responded to each question in a very casual way, almost as if she was telling a bedtime story. She began to feel horny very early before her periods started, she thought when she was eleven years old, by then her parents had bought a fairly large house which had several wings independent of each other; her bedroom and small study room were located exactly opposite to her parents wing which was quite a long distance; when she began to feel sexually aroused she didn't understand what was happening, her pubic hairs began to appear and since she didn't know anything about it, she thought it was strange, and used to open her legs in front of the mirror to check how long the hairs were getting, and also began to masturbate in front of the mirror while she observed all her bits.

She developed earlier than other girls, and her boobs began to sprout quickly at about twelve years of age, then she noticed boys looked at her boobs instead of looking at her face when they talked to her. She became friendly with a boy who lived next door, his parents were academics, and being the only child he spent a lot of time on his own; their friendship developed and one day he asked her if she masturbated. She said that she did, and then he asked her if he could watch while she did it. She agreed and after school they went straight to her bedroom, she took her underpants off, spread her legs on the bed and began to do it; perhaps she was nervous and it took a while, when she finished he had an erection and then she asked him to do it while she watched. That is how everything began.

'What did happen afterwards?'

Well, we saw each other the next day and he asked me if he could masturbate me instead and I agreed. Again we met after school and went straight to my bedroom, pulled my pants, and spread the legs for him to do it. After he finished with me his erection was huge so I began to masturbate him until the white stuff came out. After this experience we began to try different things and eventually one night I heard a tap on the window; it was him, he wanted to come inside because he couldn't sleep thinking about the things we had been doing, and he had a permanent erection which he hadn't been able to get rid of; I opened the window and initially we continued to touch each other until it was impossible not to do the whole thing.

'How did you know where to put it?'

'The body tells you, because there are tingling sensations around and inside the genitals and it's easy to guess that it goes there'.

He continued to visit my bedroom after school, and almost every night for a long time; sometimes we had sex all night long until we were both very sore down there, in some occasions we both went to sleep and when we woke up in the morning it was a real hassle to go back to his house without being noticed.

All of a sudden his parents decided to move to another city, and I was left feeling absolutely lost without him; I don't know if it was love or that we had become accustomed to each other, but his absence made me very unhappy because I never heard from him. After some months I went wild and began to have sex anywhere, and when I felt like it, and never felt embarrassed about anything that gave me pleasure.

The final exams started, I tried to do as well as possible. I wanted to give good news to Mamá Nena. In a way I disliked the imposition placed on me to help Clara, it was of no use.

Clara was consumed with the thought of sex, and her strong desire to copulate as many times as possible appeared to rule her everyday life; although the chaplain satisfied her sexual needs once a week, she needed sex everyday which was really impossible to achieve.

She told me that the days in between the weekend and her sexual encounter with the chaplain, she had to masturbate before she went to sleep; she waited until the lights were turned off and people had gone to sleep before starting the procedure; apparently, she began to touch very slowly around the edges, and a bit in the middle, until she completed the arousal because she liked to prolong the sensations as long as possible; at home she had a gadget, but she couldn't bring it to school because it made noise as it was activated.

Clara was always eager for the weekend, and to have the opportunity to feel raw; if there was no sex or the sex wasn't good enough to satisfy her needs, she masturbated with her noisy gadget which was almost as good as the real thing.

'What do you mean the sex is not good enough?'

Clara's response was quite clear. 'Oh, all men have dicks, but not all dicks are the same, and some men don't know how to conduct a proper sex session; some men think that if they just push the dick and move it in and out is enough to satisfy the other person. Those men are lousy in bed, and when I get one of those, I have to satisfy my sexual needs with the plastic gadget'.

I had fears that perhaps there would be some suspicion from the nuns; however, the chaplain was careful enough not to raise suspicion, and the sex encounters continued right to the end of the year. Clara didn't care whether she passed the academic year or not, perhaps she had other plans, it would've been difficult for her to repeat fourth year of high school. She was going to be eighteen years old in December.

Exams were completed, and in spite of the lack of time, I did well and was able to achieve the second top spot in class. Clara failed.

I thought at least she had as much sex as possible and she wasn't found out, with the good result that nobody ended up with twisted knickers.

The time to go home arrived. We packed our belongings and had everything ready for the next day. The usual theatre presentation was about to start when Clara approached me to say goodbye in case she didn't find me later on; she forgot to say thank you. Or was I the one who had to say thank you for the sex instruction?

Mamá Nena arrived early as usual, and I had the pleasure to receive some medals for excellence and some other prizes for her to see. However, the nun in charge of my class said to grandmother that the following year would be my last one if I didn't sort out my lack of discipline. Although a good student, the school would not have me anymore.

We arrived home and everything was as the previous year. Grandmother didn't tell mother about the nun's warning for the following year. She kept her word and after a couple of days, she said it was time to depart because of the commitments she had with the new church fund raising, and of course it was important that I accompany her, because the whole town expected me as well.

Mother didn't say a word, perhaps she was happy to see me leave; we packed and left early the next day. Mamá Nena said it was true that the entire town was waiting for me. The programme for the fund raising had included me in many ways with the dances, also every girl wanted to look like me, and boys asked her if they could invite me out.

I was able to ask questions to grandmother, and generally she responded in a clear and uncomplicated manner, so out of the blue I said: 'Mamá Nena, what do you know about my father? Is there any possibility that he is still alive?'

'This is rather a difficult subject' she said.

'Tell me everything' please.

There isn't much to talk about; the truth of the matter is that from the very beginning it was clear that a great deal of incompatibility between your mother and father was present. I feel guilty because I thought she wanted to marry your father, when in reality she was waiting for a boy who went to Madrid to complete his medical studies.

She was unhappy since I remarried, and I suppose she saw her own marriage as a way out. It was silly, had she waited for the medical student her life would have been very different. But that is life.

Your parent's relationship was on and off, you were barely twelve months old when the first split occurred; after that your father returned for a brief period of time, she fell pregnant and the situation continued like that until the last reunion when she fell pregnant once more. She lived with him briefly and on her return to the family said, she would never see him again. Your younger sister was born, and indeed he didn't show up or call during that time, and your mother didn't want to make contact with him either. He was never mentioned again.

All of you seemed to be happy with the life around you; none of you ever asked about your biological father. Your Papi has given all of you the love and attention a father gives, therefore your biological father wasn't needed or thought of. Your mother apparently received a phone call from one of your uncles who said your father had suffered a heart attack, and the funeral was taking place the following week. She put the information aside and kept it to herself. Perhaps she was happy that the natural flow of life finally helped her to get rid of him for good. She didn't mention his death to anybody until some months later; the reason for her silence was that by not telling anybody about his death, she avoided being urged to attend his funeral, which I can fully understand.

She despised your father for reasons she never wanted to discuss, because she claimed nobody would believe her. Your mother didn't want any contact with his family, and avoided at all cost any interaction between you and them. On several occasions your father's family tried to establish some form of communication, but your mother always refused.

Only time would tell if she has been right about it. Papi and Tuni didn't accept her story and that is the reason they opposed so strongly her relationship with Maximiliano. In addition to that, they believed Maximiliano belongs to an unacceptable social class.

Papi and Tuni have doubts about your father's death and to be honest I have doubts as well. However, what happened can't be changed and it is better to live for today. Stop worrying about what is correct in the eyes of the Church. Life is to be lived in the best possible way, try to see the positive side of life and enjoy every moment as life brings it to you.

It was always the same. Mamá Nena had the ability to release my doubts and fears, and she restored the balance in my life. She was correct; the man was my biological father, but while he was alive he never showed interest in us, why bother? Papi was my father as far as I was concerned, and I was happy with it.

We didn't stop to visit relatives or call on Anita and Isidoro's hacienda this time. After a long journey we arrived home at dusk; the smell of wet soil filled the air like a welcome sign, unfortunately those vicious mosquitoes always ready to nibble my flesh, and drink my blood without compassion were out in the thousands; my arms and legs were covered with mosquito bites, and the next day I was full of pink, itchy blotches.

The first concert would take place by the end of the following week, and we had to commence rehearsal the very next day. The mothers had made pretty dresses for the regional dances, and had prepared costumes for the dances I would organize. Vargas was in charge of the choreography. Most girls wanted to learn the dances, however I realized that in many instances they didn't even understand the way I expressed myself, I thought it was a funny situation because everybody spoke the same language, yet often, I had to explain in simple words what I had said. I noticed there was a marked difference between the level of education in the provinces and the city.

Vargas was the organizer; the concerts ran for a couple of weeks with special functions on Saturday and Sunday after the church services. It was exhausting. If anybody wanted to have a career in the entertainment industry this was a good example of life in a small theatre. After the concert small children wanted to touch my costumes and their mothers wanted to talk about organizing dance classes during the holidays.

I wanted to hear more about my future and found the right opportunity to talk to Vargas; please continue from where you left I asked him. He looked intensely into my eyes and said: 'It's murky at the moment. You can't understand that your life has been served on a silver platter because there is too much turmoil around you at present; there will be many years before life shows you the real bright side of your destiny. Don't look to the past for answers, always look ahead of you. You must deal with the future, the past is gone and nothing can be changed. You will live on a large island most of your life. In less than 10 years you will leave this land never to return, the new language you learn will be spoken as fluently as your mother tongue, and in addition you will be able to communicate in other languages. Luxury and abundance will surround you because your wealth comes from within, and what surrounds you is only a reflection of your inner beauty and riches. You will encounter lots of jealousy along your path; the jealousy comes from individuals who are unable to understand that you are a very different person'.

I didn't understand a word he said and asked him to tell me slowly so I could write it all down. He patiently obliged and as he finished his predictions, didn't want to say anymore. I kept that piece of paper together with the previous one for many years, I folded it in little folds almost like origami and hid it with the rest of my treasures until time disintegrated the paper, by then I had memorized every word.

The holidays continued and we were very busy attending parties, lunches, and lots of gatherings. We went horse riding and from time to time spent days with new relations Mamá Nena found. I had a couple of marriage proposals which made me laugh and the way Mamá Nena used to tell the story was hilarious. One of the marriage proposals came from the owner of a large hacienda, his name was Carlos. Carlos had three children but wasn't married to their mother and didn't live with her either.

He decided to ask Mamá Nena for my hand in marriage; apparently, I was the right person for him; he was affluent enough and could build a new hacienda for me. Mamá Nena said to Carlos: 'how many cows are you prepared to give me in exchange for my granddaughter?' Realizing what a fool he had been, he apologized and the proposal ended there.

The other proposal came from the notary's son Aurelio; he said to Mamá Nena that he loved me very much. He arrived at the conclusion that since he was twenty six years old, and his sisters liked me as well, we could live together at his father's house, which was quite large. He already had a job assisting his father in the notary business. Mamá Nena said to Aurelio: 'what makes you think that you deserve my beautiful granddaughter? Dear child you don't even have money to buy your own toilet paper'

Grandmother enjoyed telling these stories, and we laughed until we cried.

Time had gone! Evaporated! My holiday was about to end and we began to pack. We visited Anita and Isidoro on our return and Yesid arrived to pick us up at the train station. Handsome as ever, it was lovely to see him. Sadly, I realized his personality had undergone a radical change; a bit arrogant, he was sure to let us know the number of important people he socialized with, while at university.

At dinner Yesid sat next to me, but it wasn't the same. My heart didn't flap and the butterflies had gone. He said he thought of me often and every time he saw me he realized his love for me was still there. 'Did I love him?'

'I don't know' was my response.

Fabio arrived soon after dinner. 'Nené you have grown up, you are indeed beautiful. I may even marry you one day'.

Mamá Nena proceeded to tell the stories about the marriage proposals to everybody's amusement. Coffee was served in the courtyard, Yesid and I sat near but didn't talk much, Fabio made the comment that we looked bored and wanted to know what the problem was; he began to ask many questions about school, and the things I wanted to do when I finished high school. He even mentioned that he had been transferred to the barracks located a couple of hours from the boarding school, and perhaps he would visit me sometime.

I just nodded. Yesid stood up and left.

I didn't have anything to say.

We left very early the next day because the trip would take almost eight hours. Those trips presented a good opportunity to talk to Mamá Nena about family, school and a multitude of other things. The trip was always interesting, whether it was going down the cordillera or climbing it. I began once more to ask questions about my biological father. 'Mamá Nena, if my father was so awful why did Papi and Tuni oppose so much to mother's relationship with Maximiliano?'

I don't particularly like Maximiliano either. I think he is a horrible person, sarcastic and critical of everything all the time. He isn't likeable at all.

Consider this, Mamá Nena said: 'a woman with four children would have great difficulty to find a man who accepts such responsibility, and initially he appeared to accept that all of you would become part of his family; he wasn't well prepared for it, and he wasn't prepared to deal with your mother's character either'. He is thirty years older than your mother.

Many life experiences naturally should've prepared him well for the life he walked into, however, he'd never married, his life had been free of any family commitments, and he was and still is badly equipped to deal with the events that have followed after their union. Your mother is terribly unhappy, and now there are two more children, not much she can do but to continue with the fiasco, grin and bear it.

I know she takes her frustration on you many times, and you are correct, it's unfair. The problem is aggravated by the fact that you are absent most of the time, and consequently, not able to fit into the family group when you return, a circumstance that makes the situation even worse. I warned her about the lunacy and unfairness of sending you away, I also warned her about the possible changes in your personality due to the fact that at a very tender age you had to adapt to a totally different life; you had to fend for yourself, and therefore the situation makes you feel detached and unfamiliar with what we call the family unit. It isn't your fault that you experience the feeling of not fitting in on your return home, it is a natural reaction.

There is regimentation and discipline during six months of your life, everything is in order and there are routines to follow, all of that makes sense; however, when you return home after six months of absence, you are more like a stranger returning to visit someone you knew in the past. The immense changes you experience while you are away, are an obstacle for you to be able to easily enter the family environment; every time you return home you have grown not only physically but your thinking has been transformed, and you obviously are a different person.

Your mother doesn't appear to understand that you have changed into a little person who likes to think, a person who has become more refined than the rest, and that really annoys her. She likes adulation, the type of adulation Fena gives her. You are different.

You are a totally different person to Fena, straight forward with your opinions and comments, and that is one of the main reasons you feel totally frustrated and alone. I don't see a possible change in the situation; I wish I had the means to look after you, but I haven't.

I have tried to persuade your mother to tell me the cause of the disgust towards your father. She said it was too awful to remember it. I exerted pressure on her, and finally she said that it was impossible to live with a man that had an interest in boys. It is something so horrible to contemplate, that I didn't ask more questions.

Let's return to Maximiliano's problem; everything could've been avoided if he had been ignored from the very beginning, if Papi and Tuni had seen him as someone who was passing by and nothing else. Obviously your mother felt lonely and someone was paying attention to her, it didn't matter to her that he is thirty years older and quite unsuitable from many points of view. Yes, he has money, and he is a professional, but she should've been more attentive to other important details, because of all of you, and should've been more discriminating. He isn't suitable for several reasons.

His background is too different to ours, he is brash and unsophisticated, and no amount of money may cover the fact that he belongs to a different social class. Another important factor which she completely overlooked was that, he was accustomed to do whatever he pleased since he was free of commitments. He was also free to go out with different women, and he has continued to do so to add to your mother's disappointment, and the worst of it, is that he doesn't even bother to be discreet. He often drinks to excess and dismisses your mother completely. He must feel like he has a rope around his neck, and in addition teenagers aren't the easiest people in the world to deal with.

Well, Mamá Nena I said. 'This isn't my fault. Why do I have to pay for their unhappiness?' There is no place for me in that house. There isn't any joy in anything; they make me feel as if I am a burden. They are obliged to collect me from school, but I think it would be quite convenient for them if they were allowed to leave me at school the entire year and forget about my existence. They have a choice I don't have one at the moment. There isn't another place for me to go; sometimes I believe it could be better for me if I stayed at school the whole year. On the other hand I could spend some time with Papi and Tuni, but mother doesn't allow me to mention them or even to call them. This is too much for me. I feel it would be better if I was dead.

I understand how you feel Mamá Nena said. Try to finish your studies, behave well at school, so the nuns don't have a reason not to accept you the following year. Once you finish your high school, you may decide what to do. You will be sixteen years old by the end of next year, it could be too early to make life decisions, but things may change for the better. 'I will try to take you away once more, let's see if we succeed'.

We arrived home, with only a couple of days left to organize the school items. Mamá Nena waited to take me back to school. It would be my 5th year of boarding school.

Yvonne had been moved to the senior's dormitory because it was her final year of high school. She didn't like it since the majority of girls were older than her. They talked about boys, the parties and the holiday experiences; she usually spent her holidays with her elderly parents, and her much older siblings who were already married and had children of their own. She always talked about her nieces and nephews and the rest of the family. She didn't have interests of her own and that made her dull. She wasn't interested in boys at all and boys in general didn't like her, she appeared old for her age.

Yvonne wasn't a pretty girl; she had mono eyebrows, a round face, and straight black hair. Her front teeth had been replaced with a not so attractive plate which moved forward sometimes. She was nearly eighteen years old; she was very boyish, not at all refined, perhaps being the youngest in a family of eleven brothers had made her adopt male mannerisms.

She never talked about anybody she might have had a slight attraction for. We thought it was a bit odd, but we accepted it. One of her brothers had graduated recently, and had found a job in the city therefore he would take her out on weekends

The new situation didn't bring a change to her appearance or make her develop interests of her own either; we used to ask her about the activities she got involved with during the day out, and her reply without failure was, not much. We stopped asking.

We also received a letter from Clara, she talked about the new school and included some photographs, she looked happy. Clara had been sent to a finishing school and she was enjoying her freedom. In the letter there was a special message for me, thanking me for the effort I had put in helping her, and added that everything was wonderful in every way, and that she had some big and totally pleasurable ones. Everybody asked what she meant by that.

I knew, but didn't explain.

Pilar sent me a letter through one of the day girls, she had done well in her studies and was thinking about doing linguistics after she finished high school. Her idea was to work with a big international organization; she included photographs and asked for my home address.

I continued to receive letters from Pilar through the day girl; I didn't want to give her my address because I was sure mother would confiscate and read her letters. I found the courage to write bits and pieces about my life, and my unhappiness, but those stories didn't flow easily from the pen onto the paper.

Her parents finally found Remedios and Alfredo engaged in sex, a night on their return from the opera. The worst part was that they were doing it on the dining table, and they had smothered themselves with marmalade. The parents were very upset, with the end result that Remedios was sent to France to live with some relatives.

Before Remedios left, Pilar was able to question her about the incident and she wrote: 'It was terrible because they were absolutely naked. She had spread herself on the table and he was on top of her in the middle of the sex session, so they didn't hear anything until the parents turned the lights on. It all began in an innocent way and for some reason they couldn't control their sexual desire. Was the pleasure too intense?

Remedios met a cousin and the plan is to get married next spring. The relationship between Alfredo and my parents has become very frosty. He left home after his university course finished, and at present there isn't a lot of communication between my parents and him, which is sad.

I do communicate with both of them and know that Alfredo travels frequently to France and they spend time together, the funny thing is that they don't feel sorry about the incident, and they appear not to be able to stop having sex either. What is going to happen when Remedios marries? Maybe Remedios and her husband would live together, but Alfredo will provide the occasional sex encounter, for as long as is possible to continue. Hopefully no one will have suspicion about their true relationship. Pilar wrote.

Pilar visited several places of interest during her holidays, she talked to her parents about inviting me for a month or so and they agreed. We would visit museums and galleries it would be wonderful. What a dream I thought; I am not allowed to go to a matinee, how on earth I would be allowed to go away to Europe!

My lack of discipline continued; outspoken, not confessing any imaginary sins, disappearing during study time to be on my own, hiding in the theatre, other times I would sit in the room where visits were conducted. I spread my books on the bench and felt really happy with the solitude and silence until a horrible nun would find me. Sometimes Sister Barbarita would find me and she asked many questions about my behaviour.

I certainly had problems which made me feel that I needed space and solitude to cope with life in general. I was a closed book and the nuns didn't like it. I performed well academically, no matter how many times I was sent to stand in the middle of the corridor. I found myself in the corridor outside the study room almost every night. Sometimes I had company, and as soon as someone joined me, we laughed and talked as if we were at a party rather than facing some form of punishment. The next day every nun asked for my homework, and without failure I always presented a neat, clean and well prepared work. I started to think that perhaps the nuns believed I had an accomplice like Mephistopheles from the other world.

I began to leave my body at the desk during boring lessons; I sat outside the window and listened to whatever went on in the classroom. One morning Sister Barbarita was teaching chemistry, it was lovely and sunny outside while the classroom was cold and the lesson was boring, so I decided to leave my body and stand outside the window looking towards the classroom, everybody looked half asleep. Sister Barbarita said: 'you look like you are in another world. Wake up girl and tapped the desk. Can you answer the question?' To her surprise I answered her question. After that she told me to wait for her after the class finished.

The weekend arrived and Papi and Tuni visited me in the morning. The afternoon walk was cancelled because it looked like it was going to rain, so we proceeded to the study. I was there for almost one hour when my name was called again. Thinking that quite likely the visitor would be mother I took my time to arrive at the visitor's room; to my surprise the visitor was Fabio wearing his army uniform. Fabio looked impressive in his uniform. I didn't know what to say, he was engaging and tried to make me laugh but it was odd. Perhaps he sensed my discomfort and left soon, before he left he gave me some money, but I didn't want to accept it, I said to him that it was wrong to give me money, it was kind of him to visit and that was quite adequate. He insisted that I should take the money because he didn't know what to bring me or what I needed.

June holidays arrived and I went home. If my behavior didn't show a remarkable improvement during the second part of the year, the warning was that I would not be accepted the following year to finish high school. Mother went berserk when she heard about it.

'It isn't my fault. I told the nuns that you'd married Maximiliano in a civil ceremony'.

She couldn't say anything for some minutes, and then began to justify her decision. I didn't want to hear about it. The moment had arrived when I didn't know what would be worse, whether to stay at school or to be at home.

I believed that the truth of the matter was that I didn't want to confess, and I questioned all those religious practices that appeared to be so unnecessary. In addition I didn't fit the mould of a future nun. I showed my discontent, I expressed my doubts, and I often questioned the dogmas, didn't accept the explanation that you believe it because that is the faith. I was a person who had a different way of thinking; I didn't belong to the group, I was an individual. I didn't believe blindly in whatever they said, I saw their hypocritical behaviour, their hates and insignificant intrigues. I saw how unhappy and trapped they felt; I saw their loneliness and the misery of a life without love. I had observed their envy towards someone who had the courage to challenge them.

We arrived home to a totally different tune. Mother didn't criticize or admonish me as on previous occasions. I was flabbergasted about her mild reaction. I thought, maybe tomorrow the punishment will commence. As usual few items of clothing fitted me. I asked for some sweaters and shoes. Mother said I could go shopping the next day. I almost fainted!

Jaime, an old friend of cousin Ye, had continued to visit the family even after cousin Ye departed. Of course I hadn't seen him for a while. Mother invited him to lunch later during the week. Jaime graduated as a medical doctor and had begun to work at a private clinic not far from our house. The few times I'd seen him previously, he'd always talked to mother, this time he seemed interested in talking to me; I believed that mother had discussed with him my expulsion from school, and through him mother thought that she could find out a bit more about it because I wasn't saying much.

He asked mother whether it was possible to take Fena and me to the movies the following Saturday, and mother accepted the invitation. Jaime came home to pick us up on Saturday after lunch, to our surprise he asked whether we wanted to go to the movies or visit Papi and Tuni. We preferred to see Papi and Tuni we answered. He asked many questions during the journey. Fena was more familiar with Jaime because she was accustomed to his regular presence during lunches and dinners.

Our arrival took Papi and Tuni by surprise; they hadn't seen Jaime since the break-up. He talked for a while and then suggested that he would return to pick us up in an hour because we were going to see a movie.

He returned to pick us up within the hour, while we sat in the car my vision went dark, and as I closed my eyes all I could see was a brilliant, colourful, composition of bright dots. The sensation disappeared as soon as it had arrived, but it left me with a violent headache and a little sick. I didn't say anything about it and of course I remained very quiet.

I felt nauseous, and according to Jaime I looked pale. I didn't feel well and wanted to go home, so we left. He would've liked to take us for an ice cream, but we would leave it for next time. We arrived home and I went straight to bed still suffering a violent headache; the next day I got up with a dry taste in my mouth and my head felt like a balloon, I didn't say anything. I thought that perhaps the cause was the hot chocolate we had while at Papi and Tuni.

The days passed by and it transpired that we wouldn't go to see Mamá Nena during this school holiday. Fabio became a frequent visitor as well as Jaime. I didn't take much notice of them because they always talked to mother.

Fabio and Jaime often asked me questions and looked at me intensely which disturbed me, and they wanted to know more than I was telling. Those men appeared to be interested in me, but I couldn't understand the reason for their interest. I thought mother had asked them to question me about the school expulsion.

My birthday always fell on the last day of the school holiday, this time it was on Saturday, so a lunch was prepared for me as well as a cake. To my surprise Fabio arrived in the afternoon, as we were about to cut the cake. He brought a big bunch of flowers for me, it was the first time someone had given me flowers, as he gave me the flowers he said loudly: 'to a beautiful girl' and added that it was possible he could marry me one day. I felt very uncomfortable.

The next day mother took me to school and asked me not to be so talkative. 'It would be better if you finished your last year of high school here, rather than experiment with another school' she said. Mother's mild reaction had caught me again by surprise. Had she seen how much I suffered or simply had she given up?

I was about to start my last six months in prison. We began the second semester, no sooner had we started and it was September; a couple of months and the end of the year would take me away from here forever. I firmly believed that everything would be better once I returned and remained at home with the family. No more anguish about being alone or left out of everything.

We were playing a horrible and aggressive ball game and I felt dizzy. I told the nun that I had to sit down because I felt unwell. I walked towards a shady section of the patio when my vision turned black; I closed my eyes and saw a multitude of bright coloured dots on a black background, like the brightness of the stars on a moonless night. The brilliancy of those colourful dots gave me a brutal headache, this time my tongue felt numb and nausea followed pretty quickly. I sat for a while with the head resting in my hands and feeling extremely dizzy. The nun came to investigate how I felt; she took me to the infirmary and told the nun in charge to allow me to rest until I recovered.

The headaches returned fairly often, but the colourful dots and the nausea didn't come back.

I studied diligently with the desire to be the best at the end of the year, because that would prove to me that I was expelled not due to my unruly behaviour, but because I refused to confess, and perhaps I was right that mother's civil marriage was a contributing factor.

True to my efforts I was number one for the month of September with high marks of nearly 100% on every subject. I kept the number one position in the class until November when exams and tests followed before the final exams at the beginning of December.

On a Sunday afternoon at around 4.30 I was called to the visitor's room. It was strange because that was the time when visits terminated. I proceeded anyway to meet whoever was there. The nun opened the door and told me to follow her to the small room.

Papi and Tuni were waiting for me in the small room, a more intimate environment than the large salon with the big chairs placed against the walls. They appeared a bit anxious, we sat and after some small talk they told me that there was someone who wanted to meet me. He was waiting in the next room.

'Who is he?' I asked.

'He is your uncle Rogelio'.

'I don't know who he is, why would I want to meet him?'

'He is your father's brother and has shown great interest in you since we made him aware of the problems you have with your mother'.

'So, what is he going to resolve by meeting me?'

Papi left the room and asked Rogelio to come over. I stood up waiting for this person that I'd never met. A short man with light coloured hair and green eyes that like darts tried to penetrate my soul. Very well dressed and as he said hello his smile showed stained and crooked yellow teeth that made him look like a photo of a piranha. He smelled of cigarette.

Rogelio introduced himself and soon commenced to ask questions about mother, curiously enough didn't ask about my sisters. He then continued to say that if I wasn't happy he would help me to leave school, and I could live with him and his mother. 'Do you want to see me again?'

'No'. I responded.

He said: 'very well then', turned his heels and walked away.

'Why did you bring this horrible man?' I asked Papi and Tuni. 'Is he truly an uncle?' He is revolting.

'We are only trying to help you, it has been very difficult to contact that side of your family' they said, and now you don't wish to see him again. What a waste of time it has been. I said goodbye and began to cry. Why are they doing this to me? The very people I love and trust. As I walked towards the chapel where everybody was at this particular time, I felt very confused. Perhaps he wasn't uncle Rogelio, if Papi and Tuni made such effort to find that side of the family, probably he was my father, but they didn't want to give a shock bigger that I could handle.

Life continued as if nothing had happened. My efforts to be the very best paid off. I finished the year having the highest marks in my class, and for a change mother turned up to the prize and medal presentation. Yes I was expelled. Mother didn't say a word, I was the very best of my year and it was acknowledged during the prize presentation; the nuns didn't mention I had been expelled.

The search for a new school began almost immediately after our return home. Mother decided to talk to the Mother Superior at the school Fena was attending; on the day of the appointment mother took me with her just in case the Mother Superior wished to meet me. We were at the Mother Superior's waiting room, the door opened and Mother Cecilia greeted us. She was the Mother Cecilia who was the Mother Superior when I began boarding school six years ago.

We entered her rooms. Mother began to talk, and asked if it was possible for me to finish the last year at this school. I had been expelled for being too talkative and unruly. Mother Superior opened her arms in a welcome sign and said to mother: 'I wish all the unruly ones could be like this one, with the qualities of an inquisitive mind and the hunger to learn'.

I was accepted immediately, we left her office to fill up the forms for the school enrolment.

Why wasn't this done before? Why impose all the loneliness and unhappiness I had experienced? In view of my acceptance, I believed that mother didn't want me home, and at this moment she was the one left with no choice.

The holidays progressed in a pleasant manner; I still sensed that from time to time mother didn't want me at home. She couldn't accept any compliments people gave me; it was almost like an obsession of hers that after a person offered a compliment, she had to add some sharp criticism without failure.

Fabio and Jaime continued their regular visits, they invariably tried to talk to me and I didn't like it at all. Their questioning and the way they looked at me, made me very self-conscious of my appearance, because boobs had begun to spring out, and my long, abundant wild hair made me look like a lioness. Elsi said that they looked at me because I was a very pretty girl and I had grown so much. They admire your beauty, but la Señora gets annoyed and then takes it on you after they leave, almost as it is your fault that others find you to be beautiful.

I escaped to the terrace to read some magazines, the doorbell rang, but I didn't pay attention to whom had arrived,

I heard voices shortly afterwards. Elsi appeared on the terrace to tell me that el doctor Jaime had arrived.

'What can I do?' She asked.

'Well, did you tell him that mother is not home?'

'Yes, I did'.

'What does he want?'

I told him that you are the only one home, and he insisted that I tell you he is here, and wishes to talk to you. By the time she had finished giving the message Jaime was standing at the edge of the terrace.

'I am very pleased to have found you. Hello Nené. I dislike calling you Nené, it's a child's nickname. Why does everybody ignore your real name?'

Well, I have four names and it would be too long to call my four names all the time; mother likes my second name because it was the name of a famous beauty queen centuries ago, I hate that name! Mamá Nena likes my first name because it reminds her of the great love affair with a man too unsuitable for her, and the last two names are Mamá Nena's Christian names. There you have it. That is the reason everybody calls me Nené instead of Nena because it would get confusing calling me the same as grandmother.

'I've heard about your expulsion from the boarding school'.

'We have found a solution already' I said.

I have also spoken to your mother about you and the problems that you both have. I am aware of the difficulties your mother is going through at present, and I have offered a solution, if you don't mind I could tell you all about it.

I also keep in touch with your cousin Ye, and although his manner of communication is somehow laconic, I've found out that it is a bit difficult for you to fit in with all the changes that had transpired within the family. I have continued the contact with your mother because I want to keep in contact with you. As you know I graduated last year, and already have a good position at a private clinic, and my financial situation will only get better from now on. Soon I will be going abroad for a postgraduate course; my return is scheduled for the middle of next year. I would like you to think about marrying me on my return. I do love you. It is crazy, but I have been in love with you since I met you when you were eleven years old. After you went to boarding school I said to your cousin Ye that I would marry you one day.

But I don't love you and I don't want to get married, I have many things to do. I have to study, travel and see the world. 'Kiss me to check if it gives me butterflies'.

He kissed me. 'No, didn't like it'. 'Do it again to see if it is different'. 'Not really'.

I tried to disappear from that day onwards every time Jaime visited; as soon as I heard his voice I vanished, ignored mother's calls until she gave up. I re-appeared as soon as I was sure that Jaime had left, on the few occasions when my path crossed his, I could not stand the way he looked at me. Jaime began to talk to Mamá Nena about my rejection, perhaps he thought that Mamá Nena would be of help and that she could persuade me to marry him, and in that way resolve mother's problem. He didn't know grandmother was my ally.

Oh Mamá Nena I can't stand him was my usual reply. It was a relief when he left the country to continue his studies abroad because I didn't have to see him.

Mamá Nena arrived for Christmas and I was hopeful that she would take me with her in the New Year. The end of the year was a little more animated and jolly thanks to Mamá Nena's presence and efforts; we enjoyed delicious cakes and all sorts of goodies she so brilliantly created with my help and Elsi's.

There was a surprise for me. I was going to spend the whole month of January Island hopping in the Caribbean with Mamá Nena. I couldn't believe my ears when Mamá Nena said she had purchased the flight tickets, and we should be ready to leave in a couple of days. The first stop a Fortress City the Spanish had founded around 1500. Then we would visit some small Islands.

We arrived at a hot and steamy place. The sea was like a shiny jewel with a magnificent turquoise colour, the breeze was deliciously cool close to the water, and the smell of the ocean filled the air. It was the first time I had seen the sea, and had never imagined it would have such impact on me.

We visited many places of interest, it was important to see the enormous sandstone walls that formed the fortress the Spaniards had built to protect the city from the pirates during the reign of King Felipe II, around 1700.

We went to the markets, visited museums and historic houses, as well as the Inquisition Palace, where we saw large scales used to weigh women, who were accused of heresy during those terrible inquisition times. Mamá Nena found a relative who showed us many places of interest, until it was time to continue our journey to the islands. I met new cousins, and as we left I promised to keep in touch with them.

The small airplane flew low enough to make the islands look like scattered emeralds that just surfaced above calm, and transparent, light blue liquid; curly, little waves caressed the big, white beaches overcrowded with swinging, svelte coconut palms. We tried fruits and foods typical of those areas, had fresh coconut milk for the first time, went to the markets on every island, and visited many historic sites the Spaniards left after their conquest, and we found their unmistakable imprint everywhere. The characteristic blue cobblestones paved many streets; old colonial homes with their timber framed balconies, and timber shutters painted light, pastel colours, as well as the usual wrought iron balustrades.

People always talked loudly to be able to be heard over the loud music which played constantly wherever we went. We used the local transport which had to be shared often with chickens and a small piggy.

Mamá Nena asked many questions and always found out the best places to visit. Don't be shy to ask questions, she used to say when it was noticeable that I felt uncomfortable. Remember that people are generally kind, and are always willing to share their knowledge with you, if you ask in the right way and with a correct and gentile manner. It saves you a lot of time and effort.

It was a wonderful holiday once more. It was the first opportunity for me to see the sea and I loved it. 'When I grow up I would live in a city by the sea, no doubt about it', I said to Mamá Nena.

Sex against the wall

We returned home with enough time to sort out the new uniform and school texts for my final year of high school. The academic year started and I felt flat and depressed; I didn't seem able to apply myself, and the headaches started to afflict me almost on a daily basis, I had no energy. The environment at home was not conducive to study, I had to share the bedroom with Fena, therefore there was no room for a desk and I had to spread my books on the dining room table. Some days I didn't even bother to open my school bag to do the following day's homework.

Life was worse than at boarding school. Nobody to talk to and the house was dark and gloomy. I also felt all those ghosts that woke me up during the night and stood by the side of the bed. There was a very persistent young man with straight hair standing by the door, he was angry because nobody helped him; many times I woke up with the heart on the tip of my tongue, and so frightened and agitated it was difficult to fall asleep again. Other times it was the man who died in the room downstairs, and nobody visited while his casket stood in the middle of the room. On other occasions I woke up while someone stood by the side of the bed or just floated above my face. The more frightened I was the more I felt those people. Curiously enough it was always the same individuals. Some of them whispered in my ear, other times they just stood silently by the side of the bed waiting for me to wake up and then wouldn't go away.

I didn't think it was wise to discuss the situation with mother since I felt she didn't want me at home with them, and that would have been the perfect excuse to take me to a sanatorium for the insane. I wasn't sure whether it was my imagination, or whatever I experienced almost on a daily basis was real; sometimes I dared to think I was mad.

It was quite fortunate that a new domestic helper was hired to wash and iron, she possessed a nervous nature, and she appeared to rush all the time, walked so fast it almost looked as if she ran instead. I offered her a coffee and a piece of cake for morning break but she didn't want to sit down, she ate and drank as she ironed and all of a sudden said: 'I am sorry Niña, but I don't like this house, it has too many ghosts and that makes me very nervous, those rooms in the centre of the house are the worst'.

'How do you know there are ghosts here?' I asked her

'I am glad you don't feel anything Niña, because I wouldn't be able to sleep in this place. I only live in a shack with a dirt floor, but the other world doesn't torment me there'.

'Can you see people from the other world? Do you mean dead people?'

'Yes, I can see and hear them'.

'Who do you see?'

'There are many people in this house, mainly men, and unfortunately there are unhappy souls who haven't gone through to the other side'.

'I am sorry you feel that way, but thank you for letting me know'.

What a relief when I heard her words. She proved that I wasn't going mad as I sometimes thought.

Christine and I went to the same school; Christine was a day girl and I was a border. We developed a good friendship throughout the years we shared the same classroom. The year I was expelled from school, her parents decided to send her to live with her aunt who lived in the same city we lived, and only ten blocks away from home.

Unknown to both of us, we ended at the same school, because like me, she had been expelled as well. She couldn't understand the reasons for being expelled because she was also a good student, but like me, she disliked religion and frequently asked questions, which appeared to be the wrong type and probably she fell into the heretic label.

Christine's story was different to mine. Her parents for an inexplicable reason decided that they didn't want to have her at their house anymore and therefore her expulsion presented them with the opportunity to get rid of her; the sad part was that her mother told her that she wasn't wanted around them anymore. I felt sorry for her because there was no explanation for her mother's action.

Her aunt and her husband didn't have children, so they agreed to look after Christine who was a dedicated and good student. On the occasions I met her aunt, I had the impression that the lady was quite tense and agitated; very neurotic and when I visited Christine we normally had to walk out of the house and sit on the dwarf wall of the garden, or walk around the block because her aunt invariably had a headache or she was in a nervous state and didn't tolerate music, or laughter; even the sound of our voices irritated her; she was almost a carbon copy of mother. I didn't mind the imposition because going to Christine's place was more agreeable that staying at my home. Also when I visited Christine we made cakes and had interesting conversations without being snooped like it happened at my place. Mother used to send my sisters to stand and listen to our conversations, and that annoyed me.

The frequent shortages of bottled gas didn't seem to affect Christine's household, and we were able to bake cakes almost every Saturday, until on one occasion after our usual bake Christine's aunt arrived, and as she entered the house and the aroma of the fresh baked cake found its way into her nostrils, she went berserk and abused the hell out of us because the gas was low and the delivery hadn't taken place.

I left Christine's house and when we saw each other at school the following Monday we talked about the problem; it was strange because until then her aunt had been difficult and hysterical but not so bad. We thought that her neurosis was escalating perhaps due to emotional difficulties with her husband.

Christine's aunt had questioned the maid during the weekend about the gas which became a real issue; all of a sudden the family was in the same situation as the rest of the city's households and Christine's aunt couldn't understand the reason behind the problem. The maid kept silent and patiently listened to her patron's complaints; after the upheaval subsided, Christine's aunt went upstairs to rest her head since the onset of one of those terrible migraines began to appear.

The maid had arrived at their household approximately six months before, a country girl who settled fairly well considering the intransigent behaviour of Christine's aunt. Good natured and with a happy disposition, she befriended the other service personnel from the butcher to the drycleaners, the gas delivery man as well as several policemen who patrolled the street.

Some problems began to appear and the gas was only an insignificant one compared with the huge problem that surfaced in the maid's life. Everybody thought that the maid had gained a lot of extra weight during the last months, until it was evident that the perceived extra weight was due to her pregnancy, which Christine's aunt had discovered that morning before she left to the hairdresser. That was the reason Christine's aunt was so out of her mind that afternoon, and after I left their house, Christine was made aware of the new problem.

The neurosis and hysteria reached a climax after I left Christine's place, and the whole episode about the pregnancy burst into the open, and Christine's aunt was beside herself. She cornered the poor girl and forced her to tell what happened. Christine's aunt was raving mad while she questioned the maid; 'you are pregnant' she told her. 'What I am going to tell your parents?' They trusted that I was going to look after you, and look what you have done. 'Who did you go to bed with?' 'Was he, the gas delivery man? Was he, the policeman? Was he, the butcher? When did you go to bed with a man?'

'Señora, I swear to you I haven't gone to bed with a man', the maid replied and began to cry.

'Of course you went to bed with a man otherwise you wouldn't be pregnant. Do you want me to believe the Holy Spirit visited you during the night?'

'No Señora, on Jesus Christ I swear I didn't go to bed with a man'.

Then, tell me how did you get pregnant? 'A woman only gets pregnant after a man put his dick inside her genitals and that is why you are pregnant'.

'Please Señora, believe me I didn't go to bed with a man; my genitals whatever there are, are clean'.

So, tell me what happened? 'How did the man put his dick inside you?'

'Yes the gas delivery man put his dick inside me, so did the butcher and the several policemen who patrolled the street, but I didn't go to bed with any of them; I stood against the wall with my legs open and lifted my skirt when they put their dick inside me; they told me that I wouldn't get pregnant if I let them do it against the wall, so I believed them'.

'Why did you do it with all of them?' 'How many men put their dick inside you while you stood against the wall? Half a dozen men put their dick inside you?'

'More than six men, I counted to eight. Señora, to tell you the truth I didn't think it was bad, on the contrary it felt very good while it happened; they also told me not to tell la Señora because Señoras of your kind are difficult to please and become neurotic. If la Señora found out, she was going to be angry at me because some people thought that doing it was bad'. 'How is it possible, that something that feels so good can be bad for anybody?'

Christine and I laughed our heads off, but it was a serious matter for the poor girl; there was no way of finding who the father was. However, Christine's aunt approached the butcher first, and he begged her to keep it quiet, because if his wife found out there would be a lot of problems; they already had six children and she was pregnant again. She tried to find out who the policemen were, but it was customary that the police force alternated the patrols to avoid corruption, and to make matters worse the maid knew their nicknames or Christian names only. The gas delivery man obviously had been transferred to another area of the city, and the maid didn't know his name either.

How to break the news to her parents was the next chapter. Christine's aunt decided to wait until the birth of the child and perhaps if the maid consented the child would be adopted. The child was born and he was so incredibly beautiful and healthy, Christine's aunt and her husband adopted him with the condition that, she would remain at their household until she either got married or decided to leave minus the child. What a beautiful outcome to the story.

We used to talk about the incident, and after all the drama Christine's aunt became a better person, no so strung up and agitated. She was friendly and quite talkative when I visited. In spite of our friendship I didn't discuss my home life with Christine, but I did tell her about my headaches and how unwell I felt.

The fact that I struggled with my homework depressed me even more, I was accustomed to be the best I could among the rest of the class, for some odd reason I couldn't learn as fast as I normally did while at boarding school. Those awful headaches arrived like applied torture and only went away after taking four or more pills; the pills not only upset my stomach but also made me sleepy. My memory stopped functioning and didn't retain anything, and I became so depressed, I even contemplated suicide.

I received a letter from Pilar, it was lucky that I opened the door when the postman delivered the mail that morning, and among the letters there were news from Pilar. She was happy, was looking forward to her final year of school, and unlike me, was enjoying her life. I read her good news and I felt so sad and depressed with my life that I didn't have the courage to respond. It was the last time I heard from her.

Mother had instructed us to catch the bus provided by the school, but from time to time it was more interesting to travel by public transport or walk the ten blocks from school when the afternoon was sunny. On the way home there was a private university and I liked to walk in front of the main door, so many girls and boys coming in and out always laughing, looking happy. Hugo a friend of cousin Ye who was doing his thesis in nuclear science, just walked out as I passed by. I hadn't seen him for a very long time. I was surprised that he recognized me and called my attention. Hugo invited me for an ice cream and I accepted. I sort of liked Hugo, he wasn't handsome; he had dark hair, rosy skin complexion, lovely smile and what I liked the most was that he talked in a soft well-modulated manner. We talked for a while, I glossed over my school problems with physics and calculus and he kindly offered to help me out.

Hugo started to pick me up a block away from school on the days I arranged to walk home, and we walked together discussing many things. Hugo pulled my arm as I was about to cross the road quite impetuously; his action probably saved my life, I would have been squashed like a cockroach and my guts spilled on the road otherwise. 'Phew! That was close'. He said. Put his arms around me and kissed me. 'I like you Nené. You are so beautiful'. 'I like you too'. We continued holding hands until we were close to home. I suggested to Hugo not to tell anybody, because if mother was aware that there was something going on perhaps I wouldn't be able to see him again.

Hugo continued with the physics and calculus instructions, which was very fortunate for me at that moment, because in a way I had given up, due to the difficulties and frustration I was experiencing with each aspect of my studies. He took my books and resolved every single problem in a way that, if I didn't understand I memorized it, and if my memory failed there were some steps to follow to resolve the problem.

The year was progressing in a very slow motion. I was terribly unhappy at school and at home. Life was dreary indeed. The most frustrating situation was not to be able to be the best anymore. I couldn't understand why my mind had given up on me since I was accustomed to breeze through every subject without difficulty; it felt as if my brain had shut down and refused to learn. In addition it didn't want to remember the simplest of things.

The headaches continued to occur with more frequency; sometimes I would wake up in the middle of the night feeling like my head had been put in a vice, the pulsating pain was so strong it induced nausea. Other nights the ghosts would wake me up. Still hadn't mentioned the headaches or the ghosts to anybody. Towards the end of the year I really didn't feel well at all, and dark circles appeared under my eyes, the lack of sleep was wearing me down, and the enormous worry that perhaps I was going to fail my final year of high school filled me with panic.

Hugo encouraged me constantly; he was kind to suggest that it was difficult to adjust to a new school, as well as a totally different environment, with the added problem of the incompatibility with mother. He brought brochures from several universities which explained possible courses in the artistic field. He thought I had tremendous affinity with the arts, music, philosophy and political sciences. I would be good at any of those careers regardless of whatever I selected. Hugo was a lovely person to be with, he was gentle and thoughtful; he seemed to understand the problems I had with mother better than anybody else, because he experienced many times mother's inflexibility, and he heard her constant criticism of me, always making comparisons with the lovable Fena, and making sure that everybody knew how wonderful Fena was.

The final exams arrived and I tried incredibly hard to memorize everything I could, I didn't care anymore that I wouldn't be the best, I just wanted to pass and to be able to continue with university. I would be forever grateful to Hugo for his kind comments and encouragement, and without him I would've failed my last year of high school.

The graduation ceremony morning was shared with a diabolical headache, and the uncertainty of not knowing if I had passed the year. Nobody had said anything to me, but my deep feeling was that I had failed. I entered the theatre and saw mother sitting somewhere close to the front rows; it was unusual for her to be on time.

The palm of my hands absolutely wet with perspiration, and tremendous nausea and dizziness. I felt I was going to faint at any minute. All of us moved to the podium and stood on a line waiting to be called to receive the diploma.

I was called to receive my piece of paper. The ceremony completed we approached Mother Superior to say goodbye, and to thank her for the opportunity she gave me to be there during the final year. What Mother Superior said to mother left mother speechless. It was a peculiar moment of discomfort for mother, since she wasn't able to find words to contradict her.

Señora, she said. 'Your four daughters are pupils of this school and we like them all, I only wish your other three daughters had the intelligence, finesse and the individual mind this one has. Children like this one are rare, and a pleasure to teach because they only have to be nurtured to blossom into fine human beings'. After saying thank you several times to Mother Superior we left. Mother's only comment was how fortunate that Mother Superior appeared to like me. I laughed at the poignancy of that moment.

I wondered why Mother Superior had said all those wonderful words, because she didn't have a class with us and I rarely saw her. Maybe she was mistaken, and after she said all those wonderful praises, she realized I was the wrong girl, and couldn't retract her comments.

I can't remember what happened on the way home, there was a heated argument with mother, and as we arrived home I must have said something which made her slap me across the face. I went to bed because the headache was intense and I had to close my eyes to stop the nausea, after a while I fell asleep and woke up before dinner still wearing the school uniform.

Hugo arrived to visit me the next day while half of my face was like a purple balloon; the upper lip had a cut which left a little opening for blood to escape as I talked. Fortunately mother had gone out, so Hugo didn't have to find an excuse for his visit since my school term had finished. He wanted to take me to a friend's graduation party in a couple of weeks.

I suggested that Hugo talk to cousin Ye to find out the best way to obtain permission. We also had to avoid Maximiliano's intrusion. I don't know, I said full of frustration, life is so difficult here that at times I have the desire to run away as far as possible so nobody can find me. Hugo smiled, and kissed me goodbye.

Hugo brought cousin Ye for the first time after all those years. He looked well, was working with a foreign company which gave him the opportunity to travel abroad several times during the year. He had accepted a job offer to go overseas. Ye managed to obtain permission for me to go to the party; we also escaped the possibility of Maximiliano pushing his way to join us, and spoil our moments as he had done in numerous occasions.

I also had to buy a dress, shoes, go to the hairdresser, and I wondered whether it would be possible when the time arrived to do all those things. I bought an ice blue, satin fabric which was made into a gorgeous dress like those on magazine covers; I designed it and selected soft silver sequins to cut the neckline. Mother's seamstress created a fantastic garment. The day of the party arrived and I didn't want to push my luck by asking if I could go to the hairdresser, I got dressed and was ready to go, even mother commented that I looked pretty. It was a great party, beautiful house and garden, fantastic food, music, and a happy atmosphere.

Hugo and I walked towards the garden holding hands, he gave me a little box; it was a ring with an emerald and some little diamonds around it. It was a present for trying so hard to pass the final year. I did feel butterflies when he kissed me and I liked his kisses. He used to hold me tight and I could feel his excitement and his passion. It was time to have sex I thought. I was only sixteen but I felt I was ready for it; I had to find a way to let him know that I would like to try it. Clara's technique was a bit crass for me and I also believed that love did exist, and it would be beautiful to experience desire, lust and passion; all those emotions that the sex act may bring mixed with love, and not just because you felt like it and it could be done with anybody anytime as Clara had said.

The final exams completed and with excellent results Christine matriculated to do physics. Meanwhile, I began to search for university courses based on the brochures Hugo had brought home. I decided to pursue an art course at a private university, the forms had to be collected and filled in and also the time for an aptitude test had to be booked in, the test was a crucial part of the admission.

I told Hugo that I would meet him after I had carried out all the paper work. Hugo met me at my future university and then we went to his friend's place to collect some books; his friend had a motorcycle accident and was in hospital with multiple fractures to one leg. He had a cute one-bedroom apartment, incredibly neat and tidy, even his bed was made; also had a coffee plant by the window. We gathered the books his friend had requested, and as we were ready to leave I put my arms around Hugo and kissed him. He returned my kiss passionately and we continued kissing for a while; he began to touch my legs in the same way Yesid had done a couple of years before. The more I could feel his hardness against me the more passionate his kisses became; he then put his hands under my sweater and touched my torso. His hands felt hot, and at his point he stopped and said: 'Nené, I can't do it. You are only sixteen years old. I will be in jail for abusing a minor'.

'I won't tell you abused me. I want to do it too'.

He hesitated for a moment and after he composed himself, we walked out of the apartment and in a way I told him that I was ready to have sex. I didn't think age had anything to do with it and according to Clara if one wanted sex that was ok, and anyway why waste time instead of beginning to experience all those fabulous sensations?

The family was invited to a New Year's party at one of the clubs. Cousin Ye didn't join us, but I invited Hugo. Another distant cousin who we used to go out with also came with us to the party. We danced most of the night, the count for the final seconds of that year began and as the counting reached twelve Hugo kissed me passionately. Mother saw it and began to move me away from him. We had to dance far away from each other, every time we became close mother began to pull me away.

Then Hugo said: 'would you like to marry me?'

'Yes' I responded.

'Will I be able to continue my studies?'

'I wouldn't have it any other way, you can't be a parasite', he said.

The party over, we went home. Mother kept Hugo and I far apart. I didn't care at all, this life would finish pretty soon, I thought. How wrong I was! We arrived home and I went to bed. Next I had someone shining a torch into my eyes and slapping my face trying to wake me up.

She is coming back, I heard. 'Can you hear me?'

I nodded, I wasn't on my bed. I had been moved to the sofa in the living room. During the early hours of New Year no ambulance was available to pick me up. The whole service was working at full capacity with the several serious road accidents. After several hours trying to find a doctor, finally a locum was found and he was the one shining the torch into my eyes.

I opened my eyes, my vision was blurry, the peripheral vision was black with bright dots, the tongue was numb, and I had a horrendous headache, my mouth was dry with a bitter taste, it was exactly the same I had experienced in former occasions; this time the nausea was fairly strong.

'We almost lost you' the doctor said. 'How do you feel?'

'I have a terrible headache' was my reply.

I was given a drink of water which I threw up immediately. The doctor observed me for a while and then talked to mother and Maximiliano.

I was confused and didn't understand what had happened. I asked Fena, and she told me that she woke up because of the strange noises I made. The noises continued for a while, she touched me and tried to make me roll over, but she then realized that I had difficulties breathing. She turned the light on and saw that I looked purple and some white saliva dripped out on the side of my mouth. She called mother at once, and as mother and Maximiliano entered our room I had gone stiff and was shivering violently. They moved my arms trying to make me breathe, massaged the heart until I had become more stable; meanwhile Mario, our cousin who was spending the night at home with us, began to call for an ambulance until he found the locum doctor.

It had taken over an hour for a doctor to arrive. Meanwhile my heart was massaged and they moved my arms to try to improve my breathing, but I had lapsed into a coma. The doctor tried to arrange an ambulance but there wasn't a single ambulance available. It was then, when he decided to inject me with something and waited to see my response.

The next day I phoned Hugo and told him the events of the night before, I was still on the sofa when he arrived. We talked and laughed, I told him that I couldn't marry him because probably I would die soon.

I felt a lot better the next day, although the headache and nausea kept me company for several days. I threw up immediately after I drank or ate something. Mother took this opportunity to tell me that I had to have a medical check-up to assess if I had messed up with boys and I was pregnant.

Oh how much I hated her. During the following week she took me to the doctor for a check-up; he was a sweet old doctor, a gynaecologist who had delivered my two younger brothers. He was kind and gentle, checked my blood pressure, looked into my eyes and said I had to go to a neurologist for further tests or to be hospitalized for observation.

Mother made the arrangements with the neurologist, always complaining about the cost of the services and the inconvenience I had created with this problem. I had wires attached to my head, and when the results were made available, it was clear that the headaches and nausea were the consequence of a blood vessel inflammation on the base of the brain.

The most practical treatment was the use of tranquilizers. The tranquilizer was prescribed and it had to be taken twice a day to keep me calm. I had to avoid spicy food and the most important thing was to prevent stress. Ha! That would be a true challenge!

Mother and Maximiliano made me feel as if whatever happened was my fault and it was my choice to be ill. They were so unkind and cruel with their remarks. My heart was full of hate towards them. I had to leave that awful place called home, I thought. The effect of the tranquilizer treatment showed the results almost immediately; although the headaches continued they weren't so vicious and the medication kept me fairly calm, in that way I didn't have the energy to be bothered about anything and life continued in an uneventful way.

I guess being drugged with prescription drugs was similar to inhaling marihuana; I was spaced out permanently, and in a trance.

I was accepted at the university I had chosen, to the course I had selected and soon my lectures were about to commence. It was an exciting time ahead for me, the course required many art books and other equipment that was quite expensive; I also needed a new wardrobe and of course pocket money for transport, lunches etc. Well, what a mistake I'd made.

'I enrolled in a course that was far too expensive; as usual it was my aristocratic way of thinking which ruled my decisions'. I was so full of myself and didn't for a moment contemplate the financial burden placed on the family. Perhaps I could have selected a more economic university, maybe a technical college would have been more appropriate for me, but since I had those ideas of grandeur and saw myself better than the rest, I was imposing myself on everybody; therefore, every time I requested money I heard the same story.

A couple of months into the course I had enough, and thought it would be better to stop my studies and find a job. The university informal hours gave me more opportunities to visit Papi and Tuni and they always helped, but they had to be very discreet for fear of antagonizing mother and making my life more difficult.

Mario, a cousin was working with a bank, I talked to him about my financial problems and also discussed with him that I had to look for a job because the situation at home was unbearable. Casually I asked him if the bank lent money to students. He informed me that there was a system in place but I needed a guarantor because of my age. Being a bank employee he couldn't do it, but I should ask Papi.

Papi was delighted to help me, so we did all the necessary paper work to obtain the loan. The money began to flow and I didn't ask for anything else from mother; I began to buy quality items of clothing as well as the expensive equipment and books required. I walked a lot because I enjoyed it and saved money at the same time. For a month I felt really happy with my new found independence, and curiously enough, mother never asked where the money was coming from.

The fact that I didn't have to put up with arguments and recriminations every time I needed something was delightful, but unfortunately, didn't last. Mario innocently told mother that I had negotiated a loan with the bank, and Papi was the guarantor. He told her that it was very clever of me to do so, since the course was expensive.

I had lectures at 11am and after I finished my assignments that morning, I placed my new garments and matching shoes on the bed before I went to have a shower, on my return to the bedroom every single item had been removed.

Elsi, very quietly told me that mother had taken everything. I went to ask her the reason for confiscating my things since she hadn't bought any of those items. Her reply left me absolutely shocked. She had found out about the loan, and I hadn't given her any money, therefore, if I wanted to live there with them, I had to give her half of the monthly income the bank had allocated.

'The last thing I want to do is to live here with you. You are like vultures, you and Maximiliano are the most horrid people on earth. I think if I died tomorrow you would probably chop me up in little pieces and eat me'. I went to my room got dressed and left.

The following month I began to give mother half of my income as she had demanded, but it was quite difficult to make ends meet, and to accommodate the expense of the materials I needed, I had to avoid buying lunch. I didn't talk to mother anymore; if she asked me something I responded and that was the extent of my conversations with her. Meanwhile I noticed a great deal of activity around Fena, but it was all hushed up.

New items of clothing, even a large suitcase arrived one day. Mother and Fena began to admire some items recently purchased for Fena not realizing that I was in my room and I could hear their comments. I kept as silent as possible, then, I heard that Fena would travel during the June holidays, and that she'd stay with a friend, but it had to be kept quiet so I wouldn't find out. I left quickly before they could get a hint that I'd heard their conversation.

I wasn't jealous that Fena was allowed to travel abroad and that she had beautiful things. I never envied her. I sort of despised her lack of intelligence and her slimy personality. What made me angry was that she was a willing participant, she knew about my struggles and difficulties; she was well aware that the money I borrowed was buying her those items, and yet she continued to pretend her ignorance about what mother was doing to me.

It was difficult to find a solution to my problems, because the money I received from the bank wasn't enough to move away, and pay for my studies; while the unpleasant situation continued, I arrived to the conclusion that I had to leave home.

I met some girls at university who were boarding with families; others were boarding at special boarding houses for students. It didn't appeal to me to leave home and move to another place where I couldn't have a little freedom. I had to investigate those places. My struggle at home continued from bad to worse; since I didn't say much during the time I was there, nobody knew anything about me, and for me it was an unhappy situation.

I could've moved with Papi and Tuni but as much as I loved them and they loved me, Tuni's intense religious and controlling nature wasn't at all appealing to me. In a way it would've been like jumping from the saucepan into the fire.

My daily schedule was: I left home in the morning, returned late afternoon, did my assignments and remained in my room all the time. I really withdrew from the so called family activities. Nobody talked to me, the only affection I received was from the dog Petra. During this time Mamá Nena's visits were kept to a minimum; I didn't know why, but I guessed that Maximiliano made her feel uncomfortable with his constant acid remarks, and the general feeling was so unhappy that perhaps she didn't feel like being part of it. During the few occasions when she visited, she didn't stay long, and I didn't enjoy talking at all because I believed nobody would help me, and in a way I'd lost the belief that there could be some fairness towards me.

I did think about suicide quite often, and arrived at the conclusion that perhaps the tranquilizers could put me to sleep forever, and thus remove me from this horrible situation.

Fabio, Yesid's brother began to visit often, sometimes on Saturday afternoon. I never took a great deal of interest in him, because he was mother's age and I believed that his visits were connected to her, until an eventful Saturday when Maximiliano and mother had gone away. Fabio arrived at around 5pm. I opened the door and immediately told him that mother and Maximiliano were away, but he pushed the door and entered the hallway anyway. He walked straight into the living room, made himself comfortable and began to ask questions about a variety of subjects. I responded politely but without interest, and after a short while I excused myself because I had a fairly large assignment to prepare for the following week.

I went to my bedroom and continued the work on my beach house model. I must have been there for half an hour or so, when Fabio entered my bedroom with the excuse that he wanted to see what I was doing, and he sat on my bed. Soon he stood behind me and began to stroke and kiss my neck, I told him to leave me alone, I wasn't interested in him and I had to do my assignment. He didn't take no for an answer and persisted with the kissing, I didn't know what to do. He continued asking questions while he kissed me, it was getting dark. I wanted to get rid of him, but somehow it wasn't easy. I went to the kitchen and told Elsi to stay around because I didn't know how to tell him to leave. The hours passed by and finally very late during the night he left.

Maximiliano and mother arrived before dinner on Sunday and Elsi told mother about the problem we had with Fabio. I knew Elsi would've never blamed me for anything, however, mother began to accuse me of being of bad reputation and a lot of other things, but as usual I shut my ears and closed my senses ignoring whatever she said.

The following week I saw Fabio outside the university main entry. My faculty wasn't located in the main part of the building; it was with the arts section a block away. I felt safe from the point of view that he didn't know where I was, therefore, it was of no consequence. Yes, it was of consequence! By Friday he found my lecture rooms and there he was waiting for me as I left for lunch. He asked me to join him for lunch and I refused; he insisted and taking my hand pulled me away. We went to a little cheap place where a lot of students frequented; the food was delicious and also the music played gave this little place a great ambience.

I thought that since there was a possibility of meeting someone it was quite safe, and he made me follow him by pulling my hand. We found a table and almost immediately he said that he was very much interested in me and that we could elope straight away and get married.

A chill ran down my spine, the hairs on my neck stood up in the same way when I saw aquarelle like invisible people that hovered around some spaces. I waited a little and the lunch order was placed, then I excused myself to go to the bathroom. I felt sick and disgusted that an old man, a man my mother's age was proposing me to elope with him; the thought crossed my mind that perhaps he would kidnap me to satisfy his sexual desires, and I decided to leave the place promptly. I asked some guys to act as a curtain and cover my exit, in this way I managed to walk out of the place unnoticed.

I walked all the way home that day, it took me two hours. How much I hated my life. To add to my troubles this stupid man, what was the problem with me? I didn't think I was doing anything to encourage any of this to happen, but why was all this happening? I was just sixteen. As I began my walk I counted the marriage proposals I had received until then, Yesid, my first love. Carlos the farmer, when Mamá Nena could've received several cows, Aurelio the notary's son who didn't have money to buy his own toilet paper, Jaime the medico who was so keen to resolve mother's issues, Hugo the nuclear scientist, who soon realized that the family had too many problems, and therefore the situation diluted any amorous feelings towards me, and now this idiot of a man, Fabio the sergeant. To be precise half a dozen men wanted to marry me, why?

After that incident he telephoned several times, if I answered the phone and he tried to talk, I, with great delight used to say wrong number and terminated the call. He never visited the house again; mother must have said something to him.

Many people, including Mamá Nena used to say that I was a very pretty girl. Lots of times I wished to be like the rest of the girls. Sometimes I wished I had hairs on my upper lip, and on my nipples, so I could say to those idiots do not come close to me, I have hairs on my nipples.

The bank loan was not enough for me to rent a place and meet all the other expenses. Once again that feeling of entrapment overwhelmed me. I was in a tunnel without a visible exit. Two more years seemed too far away to continue with the routine I had to face every day, there must be a solution I thought, but the ideas evaded me. I would finish university, and as soon as I finished, I would leave this place that was called home, never to return. Perhaps the only exit was death and mother would have to re-pay the loan. I had a giggle.

At university I joined the music and dance clubs, it was great fun; the dance teacher organized performances for private parties and television. That brought me in contact with another world, people were lovely and free, some prima donna surfaced from time to time as well as famous people, all friendly to me, perhaps being so young there was no threat from my part.

After a short period of time I was offered a segment on a Sunday morning television show. There was nothing much to do, I had to arrive at the studios approximately one hour or more before the show went to air; there were dresses and shoes for me, the maquillage department to arrange my hair. 'Just look at the camera while the credits roll' they told me. I received a lot of money for doing that. This time I didn't tell anybody about my new source of income.

I Bought jewellery that I could hide and wear as I left the house, also small items such as exquisite leather belts, good quality shoes, beautiful underwear and so on. I discovered the road to good taste and sophistication which for me proved to be the right path. I became more reserved than I have ever been, analysed and observed people's behaviour with interest; at the same time began to read psychoanalysis text books, which I found by accident on the shelves at the university library; with a bit of curiosity I initially took a book, and after that I began to read an enormous amount of material on case studies. Another interest was the occult and I found books at the local library. As soon as I finished one book I borrowed another. I hid those books and treated them as treasures, made sure that mother didn't find them, because if she did, I feared she might've confiscated them.

I immersed myself in my books; I noticed that my anguish and unhappiness were forgotten while I read. Among the many books, there was one of particular interest to me, I wish the author and title of this book had remained in my head. What a wonderful book. Hundreds of case studies about women's emotional and behavioural problems. There were a lot of medical terms, which were explained in the glossary, but apart from that the content was easy to understand. It was an enormous book printed on fine paper, almost transparent, the cover was black with gold letters, the size and weight didn't present an obstacle for me to carry it everywhere, I was terrified that if left at home mother would've taken it and certainly would've disposed of it.

I devoured chapter after chapter until I began to read the problems many older females encounter as their daughters reach puberty, and the mother's inability to accept the psychological challenges presented by the young girl; perhaps the daughter is pretty, intelligent and questions the mother's way of thinking, and in a way the mother sees her as a threat. Certain jealousy surfaces towards the young adult; the feeling of a lost youth, and all sorts of other problems possibly associated with a disastrous marriage, which compounded with the young girl's beauty helps to develop negative feelings from mother to daughter. It also described the pattern of behaviour and the peculiarities to observe.

In general, the study concluded, it was a difficult problem to resolve, because of the feelings of inadequacy from the adult, and the inability to understand the unnatural behaviour; as a general rule the cause for the bad relationship was attributed to the rebellious behaviour of the young adult.

Wow! I read this chapter a thousand times! It described my situation incredibly clearly. Why was mother jealous of me anyway? She was a nice looking woman, still young, unfortunately married to an old and decrepit bloke and to me it had been her choice.

The answer to my problems was clear! As I always thought, mother had a problem towards me since my first year of high school ended, and the problem was evident on my return home. The reason for the disinterest in anything that related to me, the criticism of almost everything I did or said, I was never good enough; I was a libertine with a filthy mind, and other times mother contradicted herself with the complaint that I behaved as if I belonged to a better social class than the rest of the family; I acted in an aristocratic and aloof style, and therefore looked down on everybody.

Mother often used to talk about her lineage. She was a descendant of noble families. Her noble father's origin was Spanish and he had some sort of title, and her great-great grandmother's relations were part of a noble family who relocated from the Italian region of Emilia Romagna to South America during the late 1700's.

She appeared to forget about her presumptions, while it was time to undermine and destroy my personality. I always sensed that when the holidays arrived, and I was taken home the warm welcome wasn't there; mother's late arrival to pick me up was a silent demonstration that I was a burden to deal with. She picked me up at school, and the criticism started immediately for one thing or another, sometimes the superficiality of the criticism was beyond logic, such as a bit of hair dropped over my eye and that irritated her. There was never a sign of appreciation about my good academic performance, and when someone complimented my physical beauty the negative comments and the comparisons invariably followed.

She relished the satisfaction she brought to herself when she put me down, undermined my confidence and in a way tried very hard to destroy my personality. It provided her the means to achieve a result that was pleasing to her; consequently, she felt good about herself and also justified her actions.

At the time I was at her house, she saw me every day, I had developed a sense of my own style, and the capability to resolve my problems as I demonstrated with the bank loan, and of course it wasn't satisfactory to her that I began to buy beautiful items of clothing, and that my appearance was improved by my good grooming and good taste for that suited me. My chosen studies even brought a sense of refinement to me. It was clear the career I had chosen was the right one. I enjoyed immensely the art world, architecture, design, and literature. I was quiet and reserved. What annoyed mother the most and certainly without exception, was that people made positive comments on either my appearance or on the young and sophisticated girl I'd become.

Nobody said much about her beloved Fena, so mother's duty was to remind people that I had disgusting habits, such as reading everything that appeared in front of me not discerning at all which material to select; my personality leaned towards the libertine side of life, and I gave a lot of grief to everybody through my rebellious character. Without failure she added there was fear for my future, because in general people wouldn't accept me and that was of a great concern to her. It was almost comical to see people's expressions and not knowing how to react when I was present; to avoid embarrassment I decided to disappear as soon as someone arrived, and as I did so, curiously enough people who knew of me used to ask where I was.

During the rare occasions when I was present and people hadn't met me, invariably they would say to mother that she had never spoken about the beautiful daughter she had.

The tranquilizers continued to help with the headaches and the seizures stopped as well almost completely; from time to time I felt unwell, but I could cope with it, and the most interesting part was that my brain was functioning again. I enjoyed my lectures and didn't pay any attention to mother or Maximiliano. My goal was to complete my studies, find a job and leave.

June arrived and it was time Fena departed for her holiday abroad. It appeared that I was expected to farewell her at the airport, but I left early that morning and I didn't even say goodbye. My life continued as it had been for the last six months, I studied, did all my assignments, days passed by when I didn't talk to anybody at home except Elsi or the dog Petra.

Fena was expected to return at the end of June to complete her high school studies, but mother accepted the fact that she had decided to remain with her friends; she matriculated with the help of the family and was doing small jobs as a baby sitter to raise funds for her studies. She never wrote to me and I didn't write to her either. Mother had accomplished the destruction of the sibling relationship for good.

Fena returned towards the end of the year to renew her visa, and that caused a lot of excitement; mother tried to convince her to remain in the country, but all Fena wanted was to fly away again, and after some months and with the help of the people she had baby sat for, her visa was renewed and she left early in the new year. What a disappointment, mother had to content herself with my presence!

My studies continued well and I passed to second year. It was indeed a gloomy period. Holidays came and went; I only managed to go out on a couple of occasions. I started the second year of university which I enjoyed very much, the materials I had to buy and the books were quite expensive. I also had to pay for the cost of the semester which left me without any money, again I walked everywhere; Papi and Tuni helped me with transport money and lunches.

I didn't give money to mother for about two months, consequently, she told Elsi not to give me any food because I wasn't paying my way. Once more, mother and Maximiliano's mean, vulture like characteristics surfaced, and history repeated itself like when cousin Ye had no money. Papi and Tuni stepped in and I had lunch with them every day. Tuni made little parcels for my dinner; actually, I enjoyed Tuni's cooking, it was tasty and varied. It was happy food as I called it. The food at home was laced with bitterness and misery.

I had a big project to be done with the team the professor had selected, and unfortunately I had to work with three other students sometimes quite late at night. I didn't particularly want them to study at my place because I didn't have any certainty on how things would turn. The project was too large to be transported, so we decided to work at one place only, and that was Susana's home. Her parents' were agreeable and friendly; her father helped us to cut materials and sometimes suggested ways to hold things together. We worked very hard and went to bed perhaps at around 3am. We just dropped with exhaustion.

Susana on her bed and I rested on the sofa. When I woke up, I was told that mother and Maximiliano were waiting to take me home.

'What happened?' I asked Susana.

She said 'I made strange noises and I looked as if I was gasping for air', she called her parents and they called mother.

I went downstairs and they were waiting for me in the car, they made me feel that whatever happened was my fault. Perhaps in a way it was my fault. I thought I had recovered and stopped taking the tranquilizers. I didn't have any checkups with the doctor, mother never took any interest in my well-being, and she never asked how I felt.

I started taking the tranquilizers again, it was simple to buy the medication over the counter since a prescription wasn't required; I took the pills with no supervision whatsoever, medical or from mother. I continued to medicate myself, and made sure that I took the pills every day, one in the morning and another one at night. It seemed to work because the seizures stopped and the headaches were more infrequent as time passed by. It was very clear to me that I had to move out of home with money or without it. The time was in front of me.

I saw Christine from time to time and we talked about our lives; finally I had the courage to tell her snippets about the situation at home and she was flabbergasted. At the same time she had fallen in love with a fellow student from her own faculty and they had started a sexual relationship. She was happy because he had graduated and had a very good job, and that permitted her to move with him and continue with her studies. Our lives had taken different outcomes and we saw each other few times before we drifted apart.

A new life

I met two girls at university. They were sisters, their names, Gloria and Amparo. They had moved recently to the house of a lady widow who was amiable, and she was looking to increase the number of students to fill up the many rooms her house had. It was a large two storey house on the main road with easy access to public transport.

The main rule was not to make too much noise if they arrived late at night. The lady provided light breakfast and dinner. She was a seamstress and had lost her husband recently. While the husband was alive they lived in another city, but she relocated due to the financial problems she encountered raising three children with no assets and no family support, because she was blamed for his death.

Gloria and Amparo introduced me to Saturia, the young widow. She was a sweet woman and quite young, caramel coloured skin and big dark eyes, very slim, and sorrow was painted all over her face; I immediately felt great empathy with her, and as Gloria and Amparo left the room I began to talk to her about all the reasons why I wanted to find a place to live. It was the first time I told everything to a person I'd just met.

Her eyes filled with tears, she took my hands and told me I was welcome to stay at her house. I decided to move the following Saturday. As I made the arrangements I felt relieved, almost as if a great load had been removed from me, finally I would start a new life. I had enough money to pay her, and with the additional work I did for television, it would be fine.

Saturday early in the morning I began to pack my clothing and other things I had bought. All my possessions fitted into one big suitcase. It was quiet and nobody saw me or paid any attention to whatever I was doing. By the time I took the suitcase downstairs, mother appeared and told me that the suitcase wasn't mine and I didn't have any right to take it away.

'Don't worry I will return it'. A taxi was waiting for me, and by the time she began to scream I had shut the door behind me, got in the taxi and left.

I arrived at Saturia's place. Gloria and Amparo were waiting for me and took me upstairs to their room. I began to share a room with them while something else was available.

Saturia began to tell me her story once we became more familiar. She had been married for about ten years and her life was fairly good for a long period of time. After she gave birth to the last child, she noticed her husband developed a more quiet and reserved manner; arrived late and left early in the morning, and he appeared to be busy and doing well in his insurance business.

Time passed and when the boy was about two years old, he had become more withdrawn and absent, she then thought that perhaps he had a mistress. This possibility didn't worry Saturia; he was a good father and provided well for the family, in addition their sexual relationship after the birth of their son was almost non-existent. Sex wasn't all that exciting therefore it was rarely on the daily menu. When they had sex it was a cold, fast, dutiful affair for her.

She never asked for anything, life for her continued as it always had been. Suddenly there was no money for some luxuries she was accustomed to, but she attributed this to a down turn in business and again didn't ask any questions.

At the mere suggestion that she could begin a small business to utilize her seamstress knowledge he blew his top off. Her idea indicated doubts about him and his ability to be a provider for the family. He left in a huff and didn't return for the night. Every day the tenseness of the situation was getting worse and she was concerned about the finances; however, nothing could be said without erupting into an argument and she decided to put it aside as a bad moment and carried on with life as usual. She didn't mention their problems to hers or his family.

The situation didn't show any improvement, his absences were prolonged and his mood swings became difficult to deal with. She thought that it was probably the end of their marriage and that he had organized a mistress somewhere else, she had to think what to do. Meanwhile, she believed it was better if she waited to hear the bad news from him rather than to accelerate the end.

Two days passed by and he didn't come home or called. She contacted his office, nobody answered the phone. She was getting impatient and had to find out sooner rather than later about her fate. She found the courage to visit his office; once and for all she would hear the news, it didn't matter how bad the news was, it was better to know what was going on, than to continue with a life of uncertainty. She arrived at the building, climbed the narrow stairs and knock on the door, there was no response, waited for a while and decided to search for the caretaker.

It was possible that the person in charge of the building upkeep knew something.

No, he hadn't seen el señor for a couple of days and he didn't know whether he was travelling either. 'Is it possible to open the door to his office?' Saturia asked. The caretaker was hesitant, but decided to provide some assistance in her investigation. The door opened and exposed her husband's body hanging from the ceiling; he hanged himself using his belt.

The police were called. The body was moved and carried away. The formal investigation started. Well, she thought, if it wasn't another woman, why did he hang himself? Within a short period of time she began to receive letters from creditors, and the final one about the house repossession due to accumulated debts, the letter had the logo of a gambling company.

A month after his death she found they were destitute and with no place to go. Even the children's beds were taken away as payment for his debts. His family as well as hers blamed her for his suicide; both families accused her of ignoring the signs of a disturbed person. Not knowing what to do, she took refuge with friends who lent her a hand and provided accommodation for her and the children.

It was then when Saturia began to offer her services as a seamstress, with great effort she was able to move to a rented house and began to provide for the children; she couldn't forgive how badly both families had treated her, and decided to move to the capital to start a new life, her prime objective was to keep the children away from the bitterness that might emanate from the families' distress. Courageously she rented a house and started her seamstress business, and everything was working well, and life started to appear kinder to them all.

She wanted to rent rooms to females only because she felt more comfortable and secure. All the rooms were occupied; one had a recently married couple, she looked fairly young, long hair, and her skin was almost translucent. Her husband left to work early in the morning and she remained in her room all day, never went out or talked to anybody.

The other room housed two elderly sisters who gave the impression they were unhappy and disappointed with their lodging circumstances. The sisters worked at a government office and were very particular about their dress and their general appearance; rather old to share their time with students. They had a temporary job with a government minister, and I supposed the temporary accommodation suited them.

Selmira rented the other room, a lovely girl who had left her family and had found a job in this city. Her story was rather sad. She fell pregnant and left her family to be able to have an abortion. Having an abortion wasn't an easy experience as she found out. Finally she found someone to perform the operation with the terrible result that by the time she arrived at Saturia's place, a haemorrhage had set in and she was in great danger. Thanks to Saturia's quick thinking a tragedy was avoided.

Selmira was full of life, easy going, clever and pretty. She loved to read. She had the entire collection of Agatha Christie Mysteries. The books were beautifully bounded in leather and with her name printed on the side. The books were a gift from her late father.

Gloria and Amparo were able to go home on Friday to return on Sunday afternoon. Gloria was studying political sciences, she struggled with her studies. She really wanted to party as much as possible, and to that effect she went out every night and returned well past midnight.

Amparo was in the 4th year of business administration, she was studious. Her boyfriend was in the same year and they studied together, quite often she asked me to vacate the room because they were going to have sex. I used to say fine, and left the room. Saturia didn't know about it or turned a blind eye.

I took the opportunity to talk to Saturia while I obliged to their request. I admired her skills in cutting and assembling garments. The sex session finished and Amparo called me back.

Gloria and Amparo introduced me to many guys from their city of origin. Among them Antonio; from the beginning I had reservations about him, he seemed rather ordinary and certainly lacked a lot of class.

As Gloria and Amparo got to know me, I began to spend more time with them and was often invited to their parents' house for the weekend. I did have a good time and met their parents who on the surface appeared fine, although the mother was quite unfriendly towards her husband most of the time.

The other room was occupied with another recent arrival, she wasn't a student; she had separated from her husband and had left a child behind. Her story was difficult to piece together because it appeared rather surreal. Her name was Rosalba, approximately twenty six years old, had been married for seven years and according to her, the husband was violent and on many occasions had threaten her with a gun. She decided to leave him after an argument so violent, he forced her to lay on the bed, made her spread her legs, and placed a gun barrel inside her vagina, because he was certain she was having an affair. She planned her escape for weeks until she found the courage to leave. All this sounded more like a B grade violent movie.

Rosalba was nice looking, vivacious, and a bit plump. She went out every night with a different man; usually the man arrived to collect her in an expensive car, always after 8pm. Rosalba returned well past midnight most nights, soon she began to return the next day. She also began to show us expensive items of jewellery and a lot of cash. Perhaps four months had passed and she told Saturia that her husband had found the place and she had to leave. To us she said that one of the men, who she went out regularly with, had offered her an apartment and that he wanted her services exclusively for him. She had accepted because it was a good offer. The main condition was that she couldn't be seen with him, and since her husband was looking for her, it was better to remain a bit reclusive for a while. The man travelled constantly and he would take her with him on his trips.

Rosalba went somewhere for a week and on her return told us all the particulars of the trip, including the salubrious bits like the things she did to the man while he drove, she did it to amuse herself while she was bored. The man was driving and she put her hand down his pants and began to fondle him, after a while she began to give him oral sex while he continued to drive; he was quite taken by it because he'd never driven while oral sex had been performed on him.

Rosalba finally left Saturia's house. The room she had occupied was fairly large, and Saturia needed the money to cover her expenses; she advertised and soon new tenants appeared. Four guys, chemistry students from a Caribbean university; they had enrolled on a six month course at one of the local universities. It must have been a good proposition because Saturia forgot she only wanted females at her house.

It was a perfect arrangement, six months would fly away, and she was able to increase the rent which would provide her with a better income, and that would make her life easier. The new guys were due to arrive in a space of a month. We didn't think much about it.

It was almost the end of the year and life went fast preparing assignments and sitting for exams etc. Soon holidays would start and I needed extra income because the bank didn't provide any financial assistance during holidays.

The dance teacher from the university dance club got a gig on Sunday morning for the month of December, extending to the end of February, and with the prospects of continuing for the rest of the year if the television gig was successful; he needed some girls to form a small dance group to perform on a regular basis. He had organized an audition to take place in a couple of weeks, and we had to begin rehearsal. I took the offer. It was a great decision to accept.

We got the job and I began to meet famous actors and producers of many shows, I also met advertising agents who offered me small parts on commercials; other times my job was to prepare the set as an assistant to the principal set designer, I learnt a lot, life was free of worries and enjoyable. I got along well with the girls and Saturia. However, I still needed more regular work to make ends meet.

An advertising agent offered me a part-time position with her company, it was a small office, the company had two employees and provided a very small salary; I was glad that something had turned up for a bit of experience, because I realized as I worked assisting the main designers, I didn't know a thing. Not a clue of how to run anything or organize samples. It was embarrassing that after two years at university and so much work and expense, the raw ignorance about how to carry out the organizing of projects was so acute.

The director of the small company was a woman of about forty; never married and still lived with her parents at a large house not far from Saturia's place. She was very bossy towards men in general, but patient towards me. She couldn't draw, she didn't have any artistic fibre in her, yet she was the principal in an advertising agency. It was varied work and she began to send me to talk to clients she didn't particularly like, which I found amusing because of my lack of experience. However, this was my training ground and I was determined to learn as fast and as much as possible.

I hadn't made contact with the family since I left their house; it was more or less a long year, and due to my television appearances it seemed that mother had decided to find out where I was living, but nobody knew, because I made sure that my life was not going to be disturbed by any interference from the family.

My thought was that if they didn't like me, or care about me while I needed them during all those sad years of abandonment, and loneliness, there was no reason to communicate with them.

Mario, the cousin who worked at the bank, saw me almost every time I went to withdraw the monthly allowance, and he asked how I was and where I was living.

I said to him that like on a previous occasion he had betrayed me by telling mother about the bank loan, and as a result my life had taken a turn for the worse, I didn't want to tell him where I was living or where I was working, because I had enough of that life and I didn't want to have bad experiences again.

'Mario: if you are really interested in me and my wellbeing, and if you find out where I live or where I work, you will not tell anybody because you have to respect my wishes. I don't want to see mother, Maximiliano or anybody else for a long, long time'.

He kept his promise and I started to see Mario more often. He took me to parties and sometimes he had office functions and invited me. I never gave him my address or telephone number.

Daniel, the bank teller I used to talk to when I withdrew the monthly allowance, called Mario when I arrived, and then if Mario had any invitation for me I used to arrange to meet him in different places away from where I lived. He said it was better for him not to know. 'Not knowing where I lived allowed him to tell the truth, so when people asked him, he could say with all honesty that I was well, but the truth was that he didn't know where I lived'.

University started and the new tenants moved to the vacant room; initially it was interesting to meet new people, then we noticed the noise, the nonstop loud music while they were in their room, they also talked loudly to the point that the place became like a market. Amparo began to yell to shut up because she needed to study.

From Friday until Sunday night the loud music and the drinking didn't stop; Saturia began to participate in the new found euphoria, as well as Saturia's sister who appeared frequently at the house, because she liked one of the guys.

Selmira couldn't take it anymore and left which was very convenient for Saturia, and she offered the room to the guys. They began to pay more rent and had more say in whatever went on, two more of those students arrived and we ended up with six loud clowns.

Gloria, Amparo and I didn't fit into the scene and kept away. Those guys were rough and loud, they didn't talk normally, they shouted all the time. The first guys arranged a party to introduce the new tenants and invited us to participate, the loud music started early, the room was animated and other guys from their faculty began to arrive. At about 11pm they started to distribute white little pills they had made in the lab, they said the pills were amphetamines which would make us euphoric and happy.

Amparo had to study, I had to finish a large assignment however, Gloria who was always ready to party accepted the offer, initially she began to laugh and couldn't stop the euphoria, it was so silly; then the shakes started with strange visions of creepy crawlers invading the floor and she was terrified, after the shaking stopped she threw up her guts and said she felt awful, she looked green and dishevelled.

These types of parties continued during the weekend but soon the pill popping took place during the week as well. Saturia and her sister started to argue because they were running after the same guy. The little pills became part of the normal routine and were distributed among themselves. Those six guys took over and behaved as if they owned the house and nobody else existed.

Gloria and Amparo decided to look for a place of their own, so it was only me left alone with those guys. They left and I moved to a smaller room which suited me, the bad part was that another two guys took the room that Gloria and Amparo had vacated. I didn't like them.

I saw Rosalba when she came to visit Saturia, she talked about the building she had moved to after her first relationship ended; the building belonged to a lady who had subdivided it into small one bedroom apartments and there was a vacancy next to her apartment. I went to talk to the lady owner and to check the premises. Too expensive!

I continued living at Saturia's place, meanwhile, the chemistry students wild parties continued; the advantage I had was that I closed the door to my room and I entered another world; the noise, music and their arguments didn't affect me while I studied, I was able to dedicate my time and concentrate on my work without much effort. I ignored them completely, although they did look for my company and never stop inviting me to join them.

The part-time work provided me with more money but it wasn't sufficient to rent a place of my own. At the same time I frequented Gloria and Amparo's new place to get away from the mad house I was living in. The weekends were the worst; it was a nightmare to remain there, and because I had to complete large assignments, I was basically grounded doing my work. Amparo and Gloria had engaged a live in maid and when they visited their parents during the weekend, they invited me to stay at their place; I took my work and the maid cooked lunch and dinner, and I could spread my work on the dining table, I provided her with company and she was kind to me.

Gloria and Amparo's friends from their city of origin used to visit quite often. I saw Antonio many times and he began to invite me out, I accepted his invitations with a bit of reservation because I thought there was something odd about him. Gloria and Amparo organized a party and invited most of the guys they knew from home, Antonio wasn't there and the other guys began to talk about him and said that he had three children.

I thought he was rather odd when I met him, also he was too old to be student, he said he was thirty, he supposed to assist his parents financially he said, and therefore couldn't come to parties on the weekend.

Amparo was very keen to make me accept one of her friend's invitations, and constantly encouraged him to invite me. Amparo thought he was the perfect person for me and vice versa. I finally accepted his invitations and a relationship began to develop, he visited me at Saturia's, took me to the movies, and used to meet me after lectures sometimes.

Oscar was doing his intern year of medicine and like me didn't have a lot of time, but he was fun to be with and had a great sense of humour. I truly enjoyed his company, he was gentle and considerate and most of all we were able to discuss a myriad of topics, we discovered a lot of common interests and similarities which provided great affinity. His zodiac sign was the fish and that was in total harmony with my crab sign, we were both water people; sensitive, meticulous, loved nature, open spaces, reading and solitude; with Oscar I found balance in my life and I began to fall in love with him, he was becoming an integral part in my life; he was constantly on my mind and I longed to see him.

I had to find a job because of the necessity to have real practical experience before I could begin my final project. I began to search for opportunities with large companies which provided the possibility of a job. I cold called many places and found out that nobody wanted to employ a person without experience. I had some experience with the small advertising agent, but that wasn't considered sufficient to fill my curriculum. I had so many rejections, and every time I was rejected my thoughts leaned towards the idea that the company wasn't suitable to me, and instead of being discouraged, I continued to search believing that there would be something fabulous for me.

I had to go to the studio to assist the set designer to prepare a set for a sock commercial; we waited for about one hour and the designer didn't turn up. I was told to prepare the set, the studio had been assigned to this commercial and the producer would be furious if nothing was in place when he arrived. The commercial was shot to schedule and the producer asked who had done the set because it was quite different to the usual style. The chap who helped me told the producer that it was the assistant designer who prepared the set as the last resort, because the main designer hadn't turned up. The producer asked to see me.

I went to his office, and again it was a small business, a little larger than the other office where I had been working part-time. The company was located in a new building quite close to the television studios. The company consisted of the owner, who was the producer, the accountant, the secretary who arranged all the commercial breaks for the television programmes; and at the studios the principal set designer and his assistant.

The producer was a mature man with grey longish hair, a handsome man, who dressed impeccably. He wore a black polo neck top under his jacket, perfectly pressed trousers and his shoes were well polished. The job was mine if I wanted it, and he offered a generous salary.

I was to be part of the set design team working with the senior personnel, and part of my duties included preparing the graphics and the set for a new pilot children's programme, which was to air the following month.

I did like the offer and accepted it without hesitation. I commenced my job with great enthusiasm and got to know the principal set designer, and I soon discovered he didn't like me a bit. I was to be part of the team with the principal set designer and his assistant, but he didn't even want to talk to me. It didn't matter what I did, he ignored me completely; his assistant did respond to my questions and was helpful, however, my instructions were supposed to come from the old man, but while at the studio I just wandered aimlessly without anything to do, and he began to say that I was useless.

The day of reckoning arrived sooner than he expected when a set was prepared for a musical, and the producer arrived to check the setting. He blew his top off because the set was insipid, and with those awful sticks that didn't represent a bloody thing. The entire set had to be pulled down and redone, and there were only five hours to prepare the new set, because the programme would be a live transmission which was to commence in the morning the following day. After the producer left the set, the old man approached me and in a crotchety manner and with great arrogance said: 'well, I suppose you may give us an idea about what to do'.

I suggested that if the colour of the vertical elements was changed with more contrasting colours, and the floor was painted with a good geometric pattern using curves, the entire set would look very different and he didn't have to pull it down. To my surprise he did it, and the set was finished in less than four hours. Enough time for the quick drying paint to set. It was late night and the set designer called the producer to check the work. He arrived a bit annoyed that it was past midnight and he would've preferred to do other things, but to make sure everything was in order he obliged. Well, he liked it. The principal set designer didn't say a word about my input.

The next day I told Leito the secretary about it; she said that everybody knew how crotchety the old man was and not to worry about him. After this event, the secretary was friendlier to me, and from time to time we had some good talks.

Her name was Leanora, however everybody called her Leito. I couldn't determine her age; she looked about thirty five or forty years old more or less. Always dressed in an elegant and glamorous manner, wore expensive garments, shoes and good quality jewels. Her hair was blond arranged in a French bun style.

I felt a bit unsettled in the new office environment. I began to work and soon produced good graphics for the children's programme, also I had to design a new set every week which was quite hard, despite the assistant's help we were chasing our tails every week; the assistant mentioned that it was a bad decision to change the set every week because of the expense, and the programme could be axed earlier that predicted.

Meanwhile, I continued with the graphics, and found that I had to work during the weekend to catch up with all the work; sometimes Leito used to come to work as well, and in this manner I got to know her a bit.

Leito's men collection

It was after lunch when Leito arrived at the office and said how hungry she was. 'But you just came from lunch', I said.

'Oh yes, it was a lunch break, but I didn't have time for lunch because I had sex'.

'Do you have sex every day during the lunch break?'

'No, only twice a week' she said.

'How come you know when you are going to have sex?'

Leito said: 'I shouldn't tell you this, but what the heck' I have organized my life around married men because I don't want any ties, I don't want children. I want to be free and have a good life. I have six men in my collection, two men per week on certain days and these days can't be changed.

Married men, have either nice looking women who are bitches and all they want is to go to the hairdresser, paint their nails, play tennis and go shopping. When the poor bugger comes home, the maid has prepared dinner or they go out to a restaurant; after that if he wants sex, she invariably has a headache or is too tired from all the social commitments, or perhaps she already had sex with the young gardener or the tennis instructor. The other type, is the wife who after many years of marriage has become fat and unattractive and he has difficulty having a hard on. These men know I am discreet and they have nothing to worry about.

Once we begin a sexual relationship I establish rules, and it is up to them to respect those rules or there is no room for a possible arrangement.

I study them very carefully before undertaking any involvement; these men have to meet certain criteria because I don't want complications of any sort. I discuss with them the arrangements in a clear and detailed manner, therefore, there is no room for misunderstandings; from the very beginning, when a man and I decide to begin a sexual relationship I am very specific about how they will behave and what I offer. There are no strings attached, there is no cooking at all. They see me every four weeks on a pre-determined day, the time may be changed, but it's better to keep to a routine. Each visit requires some financial arrangement, because I need to pay for my apartment loan, and they all know it is my intention to purchase another property as an income for the future. I don't do kinky sex, anything else they can have.

Let's take Luis for example, he was the first one; I've had him for the last ten years. He is fifty five years old, is a senior executive in an international company, he travels a lot, has been married for thirty years to the same woman; she falls into the category of the good looking with nothing specific to do. She fills her time with lunches, shopping, and although she doesn't run after her own children anymore, now it's the grandchildren who take her time, and therefore, she is always tired with a headache.

I met him at one of the Christmas parties and everything began from there. Luis has been very generous; he gave me the deposit for my apartment and advised me on the purchase. He is great in bed, has an insatiable appetite for sex, every time I meet him there is little talk, we get straight into it. From the moment he arrives at my apartment and I open the door, he begins to take my garments with such urgency that it makes me incredibly horny to know that someone wants me with such desperation. He touches every part of my body, and sometimes begins to penetrate me while still standing as I close the door.

He likes to do it twice a session and can't wait for the next meeting; after he is completely satisfied and doesn't have more energy, he gives me money for the mortgage payment and says: 'four weeks seem too far away, may I see you again sooner?' He knows the answer.

Tomás is the other man. I've had him since he was forty, soon after his second marriage went pear shaped. He is the owner of a large food manufacturing company, he inherited the business from his father and there is a lot of money in the family. He married a socialite, good looking and bitchy; after a short marriage he began an affair with one of his secretaries, and was found out as he left the theatre one night.

The story goes that he had been having an affair for quite some time; the secretary had organized to see a play and asked him to accompany her. Tomás told his wife that he was going to be away for a couple of days which wasn't unusual in his line of work, unfortunately as Tomás and his secretary left the theatre his attention was called, it was one of his wife's friends.

It was a costly and acrimonious divorce, no children, but he lost a good portion of his fortune. After a short period of time he married the secretary who during their affair had been a great companion and lover. Children began to arrive, one after the other, somehow her libido was affected and she lost sexual desire. Only four years after their marriage, she didn't have any interest in sex anymore; he was puzzled, but accepted it for some time. His sex life was almost non-existent and when she accepted to engage in sex, it wasn't the pleasant experience of some previous years, it was difficult because he couldn't bring back what they had. I met him at a time when he was extremely frustrated, and although he did love her, he wanted sexual satisfaction.

He began to visit our office while the filming of a commercial, which was part of a substantial advertising campaign, we began to develop for his company. I had to deal with him for the approvals and all other particulars of the marketing; like time to go to air, the number of commercials and the programmes chosen to insert the commercials. There is a lot of work when a company big or small begins an advertising campaign, and most of the time, I get to know the clients very well.

He was a good and generous client who brought small presents as a way to say thank you.

I was leaving the office after a long meeting which finished at about 8pm. He invited me for a drink, I accepted it. We had the first drink and after another one, more drinks followed, and as usual when men have problems, the conversation is diverted to the family, children, and his previous divorce, before I am asked about my private life.

It was 10pm and he invited me to dinner which I agreed since I was starving. During dinner and after more wine he began to talk about his life of frustration, and his marital relationship.

I was quick to tell him that I could help, but I didn't want any ties, I wasn't seeking marriage, I couldn't take any infringement of my freedom. It had to be an arrangement of mutual convenience. I needed discretion from him. Absolutely nobody would know about our involvement, and since he frequented the office, I needed reassurance than he would never carry on in any way that would jeopardize my position in the company. I outlined the conditions and he accepted the offer.

'Is it possible to begin tonight?' He asked.

We left the restaurant and went to my apartment; he was a man desperate for sex; a little dick but very effective. He knows how to move it very well. The relationship has continued and it's already in its fourth year, I satisfy him every four weeks. It's a shame his member is so small, but he makes up with good techniques and a lovely gentle manner.

His generosity is outstanding. I think I will have him for a long time. The relationship with his wife has improved; when he asks her for sex and she refuses, he is quietly content and accepts it with the knowledge that I will satisfy him soon.

'Do they know that you have others?'

Leito responded: 'they are trained not to ask personal questions. Men are very peculiar, it's very important for them to have good sex and to feel that they are needed. I certainly need them to pay my mortgage'.

This was amazing, it brought back memories when Clara told me about her sex exploits with the chaplain. Sex was incredible. She was right to say that everybody does it, and as long as nobody catches you, it is fine, and nobody gets the knickers in a knot.

'Oh Leito, I can't wait to hear about the other four'.

'I will tell you tomorrow, when we finish work we can go for a coffee'.

The next day work finished early and certainly we went for a coffee.

Leito continued: the third man is Federico, he is the least sophisticated of 'my men collection'; this is the name I've given to the group of men I have.

Federico doesn't have great academic education, he is intelligent and shrewd in business; sometimes his lack of refinement makes me nervous because this is the type of man who lets his emotions come to the surface. I am very strict with him. He loves oral sex and he gives it to perfection, he also likes to receive it as many times as possible. He is so incredibly handsome and charismatic; his body is athletic and always shows a healthy suntan. Federico started his business the humble way, he began to work as a junior in a construction company and he did chores just above the labourers. The company owner had given him employment as a favour to his father, who was one of the company's loyal employees for many years; after Federico's father's retirement, Federico began to work on a permanent basis; he undertook courses at the Technical College and received adequate qualifications to succeed in the building industry.

He'd been working with the company for several years, and when the owner retired he offered him his shares in the company; he purchased them with a bank loan. Federico's finances improved and with this improvement he was ready to marry.

He married a simple girl of similar background, and everything appeared fine on the surface until she became pregnant with the second child, from that moment onwards she consumed incredible amounts of food, and therefore, she gained weight rapidly in spite of doctor's warnings.

The child was born and a caesarean had to be performed due to her obesity, after the birth of the child her weight didn't return to normal, she continued to be morbidly obese, and to his frustration, she didn't show any interest in any weight reduction. The problems started then. She was eager to have sex but he couldn't perform. Many visits to doctors, psychiatrists and even sorcerers didn't help his condition. He was faithful to her, and didn't try other methods until he met me at a function organized by his company.

The owner and producer received an invitation to the lavish function at a fairly exclusive hotel, but he had previous commitments and sent me to represent the company. Everything begins with a drink. I felt a bit tired, and at about 11pm I approached Federico to say goodbye, he was under the weather and in a mood to talk. I sat with him and accepted a drink, and suddenly he began to pour out his soul. He told me everything including his impotence; it must have been very difficult for him to open his emotions. He described the repulsion he felt at the sight of his naked wife, all that fat which spreads over her sides, those awfully big tits which touch her waist, the skin folds on her legs and abdomen, those huge buttocks that wobble as she moves, the skin is always clammy and moist, is like touching an amphibian.

'When did it happen for the first time?'

I recall, he said. 'It was our anniversary; she insisted I come home early because she had a surprise for me. I obliged and arrived home at the specific time. I opened the door and there she was waiting for me naked, she was spread over the divan with a leg on the floor and the other on the seat, she also had attached a red ribbon to her grossly obese waist. She was amorous and eager for sex. But I couldn't do it. Time and time again I tried to do it, but I couldn't'.

Some other time I tried to do it while the lights were off, imagined that I was having sex with a beautiful slim woman with a normal body, but as I touched her blubbery, sticky, and clammy skin no amount of fantasy made it happen. After I listened to his story I asked him whether he had tried any conventional methods to find if the situation was localized to his wife only.

'No, I haven't done it, first because I am a deeply religious man, and believe in the sanctity of marriage, and second for the fear of finding out that perhaps the situation is permanent, and that is a terrifying thought when you are a forty five years old man'. I had let it go for a while, and try not to think about it, but to be perfectly honest, I have been depressed for a long time.

'Would you like to try with me? I have several rules and conditions which must be followed'. I began to explain my rules and conditions in case he wanted to begin an arrangement of mutual convenience.

'Very well, I believe your conditions are fair, I've drunk a bit trying to forget my sorrows, but let's give it a go, it can't be worse than the present situation; I will deal with my religious beliefs later'.

We went to the hotel room he had booked for the night, had a shower together and went to bed.

I said: 'stay still. Don't do anything'.

I began to give him oral sex, to his amazement and in spite of the many drinks he had consumed, he responded quite well, he gave me oral sex and climaxed with normal sex. He was happy; all the alcohol he had consumed that night dissipated, and the night was an orgy of sex as if he was trying to recover those lost pleasurable moments. He is well endowed, has a terrific large member, hard like a metal rod, and great energy, having sex with him makes me feel absolutely filled with him, he touches well inside. He is able to satisfy the most ardent of lovers. Federico is a delightful person to be with; he dutifully contributes to my mortgage, and I have imposed additional demands on him, like if he decides to have sex with someone else he has to tell me. I have to protect myself against infections.

He swears to have found out the perfect solution to his problems, he continues to let his wife believe that he is impotent. He suggested his wife to take a lover because it isn't fair that his condition is affecting her.

'What about his deep religious beliefs?'

'Good sex is the best therapy to erase religious beliefs'. Leito said and let out a big belly laugh.

I also have a government minister, whose wife has turned out to be a lesbian after fifteen years of marriage. This is the most peculiar man in my collection. He has to be incredibly discreet. His wife has agreed to continue their marriage for the sake of his career, and the good life and privileges she has become accustomed to.

I can't tell you if this story is true because he is very reserved about it all. Anyway, he loves his sex every four weeks. He is meticulous, has exquisite manners and taste. This one brings me beautiful jewels from every corner of the world he visits. He relies on me for his sex, he feels comfortable and secure. He is an average lover, not too exciting, but competent. This one depends on his income and the perks of the job rather than a personal fortune. However, he also contributes to my mortgage every time he visits.

'Do they know that everybody is paying your mortgage?'

'Why do they have to know?' One thing all of them know is that I must pay my mortgage as fast as possible, because I need another property as security for my later years.

'It's late. We finish another time' Leito said.

Those stories were terrific. Why was she telling me her secret?

On Monday I said to Leito 'I can't wait to hear about the other two in your collection'. Unfortunately work didn't permit the luxury of time for the story telling. Weeks passed by and we couldn't meet to continue. Perhaps she was testing my discretion as well. I didn't disappoint her.

The children's programme progressed very well and with good ratings, but the purse began to show signs of financial difficulties due to the expenses incurred on a new set every week. It was decided that the sets remained the same for two weeks. This modification would save money and give some extra time to gather more sponsors.

Another weekend filled with work; I was getting tired of it. My salary was generous, but I wasn't told that I had to work all those long hours to make things happen. Leito finished her schedules and I almost completed my tasks; it was 6pm on Saturday. I was exhausted. Leito moved to my desk and said: 'gosh, you look terrible. Come with me for a coffee and a cake'. We ordered a coffee and while the cake arrived, Leito asked me if I've had any sex experiences yet. I told her that I hadn't found the person I would like to do it with.

She said: 'you can get a lot of money for it; men love to be the first one to do it to a girl'.

'What do you mean a lot of money?'

'Probably thousands' she said confidently.

'No, it doesn't sound nice to me', I said.

Tell me about the other two men in the collection. I've been waiting for long time to hear their story.

Hernando is an architect. This man is adorable and charismatic, handsome, a bundle of energy, funny, intelligent and successful. I could have sex with this one just for the pleasure of it, but I have rules. He is married for the third time, has children with two of his previous wives and at present his marriage is on the rocks. He has the good fortune to be successful otherwise he would be a pauper with a wonderful dick.

I met him while I was waiting for documents to be signed for a campaign we were about to start. He had an appointment with the director and I was waiting for the same man to sign the documents. The secretary came to the reception and informed us that unfortunately the director was delayed and that he sincerely apologized; she then asked if it was possible to wait. Would we be prepared to wait in the waiting room and have a coffee?

I said yes, and explained that the campaign couldn't start without the documents. Hernando said he had some minutes to spare. We moved to the waiting room while the secretary brought a coffee; meanwhile we began to talk about trivia, the movies, books, music and he informed me that he had started to build a large apartment complex.

I queried him about the apartment prices and the completion date; he asked me to visit his office, he would show me the apartment's layout, the location site, and the good design features included in the construction.

The director finally appeared with my documents and greeted Hernando like an old mate. Hernando had given me his business card, I kept his card but wasn't sure about the purchase of an apartment yet. I needed more cash.

Hernando must have questioned the director about me, because within a week he called the office to ask if I was still interested in the apartment. 'Come to my office, I will send a car to pick you up and when you finish looking at the apartments we can have dinner somewhere'.

I said yes.

The very next day he sent a car to pick me up. I arrived at his fabulous office which had a view to infinity and the blue sky. Hernando's charm was as irresistible as the magnificent view. I looked at the layouts and the architectural models with the gardens and swimming pools.

'How much are they?'

'Well, it depends whether you buy off the plan or after completion. The complex is selling well off the plan, and there are still many available, but not for long. Talk to the sales personnel they will tell you'.

'I've booked the restaurant. Let's go'.

We had an exquisite dinner the conversation was most enjoyable; he had so many stories to tell. The stories included his failed marriages and the difficulty with the children. He also included comments about the current state of his marriage which was doomed to failure, because both of them had lost patience with each other. He wanted to know if I was in a relationship, where I lived and other personal details. It was a good evening, he brought me home and we said goodbye.

Hernando didn't stop there, he contacted me frequently, but I wasn't sure about this one. Had he too much baggage? His persistence was something to be wary of. It took him several months of invitations and flowers until I told him my rules, and that he had to adhere to them otherwise it wouldn't work. He was too unruly and uncontrollable to accept them, was my belief. I was surprised to hear he also thought it avoided trouble.

Hernando looked happy every time I met him, as I had expected, he wanted to break the rules several times. I had to be firm and didn't allow it. This relationship is only two years old, but he has become one of the men in my collection. I tamed him.

Hernando's marriage appears better; in many cases the marital problems revolve around sex. How can any woman reject this guy? He is delicious to be with; sex is like a fantasy every woman dreams of. His sexual habits are varied like the seasons, it feels as if the energy of the universe enters his member to make his erection long lasting, and there is never a dull moment. When he wants to try something new he even draws it, I laugh my head off when he illustrates elaborated sexual positions like in the ancient books. He improvises with chairs, ladders and other paraphernalia in lieu of servants. He is amazing. We meet for sex sessions that last up to three hours, and by the time we finish we are totally spent.

I bought an apartment off the plan with his help, and I intend to move there when the complex is finished; I will put my other apartment on the rental market.

The newest man I have collected was totally unexpected. After Hernando I thought I had enough variety in my life. Everything marched in an orderly and in an exciting way. My sex life was fantastic and as I always wanted it to be. I had five men, each one with different erectile qualities and sizes, from small but competent to very large and extremely pleasurable, and Hernando's member is not only delicious is also beautiful, and he moves it with such perfection, that makes me think he has been practicing all his life.

I was in a terrible rush to drop some documents, and as I entered the building I had a collision with a man carrying a bundle of papers. He was a solicitor on his way to court. On the course of our collision his folders opened and papers were scattered all over the floor; I apologized, he apologized and we began to gather the papers. He left and I delivered my documents.

I didn't think much of such incident until several weeks later, when our producer had to attend a meeting, but he was delayed filming a commercial, and called to ask me to attend. I went to the meeting which finished about 2pm. I recognized him immediately.

The lift opened and a man entered. He looked at me and said: 'are you the lady I collided with, some weeks ago?'

'Oh, yes I am sorry about it, it was my fault'. I was in a terrible hurry, our messenger wasn't available that day and I had to deliver some documents.

'It was lovely to collide with you' he said. 'Let me take you to lunch to make up for the incident. I am a lawyer, my name is Francisco, but everybody calls me Paco'. 'I am Leanora, but everybody calls me Leito'.

We drove to the city outskirts to one of those classical, stylish restaurants everybody talked about. Lunch was superb; the conversation flowed with ease as if we had known each other for years, the conversation turned to personal details, he wanted to know if I had sentimental ties with anybody. I responded as I normally do. I don't want to marry because I don't want to have children, I love my freedom. I have a good life, and enjoy my work. After some glasses of wine, Paco started his story.

He was happily married, and they worked well as a couple, and enjoyed each other's company. Both had similar interests, but something was missing. Early during their marriage his wife wanted children, but couldn't conceive and she subjected herself to a multitude of operations with a negative outcome. He always said to her that it didn't matter to him, but she pursued it, until the last operation when something went wrong, and after her recovery she didn't have one bit of interest in sex.

He was patient. He initially thought it was a passing phase and soon everything would have returned to normal. The reality was that she didn't like sex anymore; she complained that sex was a painful experience, and no matter how many times she visited the gynaecologist no solution was offered. She apologized and cried which made him feel terrible because he still wanted sex. Paco decided to work longer hours, to search for more clients and to build a good business; as a consequence his work load was extensive and quite demanding; it also took his mind from other matters.

Leito met Paco several times before deciding to add one more man to her collection. She outlined her conditions which he accepted, and the relationship began. Paco hadn't had sex for the last four years, and he was as horny as a man can be.

'This is like fiction', Leito said. So many men incredibly frustrated because they are deprived of sex. I've given them fantastic moments; each man is so different, yet the problem is the same. Do you know that the best erection happens in the morning? Women don't want to have sex in the morning. Imagine 100's of men drive to work after they had a stiff dick and couldn't make use of it; following a frustrating start to the day, they are aggressive on the road and they are aggressive when they arrive at the office, and we have to put up with it. However, once I begin the therapy they are all generous, they don't impose demands, all they want is sex, unrestricted and pleasurable with no strings attached. I've become a sex therapist I tell them and they laugh.

'Does Paco want anything different from the rest?'

'No. He is happy to do it a couple of times every time we meet'.

That was it! I've heard about Leito's men collection; it all sounded like collecting jewels and keeping them in a box. All these stories were very interesting; yet she never mentioned love. I believed everybody needs love, not just to be needed for sex. Perhaps for Leito to be needed for sex was a form of love.

I was with the company for over six months. I did learn something invaluable. No matter how much you want to progress, there is always someone who wants to be an obstacle to your success. In my case, it was the old crotchety set designer who didn't give me a chance, and on the few occasions I had the opportunity to show my ability, he took credit for the good result my input provided.

The children's programme was axed and my position was terminated. I was going to miss Leito, her friendship as well as her stories. I wished her well and thanked her for the friendship and support.

New opportunities

Mario came to my rescue once more. He introduced me to the general manager of a large design and construction company. I told the general manager that I was looking for a job and the man said that they always needed pretty girls to fill up their offices. 'We called them VGS'.

'What is VGS?' I asked

'Very good sorts', was his response and he winked. 'You fall into the VGS category and I believe I can help with a job. Give me a call next week'.

I thought he was joking, but I took his business card, and the next day called his office to make an appointment to see him the following week. I did my best to look good for my appointment. His name was Doctor Pacho or Doctor Pachito as some people called him. I arrived at the reception and his secretary showed me the way to his office.

He remembered me and asked about my experience and qualifications; after I provided him with the relevant information, he said that the head of other department was looking for new people. Let me call him.

Dr Pacho took the phone and talked to him. Yes, she is here, he said, and she is a VGS, he added. He instructed me to proceed to the next department to see the man he had just spoken to; my secretary will take you there. He wrote on the back of his card. 'Dr Jimenez, this is the girl I have just spoken about. A true VGS as you can see'.

I took the lift and went to the other floor, as I arrived I saw an old lady with reddish coloured hair sitting behind the reception desk. I showed her the card Doctor Pacho had written his message on, and told her that Doctor Jimenez was waiting to interview me for the vacant position in his department.

She looked at me from head to toe and said: 'the position has been taken'.

'Doctor Pacho said it was still available and that is the reason I am here, he sent me to see Doctor Jimenez'.

'These men do strange things for a pretty face, I don't understand what they see in you', and looked at me with disgust.

There were two armchairs and a sofa in that waiting room; I sat in the middle of the sofa because it faced the door to Dr. Jimenez's office. My skirt was quite short; I crossed my legs and let them fall sideways, put my chin up and waited for the door to open. The door opened and I had a glimpse of Doctor Jimenez sitting behind an enormous desk, a short man with straight hair brushed back. He stood up and walked some steps. The red haired lady approached his desk said something then, turned back and as she was about to close the door Doctor Jimenez saw me.

He stood up and walked towards the door, he had a limp. He looked at me and asked me to come into his office. By the end of the interview I knew the job was mine, because he asked if I was available to commence soon.

I left the premises and said to the red haired lady: 'this job is mine, you will see. I will begin to work here in a week's time'.

Dr Jimenez sent me a letter confirming my appointment as a junior designer at his architecture department.

I was eighteen years old and had discovered the power of beauty, how to use it properly, and the confidence that it brings to oneself. How could I forget what Leito told me the day I was terribly upset, because the crotchety, old, set designer had been obnoxious to the extreme. Leito was very kind to tell me not to forget that my beauty opens doors, to treat my beauty as a great tool, and to use my beauty to obtain what I want. 'If you are beautiful and intelligent half the world is yours, you only have to work the other 50% and if you possess sex appeal, this brings success to you because men's lives revolve around sex'.

'Men fall invariably for a pretty face, and if the girl has sex appeal, they want to get there for some fun. You must always act on your best interest, because sex is a tool to be used wisely; never waste your assets'. By the time she finished my tears had disappeared.

I wasn't very good at my new job, but all those architects and engineers were kind and patient because they needed pretty girls in the office. Until I arrived there was a vacuum of VGS's so they said. Sometimes people from other departments entered our office and asked where the new beauty was. It was bizarre when people I hadn't seen previously, arrived at my desk to look at my pretty face.

I began to learn and understand how things worked in a big office. The stories followed quickly that prior to my interview, an architect had been interviewed and a very experienced draftswoman had presented an excellent portfolio, but Dr Jimenez had consulted with the architects and everybody agreed to hire the beautiful one, because it was better for the office moral. They needed a VGS and I got the job!

I was still living at Saturia's house. Unfortunately, Saturia's place was no longer the place to be. The parties without exception finished well past midnight and always with a fight; the little pills were showing the long term effect because everybody needed larger quantities more often, and the initial laughter terminated with aggression. Through Amparo my friendship with Oscar continued and we became quite close. I did like him and Leito's sex stories had woken up my desire to experiment.

Lust, desire, love

Oscar arrived at around 9pm when the party had just started, I introduced him to the guys and immediately he was offered the little pills which he refused; it was impossible to talk or be heard over the loud music, therefore, I invited Oscar to come to my room.

I had a desk as well as a small sofa, we closed the door and the window to the courtyard, and the room was instantly more pleasant. We began to talk, the kisses followed and in very short period of time we were rolling in bed. I became nervous, because I knew what was going to happen, and in a way it was time it did. I had expected it for a while.

It wasn't as Clara had described. It was uncomfortable and it hurt. I didn't think much of it at that moment. Oscar was sweet and realized that it was my first experience and apologized he had to leave; his shift started at around midnight. I thought it was better that way.

My friendship with Gloria and Amparo continued, we went to parties I visited their place on weekends since they travelled home less often. Sometimes when they went home for a long weekend they invited me, and if Oscar was available he used to travel with us. Their parents were strange, their mother appeared always angry towards their father; at times he would approach her and touch her arm, she quickly moved it away from him. I asked Amparo what was the problem. Apparently her father had an affair with somebody in town and her mother had found out. He was regretful, but she didn't want anything to do with him anymore. They had money but refused to come to an agreement about finances and had continued living together. She and Gloria were lucky enough not to live with them and experience their permanent frosty manner. It was disturbing and difficult enough during the few days we were there.

Following our first sex encounter, Oscar and I continued to see each other often. Our pattern of behaviour changed, and I began to realize that all those stories Clara had told me and Leito's tales about her experiences were true. Sex was magic. It became an obsession, and I began to discover lust and desire. Oscar was a hot lover, and very passionate. Every time we met the first thought was to find an opportunity to have sex, sometimes he called at my new job and asked me to leave an hour earlier; we met and began to have sex as I entered his premises. I met him at his apartment; I took a taxi and while I arrived he prepared something for lunch, but the desire to have sex was always stronger and at the end little time was left to eat.

My new job gave me good financial freedom and more time to do other things. The new job was very different from the last one, it was Monday to Friday, deadlines to complete a project did exist, but it never interfered with our private lives. The architects were fun; most of them in their mid thirty to late forty's and the office seemed divided in two groups. I was given a place among the older group, they pampered and spoiled me. Among this group were two girls, Isabel and Nancy. I instantly became friendly with Isabel since we were compatible in many ways; she was some years older than me, nice looking girl, sophisticated and fairly serious. Nancy was the opposite abrupt and impatient, rather difficult to get along with until we got to know each other better. Nancy was the oldest of the three of us.

My love affair with Oscar absorbed most of my free time, we often spent the entire weekend in bed and we had sex as many times as possible. Only then I understood what Clara had said to me about being raw; the more sex we had, the more we wanted it. It was addictive.

The times when Oscar arrived at Saturia's place, the hunger and desire to commence a sex session consumed our energy; we closed the door, and took advantage of the noise and the tenants' disorderly behaviour to involve ourselves on our new interest. As soon as we closed the door and sometimes without undressing we began the urgent task of having sex to calm the accumulated lust.

The owner of the first office where I had worked part-time, called to ask if I could help her with a project that turned out too large for her. I accepted and went to work on Saturday. I asked Oscar to call me when he finished at the hospital.

It must have been 7pm when the owner said she had enough and left. She gave me the key to lock up, and I would have to return the next day to complete the work if I couldn't finish that night.

Oscar called. I told him I would wait for him at the office rather than go to Saturia's place and wait for him there. Oscar arrived and asked me if I was ready. I said yes, then opened my overcoat and showed him that I was absolutely naked under it; he then touched me in a delicious way while we used the reception desk to have sex on it. It was as Clara had described it. I was absolutely wet with pleasure. We finished, cleaned up and locked the door.

I returned to complete the job the next day; I saw the desk and the image of the night before passed in front of my eyes and it made me laugh. We'd begun to have sex everywhere and anytime.

I left Saturia's house. My friendship with her continued and I was able to visit her regularly. She was a very accomplished seamstress, and quite fortunately she had many clients who happy with her work, returned to use her skills and that contributed to her financial stability.

All those male students left and she decided it was time to have a more sedate life. The relationship with her sister soured since the fiasco with the student, and she found that once again she was isolated from the family. I asked Saturia if she had sex with the student since she was there and he would've been able to find his way under her blankets during the night. She gave me an evasive answer.

I added: 'Was it better than the sex you used to have with your husband?' She smiled.

'See, you aren't cold and uninterested; your husband wasn't the right man'. She didn't want to talk about it and I left it at that.

Saturia moved to an apartment in the city centre, she began to make all my dresses and suits. It was lovely to see her, sometimes Oscar picked me up and she was glad to see him as well. I started to dress in a stylish and smart way and never bought any garments from the readymade racks; Saturia had a subscription to international fashion magazines and we took and modified the fashion styles to suit me, and in that way designed and made fantastic outfits.

Time passed fast at my new job, I didn't even think about my immediate family, I did visit Papi and Tuni as frequently as I could, they had moved to a town approximately eight hours from the capital, because Tuni wanted to look after my great grandmother and Papi obliged. I missed them terribly, maybe it was better that way, Tuni a very religious person would've been mortified if she had found out about my sex sessions with Oscar.

I didn't know if my emotions were true love, lust or desire; certainly, I loved to see him, I loved his touch; just thinking about him gave me goose bumps. Was it because of the sex or because I was in love with him? It felt good anyway. It almost felt as if I didn't need anybody else in my life. I felt complete. We were so different yet so similar.

We went away for a weekend to a popular town two hours away from the capital; we explored the surrounding area, followed the winding path under the trees and walked up the hill, not a soul in sight. We descended on the other side, found a stream of clear water which felt cold; it didn't matter we undressed and Oscar jumped into it, I just wet my toe. The water was freezing. Oscar quickly jumped out of it, even his dick looked purple. Of course we had to warm up and began to have sex on the little sandy beach under a tree; we had just finished dressing when a group of people descended. I must confess that on all those occasions we had sex in public places, it was extremely exciting.

We went to the movies fairly often. I don't even recall what film we intended to see because we didn't see anything; we sat in a remote corner of the theatre, it must have been a bad movie because the theatre was nearly empty, Oscar let his hand walk under my skirt and began to touch me, he continued to touch me until I almost fainted. We left the theatre and went straight to his apartment.

Oscar was the centre of my life, and for the first time I felt that my feelings for him represented happiness and fulfilment.

He was invited to a party at one of those beautiful colonial houses that often are used as reception places; it was a magnificent building with an enormous garden. Saturia made me a long dress; it was a chiffon fabric with a flowing skirt which was the fashion. Just before Oscar picked me up, I decided to take my underwear off, out of curiosity, to check if Clara once more was right about the story of no underwear. Not wearing any underwear and the thought of Oscar's possible reaction aroused me, and I was full of lust.

We arrived at the party and I could hardly contain myself, and after about an hour I said to Oscar: 'have you noticed that I am not wearing any underwear? If you pull the zipper down I will be stark naked for you. All I have to do is open my legs, and I am ready for you to get inside me'.

Clara was absolutely right! He went wild. During the following minutes he looked at me trying to decide what to do, we continued to dance but the emotions changed. Lust and desire had taken hold of both of us. I wanted him, I was already aroused and he couldn't resist my offer.

It was a crowded party, and we were sure that if we walked into the garden and disappeared behind a tree nobody would notice; we began to walk away from the house until we reached the remotest corner of the garden where we still could hear the music in the distance.

It was a quiet moonless night, no stars either, only the deep blue darkness, and trees around us. Oscar lifted my skirt and touched me, I was already wet with desire, he lowered himself and began to give me oral sex until my legs began to tremble, and then he penetrated me while I leaned against the tree. Clara had said: 'all that liquid running down my legs and I still wanted more'. She was absolutely correct.

We sat on a bench for a rest; then Oscar said: 'aren't you wearing anything at all under that dress?'

'Check it out', was my reply.

He pushed the zipper down, and as the dress fell over my shoulders exposing my breasts, I let the dress fall to the ground around my ankles, all my body exposed, he began to kiss and caress my breasts; again we wanted more sex. His hands caressed me while his kisses were full of passion and desire, and we did it all over again. After the second time and temporarily satisfied, we composed ourselves, and he helped me to put my dress back still touching every inch of skin as the garment slowly covered it.

We went back to the guest house and continued to enjoy the other aspects of the party; when we returned to Oscar's apartment at about 4am the insatiable appetite for more sex was still there.

Some months later Oscar's distant friend was getting married, and we were invited to the service as well as the reception. We arrived at the wedding reception to discover that we were seated at a table with people we didn't know. We sat down to share a meal with twelve unhappy couples. Some of them were clearly arguing as if nobody was listening to them, it was very boring. I whispered in Oscar's ear: 'would you like to go somewhere and check if I forgot my underwear?'

'I would be delighted'. He said

The reception centre was a large complex with many rooms; we began to inspect the rooms on the first floor until we found a smallish room perhaps used for meetings. We walked in, Oscar made sure the door was locked. Meanwhile, I unzipped and removed my dress. I rested on the table with my feet touching the ground. I opened my legs and remembering what Clara told me I said to Oscar: 'look, I am ready and everything is waiting for you'.

He moved close to me and touched every bit of exposed skin, the pleasure was intense, and he was ready in an instant; I lifted my legs and we began another sex session in a public place. It took a while to complete our interlude, it was hot, the air conditioning wasn't working in this area of the building; the room was dark, the only light was the exit sign over the door; we almost needed a shower, especially me with all that liquid running down my legs.

We rested on some comfortable chairs, I was totally naked still wearing my shoes and Oscar had removed his pants. We stretched our legs while we tried to cool down, but I was on fire and wanting more sex I moved each leg over the chair's arm rest to expose everything. I felt very aroused doing it and Oscar was delighted I did it again. He moved closer and caressed me. At that point our arousal was phenomenal. We had sex again.

We left the room and returned to the area where the reception was taking place, the speeches had passed and the dance floor was full of people. We joined the dance, and as we began to dance I said to Oscar: 'I don't want to be here, I want to go to your place, have a shower, go to bed and continue to have sex until any bit of energy left walks out of our bodies and we fall asleep'.

We left immediately, arrived at Oscar's apartment, had a shower and went to bed. Then he said: 'please do it again I feel aroused just thinking of it'.

'Did you like it?'

'Yes, I want more of it. It's wild'

Once more, Clara was right. The element of arousal was beyond description. How did she know so many things about sex?

Our antics continued. Everything was incredibly exciting, and every occasion was different and thrilling. However, Oscar turned into a possessive individual and I didn't like it, he began to talk about marriage, but I didn't want that. My idea of marriage was into the distant future, probably another five years or so. He was beginning his career and after all those years of hardship, I didn't think marriage was the correct approach to life at that moment.

I was happy to experiment, to continue the enjoyment of that sexual passion I had heard about and have finally discovered. He was of the opinion that he wanted marriage. We began to argue, we had never argued before, we continued to see each other and as long as he didn't mention marriage we had a very good time.

At the office, I heard when one of the architects said that someone had been caught having sex in an elevator car on the weekend. Unfortunately they whispered and I couldn't hear the details. I'd love to do that I said to Oscar, but I thought it would be almost impossible, because the lift goes up and down and the risk of being caught is too high.

'Let's try' he said.

We began to search for an elevator car in a small building, we had to find a building that was open after hours, but nobody worked there after dark or during the weekend; also it has to be a building without a caretaker.

We left a movie theatre and passed in front of a cute newish building, the main door was open; we walked into the lift car and stopped on each floor to check for tenants working after hours. All the offices had the lights turned off. Nobody seemed to be there; obviously someone forgot to lock the main door.

I had developed a taste for not wearing underwear, it made me feel free and ready when I was with Oscar, and he seemed to get sexually aroused every time I told him that I wasn't wearing any. We entered the lift car again after we had inspected every floor; pressed the button to go to the top floor. The elevator car began to rise and Oscar's hand went inside my legs and as we reached the top floor I held the stop button while he penetrated me. I rested my head on the handrail and curled my legs around him. Again the problem of all that water running down my legs, we had to find a bathroom. It was exciting and a lot of fun.

The end of the year arrived with great speed and soon Christmas's holidays would give us a break from work. Oscar decided to work during the festive season and take holidays in late January. I did take the festive days and went to visit Papi and Tuni; I spent the whole week with them, and the last days of the holidays with Gloria and Amparo before returning to work.

Oh I missed Oscar. After nine days I was desperate to see him, his long shifts at the hospital continued until the end of January. He was exhausted because of the lack of sleep. We saw each other sporadically and began to plan our next holiday.

We decided to book accommodation on a deserted small coral cay in the Caribbean; it was a truly remote little place, they called the nearest island, which perhaps was double the size of the coral cay, the mainland. No television, no telephones, no shops. There was only a small place where food was prepared and served, and some motorbikes were available for rental. The compact self-contained thatched roof structure was located on the beach under coconut palms. There were only three self-contained rooms available for tourists all built far apart from each other, so privacy was assured. It said on the brochure.

We flew away and arrived on the main island, a blue painted timber boat transported us to the small coral cay. The fishing boat moored into a tiny inlet, in front of the jetty there was one building that served as the information centre, post office, restaurant, hiring equipment, and shop.

We hired a small motorbike; the little motorbike was all the transport we needed to move around the island, we filled the basket with our small bags and with the aid of a faded map and some finger pointing directions we followed the dirt road that took us towards our accommodation. The place didn't disappoint us, it was absolutely beautiful. Turquoise water as far as the eye could see; the room floor was covered with grass mats, the window panes just lifted to allow the sultry air to enter the space. It was really delightful and serene.

We went back to the central shop to arrange meals; by that time the sky was overcast and the shopkeeper talked about bad weather coming up unexpectedly, totally out of season, he also talked about the restrictions the islanders encountered while the weather was rough. They had some spare fish in the refrigerator, enough to last for two weeks, but the food from the mainland would be rationed. The storm appeared to be a tropical one which could last for several days.

We thought it would be interesting to experience a tropical storm; it would be magic to listen to the howling wind and to see the coconut palms swing under its force, apart from that, we had many ways of getting entertained, and we were certain time would fly away.

We drove our motorbike the length of the island that afternoon. The rain arrived with strong wind which whistled ferociously, and by the time we stopped under the coconut palms, we were absolutely drenched so decided to return to our room. Since we hadn't seen each other much during the months of December and January we were sex starved. There was an indescribable energy between us, Oscar touched me and kissed me as we entered the room. My body behaved as if an electrical current passed through me and made me instantly receptive to him, we had discovered that our bodies behaved in unison and the desire to be together was like a magnet, and once we began to have sex it was almost unstoppable. Unfortunately we had to get up around 7pm and in the rain went to the central place for dinner.

Everything was in darkness, the generator wasn't working and dinner was served with the help of a candle light. It appeared to be that we were the only guests on the island the others were left stranded on the mainland. The shop was empty apart from the few locals having a beer. Dinner consisted of grilled fish, prawns and plantain served on a banana leaf.

The return trip on the motorbike was a disaster, because of all the big paddles on the road we were covered with mud. The best option was to stand under the heavy rain outside our room, and let the power of the water remove the mud. The heavy rain washed us and removed most of the mud and we began to undress outside the room while we fell into each other's arms. We had torrid sex many times before, but this time was different; perhaps we needed to catch up and satisfy the lust and desire that had been suppressed by a busy schedule, or possibly, the tropical storm over us charged our bodies with a kind of wilder, deeper passion.

Maybe the absolutely deserted place allowed us to let our desires surface without inhibitions. Not that we had many inhibitions, but it was obvious our relationship was changing to a higher level of understanding and intimacy and we needed each other. Oscar explored my body with great hunger and I let myself be explored. We climaxed many times but didn't move apart, we just remained together until some minutes later we started all over again. For the rest of the night amid the storm and the wind we created our own storm with our bodies, we fell asleep and woke up to a desire more powerful that in the previous hour.

The sun began to shine on the horizon like a sliver of light through the dark, grey clouds and we started our sex storm once again, every pore on my body was charged with a desire for more. It didn't matter how many times we had sex, I wanted more. Oscar wanted more. We went for a swim before the storm arrived, got dressed and went for breakfast, deciding to walk under the rain, in that way we didn't get splashed with mud. While we walked I asked Oscar if he had any fantasies. He said he had fulfilled them all and couldn't think of anything else he would like to experience, and for that very reason he believed we should get married.

I am only eighteen years old, I said. I really like everything we do but I don't want to become like those awful married people we met at your friend's wedding. They all looked so miserable, so unhappy, so bored with each other. Remember we had to be resourceful that day. We had to find a room. I had to rest on the table, showed you that I was ready to relieve the boredom. Wasn't that a great moment? If we were married we would be like those people. We wouldn't have sex against a tree, and then after a couple of minutes you undressed me to have more sex on a bench, without fear of being caught. All we wanted was to be with each other.

We wouldn't search for an elevator car, inspect the office floors, and hold the stop button while you were inside me. You wouldn't be eager to have sex on a reception desk; I don't think you would put your fingers inside me while we pretended to watch a movie in an empty theatre. Remember how wonderfully horny I was? And the virilis cramp you only got rid of after we arrived at the apartment?

I am ready for you any time, you can do anything, and I am happy to offer you my body. I love you with such great passion I can't even describe. I can't find words to express my love for you. I love to have sex in public places, the tension and the excitement it provides is unreal. However, I do have a fantasy. Many times I dream about having sex and when I wake up, I am moving, breathing heavily and have tingles all over; my fantasy is to have sex while I am asleep. If you see me moving and breathing heavily, just get inside me quickly before I wake up.

The weather was set to continue with tropical storms; there was thunder, constant heavy rain, and we had to spend most of the time indoors; when the thunderstorms stopped we had swims and walked the surrounding areas which were blissfully empty of people. My sexual organs were on fire and Oscar began to feel quite sensitive too. We decided to be celibate for a day. It was incredibly hard to do it. The sex curfew lasted from breakfast to dinner, and after dinner on our return to the cute quarters, we started again with the same fury the tropical storm carried on. The night followed the pattern of other nights, and during the day we filled each other with tenderness and deep passion.

We went to the central place for lunch it was very steamy and hot, everything saturated because the rain hadn't stopped since the day we arrived, after lunch we walked to our room and went straight to bed and fell asleep. It was almost dark when I woke up and saw Oscar looking at me with a smile on his face. 'You just did it' he said.

'What did I do?'

'You moved gently and made some just audible, delicate sounds. I presumed you were having one of your dreams and penetrated you as per your instructions. I climaxed and you continued moving until you woke up right now'.

'Yes, I was having a sex dream. Wow, a fantasy fulfilled. It felt very good in my dream. How did I move?'

'Gently with slow contortions and soft sounds, you had an orgasm before I did, but continued to move'.

'How do you know I had an orgasm before you?'

'You were very wet, almost as if you had peed on the bed'.

'See, we wouldn't have this fantasy fulfilled if we were married'.

We got up and went for dinner; we had to drive the motorbike because our legs were very tired from all those exercises. The locals were curious about us and what we did during the day. We told them that their island was so incredible beautiful and even in the rain we went for walks, took advantage of small breaks in the weather to go for swims, and enjoyed the magnificent colour variation the storm brought to the sea.

It was our last day; if we'd wanted to experience a tropical storm, certainly we'd felt the fury of it. The sky still grey and our bodies were also spent. We returned home.

Oscar returned to his hospital duties which offered him a more sedate timetable, we took advantage of it and we began to see each other for lunch every day. He prepared lunch while I took a taxi to his place and as soon as I arrived we had the first sex session, had lunch, and before I left a quickie for the road as we called it. During this time I noticed an interesting pattern with the guys at the office. Some days the sex Oscar and I had was incredibly torrid and when I arrived at the office after lunch break, most of the guys made comments about how beautiful I looked, and they looked into my eyes; since I met Oscar every day, I began to notice their reaction was very much tied to the intensity of our sex sessions.

Life continued its course, everything was well, I was happy with work, but Oscar began to put pressure on me to marry him. He became more possessive, began to be suspicious of me if I couldn't meet him.

Oscar had to attend a conference that lasted five days, on his return we arranged to meet at his apartment. I left my place and on the way to catch a taxi I thought of something really crazy just to see his reaction, I returned to my place, took everything off, rubbed honey on my nipples and genitals, put a trench coat over and packed a pair of jeans and a top in my hand bag. I took a taxi.

He saw me arrive and he was standing by the door as I went upstairs. He kissed me and embraced me as if we had been apart for a century. Oscar began to unbutton the trench coat and started kissing my neck and chest until he tasted the honey on my nipples. His hands moved all over me and soon discovered the honey on my genitals. He said: 'lady we may have to use several instruments to remove all this honey'. As he said that he lifted me off the floor and placed me on the dining table; he sat on a chair, opened my legs and began to lick me. He started cleaning the honey gently on the sides and on top until he had me in such state of arousal that I begged him to penetrate me. At that moment he carried me to bed. He began to undress while I stroked his magnificent erection, licked and kissed it. I was on fire and I wanted more, after a moment he penetrated me with his wonderful instrument. Certainly a lot of honey came out. Every time Oscar caressed me like that I became insatiable.

We had been invited to dinner to a hacienda, the place was on the city outskirts, a distance of more or less over an hour, and the drive was along a deserted country road. We left Oscar's apartment just before the sun began to set, it was a relaxing drive and from time to time we stopped to admire the landscape; as we were getting closer to the destination I pulled his zipper down, unbuckled his belt and began to stroke him while he drove.

'We will be killed. Stop it', he said.

Let me see if you can do two things at the same time and continued to fondle him. It was already dark. The car stopped, Oscar opened the door and walked towards my side with a full erection through his unzipped pants; he opened the passenger door, invited me out and said: 'let me check if you are wearing underpants. He lifted the skirt, caressed me as usual, and on the side of the road we had sex against the car. What a delicious experience we had.

It was so incredibly exciting; I loved him. Sex was like an electrical current through my body and it filled my senses. Sex with Oscar was like a dream every girl wants to fulfil. He was handsome, intelligent and a magnificent lover. Why didn't I want to marry him?

Sex was wonderful, I was in love with Oscar and there was no remote reason for him to think that I would be interested in someone else, but he began to behave angrily towards me like if I'd done something wrong. When we met, although, we continued our sex sessions in the same torrid manner, some abruptness was present sometimes. I arrived at his apartment, he quickly undressed me and carried me to bed opened my legs and began to kiss me. Initially I thought it was funny and his behaviour even aroused me, until on one occasion as I arrived he took me to the bedroom which was normal, however, he undressed me in a hurry and spread my legs; the kisses didn't start as it usually did; he smelled in between my legs, and said he was just checking whether I had been with someone else, then apologized. We had our usual sex, but everything began to change that day.

I was deeply in love with Oscar, but I didn't want to marry him, it was strange. I couldn't see myself living with him forever and ever, in spite of the great moments we had. I began to withdraw and like a hermit crab I started to take refuge inside my shell. I continued to meet him for lunch, although, his jealousy and possessiveness fluctuated from irritating to non-existent, and the relationship began to experience a dramatic change.

The day arrived when I didn't want to meet him for lunch. I tried to find an excuse, but my body missed his caresses and I found out that I gave in to his requests. I felt the desire to see him but it didn't have the same intensity; the passion that joined us initially and we had experienced throughout our relationship was beginning to disappear. I didn't feel comfortable anymore and he knew it. He often asked me why I appeared to be distant, although I responded to his affection and sometimes possessiveness.

I wanted to be sure that I didn't desire him anymore; our sex sessions became less frequent until the feeling after sex wasn't as fulfilling as it had been during the past eighteen months. Oscar called me and often told me how much he desired and wanted me. I met him many times, he caressed me, but my body didn't respond in the same way anymore. I let him explore me as he had done before, he kissed me with the same intensity he'd kissed me before, and he did exactly the same he'd done before, but the fire and the wild passion weren't there anymore.

I met him for lunch, and as usual he was amorous. In previous times I was so receptive that on my way to the apartment I was already filled with desire and excitement, my body was on fire and couldn't wait to arrive to receive his caresses. As soon as I saw him he used to run his hands under my skirt to check if I had forgotten the underpants, during those times his fingers walked inside me and we just had sex on the table while his hands touched every bit of me and moved deliciously all over. I used to have consecutive orgasms until all that liquid ran down my legs, and a very intense pleasure possessed my body, those days after we finished a sex session I wanted more and he always obliged after a couple of minutes.

Oscar tried to revive the past, but unfortunately the past had already gone. Yes, there was sexual pleasure, but the pleasure of the mind and the heart had moved on. It was the end, I knew it, but didn't say anything. We kissed and said goodbye.

By the time I left Oscar's place I'd made a decision. I wouldn't see him anymore. It wasn't as easy as I thought; as I started to avoid him, Oscar began to chase me more. I didn't answer his telephone calls anymore, at the office I told the girls to say that I wasn't available, but if the guys answered the phone I had to talk to him. Oscar began to wait for me outside the building, and at that point I decided to stay at the office during the lunch break, and the girls brought food for me. It meant that I went to work in the morning and left at 6pm. Isabel and Nancy used to call me to let me know if Oscar was outside waiting for me, and if it was the case I delayed my departure, until the day he arrived after Isabel and Nancy had left.

There was an exhibition of art works in the boardroom and I decided to have a look; while at the exhibition a girl from another section brought Oscar with her. He followed me home in spite of my refusal to be with him, we arrived home and of course he wanted to enter the premises, I didn't show any interest, but he forced his way in. Once inside my place he began to caress and kiss me as he had done in the past. He undressed and touched me in the same manner that used to make me feel wild with passion. I didn't want to be with him anymore. I allowed him to undress me and then he pushed me on the bed and as before kissed me all over.

There was pleasure, even though, at that precise moment I thought I didn't want him anymore. I cried. He became annoyed, and then slapped me on the cheek. I continued to cry while he apologized profusely; kissed me and penetrated me once more. I remained under him until he finished. He stayed inside me as we always did, that was until his member languished.

I got up, went to the bathroom and cleaned myself I didn't like his smell anymore. The love I had for him hadn't disappeared completely, but I was experiencing a range of confused emotions, and it appeared to be that there were only the remnants of happier times. It was so sad. The tears continued to flow, and the more he kissed me the sadder I felt. He was aroused again, and again he tried to excite me; I allowed him to touch me and kiss me because I also wanted my love and desire to be revived.

Gonzalo, one of the architects began to ask me out once he knew that my relationship with Oscar had finished. This chap had constantly invited me out, but I had always rejected his attentions. During the time I was with Oscar there was nobody more intelligent, better looking, more desirable man than Oscar, there was such emptiness without him.

I wasn't looking for a replacement; my heart was just beginning to overcome intense pain. I often thought about Oscar and whatever had gone wrong. Our love affair lasted eighteen months; it had been so lovely and sex was such an important part of it. For me, it was a period of discovery. Oscar showed everything and had confirmed everything. Even Sister Barbarita's warning about men and how they like to open the woman's legs and look inside and touch. Oh I really liked that. I liked everything Oscar did and I would remember him forever.

Oscar continued to follow me and waited for me outside the building, less often but quite regularly. Every time he followed me we had sex. Oscar always pushed his way into my place, and once he was on the premises, I didn't want an ugly argument, so I always obliged.

I hadn't seen Oscar for almost two months and I accepted Gonzalo's invitation for a cup of chocolate, it was late afternoon. Gonzalo and I left the office and walked towards the coffee shop, as we were about to cross the road, Oscar came from behind and embraced me.

'Where are you going my love?' He asked.

'For a cup of chocolate', I responded.

'I may as well join you and then I will take you home'.

'Fine' I said.

The three of us went to the coffee shop had the chocolate and left after some tense moments; Oscar took me home. We arrived home and I didn't invite Oscar to enter. 'I am tired' I said. He didn't want to listen to my excuses and he pushed his way in. Once inside my place, he began to kiss and touch me, Oscar knew me well, he was my first man, I allowed him to undress and touch me as he had always done; he covered me with kisses. I was wearing underpants he noticed; after two months of no sex I accepted him because there was some love left and because I needed a man at that moment. It was a strange feeling. It was the first time I was aware of it. Until then I never thought about needing a man. Oscar was so handsome, and athletic looking, but sex didn't feel the same, and I thought he finally realized he had lost me.

'May I visit you again?' He asked.

'Yes, I will always open my legs for you' was my response. He kissed me and then left.

Gonzalo continued to pursue me, although, I wasn't interested in him. Other guys began to invite me out as well, I didn't have any desire to go out or do anything with anybody, I had a great void in my emotions; however, I welcomed the odd invitation because I felt lonely.

Gonzalo invited me to a party and I accepted. He arrived to pick me up and at the same time Oscar appeared at the gate. I opened the door it was a very sticky situation. I felt sorry for Gonzalo but asked him to leave. Oscar entered the premises, he was a bit agitated. I told him I was going to a party Gonzalo had invited me, nothing else. He became angry and asked me if I was going to have sex with Gonzalo, he then put his hands under my skirt to find out if I was wearing underpants.

'Of course I am wearing underpants. I only did that for you'. It's just a party. I don't even like the guy. I feel lonely. I don't like what you are doing. I don't love you anymore. But I do, was his response and began to kiss me and unbuttoned my blouse. I wanted his familiar touch once more, and I allowed him to continue to caress, kiss my breasts, while his hands moved over my body. I felt sexual arousal with the man I had loved. He undressed me and showered me with kisses like in the past. The arousal was only in the sexual organs. Clara was right again, love is not necessary to have sex with a man.

I did enjoy sex without love, but it wasn't the same as when love was present. Sex moved into a different dimension when love was part of it; perhaps a figment of my imagination, but the orgasm felt just like an orgasm without love. We had sex several times as we did before and Oscar finally left. From this day I felt a bit nervous about going out with a new guy since I didn't know if Oscar was going to show up unexpectedly.

I decided that I should try to find another place to live, or perhaps go on holidays, and I felt the need for a change at that moment. I began to look for new accommodation and to talk about a holiday.

Nancy had never been in the Caribbean. We agreed that the month of January was the right time to go. Four weeks in the Caribbean would be great. She was interested in architecture and seemed like a good companion since she was much older than me. We began to arrange the required paper work and visas to go in January; with everything arranged for the trip, I thought it was better to keep my rental accommodation to the end of the holiday, and wait until my return to make the changes required.

It was close to Christmas and the office would be closed for the week in between Christmas and New Year. I'd visit Papi and Tuni. Also began to buy presents and decided to buy some for mother, brothers and sisters whom I hadn't seen for two years.

I bought the presents, placed everything in a big bag and went to mother's house, rang the bell; a new maid opened the door and I said to give the bag to la Señora and left. It felt strange and I began to walk as I normally did when it was necessary to clear my mind. I passed a new shopping centre, some boring Christmas carols were playing through the loud speaker and lights illuminated the space. Oscar entered my mind as well as the happiness we had experienced the previous year, all those thoughts made me feel sad. I lifted my head and there he was, Oscar in front of me looking at me with great tenderness. I was lost for words. He embraced me and asked me to lunch, with hesitation I accepted his invitation. He'd cook lunch for me the next day.

I arrived at his apartment feeling nervous, but thought this would be the best opportunity to make sure Oscar was out of my life. He was affectionate, and rather amorous, I could feel he restrained himself from caressing and touching me as soon as he saw me. We had a good talk. He told me how much he'd missed me; I also let him know that I was finding difficult to adjust my life without him. He finally asked once more to marry him. I said no.

We finished lunch, began to clear up the dining table, and he reminded me how many times we had used this table for activities which didn't involve the consumption of food. I looked at him, smiled and said: 'yes, it was food of another kind. What lovely memories, I wouldn't change what we had for anything in the world'.

'We can bring it back'.

'No, it's gone', was my reply.

'Can we do it once more?' He asked. A tear ran down my cheek and my heart ached. I embraced him and kissed him. He began to kiss me with all that passion I had known. It was more that I could bear and I started to cry. He covered me with kisses while he undressed me. Once again, I was under his spell. He knew me. He knew how to touch me until I was ready for sex. He penetrated me and I enjoyed him because I somehow knew there wouldn't be a next time.

I went back to work, that afternoon we had an office party; drinks and small finger food were served, everybody was animated and in great spirits, but I had a tremendous pain in my heart. I didn't wash after sex with Oscar, I left his finger prints and his sperm in my body, for some strange reason I wanted to feel his manhood still with me. I had a couple of margaritas and they truly went to my head.

Gonzalo took the opportunity to invite me to carry on with the party and we went to a night club. We sat at a small table at the back of a dark space; he ordered more drinks, after the first drink I was truly dizzy but fully aware of what was going on.

Gonzalo put his hand on top of my dress and touched my breast. I left repulsed by it but didn't say anything. I left the table and went to the bathroom, and when I entered the bathroom feeling very dizzy, rested my head against the wall and felt sick. A girl I hadn't seen before asked me if I was sick.

'I feel very dizzy'.

'Some drinks had been spiked' she said.

She asked for my address and said that she lived two streets away from me; she was leaving the place immediately and could take me home. On the way out she asked for a strong coffee at the bar, and she said it would make me feel better. I drank the coffee, and indeed I began to feel a lot better. We took the taxi and she delivered me home.

I went straight to bed. Late during the night, perhaps 2am the bell rang many times. I was too tired and dizzy to answer the intercom and I wasn't expecting anybody. The next day at about 11am the bell rang again. I'd just had a shower and was drying my hair; with the towel wrapped around my head, I went to the front gate rather than to answer the intercom. It was Gonzalo with a bunch of flowers and apparently, very concerned about my wellbeing. I didn't invite him in and didn't accept the flowers either.

At work it was rather difficult to brush him off. He began to bring me presents which I didn't accept and he also waited outside my place to my great annoyance.

The Christmas break arrived and I went to spend the week with Papi and Tuni. It was lovely to see them, and to be with them, was not only relaxing, but restored the energy in my soul, their company brought balance into my life. We made special dinners and cakes with the help of the young maid and with Tuni went to the markets as it was the custom. Once again my life felt normal.

I thought about Oscar often and I did miss him terribly, at night before I fell asleep I almost felt his caresses, I missed his kisses and his embrace, I desired him and wished I could feel his touch; he was my first man and I still loved him.

I felt lost without him, but his jealousy was an impossible characteristic to accept in one's life.

Jealousy is destructive, and it makes people unhappy.

Torrid wonderful sex

January arrived and Nancy and I left to spend a month in the Caribbean. We selected one of the many islands that had been conquered by the Spaniards, lots of history, ancient buildings, and the usual fortress to inspect as well as beautiful beaches.

I didn't envisage having any problems since we had arranged everything in great detail. Nancy was very different to me; I knew that because seeing her at work every day we got to know each other, I thought.

Nancy was already twenty eight years old and never had a relationship not even a platonic one, had never been in love, and she had until then, a sad life. As we commenced our journey, she began to tell me that she basically supported the family of six and never had time for herself. She often talked about doing the washing, ironing from 4am but Isabel and I didn't take much notice of it. We simply thought she was having us on.

Nancy and her family lived in a village established by a priest called Father Rafael who had decided to help the very poor. Her story began with a violent, alcoholic father and the abused mother; Nancy, four siblings and the mother lived in a little two bedroom house they had managed to obtain from the priest. Father Rafael had established quotas to fill up the village; as the little houses reached completion and depending on the urgency of the situation, the priest allocated the properties to needy families.

The priest imposed draconian rules on the village inhabitants; everybody had to attend Mass on Sunday, no ifs or buts. Alcohol was prohibited, relationships between boys and girls were closely monitored, Father Rafael had an eye on everybody who lived there, and he also had informants among the group of residents as it's expected in a close society. Behaviour that met the priest disapproval incurred the loss of the house. As soon as a relationship developed, it was either marriage or nothing else; if any member of the family didn't comply with the rules the whole family was thrown out of the village.

It was true that Nancy had to wash all her siblings' clothing, because the mother couldn't attend to everything. Nancy was a serious girl with a lot of responsibility. She had some liking for someone, but the fear of being spied on, had stopped her developing a relationship. The other problem was that she considered herself unattractive; her abrupt manner and lack of femininity didn't help her either.

My problems with Nancy started fairly soon, because she desperately wanted to attract men and I didn't. She said, she wanted to make up for lost time, and that placed me in a tricky situation. As soon as we entered a place, she would eye the potential; she did attract them eventually, but it was my misfortune that her newly acquired suitors stuck to me, and then I had to get rid of them.

We travelled to a little town, looked for the best hotel in the area, not much to choose from, but we decided on the best looking building. We entered the reception and asked for available accommodation, they had vacancies and we were escorted to our room; it wasn't too bad considering it was a very small town. We dropped the bags and left the hotel to inspect the surroundings, which had lovely beaches and hundreds of svelte coconut palms scattered all over.

We went for long walks and talked a lot about life and our expectations. After a long day at the beach we went back to the hotel and didn't feel like going to the restaurant for dinner, so we asked for room service. I showed Nancy that I had the precise amount of money and I would pay for the service.

The room service arrived. It was delivered by a rather handsome fellow. Nancy took a large note to pay for a small bill. I said once more that I had the correct amount, but the waiter pretended not to hear me, obviously the man had to return with the change. It took a considerable amount of time for him to return. I said to Nancy: 'your money has gone. You will see that to recover your money we may have to call reception'. After over two hours the service man returned with the change, but he no longer wore his uniform. He gave Nancy the change and she began to talk to him like he was an old chum.

He was chatty and perhaps thought that we had planned it that way. I was sitting on the bed against the bed head, with my legs stretched over the bedspread, with a map and some tourist brochures over my lap, and tried to ignore the chat that went on between Nancy and him.

On the way out the man touched my legs and asked me for a drink. I told him that if he didn't leave the room immediately I would call reception. I took the telephone and began to dial. He left.

I turned to Nancy and furiously said: 'Satisfied? We go out and you desperately try to attract men with the consequence that I have to get rid of them, and now I was the one he touched, not you. Can't you understand?'

I didn't know whether the hotel experience made Nancy understand how to behave. I truly hoped Nancy had learnt something for my own peace of mind. The next day we went to the beach, sat under the coconut palms near a rocky outcrop where there was a man fishing; we must have been there for a little while when Nancy began to talk to the man about the fish. I was ready to go, but Nancy insisted on remaining at the beach and continued to talk to the man. The man probably thought that we were looking for someone and finally invited us for a drink.

I said 'No thank you', of course Nancy said 'yes'.

I found myself following Nancy and the old grey haired man to have a cold drink, when we could've bought it ourselves. The grey haired old man went for me and began to ask if I wanted to have dinner with him. I said 'No thank you'

He somehow convinced Nancy to accept his dinner proposition and even arranged a time to pick her up. I said to Nancy: 'you will go on your own, I don't want any of this'. By the time the man was supposed to pick her up, Nancy had convinced me to accompany her to the dinner date. The man's name was Angelo; he took us to a bar – restaurant. I thought the place was seedy and awful. However, Nancy was happy that she was dancing with someone until it was my turn. Angelo clearly indicated that he wanted to take me out. I said: 'no thank you, if there is a next time you will go with Nancy because she is the one who wishes to go out with you not me'. I returned to the table and said to Nancy: 'I am going back to the hotel'.

I took my handbag and left. I was on the street waiting for the taxi the bar attendant had called for me, when Nancy appeared. Apparently, Angelo said to her: 'if your friend isn't here, you may as well go to the hotel'.

'Have you finally learnt?'

'I am sorry' Nancy said.

Those incidents happened within the first week. We had three more weeks in front of us. The next day around 7pm the telephone rang, Nancy answered the phone. It was reception. Nancy said: 'yes she is here and passed the receiver to me'. The caller was Angelo who suggested I would go out with him. I hung up the phone and said to Nancy: 'are you satisfied now? That man from the beach is here at the reception and he has just asked me to go out with him'.

'Nancy: I've had enough. I've put up with your economical ways, but from this very moment you will do as I say. We leave tomorrow morning after breakfast, we'll go to the capital and stay in a five star hotel; if the money runs out we'll stay for two weeks instead of four. I am sorry, but I don't want to hear anything else'. I began to pack.

We left soon after breakfast, took the bus to the capital and from the bus terminal took a taxi to the up market hotel I had booked that morning. We had a double room with a balcony and views to the beach; it was a spacious room with two comfortable beds and white sheets. There was a large pool and deck chairs as well as several restaurants and bars.

Nancy was amazed and couldn't believe the difference in the quality of the accommodation and surroundings; she had never experienced anything like that, and consequently, was worried about the money. 'Well, let's check it out. We have enough money to stay here for two weeks. The alternative we have is to find accommodation more suited to our financial needs. Perhaps find a family who offers a room, and since we can't travel look for a job'.

We began to look for a job and quickly found a part-time position with a surveyor. I called and managed to arrange an appointment. He only needed one person to draw the road profiles, but I convinced him that if we worked together we would finish the job faster. He agreed and employed both of us. We had found a job for two weeks.

We then looked for a family who was renting a room in an area close to public transport. We found it. Talked to the lady over the phone and made an appointment to see the room. We arrived at the house, and after a brief inspection to the premises, we answered many questions the owner asked, and then took the room.

The house owner was named Isabella and the other lady was Alcira. Alcira was a cousin of the lady owner. She helped with the general housework and cooking. One of the many questions Isabella and Alcira asked was if Nancy and I were sisters. I felt horrified that they thought we looked alike, because I believed to be quite different from Nancy.

We liked the surroundings and paid her for the first two weeks rental. Then went back to the hotel settled our account and left. I knew everything would be fine from now on.

The work at the surveyor's office was easy and he was a very nice man, his name was Justino, we told him we were on holidays but had decided to stay a little longer because we had a three month visa but not enough money. He later put us in contact with a small architectural practice. We met the architects; they had excellent work to keep us occupied until our visa expired. Once again, I managed to convince them to employ both of us, which they did. We finished the surveyor's work and started to work with the architects the very next day. It was fantastic work. Great looking houses. We had to do sections and levels. Nancy was very good at it and fortunately, my skills had improved a lot since the first year I worked with the large architectural company. After a week with the architects Nancy decided to return home because she was preoccupied about her family's financial situation.

I remained with Isabella and her family; also developed a good friendship with Isabella and Alcira, and everybody made me feel welcome. The family was warm, affectionate and caring. I also enjoyed the architectural work because it was very different from the work I did while at the big company.

I sent a letter to Doctor Jimenez asking him to extend my holiday until after Easter. When Nancy returned she called to advise me that Doctor Jimenez wasn't too pleased with my decision to prolong the holiday. She suggested that I talk to him as soon as possible, which I did. At the end of a long conversation he agreed, and said that he would write back approving the change.

I had two long months in front of me, and for a strange reason began to plan my future trips abroad. At the same time I often thought about Oscar, and how much I missed his company and the fabulous sex we had. I was wrong to think that I didn't love him; the truth was that I did love him. I didn't have a desire to be with anybody else. Several guys from the architectural office began to ask me out, as well as the young lawyers from the office where the lady of the house, Isabella worked. I used to walk to Isabella's office to get a lift home, and in that way I met the lawyers she worked with. I even got a serenade with guitars and violins. Soon I had to leave.

Isabella and her family were absolutely lovely to me and they made me feel as a member of the family. Alcira and I had fantastic conversations and I made her laugh with my theories and stories. She used to make me laugh imitating my response to one of the questions she asked me the very first day we arrived at the house to inspect the room.

Alcira used to imitate my facial expression and tone of voice when I was asked the question whether Nancy and I were sisters. Apparently I didn't respond yes or no and looked absolutely shocked. I tilted my head sideways, pointed my nose up and said: 'why do you ask, do you think we look alike?' We laughed our heads off about the incident.

I decided to send a postcard to Gloria and Amparo. I informed them that my holiday had come to an end, I was ready to go back, and that my feelings for Oscar were clearer. My return would be just before Easter. They responded quickly and invited me to spend Easter with them.

Isabella and her husband José Tomás drove me to the airport; while we waited for the flight, photographers asked if it was possible to take some photos of me for an article in the social section of the weekend newspaper.

I was perplexed about the interest showed in me. The photographers said that my beauty was so exquisite it had to be captured through a lens, and would make a good article for the social pages; I agreed to a short interview and the photographs. While posing here and there a crowd started to gather around to check if I was a famous personality. I was told that the title for my article would be: 'even her name is beautiful'.

I boarded the plane and arrived on Easter Wednesday, midday flight. Gloria and Amparo were waiting for me at the airport and we left to spend Easter with their family. Amparo confessed that she had taken the liberty to talk about my return to Oscar, and that he expressed his interest in seeing me. I was happy she'd spoken to Oscar about my Easter holiday with them, my thoughts and feelings for him were a bit clearer; hell, I'd missed him terribly. Oscar appeared unannounced fairly regularly at their house. On several occasions we were ready to go out when he arrived and innocently asked: 'may I join you?'

'Of course you may do so, we love your company'.

Oscar coincidentally, appeared at the gatherings we frequented as well. He always talked to me and demonstrated an interest on my wellbeing and how I looked, what I was wearing, the perfume I used that particular day, I didn't mind. The lust and desire were impossible to hide. I wanted him, I missed him; I hadn't had sex for four months and felt a bit horny every time I saw him. He was as handsome as ever and when he looked at me I felt I wanted to feel his embrace, his kisses and his passion once more. On Sunday after lunch Oscar asked me if I wanted to return to the capital with him instead of the next day as it had been planned with Gloria and Amparo.

I said 'yes, it is a good idea. When do we leave?'

He suggested that it would be appropriate to leave around 4pm. We'd only drive half way in the dark. I agreed and began to pack my things, then left with Oscar. Amparo wasn't surprised at all, and in a way she felt elated that her efforts paid off. On the way to the car, he asked me if I would like to spend the afternoon with him.

'Yes, we are driving back, so why wouldn't I be with you?'

Well, Oscar said: 'we could go for a walk along the river bank which has been planted with new tropical trees and grass, apparently it is quite peaceful, and then we could spend the night together before leaving early in the morning. I can't wait anymore. These four days had been hell just wanting you'.

'It seems a great idea', was my response.

We drove to the river bank, the breeze was fresh and the ice cream vendors offered good treats; after a walk admiring the new planting and the embellishment of the area, we went to the hotel. We were a bit sticky after the walk because it had been a hot day. We went straight to the shower and showered together like we always did. As we showered with the droplets falling on my head I lowered myself, and began to kiss his lovely erection. Oscar turned the shower off, lifted and carried me to bed still dripping wet, and we made up for those lonely four months. We continued to have sex until dinner, got dressed and went out to a little restaurant by the river. We began to talk and discussed the sad issues that had separated us. Oscar said: 'I don't understand why you don't want to marry me. You obviously like to be with me. Have you missed me?'

'Yes. It'd been extremely lonely without you. The uncertainty of a life without you made me feel lost. I longed to feel you embrace and your body pressed against mine. I missed your kisses, caresses and your virilis erectus'. We laughed.

'I have missed you too. Very much', he said.

'Have you gone out with someone else?'

'No, I had a great void in my heart; I never thought we would be apart and I still want you to marry me'.

'There're times when is difficult to say what we really feel', I said.

'What is the problem?' Oscar enquired.

'Let's finish dinner, go back to the hotel and I'll give you the response to your question'.

We went back to the hotel, I undressed and dropped on the bed, open my legs and said to Oscar: 'smell me. You are the only man you may be able to smell on me. I never had anybody else and I don't have any interest to be with anybody else either. I loved you, yet I didn't receive the respect I deserved. Your blind jealousy and possessiveness spoiled a wonderful relationship. How can I marry someone who doesn't trust me? It isn't my fault that men look at me; there will be many times in the future when people will look at me for one reason or another, there will be many occasions when men will approach me perhaps to justify their ego or for other reasons unknown to me. This is the way I am, this is the way I look'.

He was silent. After a brief silence he said: 'I understand. Can I make it up to you? I truly love you and I don't want to face life without you'.

'People don't change their personality. We can certainly try, but I feel you will be the same, soon'. We agreed that we would begin to see each other sporadically, no expectations and no demands.

We fell into each other's arms. This was a different beginning and it was absolutely worthwhile to try again. There was plenty of love for Oscar; I couldn't deny that although he had hurt me with his behaviour, I couldn't see myself with anybody else. We had a passionate quickie for the road before a wonderful sunrise illuminated our day.

It pleased me that we'd arrived at a solution, because I had felt really lonely during the time I didn't see Oscar, and it was absolutely true that I never felt the desire to be with anybody else, and on the occasions when men showed an interest in me, I got rather annoyed and rejected them pretty fast.

After a long journey we arrived home to Oscar's apartment and we spent the night together. It was a fantastic night it was as if we hadn't been apart at all. We kissed and embraced with great tenderness and affection, we had sex several times during the night. A new day arrived with a resumed love which we consummated before we parted. Tuesday arrived. We had to go back to work.

I did enjoy my work, but I felt restless; I had the need for a change. I'd been with the company for nearly two years and it was time I tried something else. On my return to work, Gonzalo continued to be a pain. Gosh, I couldn't get rid of him; no matter what I said he still pursued me with his gifts and invitations which I always rejected. It seemed that the more I rejected him, the more tenacity and determination he showed to pursue me. The Gonzalo problem was beginning to annoy me to the point that I discussed it with Isabel. She was a friend of his family and would have a chat with Gonzalo to see if she could convince him to leave me alone.

On the other hand Oscar and I started our casual rendezvous. At work his responsibilities increased which he enjoyed. Oscar went away often for seminars and conferences; before he left the place he called and asked me to see him the next day if his arrival was late at night, and other times I waited for him at his apartment. It didn't matter what I had organized with the girls, I always cancelled just to be with him. They understood that I was in love with Oscar. It didn't matter to them that sometimes I was unreliable.

We spent most weekends together, he took me to lunches and dinners frequently. We went to many parties. The public sex was subdued, but at times we did engage in activities that if we had been found out, it would have been embarrassing for a young promising doctor.

The morning of my birthday Oscar brought me a gold chain with seven pearls in a beautiful arrangement and a gold ring. He arrived early in the morning before I was ready to go to work. I'd just showered when the bell rang, I answered the intercom and he said: 'may I come in?'

'Yes', I said and opened the door.

He entered and quickly closed the door, he pulled the towel away and began to kiss and touch me all over; I just melted. Before long we went to bed. It was absolutely wild, sometimes it happened like that. We were like two desperate people who had never had sex. There was intense love and a powerful desire; when we finished he gave me the presents and put the ring on my left finger.

He wanted to cook dinner for me that night. I had a new dress made, it had buttons at the front and a little belt; the fabric was soft and snugly, it followed the line of the body. In the morning I wore underwear, but as I got ready to meet Oscar I took everything off including the panty hose. I only wore the dress and an overcoat.

I arrived at Oscar's apartment; he greeted me at the door and as usual let his hands walk under my skirt and realized I didn't have anything else under the dress. He unbuttoned it, kissed and caressed me, my dress fell to the floor and he penetrated me as we continued walking towards the bed.

The sex was hot and torrid, Oscar knew how to arouse and make me ready for an orgasm. We'd just finished when the bell rang. There was no time to enjoy the tenderness of the moment. We got up quickly, Oscar got dressed while I just threw my dress on with nothing else underneath. 'Maybe it is a religious group distributing pamphlets', I said.

Oscar answered the intercom, while I dried myself. It was Gloria, Amparo, as well as Amparo's boyfriend. They arrived earlier than expected thinking than I didn't know about the dinner and wanted to help Oscar with the preparations.

Oscar embraced me constantly, and I moved closer to him. While he talked, he put his arm around me and I moved my body to feel his. Just the touch of the fabric against my breast aroused me. I could feel more and more liquid coming out of me; it felt like a constant orgasm, if that was possible.

He had bought a chocolate cake and twenty candles. We had a great dinner, cut the cake and opened the presents. During dinner they kept asking: 'are you ok guys? What is going on? Do you have a surprise for us?'

I showed them the ring and the pearls; they thought I had accepted his marriage proposal. It wasn't that. The energy they felt was our lust and desire to be in each other's arms.

They left around midnight and their departure unleashed that passion which I thought didn't exist anymore. We didn't clear the kitchen or anything else. As they left we thrust into each other's arms and quickly undressed to continue the love making we had started earlier. The passion had returned. My breasts felt swollen with desire, every part of my body wanted to be absolutely possessed by this man who had taught me everything about sex.

It was the best birthday party I ever had. Wild passion woke us up many times during the night. We were drunk with desire and lust. The new day arrived and we had to get up to face work. A long day would follow the previous night.

Oscar called me at work around mid-day to find out how I felt. The office was deserted, so I was able to talk freely. 'All I feel is this tremendous love and desire to be with you, I feel desperate for more, everything is on fire and as I listen to your voice I feel aroused. May I have more?' I said.

'What can I expect?' He responded.

'What do you mean?'

'Will it be honey or something else?'

'What would you like?'

'Surprise me'. I will pick you up at 6.30pm

My work finished at 6pm. Before I left to meet Oscar I went to the bathroom and took off my dress and everything else. One of my birthday presents was a French perfume, Isabel and Nancy had given me. What a great idea to put small amounts of perfume all over and then wear just my overcoat. It was cold, the wind blew under my coat while I waited for him downstairs at the main entrance; it was 6.25 pm. I opened the door. I waited for five long minutes than resembled five hours. Oscar arrived on the dot and I jumped in the car.

He asked if I wanted to go somewhere for a hot chocolate before we went home; we stopped at a popular coffee shop, quite well known for the good quality of its food and the stylish surroundings. While we were waiting to be served, Oscar asked me if I had any surprise for him.

Well, I don't know if this is a surprise at all, I smell really good. I used a bit of the perfume the girls gave me. I then turned sideways, brought myself closer to him so he could smell the perfume, and opened a couple of buttons to show him that it was only skin and perfume under the overcoat.

There were many people waiting to be served and our bodies and desire couldn't wait, so we left. Went straight to his apartment, we had barely closed the door when Oscar was inside me. I asked Oscar why he went wild every time I didn't wear anything under a dress, or he discovered I wasn't wearing underpants.

He said, he didn't know. Perhaps it was a primal instinct that made him feel very aroused every time it happened. We spent another night together, and the next day I had to go to my place early in the morning to get a new outfit. He drove me there, then said that he would like to choose my outfit for the day, we went in and I began to undress while he looked for something for me to wear; I said I am ready and as he turned his head, saw me totally naked on the bed, legs spread and as Clara had told me with all my anatomy exposed; we began to kiss and within minutes we found ourselves making love again.

It was crazy how we felt. Clara was correct once more. There was no shame at all in doing something that in principal appeared vulgar, it was liberating, arousing and certainly increased the pleasure.

Following my birthday we saw each other almost every day for a month. It looked like the love and the passion we had before we broke up had returned. It was scary. I was more involved with Oscar than before we parted. I couldn't say no when he requested that I join him. My body wanted him, I was sexually and emotionally fulfilled, I also enjoyed his company, and I could feel his passion for me. Oscar was thirty years old.

Oscar had been looking for a post graduate course abroad, his intention was to take me with him; although I wanted to go away and see new places I wasn't ready for marriage, but I loved him so intensely that my feeling against marriage didn't make sense. I was twenty years old and a bit.

The end of the year was just around the corner once more, and we planned a holiday in January. We thought it'd be good idea to go to a cold place high up in the Andes, if it was possible to find good accommodation somewhere. It wasn't easy to find something that attracted us, and after many enquires we decided to go to a southern city high up in the Andes Mountains.

I spent time with Papi and Tuni during the Christmas holidays. They told me that Mamá Nena wasn't well. I hadn't seen grandmother or any other family member for three years. I told Papi and Tuni that I would call Mario in the New Year to find out. I contacted Mario on my return. He didn't know either.

Oscar and I left for our holiday before Mario contacted me. We arrived at the southern city which was founded by the Spaniards in 1539. There was a great central plaza with all the important buildings around it. The entire plaza seemed to be paved or concreted and had a couple of trees here and there. We noticed groups of native Indians standing on the plaza, the women wore black skirts and lots of beads around the neck. The small beads were of many colours with a predominant yellow colour. Men and women wore the beads; the women had long hair woven in plaits placed in a semicircle either on top of the head or at the base behind the ears. Their skirts were adorned with ribbon of many colours on the lower edge of the skirt, on top they wore a colourful wool poncho with complex, ancient patterns, and some of them a black bowler hat.

The city was terribly cold and grey, the Andes Mountains dominated the city from every angle with their majestic and imposing height; the snow covered peaks in the distance diffused the sun rays into the atmosphere like sparkling diamonds, while the sun made its brief appearance in the morning until midday, and then the city was covered with a grey mantle of clouds which discharged its contents around 3 o'clock in the afternoon.

Oscar had booked a hotel which in the past, at the time of the Spanish domination, had been the property of an upper class Spaniard. It had a typical Spanish courtyard, red flowers in pots and the obligatory fountain in the middle; all the rooms had timber balconies and elaborate timber balustrades. The room had a ceiling higher than normal, adorned with large chandeliers; it had dark polished timber floors, and several oversized antique furniture pieces. The restaurant served authentic regional food.

The hotel reservation was made under the title Doctor and Señora. It was a very conservative city and we couldn't pass just as lovers; we supposed to be a conventionally married couple, and since he was a doctor of medicine everybody bowed and showed respect. It was interesting to observe the great deference people addressed him with just because he was a doctor of medicine.

The room ambience made us feel as if we were still under Spanish domination, the bed had a wrought iron bed head with swirls and gold painted leaves, it was a bed quite high off the floor with a thick mattress, which reminded me of the merino wool mattress I had when at boarding school; I described it to Oscar in great detail and we both laughed.

There wasn't a great deal to do in this city; the museum and some historic buildings were open in the morning only, everything was closed after lunch and the shops only re-open well after 3pm. Oscar hired a car which arrived with a driver; he felt sorry for the man, perhaps he was expecting to make some money from the tourists. Oscar paid something extra and told him that we preferred the freedom to drive.

We found small villages at the foot of the volcano, green hills and verdant forests, went for walks and followed well-worn ancient paths; as we climbed we could see the high peaks of the Andes with their permanent snow, it was truly spectacular; scattered plants here and there, semi-arid one moment windy and cold the next. We found ancient pathways with big granite boulders on their side but didn't see anybody. 'I am positive there are some natives around here, they are hiding behind the rocks as they've done for centuries'. I said.

When Oscar made the booking he was told that it didn't rain much during that time of the year; we began our drive along a bendy, scary road with the belief that the weather would be fine; all of a sudden the sky opened up with a deluge. It was impossible to continue, it was a dirt road and the surface was like soap, the force of the water combined with the thick fog diminished the visibility to zero. We found a narrow area on the side of the road which permitted us to wait until the rain ceased.

We moved to the back seat, Oscar stretched his legs and I sat against him feeling his embrace. 'Why do you want to marry me, Oscar?'

'The main reason, because I love you. You are beautiful, intelligent and you have a sensuality that drives me crazy'.

'What about if I became ugly, my body becomes pudding shape and my nipples touch the waist, what about if I develop folds around my stomach and legs, my flesh begins to wobble and my body feels clammy and sweaty like an amphibian'.

'That is nonsense! You will never be like that because you know you are beautiful and you are vain'. Let's talk about the things we like. 'We like to be alone, we don't need anybody around us, although, we enjoy other people's company, we like classical music, opera, and art. We both have interest in archaeology, history, psychoanalysis and the most important interest of them all is that we like sex, our bodies are well suited to each other and I fit perfectly into you. You are neat and tidy, and so am I. We both like cooking, the movies, we like walking, and exploring deserted places. You are wild and I adore that characteristic. All those reasons seem to be valid for a life together'.

Let's presume I say yes. 'Do we have to marry at church? Or may we choose another venue?'

'Another venue would be fine with me', Oscar said.

'Why all those questions? Have you changed your mind?'

'My life was truly empty without you and I don't want to experience that again. The passion that drives me to love you makes it impossible to detach myself from the essence of your being. I have a permanent desire to be with you, to be loved by you, for you to possess me, to kiss and caress me; my world is you and without you, how can I exist?'

The rain didn't stop for a long time, either the windows were foggy or the fog had covered the mountain and we were disappearing in it. The day light was diminishing which made us hesitant to drive back along that narrow, slippery road, with deep precipices on one side and a tall mountain on the other.

We had blankets to keep us warm and plenty of food in a basket the hotel had prepared for a picnic. We decided to stay.

This one was an adventure and the back seat was comfortable enough, we didn't have to undress, my skirt had buttons on the front I just unbuttoned it and opened my shirt; Oscar pulled his pants to his ankles and we began to have torrid wonderful sex. We were 2,600 metres above sea level, the heart pumped faster and the moments seemed to last an eternity. We became one body with no beginning and no end, I don't know for how long we lasted. We finished and the harmony of the surrounding landscape with the feeling in my body and heart made me say: 'Yes, Oscar I will marry you, because I love you and because the time we spent apart made me realize that I am a lonely soul without you'. I remained on him, we kissed, and caressed, until he was ready to begin again as we always did.

The rain stopped; it must have been quite late and we managed to go outside for a pee. The fog was very thick, we had something to eat and drink. The proximity made us carry on with the same ardour we had during the previous moments until we finally fell asleep, and woke up when the sun began to display its golden colours and the mountains showed a radiant, emerald green.

It was a magic moment. We embraced again and Oscar said: 'this time we won't do it for the road we will do it to consummate our marriage'. We drove back to the city, went to our hotel and ordered room service which they didn't have. We showered and went to the dining room. We were very hungry.

Luckily we had only booked for a week at this place, in reality there wasn't much to do apart from having sex, and in a hotel with so few guests it appeared that everybody checked the time we went to bed and the time we left the room.

We flew back and had a couple of spare days before returning to work. Oscar wanted me to move with him immediately. I resisted. I had that inner fear that I wouldn't be with him forever.

Once more I felt the need for a change, I liked the office, the work was constant, and in a way secure; I found that security in the work place wasn't important to me; work had to be exciting and interesting as well.

The Gonzalo problem surfaced from time to time, but it was more bearable since Isabel had a chat with him. Gonzalo had become rather nasty sometimes, and when it happened the other architects reprimanded him. Ernesto, who was one of the more senior architects, was quite severe with his reprimands.

I reached a point when I wanted something new and began to look for another job, a good job mainly appeared by word of mouth and I began to enquire. I remembered Leito and her architect friend who she serviced every four weeks. I hadn't spoken to Leito for some months. I called her. She said, she would ask him, but I had to wait four weeks because she'd just seen him for his monthly sojourn, and she never broke the rules.

I had the courage to talk to Ernesto, the senior architect in the office. I told him the reasons for the desired change. He was very understanding and said to keep it quiet, meanwhile he would investigate. I really wanted to work freelance and experience the difference in styles of architecture and office organization I said to him.

Leito was the first contact to call me. She said that her architect friend had given the name Guillermo for me to contact, and that in the meantime he would talk to him; he did, because when I called Guillermo to request an appointment, he already knew about me. Guillermo said that it wasn't necessary to take any samples of my work, because as part of the interview he would give me something to draw to check me out.

Meanwhile, Mario called and gave me bad news. Mamá Nena was in hospital and had to be transferred to the capital for further tests. He said that as soon as he knew the time of her arrival he would contact me. I hadn't seen Mamá Nena for nearly three years already.

I had an interview with Guillermo. He asked me to prepare some sections of a complicated house which had many levels. I finished the task and after he examined my work he said: 'when would you like to start?' He took me by surprise. I told him that I hadn't said anything at the office yet, but I thought I had to give at least four weeks.

'Fine, I will wait for you'. He said.

Ernesto told me that a friend who owned a large company wanted to meet me. He arranged the interview and I went to his office. It was plush and enormous. This man had a fairly large design and construction business, there were around ten architects working for him and other staff members. I told him that I wanted to work on a freelance basis; he liked the idea and asked me when I wanted to start. I was surprised with the response, and hesitated for a moment. I finally responded that perhaps I needed four weeks before I was able to commence the new job.

He said, 'it was fine'.

I returned to the office and told Ernesto how easy it was to get those jobs.

He said: 'you must have used your beauty to impress them'.

'If my beauty can be used as a tool, what is wrong with it?'

'There is nothing wrong with it little girl', he said. Life has given you an extra asset, use it well, at times others may encounter disadvantage because of it, but it isn't your fault, it's how the rest of us react to your beauty and sensuality.

'Oh. I didn't know that', I said feeling a bit embarrassed.

Within a week I received two letters which confirmed my new jobs.

Oscar wanted to get married soon, but I had other things in my mind, like my new jobs, and Mamá Nena's illness. I had been so close to her during my childhood.

Mario called to let me know that Mamá Nena had been transferred to the city hospital and she was undergoing more tests. It appeared to be cancer, but it wasn't known yet how serious it was. Mario gave me the hospital name and her room number. I didn't call. I went straight to see her. She was resting in bed, a bit pale but in good spirits. She asked many questions about my life and the reasons for my departure and my silence.

I told her everything I had found in the books I had read, in relation to the psychology of relationships between mothers and daughters. Mamá Nena didn't believe it to be possible because it was unnatural. She said: 'a mother loves her children, no matter what'.

'Not in this case' I said. Ask mother when you see her. After a long talk I left. I visited Mamá Nena several times but didn't discuss the day I would visit again. When I arrived at the hospital, I always asked at the reception if someone was there, if someone was with her, I left to avoid meeting anybody.

Mamá Nena told me that as soon as she was discharged, she was going on holidays with some friends. She was discharged and she continued her normal life for several months.

My life continued well. I changed my job. I found that to work for Guillermo was fun. Guillermo was a little chubby man, with more hair than stature. He was consumed with the thought of sex, and made me laugh with the things he said because they were so incredibly outrageous.

I worked on most of his projects which were varied and complicated; very complicated indeed. Many times I had to show him that things weren't working on paper, and that I didn't believe things would work on site either. Guillermo was very impractical. He always said that if aesthetically it looked good, it didn't matter if it didn't work. It was mere lunacy.

Guillermo dressed really badly, he wore ill fitted pants, and unbuttoned shirts at the top to show his hairy chest which he considered to be a great turn on, the shirts were also tight around the belly because he thought that those tight shirts made him sexy. He sometimes looked so atrociously untidy that I didn't understand how he managed to maintain such a long list of loyal clients.

He was going to a meeting after morning coffee, which was one of the many duties I had to carry out. I looked at him as he had sips of coffee while he gathered the documents and said: 'please, Guillermo pull up your pants, your underpants are showing holes under the elastic, and you wouldn't want the client to see them'.

He turned around and said to me with a very serious face: 'do you know why I have holes in my underpants?'

'I think you have to buy new ones'. I responded.

'No, you fool. I have holes in my underpants because I think about sex all day long, looking at you and working with you makes me horny and nervous; my balls and my dick are too heavy, my parts feel like are made of cement, and by the time I get home with so many bloody kids there is no time for a screw, and if I screw my wife I may have another kid'. He then left and I was laughing.

Guillermo returned to the office after I left; Oscar came to pick me up that afternoon, he parked the car just in front of the main door. I used to tell Oscar about Guillermo and how crazy he was.

The next day, Guillermo said to me: 'who is that Adonis you left with yesterday? I parked the car then I saw him open the car door for you. My goodness what a stallion you found; you both make a beautiful couple'.

'He is Oscar, my boyfriend. 'He is a doctor of medicine, he finished his studies not long ago and now he is an intern'.

Hundreds of questions followed after my response. I only answered half of them because his questions were all related to sex. At the end he said: 'I bet he wants to marry you'.

'Why do you say that?'

'Ah, I am sure that man has permanent cramps in his dick and every time he sees you he wants to eat you on the spot. You are not only beautiful but you are a hot chick as well. Either you are a difficult chick or you are obliging and every time he wants sex, you have him because you are horny as well. Am I correct?'

'Let me say, you probably have sex three times every time you meet, and sometimes during the weekend you spend the entire day in bed screwing until all your parts are red and worn out'.

'Am I right? Bloody hell! I am salivating, and I will begin to dribble in a minute, and my pants will get stained'.

I just laughed. I found Guillermo irreverent and funny. It was impossible to be offended by his comments and statements, or the manner and the words he used to express his thoughts. He seemed to be an agnostic and the only thing he believed in, was sex. According to Guillermo, sex rocked the world. The biggest problem was that he didn't have enough sex and he felt stiff all the time, perhaps he had to wait for his bloody kids to grow up, and probably by then his dick wouldn't work.

There was another girl working in the office, she had been there for a year. She just rolled her eyes every time Guillermo made comments of this sort.

The news about Mamá Nena wasn't very good. She had to return to hospital because further problems had developed. New tests were carried out, and then it was discovered that she had some voracious cancer already spread all over. She had a further operation, and one of her toes was removed as well as some glands. She improved, but the scars didn't heal properly, and after many visits to hospital she decided to continue her life. Everything was fine until she had to return for further tests. Then the cancer had spread to her liver and lungs, lymph nodes, and the prognosis wasn't good.

I also began my other job, there was discipline in the office; quite different from Guillermo's chaotic business. The work wasn't as varied and refined as the work with Guillermo; it was more a sausage factory of average expensive houses and apartments. Sometimes I was taken to site to check the construction progress, and I truly enjoyed the experience.

Ernesto's architect friend and company owner took me to sites on several occasions; he drove the latest sport Benz on the market. He liked to talk and while we carried out the inspections, he used to show me how to avoid mistakes on the plans and on site.

One day he said I reminded him of a lady he met while he was a student in London. 'I had a torrid affair with her, but she was married at the time to a Lord and didn't want to divorce him to live with a student. I was madly in love with her, but she just had me for sex and was very honest about it; her Lord was impotent and whether he was aware of her sexual escapees, we never discussed. She told me that I would be tired of her as a consequence of the age difference, but I was besotted with that woman; her sophistication and refinement are qualities very few possess. When you mature you will be just like her; beautiful, stylish and sophisticated. You should wear your string of pearls more often'.

'Oh thank you. That is a true compliment'.

Oscar wanted us to get married, and I accepted with the condition that we didn't tell anybody and that we married at a civil ceremony. He said we needed two witnesses.

'Do we have to know the people?'

'Not really', he said.

'Let's marry on your birthday. You'll be twenty one' Oscar said.

'Yes, that is a good idea'.

My birthday was three weeks away. I felt nervous, and Mamá Nena's illness made me feel anxious. Oscar and I got married, the old ring he had given me had a pearl attached to it, and a new ring with little diamonds appeared on my finger. We didn't mention our marriage to a soul, not even to Gloria or Amparo. I moved to Oscar's apartment, the new life didn't seem new, it was a familiar environment and our sex sessions were more torrid and prolonged than before, sometimes it was difficult to stop, the fact that we lived together didn't change anything. We still met for lunch, I still got a taxi while Oscar prepared something to eat, as I arrived he was ready waiting for me, and we began to have sex immediately after I entered the apartment.

We had many invitations to dinners and other social occasions; fairly often we were ready to leave, and Oscar let his hands walk under my skirt to check if I was wearing underpants, most of the time I wasn't. We normally undressed and began to have sex, it was better at home than to look for a corner in a garden; we were late for almost every event.

Oscar didn't tell his family we had married; however, we did visit them some time later. On that occasion Oscar told his family that I was travelling with him and that he would like to introduce me, but nothing else. His mother prepared lunch and invited a girl who she would've liked to marry Oscar. The girl looked like a pudding with wobbly legs, big belly, and her wide, fat waist poured over the side like a soufflé; quite likely when she removed her bra the nipples fell on her waist, and the folds on her stomach looked like an accordion; perhaps her skin was clammy and cold like a reptile.

Oscar's mother candidly and with certain degree of confidence, said that Oscar and whatever her name was were destined to marry, the families had been friends for many years, and it would be a natural development to their friendship.

Oscar looked at me and smiled.

Oscar's father was more in tune with life; he approached me and said almost as if he wanted to apologize for his wife's silliness, 'if I were Oscar I wouldn't let you go. You are truly beautiful'. I mentioned to him that we were mutual friends of Amparo.

Mamá Nena didn't leave the hospital, it was the beginning of September; I visited her several times and decided to tell her I married Oscar in a civil ceremony, but not to tell anybody. It was our secret and I was sharing it with her only. The following time I visited she had a little silver spoon and a rococo porcelain ornament for me. A nurse had bought it for her. The spoon was to be for my first child and the little rococo porcelain chest was for me. It was almost as if she knew her life was going to end soon.

I went back to see her on Friday the following week and she behaved in an strange way; didn't talk much, didn't ask many questions as she normally did, it was almost as if she was tired of life itself. I kissed her goodbye and told her I was coming back, and how lucky I was that never saw any member of the family while I visited her. She died the following Sunday after my last visit. Mario gave me the funeral details; I went to the service and the burial. I made sure to remain in the background because I didn't feel like talking to anybody. Some distant cousins saw me and approached me, but I left quickly before mother or my sisters saw me. I felt very sad and from that moment I began to send her my love every day, and I will continue to do so until the day my brain doesn't function anymore.

Oscar was lovely to me. He was considerate and affectionate. He cuddled me and let me weep without saying a word. Two weeks passed by before I was ready for him, his tenderness and love made me ready; I began to caress and kiss him with the passion that melted our bodies together. Apart from Mamá Nena's death, life continued its course, the world moved on. The jobs I had taken recently were better than when I had started. My relationship with Oscar made my life complete, he also made me a better person; it was the knowledge of that immense love we reciprocated, and the care for each other that made life so enriching.

Christmas came around and as the previous years, it was an extremely busy time for Oscar. I left as late as possible to be with Papi and Tuni. I arrived the day before Christmas, this time I was torn between the love I had for Papi and Tuni and my love and need for Oscar. I liked to be there for him when he arrived exhausted in the early hours of the morning, yet I enjoyed the time spent with Papi and Tuni.

I returned after New Year, it seemed an eternity the time I was away from him. This year we decided to remain in the city. Oscar didn't want to book anything while I grieved for Mamá Nena. It was fine with me. We had two weeks to ourselves before I had to return to work. We explored the city, went to the movies, listened to concerts at the conservatoire of music, went to the art gallery, took short trips away and had picnics under a tree. Every afternoon on our return we had wonderful sex sessions.

His parents announced a visit and we selected a hotel for them. Oscar decided it was time to let them know that we had married. He was certain of their approval, because they would be able to see how close and truly happy we were with each other. I was of the opinion that I shouldn't be involved at all; we could experience a nasty response. My thought was based on his mother's reaction on the previous occasion when I had met her. Oscar insisted, and said that he knew his parents and everything would be fine.

Oscar organized dinner at the finest restaurant the city had to offer; unfortunately, from the moment we arrived Oscar's mother was quite rude to me. She didn't expect to see me, she said, it was a real surprise to her that I turned up with Oscar, and she wanted to know what was going on. The first course hadn't been served and the situation was already unbearable and tense. Oscar's father was polite and on several occasions asked her to mind her words, but she didn't take any notice of him, and continued with her sarcasm and nastiness while he remained silent.

I excused myself, called Oscar away from the table and told him I was leaving, which I did. I left without saying a word to them and felt really terrible, returned to the apartment, had a shower, brushed my hair, daubed some perfumed on my clean skin and went to bed.

It didn't take long for Oscar to return. The whole episode had been a disaster. He managed to tell them that we'd married; instead of accepting the situation, his mother became hysterical. Her great argument was about the embarrassment she would go through, when she told her lifelong friends, who had their hearts set on marrying their daughter to him. So very absurd, it almost sounded like a middle ages novel.

I threw the covers away while he undressed, opened my legs and invited Oscar to possess me, it didn't matter what his mother thought, he was mine, I was his and nothing would change that. 'Come to me my handsome lover, look I am ready for you. Make love to me before I become a pudding with nipples that drop to the waist, and several skin folds on my abdomen appear to make me look like an accordion, and maybe hairs on my nipples will grow as well'. Hurry up! We laughed and began another session of torrid sex; the rest of the world was forgotten in an instant.

Oscar didn't communicate with his parents while they remained in the city, and didn't communicate with them at all during the following months. His father called him to offer an apology for his mother's impossible behaviour, eventually she would come to her senses he told Oscar.

Oscar's reply was as stern as his tone of voice. 'You both insulted my wife, you with your silence and mother with her rudeness; you also have offended me deeply. I have married a great girl, she is not only beautiful, she is intelligent, and we have a degree of compatibility, I have never encountered with anybody else before. She loves me and I love her and that is the end of this matter'. That was the last time Oscar spoke to his father.

Life continued on a positive note and we were truly happy with each other as well as work; our life was well balanced, we enjoyed each other's company, and saw friends from time to time. My birthday arrived. It was a year since we had married, and I turned twenty two that day. 'What would you like for your birthday?' Oscar asked.

'Just love me' I said. His warm passionate embrace was all I needed to feel his love for me.

Wait a minute; I haven't seen Vargas's predictions for a long time. I went to fetch the box where I had the little pieces of paper, I said to Oscar: 'listen to my life predictions made by Vargas when I was just fourteen years old. I wrote everything here. My life has been served on a silver platter, but at the time I couldn't see it. I would eventually find happiness and have everything my heart desires. 'Do you know what hasn't happened? I don't live on an island'.

'Well, we can always fix that', Oscar responded. 'Let's relocate to an island. What do you think about Easter Island? The natives believed it was the navel of the world'.

'Why Easter Island?'

'It is remote, really isolated, wild, and mysterious'.

'What would I do there? You'll always be needed, but I'm superfluous. I could be put in a rocket to the moon and nobody would miss me'.

'I'll miss you and before you are placed in a rocket to the moon, we'll have sex thousands of times'.

Life continued its course. We were happy. I spent time with Isabel, had lunch with her when Oscar was at work, but didn't see Nancy again. Amparo and Gloria continued to appear on the scene. Amparo's boyfriend found someone else and left her. After so many years together, Amparo was lost for a while and cried a lot. She was so heartbroken, and I felt very useless when she began to cry. All I could do was to listen to her sorrow and ask 'why did he leave you?' You looked so happy together, so well suited to each other. It was my only comment.

Gloria didn't complete her university studies, she dropped out at the end of her third year; she went abroad, and the last I heard was that she lived in Italy with an old fellow she met in the last six months; he had a noble title, and apparently owned an ancient castle; those two positive features would've impressed Gloria very much.

Their parents finally separated, the father went to live with the woman he had the affair with. It was an acrimonious separation, lots of bitterness and enormous legal fees.

Papi and Tuni continued their life in the small town where they had moved to, several years before; it was a hot place, although close to the river there was no relief from the heat of the day, and the proximity to the water only brought mosquitoes.

Great grandmother was still with them. Sometimes Papi used to tell me how much Tuni and her mother argued. It drove him insane. I continued to visit them every time I was able to; if Oscar went to conferences I made the effort to spend those days with them. That was the advantage freelance work gave me.

From time to time I did the odd commercial on television. The university dance teacher still had gigs, but Oscar wasn't too keen on my participation, and I finally declined all offers.

Christmas arrived again and this time Oscar didn't work as usual; we were able to take two weeks during the holidays. We decided to drive and see the country; we visited Papi and Tuni on the way to some new archaeological site which was the talk on magazines and newspapers.

The idea to relocate to an island was very much on the agenda; we gathered brochures and enquired at consulates about the possibilities of visa and work prospects. We were determined to pursue it during the first part of the New Year, before Oscar decided to apply for a postgraduate course; with new plans for the future we returned home full of enthusiasm, and very seriously continued to enquire about different aspects of island living.

Why so much sorrow?

It was a morning like other mornings, we were happy to be with each other and as soon as we woke up, kissed, embraced and as usual, had our morning sex. When he got up I said to Oscar: 'Show me your virilis erectus, show me your virilis erectus' and I imitated the construction workers whistles and calls to girls who passed in front of the construction site.

'You are a lunatic', he said affectionately.

Show us your tits the construction workers used to scream, and the screams were followed by loud whistles. So embarrassing!

Oscar said that probably he wouldn't be able to meet me for lunch because he had a late morning meeting.

'Oh well, we will do it three times tonight to make up for the missing entrée lunch'.

'You're a nymphomaniac. If I wasn't a physician, I would have to take you to one, as they used to do in the 15th century, when old men couldn't cope with a sexually demanding wife'.

'What did they do to them?'

'According to the old books and their drawings, it was a rather bizarre technique they used. The physician stimulated the clitoris to make them have an orgasm. Later on, machines were invented with the same purpose, and the physician supervised to make sure that an orgasm occurred every time the machine stimulated the sexual organs. The intent of these sessions was to pacify the sexually demanding wife and minimize the neurasthenia'.

'Oh, well, you have permission to stimulate my organs'.

'You can experiment with gadgets and other paraphernalia at hand, and I will obediently accept any treatment because I am not only your wife, you are also my physician'.

He looked at me, laughed and blew me a kiss.

We left the apartment, he opened the car door for me and I said to Oscar: 'I am so much in love with you I need to know how much you love me'.

He kissed me and said: 'from here to the moon and beyond the last galaxy'. He then left me at Guillermo's office.

It was midday and I received a phone call from the hospital, the person on the other end requested that I leave immediately because Oscar wasn't well. 'He was fine this morning', I said.

I took a taxi and asked the driver to go as fast as possible because my husband wasn't well. He did his best and I arrived at the hospital, entered the reception, identified myself and let the receptionist know the reason for me to be there. A senior doctor approached me and in silence we walked towards one of the intensive care units.

'What is wrong?' I asked.

He explained that Oscar had collapsed that morning, and after the tests, they had discovered it was an aneurism located deep in the motor area of the brain. 'There isn't much we could do at this moment' he added.

We arrived where Oscar was; my healthy beautiful man had no colour. He was absolutely translucent, barely conscious. I kissed him, he recognized me, and then said: 'I am sorry' and closed his eyes.

I cried. My tears dropped on his face as I kissed him.

'Is it painful?' I asked.

'Yes, very uncomfortable'.

'Do you think you will be able to come home soon?'

'I don't think so', he said touching my hand. I put my face close to his and cried my eyes out. He said: 'I love you'. Before I said I love you too I heard a sound like a short breath, he closed his eyes and in an instant my love was gone forever, it was as if he just waited for me to say goodbye. The senior doctor left me in the room while I cried.

He returned to the room and told me that the other doctors would organize everything and I didn't have to worry.

I went home and couldn't think of anything else but my grief. I rested on the bed while a torrent of tears continued to fall; the pain in my heart was so horrendous and the desolation I felt at that moment was devastating. I fell asleep and when I woke up Oscar was standing by the door. He smiled at me and began to walk towards the bed. 'Hello' I said and for a moment I forgot the day's events.

I accepted his death very rationally. I took some of the tranquilizers given to me by the senior doctor while at hospital; then contacted Amparo, as soon as she said hello, I began to cry and couldn't tell her Oscar had died that morning.

She kept on asking: 'what is the matter, please tell me'.

Finally some words came out of my mouth and she said 'she would be with me shortly'.

'No, don't come right now. I took some tranquilizers and it's possible I would fall asleep. Please come later when you finish work'.

Then I thought that I should contact his parents, which I did. Oscar's mother answered the phone. I said good afternoon and identified myself, before I could say anything else, she screamed: 'I don't want to talk to a whore' and hung up.

Well, I thought you can't be angry with me for not trying to let them know that you are gone. I will not try again. They have to find out sooner or later.

A cremation was organized, because I didn't want worms to eat my lovely handsome man. During the service the aria 'L'amour est un oiseou rebelle' from the Opera Carmen was played. I didn't want anybody to say anything. The service was in absolute silence.

Amparo was there for me, I didn't tell anybody else. Amparo was surprised that Oscar's parents didn't come to the funeral, I told her what his mother had done. She said: 'I agree with you; let them find out for themselves'.

Amparo was very kind to me and kept me company, but we had to share the bed, she said it didn't matter. She was there for me. Amparo also called the office to tell them that I wouldn't be able to come to work for a couple of weeks because I wasn't well. After a couple of weeks I felt a bit better and decided to continue with my work. I kept the terribly profound grief to myself.

I thought if I told Guillermo, he probably would try to get onto me. The other office was full of men and I preferred not to say anything. Everybody made comments on how skinny I was and they wanted to know whether I was sick or pregnant. It was difficult to keep the tears away and decided to tell them that my grandmother had died all of a sudden, and that I was very close to her. They all seemed to accept my answer and I wasn't asked anymore. There were days when I felt absolutely awful, and it was difficult to get out of bed, but I forced myself to continue with my work.

Work gave me solace during one of the most difficult periods of my life; the people in the office seemed to accept and understand the moments when I was a bit teary and quiet, they were kind to me, and sometimes even brought me lunch when I didn't feel like going out to buy something to eat.

At that time I saw work as a true distraction from my sorrows; I was involved in interesting projects and as long I didn't have to talk to a client everything was fine.

My decision not to say anything was taken after I read a story in a magazine regarding a woman of about forty five who had lost her husband. He suffered a heart attack. They were members of a posh tennis club and formed part of a large group of people they called friends; they dined and spent lots of time together after the tennis games they played on the weekend. After her husband's death, she became a bit of a recluse and didn't participate in the tennis club activities anymore. The other men's wives kept in contact with her and encouraged her to meet them; finally she was convinced that after six months, she was ready to resume the visits to the club.

She was nervous when she left home; it was the first time after her husband's death that she was going to participate in a tennis game. The game finished and the group proceeded to the dining room for lunch, she was behind the other women feeling sorry, but having been encouraged to participate, she was willing to put herself through it. She was walking when one of the women's husbands slipped the racket handle in between her legs and said: 'I bet you are missing it after six months' and laughed. She was flabbergasted, and couldn't believe the cruelty and crudity of that man, who had been a so called friend for many years.

I could see that if I said anything to the office men, they would ogle at me and perhaps would try to touch me and leave their finger prints all over me. In my imagination I could almost hear the sniggers and the jokes men are capable of. My good friend Amparo was there for me, she was still upset that the boyfriend of many years had left her.

Time went by so very slowly. When I was on my own and sometimes even when Amparo kept me company, I continued to feel Oscar's presence. On several occasions I woke up with a kiss, or I felt him standing by the side of the bed. Amparo was sitting on the sofa while I made dinner, and she saw when Oscar walked across the room towards me.

Amparo went to the movies with a new guy she had met at a night club. I was alone and had pulled the blanket to cover my torso, had just fallen asleep when I felt the blanket removed and a soft touch along my leg. Other times I saw Oscar standing by the bedroom window, I also heard noises similar to footsteps, and I had the impression that the books moved on the shelves.

It was a stormy night. During stormy nights we used to cuddle and talk about all the things we wanted to do. I remembered the storms we experienced the time we had a holiday on the little coral cay in the Caribbean. I began to cry and felt when Oscar entered the room. I stood up and said: 'please don't do this to me'. I was on the bed, closed my eyes and I waited for him to touch me. I felt a soft cold air current just over me, and the door to the apartment sounded as if it had been shut by the wind. I Just cried until I fell asleep; while I was asleep, I had sex with Oscar, it was so vivid that when I woke up he was on top of me and it took me a couple of seconds to realize that it was a dream, but it didn't feel like a dream it felt very real, because I felt his presence in the room.

Amparo was concerned about my wellbeing, and therefore, tried to spend as much time as possible with me, and in many occasions she continued to see Oscar as well.

Guillermo relocated his office and I couldn't walk the distance anymore. I had to catch the bus. It was a clean route that went through nice looking streets adorned with trees and good looking houses. The same people boarded the bus every day, and after a while everybody began to talk to each other. A girl called Rosemary sat next to me almost every day, she was preparing visas to travel abroad, but the friend she had planned to travel with had changed her mind. Since I saw Rosemary almost every day and as I got to know her, it was easy to ask questions related to her intended trip. She intended to travel along the length of the Americas, stop in Japan and continue through Asia towards the South Pacific. From those regions, she wasn't sure where to go, but her intention was to work as she travelled. It sounded quite interesting, and I started to think about it, perhaps this was the opportunity I needed to embrace a much needed change.

My next question to Rosemary was related to the time she intended to leave. It transpired that she wasn't sure because she wanted to obtain as many visas as possible before leaving the country; it was her belief that visas were difficult to obtain in a foreign place. I didn't know anything about it or who to ask for information.

Rosemary was studying computer science, she had a boyfriend who had graduated as an agronomist, but her parents opposed to the relationship, and it appeared that it was the reason for her decision to leave. She seemed to be a nice girl; she talked about her parents and the family frequently, and sometimes we laughed at the same things.

I finally told her about Oscar.

It was November, and five months had passed since Oscar's death. The deep sadness and loneliness hadn't diminished, I still cried a lot and found myself lost, totally lost in a big world. Sometimes I felt as if the energy in my body had completely abandoned me, the grief had squeezed all the essence of my being, and from a state of feeling complete while Oscar was alive, I felt the most incomplete creature on earth. I felt like a butterfly that had lost the colour of her wings.

I saw Papi and Tuni as frequently as possible and their company restored the balance in my life. Strangely enough I tried not to talk about Oscar with them, but I did mention about

Rosemary and her intended trip abroad. Tuni encouraged me to go and see other places as I always wanted to do. Papi was more conservative about it. 'It was a big decision to make' Papi said.

My work continued well, I had good and complex projects which kept my attention away from my grief, but I had lost the will and the interest to live. Soon after Oscar's death I had the telephone disconnected, Amparo had to contact me at work and she didn't mind. The main reason to disconnect the phone was to avoid any contact with Oscar's parents; I wasn't in a condition to take abuse from his mother, and I believed that his father would probably try to make contact once more, and I didn't want to expose myself to further anxiety. Also the lease supposed to terminate sometime in the middle of the first six months the following year. I had to think fast about what to do. I didn't feel comfortable living there anymore.

Oscar's presence was driving me insane. As much as I loved him, missed him and wanted him to be with me, the cool breeze that often passed in front of my face disturbed me greatly. I felt constant movement around the room and that agitated me to the point that I thought I was going mad.

I arrived from work early in the afternoon and as I entered the apartment, Oscar's presence was so strong I decided to do something absolutely crazy. I undressed and totally naked stretched myself on the bed, I closed my eyes and said to Oscar: 'take me like you used to take me, love me in the same way you loved me, let me feel you body pressed against mine, let me feel you are inside me and let's be one like it was before'. Something really strange happened. All of a sudden there was a gust of wind and I felt a cold breeze all over me, then something pressed over my entire body. I couldn't move, I felt as if I was paralysed in an instant. It lasted for several seconds and in the same way it began, it moved away.

I discussed the experience with Amparo, and she thought that it would be prudent to contact a medium to find out if these experiences were part of the normal cycle of grief.

We did contact a medium and made an appointment for 10 am on the following Saturday. Amparo didn't turn up on time, so

I went on my own to the medium's house. I arrived at a house elevated from the street footpath, the house was painted white. I climbed the steep steps from the path and arrived in front of a black door. I rang the bell, I felt very nervous; a rotund man in a black shirt and black pants opened the door. He welcomed me and asked me to enter a narrow corridor with black painted walls and dark timber floor, it was 10am and the lights were on. I followed him to a room where all the walls were painted black; the windows were closed and covered with black curtains. All the lights were on in that room.

He asked me to sit down. I was shaky; he assured me that there was nothing to worry about. He took my hand and began to describe my anxiety and all the multitude of events that had occurred during my childhood. Curiously enough, he asked if I was an orphan. He turned some lights off and lit candles. He recited some strange words and began to call the spirits.

My heart was pumping faster by the minute. Some spirits arrived and he dismissed them, until he called Oscar. He waited for a couple of seconds and began to ask questions.

Oscar was with me all the time. He discovered his spirit hadn't gone through to wherever they go when they leave this world; he had been trapped in the land of the living because of his concern about my wellbeing.

'Do you want me to send him free?' He asked me.

I hesitated, and then asked him to ask Oscar if he wanted to go.

'Oscar didn't want to leave' was his reply. 'He was worried about me'. I didn't want him to leave me either.

'May I call you when I need to talk to you rather than you hovering around me all the time? It spooks me, and I don't like that cold air. What I mean is that you may hover around me, but without the cold air'.

'Sorry' he said.

'I need help about making a decision to go abroad with a girl called Rosemary'. I don't know much about her, but I think she is a good girl.

'Yes, travel abroad. When you are ready everything will fall into place'.

The medium passed cryptic messages from Oscar, there was no way this man would have known about those matters. I asked the medium to ask Oscar if he still loved me.

The medium's answer left me cold and gave me a terrible stomach ache. 'Yes, I love you from here to the moon and beyond the last galaxy'. It was truly bizarre.

The medium asked Oscar to listen to what he had to say and to communicate only if he didn't agree. Oscar was quiet and the medium started to tell my future in more detail. He began to predict my future from the point where Vargas had stopped. He mentioned the various countries I would visit and the island continent where I would live for the rest of my life. He even described where and how I would live, and also mentioned a new man in my life and provided some details.

The island continent had several cities by the sea he said, but when I visited a particular city I would feel happy and comfortable to take residence there; he saw me living in a large house among great big trees that had a perfume, the perfume was like a clean smell. There is a new man and his full name has three initials. You will meet him at a place of work; you will get to know him for a couple of years and then marry him. At that point I interrupted, and reminded him that it was impossible for me to think about those things at the present moment, when grief was consuming my soul.

He continued without batting an eyelash: 'You have a lot of love to give. Live a happy life'.

'It's difficult to see all that from where I am at this moment' I said.

His reply was dry and straight to the point. 'All will happen when you are ready, and there will be signs along the way'.

It was a relief to know that I wasn't going mad. It was real. Oscar was with me all the time. I left the medium's place feeling a lot better, and with a good positive feeling that whatever decision I made, it would be fine. Oscar will be with me, minus the spooky feeling.

I saw Amparo in the afternoon, while we had a coffee I told her what the medium had said. In my opinion, I made the comment to Amparo, reality is so strange at the moment that I can't think straight anymore. The medium did say some things that he didn't have any way of knowing, and that gives me reason to believe that perhaps he is correct in his assumptions about my future. Oscar is going to leave me alone, he isn't going to hover over me as he has been doing since he died, he will be with me and manifest himself when I call him. It sounds better that way, it gives me some confidence that everything will work well.

Amparo decided to continue the relationship with the new guy. However, I wasn't so sure about him; something strange in relation to his behaviour and that disturbed me a great deal, but unfortunately, I couldn't pinpoint what I felt. I told her my feelings about him but she thought he was fine. She dismissed my observation saying that I was supersensitive about everything because of my emotional situation.

Before I communicated to Amparo that perhaps I would travel with the girl I had met on the bus, Amparo had decided that she was going to travel with the new boyfriend. He wanted to go to Europe. 'When will you go?'

'Soon' she said. When I heard her reply I felt sad. I said to Amparo: 'don't go. I don't see you happy and I feel I will never see you again'. It didn't matter what I said, she had made her mind and was determined to go. Amparo visited her parents before she left. On her return she called me to let me know that while at her mother's house, Oscar's mother called. She mentioned that Oscar hadn't contacted them since their visit at the end of the year. Did she know anything about him? His phone had been disconnected and they weren't sure of the hospital's name where he had been practicing.

Amparo's mother suggested she talk to Amparo who had just arrived. Amparo took the phone and answered her questions. She also reminded her that I had called the day Oscar died, and before I was able to say anything, she had called me a whore and hung up the phone. There was silence.

Amparo and her boyfriend left before I made my decision to leave. She had gone for about two months when I saw an article in the newspaper and a photo that seemed to resemble her. I read the article many times because to me it didn't appear to be true. Amparo had been detained in France. The police had been following the guy Amparo was having a relationship with, and called her boyfriend, for quite a long time. He had entered France three times during the last twelve months and drugs appeared to be the reason for the arrest. According to the article, the lovers had rented an apartment in a leafy suburb, and when the police arrived at the apartment, Amparo couldn't explain what the content of the boxes was. The police proceeded to open the boxes and apparently, to Amparo's surprise drugs began to emerge. She claimed her innocence to no avail. The police arrested her. At the time the article was written, it looked like Amparo would receive a very long prison sentence; the police thought that she was aware of her boyfriend's whereabouts and was protecting him. Oh, how sad. My heart shrank.

I didn't see Rosemary for several days. Finally by the end of the week she boarded the bus and sat next to me. She had been sick with the flu and hadn't gone to university.

'Guess what Rosemary? I may be able to travel with you'.

'Are you serious?' She asked with a big smile.

First I have to wait for some money to arrive, then I have to terminate the lease and after that I will be free. I will begin with the vaccinations and the medicals for the visas. You have to give me the list of countries we'll visit. She began to write the countries on a loose page.

I continued to work with Guillermo and the architects while all my documents arrived. Work became a boring routine once again. I worked to keep occupied and not knowing for how long I had to wait for the money it was better to keep at it. Somehow the guys at the office realized that I didn't have anybody to go out with and began to invite me to lunches and parties during the weekend. I turned down every invitation because I couldn't make myself go anywhere, and the thought that maybe inadvertently I let slip that Oscar had died made me feel very insecure. They always said how difficult to please I was. So pretty and so reserved, it didn't make sense to them that I wasn't looking for a boyfriend.

I received a letter, the letter mentioned the completion of all the relevant investigation in relation to Oscar's death, the letter mentioned a large amount of money as payment for Oscar's insurance and other particulars. The money arrived faster than expected. I didn't know how long the visas to various countries would take to obtain, and the apartment lease arrangements just gave me enough time to resolve everything.

I spent Christmas with Papi and Tuni. I told them I was going to travel, but wasn't certain about the time of my departure.

A New Year began, and finally I had a bit of optimism in my life; I had a couple of visas, some more to arrive. Then I thought it was silly to have so many visas because it may not be practical to go to all those places, and things may change along the way. Also it would be possible to acquire visa to other countries while we were tourists, if we couldn't obtain the visa it didn't matter; we were free to go somewhere else.

I discussed it with Rosemary. We agreed to omit some visas and just keep to the essential ones, where we thought it would be fun to stay. The prospect of going away alleviated the tremendous loneliness and sorrow my life was enveloped in. The letters and news that arrived created a distraction, and gave me the strength to pursue a different life. It was very hard to march ahead when I just wanted to curl up in a ball, however, every day arrived with a renewed energy, and happiness began to show its face once more.

Oscar's presence made me feel better. I talked to him regularly, it was weird; I knew Oscar was there next to me, because there was a very gentle breeze that followed me sometimes. Other times I saw a shadow and movement like when someone enters a room silently.

I called him and I felt his presence instantly. I had strange dreams where he stood facing me, answered my questions and cleared doubts that worried my mind. He gave me the answers but he didn't move his lips, it appeared to be more like a mental form of communication; it was similar to when I'd seen spirits in the past. At other times I asked him if he wanted to touch me. Immediately I could almost feel his touch as he hovered over me, when that happened I began to cry.

I didn't want to terminate the lease; if the most important visa didn't arrive I had to find alternative accommodation. I discussed my projects with Isabel she thought it was very exciting. Finally, I had to make a decision about the lease and one of the important visas hadn't arrived. The company didn't want to extend the lease for a short period of time, but they were prepared to accept six months as a minimum commitment which I decided to take, otherwise I would have to move out of there in December. That was a real inconvenience but I took the chance.

I spent my birthday on my own. I turned twenty three. I wasn't on my own really, Oscar kept me company.

The rest of the year continued its march and I didn't receive the important visa. Rosemary had warned me that that visa was the most difficult to obtain. I didn't think it would take so long, but it did. December arrived, just before Christmas I had to vacate the apartment. I sold or gave away everything apart for the few items of jewellery and some of my personal belongings. Free of possessions I decided to spend an extra long holiday with Papi and Tuni before going away. I also called mother to discuss if there was a possibility I could return to her house for a brief period of time before my departure. It would have been better to stay with Saturia, but her apartment was small, and I would've had to sleep on the sofa for the time needed before the visa arrived, and I felt it was an imposition on her.

The decision to call mother was based on my belief that I wouldn't return ever again, and it would be the last time to see her, and make sure that it wasn't me the one with the problem, and after all those years without communication, I expected that perhaps something had changed, and she would accept me since I had proved I didn't represent any threat to her; after my initial enquiry she said to contact her after the holiday, she would think about it. She wasn't sure whether it was wise to have me living there.

On my return from the Christmas holidays I called mother to ask if she had made a decision. She informed me, that she could offer a room at market value, and if I didn't intent to pay for it, to look elsewhere. She was matter of fact and very clear.

I was at Saturia's apartment when I made the phone call, and Saturia overheard the conversation. She looked at me with disbelief. I said to mother that it was fine and that I would arrive on the weekend. I made the wrong decision, it would have been better to sleep on Saturia's sofa.

I arrived at mother's place, the first thing she demanded was to be paid for three weeks in advance, and then continued to outline the rules which I had to follow to avoid problems. I had to be home by 9pm at the latest, including weekends. I was not allowed to go to parties; in the event that I went to a party, I had to sleep somewhere else because the main door was looked at 9pm. 'Fine' I said. I knew it would be for a very short period of time anyway.

It was truly awful to live there. I left in the morning, and arrived around 7pm. Sometimes didn't even have dinner. I went straight to bed and read. Books again were my best companions. The days I didn't work I went to Saturia and helped her finish some of her work. I did hems, fixed buttons and general finishes which I liked. I used to leave Saturia's place to arrive at the same time I arrived from work every weekday. Nobody asked where I had been or what I did during the day. For me it was better to be away from the confines of that awful environment.

I had one weekend day to sort out. I had to be away from that horrible place that was called home; however I still had Sunday. I didn't want to go anywhere; all I wanted was to be left alone which was a very difficult thing to achieve. I began to work at Saturia's on Sunday as well. It was a relief to find something to do. She had lots of datelines to meet and for me was a pleasure to help her. My visa finally arrived, it was February. I called Rosemary with the good news and decided to confirm the departure date for the first week of March.

Mother didn't show any interest in my trip, didn't ask anything related to it, it appeared that she was relieved I was finally leaving. The day I was ready to leave I organized a taxi to take me to the airport. At the very last minute Maximiliano suggested that they would drive me there. He had bought a little present for me. Mother and Maximiliano took me to the airport, we arrived late. The airline had put through the speakers the final call. I said goodbye and started the walk along the international departure lounge with tears in my eyes.

The Oracle

I couldn't understand the reason for the sadness I experienced at that moment; it was as if all of a sudden a range of emotions took possession of me although I was truly happy to leave. The last two months had been difficult to say the least. I finally was getting out of a situation that gave me grief. Papi and Tuni were the big issue for me; I didn't know when I would be able to see them again.

I took my seat on the airplane, it took off and then we had a vague idea how long the flight would take to arrive at our destination. A new stage of my life had just begun, at the time it was impossible to imagine what the future would hold for me. Everything was so uncertain.

My life felt unreal. In such a short period of time so many events had filled my existence. I had experienced a range of emotions, from the university days when I met Amparo and Gloria, and then Amparo's persistence for me to accept Oscar's invitations, and thanks to her I had the most incredible experiences with Oscar.

I learnt about lust, desire, love and complete dedication to another human being; if nobody loved me again I had all those marvellous memories within myself. I had experienced intense love, torrid wonderful sex and most of all a bond that would be with me forever. I had loved Oscar with intense passion and he had returned my love threefold.

There was an enormous amount of grief still within me, the void Oscar left in my life was impossible to fill, fortunately, through my unusual gift, I was able to communicate with him, and I didn't feel alone while I felt his presence. He was always by my side. I knew he protected me with his love.

I survived the early years of boarding school when I was overwhelmed with emotions of sadness, rejection and loneliness, this was another moment in my life when I decided to allow the good and happy memories I had experienced to take me away and to show me a new path. I didn't fight or argue with what life was bringing, I accepted it. I felt like a little insect floating on the waves of a very big ocean.

I thought about the fabulous moments I lived with Oscar, however, the pain I felt was very raw and big tears rolled down my cheeks. I could almost hear his voice telling me that everything would be fine, to take a deep breath and take one day at the time.

The flight seemed quite long and I developed sore throat. We finally arrived at our destination and Rosemary's cousin, Elena was at the airport to pick us up. She took us straight home, we unloaded the few items we had, met the children and the maids.

Elena and her husband appeared fairly affluent, the house was large, had a big garden and a swimming pool. Children were running everywhere. Elena had five children from six months old to nine years of age. Elena looked like the sap had been extracted from her, although a nice looking woman, she appeared absolutely disinterested in her surroundings and the children.

The nanny looked after the children. There was the kitchen maid and the maid who cleaned, ironed and maintained the house in order while Elena painted her finger nails and toe nails.

I met Maurizio her husband, a tall man, he had lost his hair already. I didn't think he was older than forty. Affectionate towards the children but rather cold towards Elena and she was the same towards him. During dinner the children took all the attention and there was no opportunity for anything else. After dinner the children ran wild until they went to bed.

Our intention was to stay with Maurizio and Elena for three weeks, then to continue with our trip. We woke up early next morning to the sound of children running and screaming; it was awful. By the time we got up for breakfast, Maurizio had left for work and the whole house felt like a lunatic asylum. Nobody paid any attention, all those children pushed, screamed and cried.

I said to Rosemary: 'three weeks of this will drive me to insanity'.

There were places to see and museums to visit, but Elena always insisted on taking us to those places, the bad part was that she always had one or two children with her, and without fail we had to leave the museum because of one thing or another.

The first weekend arrived and Maurizio kindly enough thought that he should show us the country side. We left with five children in the jeep, all talked, screamed and fought at the same time, but the adults seemed not to be bothered by it. It was insane! Maurizio and Elena were kind to us and paid for all the expenses, but for us it was really hard to be with such large family. We also noticed Maurizio's poor driving skills when we had several near misses along those narrow, dusty country roads. Somehow he always tried to drive on the wrong side of the road.

We decided that it was better to catch a bus and see the little towns which weren't far away from the city. There was always a market place where the natives showed their beads and beautiful weavings, and we did enjoy our trips minus the children.

Elena painted her finger nails and toe nails constantly, she matched the colour to the dress she wore; the nail painting appeared to be an obsession, and while she painted the nails she also talked on the phone to friends and relatives who lived far away. Every day was the same.

The middle of the second week was the turning point for us, we'd had enough and decided to leave the following Monday. We told Maurizio and Elena that on Saturday, if we woke up before them, we would leave early to catch the bus to a little town that everybody told us not to miss.

We did so. On our return the road was blocked due to an accident, and we were trapped in the traffic for several hours. Finally, it seemed to have been cleared and the bus began to move, it passed the scene of the accident and we noticed children laying on the grassy areas, the children were covered in blood and the jeep was absolutely smashed. Rosemary said 'get out I can see Elena and the children'.

We asked the driver to stop, left the bus and moved towards the children and Elena who appeared to be stunned by the impact. Everybody was bleeding, crying and their garments absolutely stained with blood.

The traffic was congested because whoever passed by stopped to view the accident in more detail, but nobody helped. Finally an ambulance arrived and took everybody to hospital, Maurizio was still unconscious. We had to wait until the next bus passed by and we were able to take it. After many hours of changing buses we finally arrived at the hospital, Maurizio had regained consciousness, didn't appear to have any lacerations but he was kept in hospital for further tests and x rays. Everybody else was able to go home. Not a broken bone not a scratch. The children had bleeding noses because of the impact. The jeep was absolutely destroyed.

Elena was in shock, paler than ever and we had to stay until things returned to normal. Maurizio was discharged from hospital towards the middle of the week, but things didn't get any better. Elena was hysterical. She wanted our company and cried constantly. She was truly desperate to go home. We felt sorry for Elena's condition and decided to stay an extra week. There was nothing we could do; it was more or less up to her to sort out whatever problems she had. Perhaps this was the incident which would force her to make a decision about her marriage and her life; she was obviously dissatisfied with how things were.

We decided to leave when normality returned to the household; children were running out of control, Elena was painting her finger nails and toe nails while she chatted with her friends on the phone.

The next country would be quite a different story. Full of archaeological sites to visit and being a larger country, if we decided to stay perhaps we could find work. We weren't disappointed. We went to see every pyramid and every site of interest. Hanging gardens built many centuries before by an amazingly, developed civilization; beautiful museums and architectural treasures abounded. Towns built by the Spaniards, magnificent churches and buildings absolutely intact, the buildings in perfect condition as they were left when the country found independence. It was magic to see all those treasures.

We experienced three weeks of chaos surrounded by children, so the present circumstances made the days almost too quiet. We travelled as much as possible; Rosemary didn't have any financial problems and every time she needed money she contacted her father, and he happily obliged sending more funds. I didn't have any financial worries either, my bank account was a healthy one and the money would last me some years.

We travelled for several weeks and visited various countries, went everywhere, ate fabulous food. It was time to continue with our trip of exploration. We began the trip to the islands of the Pacific; each island had its own charm, some with large volcanoes and green luxurious mountains that appeared to rise straight from the sea. The islands we visited were surrounded by beautiful turquoise waters, the inhabitants were jolly and friendly people, the food was tasty and abundant, the islands were blessed with great atmosphere; the ambience was so holiday like we didn't feel inclined to look for a job. There were so many things to see and Rosemary, like me loved to explore towns.

Each island was vastly different from the previous one, it was a true paradise. We spent the days either on the beach, or taking the local transport to places where we found a peaceful, beautiful world.

Our trip took us towards the South Pacific, we had left our native land nine months ago, and we had to make a decision where to spend the end of the year. We didn't know anything about that little island we had spotted on the tourist brochures, but we chose to go there out of curiosity. We read that only 300 people resided permanently on the island; the government only allowed 200 tourists at any time mainly to preserve the Island's ecology. Also the accommodation was limited, as we found out on our arrival.

We had the good fortune to buy our air ticket as the quota was almost closing; the transport was a small airplane and for that reason at the airport before the flight, everybody had their personal weight checked and registered in a folder.

We didn't even know the name of this little island, it appeared to be quite close to the mainland because after a two hour flight, we began to see clouds and seconds after the clouds the island appeared, and like an emerald, emerged surrounded by a magnificent light, green blue sea. From the airplane we saw enormous turtles suspended in that glorious coloured liquid. The plane landed, and we saw what appeared to be coconut palms and green pastures, the air was sultry and sticky; however, it didn't have the smell of the tropics, and banana trees weren't visible. Small buses waited for the recent arrivals to transport them to the hotels, there were no other cars on the island. People used bicycles as the form of transport or walked.

We arrived at our destination, an old place. On our way to the room we passed through a bar its front and walls covered with bamboo panels. Ugh! We opened the door to our room it was spacious, basic and full of light, there were two single beds which looked like they had belonged to a hospital at the time of war. Cotton blankets and really old bed side tables not made with real timber, but some sort of plastic finish which imitated timber grain. The room had a wall which separated a pseudo kitchen from the sleeping area; there was a small bench with an electric frying pan and some kitchen utensils. It was good enough for us.

The rooms were arranged on a square around a dilapidated courtyard; the courtyard had a couple of banana plants loaded with ripe fruit. Most of the rooms appeared to be taken by elderly people in pairs, there were some couples and plenty of fat, wrinkled, old ladies who sat on some awful green, plastic chairs drinking tea and talking most of the time.

We changed into our swimmers, and walked straight down the path from our accommodation to one of the many white beaches. Beautiful, clear, warm water, plenty of small, colourful fish wherever we looked. The bird life was equally abundant. We sun-baked and enjoyed the magnificent surroundings; it was like being part of a dream.

The island had a cinema, a shop which opened only a couple of hours in the morning and in the afternoon at 3 o'clock. People just walked everywhere under a canopy of palms without coconuts, the palms were different but that didn't matter, the palms provided shade and a tropical atmosphere; even without the coconuts the palms gave the island that paradise feeling anyway. We went to the shop and found brochures and maps that showed the location of beaches and walks, the vantage point from where to see the turtles and the many birds that called the island home; bought some provisions and went to our room to leave everything in the small fridge, then we left the room to have a hamburger. We followed every walk on the brochure, sat on the grassy areas under a tree to observe the turtles. Several turtles appeared to be suspended with their limbs extended in that clear water, while the birds flew over our heads and played in the thermal winds.

Other afternoons we went to the beach where the fish were fed, large silvery fish nibbled our legs and asked for the food pellets. Colourful big fish came close to our face masks and put their lips on our cheeks, completely relaxed and unafraid of our presence. It was so magic.

'This is paradise. What are we going to do after this week passes?'

'Don't know', Rosemary said.

One thing I am certain of. I don't want to go back to where we come from; I think I found my place, I am almost certain of it. The week just disappeared in front of our eyes. We had experienced a magic environment, and the beauty nature had presented me with began the process of restoring my soul. I cried every night, the silent tears that mourned my Oscar dropped on the pillow while I fell asleep. I could almost hear his voice, good night my love, see you in the morning.

Restless and with the desire to extend our travel experience further, we booked a flight to return to the mainland where we would continue our travel towards the centre of the island continent. We both agreed that would be interesting to travel by road instead of flying, and purchased tickets with a tour company which travelled through main towns and the centre. Some twelve hours after we left the city, red fine soil covered everything, from our eyelashes to the underwear which was packed well inside our luggage.

We arrived at the main destination, walked around a really gigantic rock, observed the surface colour which changed with the time of the day. It was hot at mid-day and cool at night. The vast spaces appeared to merge with the rest of the universe which appeared like a fine line painted on the horizon; the intense heat of the day seemed to bring a strange form of tranquillity.

We left the centre to continue our trip north to a completely different land altogether. Hot, humid and green as if a pot of paint had been dropped, and the rain had taken the task of dissolving the green paint, leaving the odd pond here and there where the calm water reflected the blue sky like a mirror. It was crocodile country we were told. We had never seen a crocodile in real life.

The storm cloud formations were out of this world. Ferocious lightning illuminated a dark grey sky for a couple of seconds, until the next one started a new display of energy, which culminated in a brief interlude, when the sun managed to show it was still there behind the massive grey clouds.

We walked in the rain, climbed rocks and viewed the water beginning to form small lakes where the trees reflected their exuberant green. There were limitations as to where we were allowed to go, the wet as it is called, presents restrictions which humans have to obey.

We travelled towards the sea to view one of the magic wonders of the natural world. It also rained, but the sunny periods were longer, the humidity wasn't as oppressive and it was on the land that had been painted green as I called it. We were able to experience lovely walks on the beach under a curtain of heavy rain.

It was very fortunate that Rosemary and I got along so well, we seemed to like the same things. She was quiet and disliked to call attention, although, she was a good looking girl. She was wise and after so many months together we had very sincere talks; we discussed intimate details, like my relationship with Oscar and the insecurity that his early death had left me with.

Rosemary's kind and supportive words slowly helped to restore my confidence and made me feel better. My emotional recovery started, although at times my intense grief seemed to take hold of me, but at other times it disappeared and I had really good belly laughs.

A decision had to be made because Rosemary's father was getting impatient with her lack of commitment towards her studies. He gave her a dead-line when the money would stop if she didn't matriculate at a college or university. We had to decide where to go next, perhaps rent an apartment and find a job. We flew south again and arrived at a large city, where we found a little place on the top floor of a rather old building, where the ants had a home during the rainy days and marched in big columns towards the sugar bowl. We also had overweight brown cockroaches which roamed every cabinet anytime of the day. The apartment had furniture which made me feel depressed, it was so horrible and dirty I couldn't cope with it. Rosemary didn't seem affected by it as I was.

I suggested to put all that awful furniture in the garage, since we didn't have a car and had no intention of buying one. We went looking for furniture but disagreed a lot. I liked good quality items, while Rosemary was content with cheap stuff, even second hand.

I ended up buying everything. I thought it was better for me to own good quality pieces of furniture. One day I realized I was on an island, well an island continent, in a city by the sea and I liked the city.

Was this the remote land the oracle had predicted through the rotund man, who lived in the house with black walls? Vargas had also mentioned that I would speak another language and that I would live on an island. Was this the one? Although a continent it was an island, far away from my native land.

English was the language. I had to learn it as quickly as possible. It felt as if this place would be my new home. I didn't belong yet, but one day I would.

Rosemary's English was good enough for her to enrol in a computer course, meanwhile I attended adult English classes and I also found a correspondence course which I finished really fast. I wanted to accelerate the learning process and within a short period of time I was able to matriculate at one of the universities in an advanced English course.

On weekends we went to the beach not far from where we lived, a little cove with yellow sand and green clear water, we sat on a fairly remote corner of the beach far away from the crowd, but invariably men appeared and spread their towel nearby, always wanting to talk. Initially they were all ignored, until Rosemary decided it was time to meet some of them.

I didn't agree. I wasn't ready to meet anybody.

Rosemary met a girl while working at a pizza restaurant and they became good friends, the girl was married, but every time the three of us went out she invariably wanted to call attention, either by speaking with a loud voice or laughing quite loudly and then checking if someone was looking at her. I didn't like it. The girl was fine if we were somewhere quiet and no men could be seen. However, Rosemary began to change and when we went to the beach she wanted to call men's attention. The ones who were sitting nearby wanted to talk and asked many questions, wanted to invite us out and then it was me who had to get rid of them. It was Nancy's episode all over again.

Rosemary and I argued about it, and she said, 'it wasn't her who attracted men, it was me with my dismissive and uninterested behaviour; it was as if in the process of trying to repel flies I used honey as a fly repellent'.

'It isn't true' I said. 'I don't want anybody to ask me out and I think all they want is sex'.

Try Rosemary said, 'go to the beach on your own and see if what I have told you is true'.

I did go to the beach on my own, sat on a remote corner not a soul around, just mothers with their babies in the immediate distance. Sure enough within 30 minutes the first man stretched his towel about two metres from me, and the second one and the third one.

I continued reading my magazine and totally ignored them. As they returned from the water they said hello and I had the impression the towels had moved closer to me than when they had left for a swim. How annoying! I left before anybody was able to start a conversation. That was the first excursion on my own.

I decided to try again with exactly the same result. What was the problem? Were my pheromones too high? I'd read that male rats follow the female rat just by the smell she leaves as she moves. Maybe it was the same with men and I had taken the role of the female rat. Sheepishly I apologized to Rosemary, she had been right; it was me.

I was progressing with my English, did a lot of extra work. I needed to become proficient as soon as possible to be able to work. I knew that perhaps the beginning of my working career would be a simple one due to the language barrier; although I could draw, the architectural terms were totally unknown, and after ten months, I was getting bored just being a student.

Rosemary enquired about job prospects for me with someone at work; by then she had a part-time position with a computer programming company. She found out that I could find a job through an agent, so she brought the name of a couple of companies which specialized in contractors for the architectural field and the building industry.

I had an interview and the following week I began a job as a draft-person in a large company. It was truly funny, when I arrived at the office which was full of engineers, the person who greeted me was and old wrinkled lady, her age could have been between a hundred and close to the grave. Grumpy and unfriendly, didn't say a word to me; while she walked in front of me she made some grunting noises and asked me to follow her to the main office.

There was a large space full of drawing boards and the people working were all men; then I followed her towards a small room, she introduced me to my future boss who was sitting in a small, crowded, room with dusty and ugly, brown shelves, also piles of rolled drawings on the floor. She left me there while I introduced myself; after a short introduction, he showed me the drawing board I would use, it was located at the very back of the large room, then proceeded to show me the type of drawings I was to do and in this way I began my new life.

I worked in that office on contract basis for longer than eight months, by then I befriended almost everybody except the old lady who never uttered a word to me. It was time for a holiday and my boss said, that after the holiday I could return to work if I wished.

I went on a holiday to visit Papi and Tuni. Although I wrote to them from every place I visited, I still had many stories to tell about my new life. I spent four weeks with them. I saw Isabel and went out a couple of times with her. I also visited mother for a day or two before leaving, when I arrived at mother's house, I offered to pay her for my lodging, which she accepted. While I was back at her house, I felt like a stranger who was recalling the previous footsteps. I didn't belong there at all and she didn't make me feel welcome.

My roots were with Papi and Tuni, but they had lived their life and I'd just started to live mine. I also visited Isabella, Alcira and the family in the Caribbean. They treated me with great affection. While at Isabella I offered to pay for my lodging, but I unwittingly offended her. Before returning to the island continent I decided to send some postcards, and for some odd reason I thought about my boss. I began to write a postcard which I wasn't able to finish, because my thoughts couldn't be put on paper, perhaps others would read it. It was strange.

I returned to work, after eight weeks away, everybody greeted me with affection and enthusiasm; my boss was especially glad to see me. I noticed that he stood next to my drawing board while revising drawings; something which he didn't do before. He also began to talk to me more often. Some time passed by since my return, and I was going out for lunch to a large department store not far away from the office, when I heard my boss calling. 'Where are you going?' He asked.

I said I was going to the department store to see if there was anything nice to eat at the new coffee shop. He offered to accompany me and I accepted. We looked for a seat near a window, ordered a coffee and a sandwich. We sat and almost immediately my boss told me that he'd missed me during the time I was away, and that he'd often thought of me. The office appeared empty, and fairly frequently people asked about your return, it felt very quiet without you, the others missed you too, he added. But I think I missed you the most.

I told him that I started to write a postcard, but couldn't send it because I didn't want people to know that I thought of him. It was a very personal conversation; it gave me butterflies in my belly. Something had changed and I began to see him differently. The first impression I had of him when I started to work at the office was that he was untidy, messy, and somehow a distant person, not very interested in others, and a bit impersonal, but my view of him seemed different now.

I began to look forward to go to work. I saw him arriving one morning as I walked into the big yard on my way to the office, I felt sickly with stomach ache caused by those unruly butterflies.

My boss stood most of the morning next to my drawing board revising drawings and talking to me. All of a sudden he said that we should go to lunch, I know about a good Greek restaurant. We went to lunch that day, and when we left the restaurant, he kissed me on the cheek and touched my arm in a really affectionate manner.

Following the lunch with my boss I had a very strange dream. I was outside a large room which had big windows on one side and the far end was open; many people stood there talking to each other; they were waiting for something or someone. I looked towards the entry and I was face to face with Oscar who smiled and said, 'he was waiting for his name to be called and then he had to go. He had expected to see me there to say goodbye'.

On my left just behind the large glass windows and on the far open end of the room there was an intense, white, bright light, which my eyes couldn't tolerate; I saw the brightness of the light reflected on the wall behind where Oscar stood. I turned my head and I tried to look directly into the light at the end of the room but I had to close my eyes. While I continued to talk to Oscar, I realized that he looked really well and very handsome; his complexion was radiant and his outfit was immaculately pressed, he looked at me and smiled, then he said: 'my love I have to go my name was called'.

'Please don't go. Where are you going? What do I do without you?'

'Don't worry you will be fine; I am at peace now. There is someone who will look after you'.

His lips didn't move. I understood what he'd said; it was like a mental form of communication. I didn't hear anything. He started to walk away from me, he smiled and moved silently towards the intense light that appeared at the open end of the room, other people moved forward as well, and I stood there without moving, until I saw him disappear beyond a bright mist. I didn't feel sad in my dream, the ambience was peaceful and serene, my dream terminated. I woke up and didn't feel Oscar's presence anymore. I called his name and the cool breeze didn't come either. I closed my eyes to feel his presence, but he was no longer there.

The old lady at the office retired and her replacement was a lovely girl about my age, lively and funny, she energized the office. We used to talk during lunch time and one day she said to me bluntly: 'I think we should do something about it'.

'What do you mean to do about it?' I said.

She was quick to respond. 'You are in love with him and he is in love with you. Let's go out to a disco and then you both can sort it out'. Christine was very perceptive.

She also had a sad story to tell. She'd been engaged and had the date of her wedding organized. Just a month before the wedding the future husband was involved in a car accident and died instantly. She was a broken person for a long period of time; she found help from a couple of counsellors and eventually recovered emotionally.

I never asked her any questions because I knew and understood how painful all that was. She volunteered the information and I just listened. As she told me her story I began to cry, she couldn't understand why I was so emotional. I didn't tell my story.

Christine organized everything for a night out. She brought someone with her. We went out to a restaurant and then to a new disco which was all the rage. About midnight Christine said she had to go and left us alone.

I felt comfortable with my boss, all I recall is that he kissed me and we left the nightclub to spend the night at a nearby hotel. We ended up having sex most of the night; it was tender, almost as if we had known each other forever.

The next morning it was a bit uncomfortable because I thought it would be difficult to work together. I didn't think I could work at the office anymore. I told him. No worries he said. 'As long as you don't tell anybody, there is no reason for people to find out'.

We got up and left after breakfast. Went to the Art Gallery to see a Picasso exhibition, I was very keen to see it, because among the many paintings in the exhibition, one of his most famous paintings on display was 'Les Demoiselles d' Avignon' as well as some paintings from his blue period. We arrived at the gallery before it open and found parking few metres away from the main entry. Unfortunately, I left my overnight bag on the back seat, the car was locked and we entered the gallery. We spent some hours admiring the exhibition, and then went to the coffee shop for a light lunch. While we waited for the order my boss removed his watch and placed it on the table. He placed it upside down and I noticed the engraving had three letters.

'What do the three letters stand for?' I asked.

'Those are my initials, my boss answered. This watch was given to me by my parents when I graduated'.

I felt a chill down my spine. Those were the initials the medium dressed in black, at the black house, had given me. I had to make sure when I returned home that night that those were the initials I had written on the paper.

We left the building and walked towards the car, when we arrived we noticed the door had been forced open, and my overnight bag had been stolen, my beautiful pearl necklace and the ring Oscar had given me on my twentieth birthday in it. I felt so sad.

I told my boss that my precious pearl necklace and ring were in that bag. I have great emotional attachment to those pieces. Those pieces of jewellery were given to me on my twentieth birthday.

What a shame, he said. 'Don't worry about it, you will be able to have many more, and gently patted my bottom, then kissed me with incredible tenderness'.

My boss drove me home, and as soon as I arrived I went straight to look for the notes I had taken after I saw the man dressed in black. Yes, the initials were correct, and this man was the new man in my life as the oracle had predicted.

I understood that Oscar's farewell and the loss of my pearls were connected. Were these the signs that indicated a new life for me? One thing I was certain of, love had returned to my life, and that night I expressed my gratitude to the universe for its generosity.

My boss and I continued to see each other and tried to keep our affair secret from the rest of the people at work. The only one who knew about our relationship was Christine and she kept the secret. It was time for me to leave. I heard one of the guys said to another: 'did you notice how that girl looked at that guy?' 'If someone looked at me like that I would melt, but these cold blooded British descendents are cold like tadpoles in a pond'. I called the agency and they found another contract job for me.

Our love affair continued to develop, and torrid wonderful sex returned into my life; deep emotional love and passion grew as the days passed by. After a year we decided to move together, and ended up purchasing a house, which we transformed into a beautiful villa by the sea, we did plant large trees that gave a clean aroma. We both found happiness. Our relationship consolidated and after two years we got married.

In spite of the difficult circumstances I had encountered while I lived at mother's place, I did contact the family through phone calls and letters, which they did respond during a short period of time, but as the years passed by, silence dominated the relationship that I thought I would be able to maintain since I didn't cause them any harm.

There was a time when some individuals, those ones we call Bible bashers, began to make contact with me and demanded that I respond to their phone calls.

Letters, pamphlets, and books were dropped in the letter box. I couldn't understand where all that came from since I hadn't given my address to anybody connected with that religion.

The communication with the family that until then was fragile suddenly stopped, and I didn't receive letters or cards from anybody within the family. Eventually I received a letter from an old friend of mother's who quite upset about her exclusion after forty years of friendship, complained about the new religion mother had embraced, and the belief that she had to convert everybody around her.

I understood their silence; the new religion was just an excuse the family used to justify their behaviour towards me, and it was also the final confirmation to the findings through the psychoanalysis books. At the age of eleven after my return from boarding school, I had been excluded from the family I was born into. This was the conclusion to what I had always known. I was free of guilt.

My communication with Tuni continued, unfortunately, Papi died soon after I returned to the island continent, and through Tuni I learnt about the treatment she received from the members of the family; it was cruel to treat the family elder in that manner, and she suffered a lot because of it. During our frequent telephone conversations, I used to comfort her, and tried to minimize her sadness by telling her, it was fortunate she didn't have to live with mother.

Mother and the rest of the family stopped communicating with relatives they couldn't convert to their new religion. Tuni, as well as I formed part of the undesirable group who didn't follow their new religious opinions.

My contact with cousin Ye has continued throughout the years and even to this day we communicate regularly. It's so lovely to have that contact which I call my only blood relative in the entire universe.

The oracle was correct and everything has happened as predicted. The accuracy of Vargas's predictions, as well as the man who lived in the house with black painted walls, the medium, had been outstanding.

It is true that my life has presented itself on a silver platter. Papi taught me that there aren't bad moments, there are transition moments, a link between good and brilliant moments; when a transition moment arrives, to say, 'from this moment everything is fine'.

My unusual determination to embrace life changing opportunities has brought great rewards.

www.ingramcontent.com/pod-product-compliance
Lightning Source LLC
Chambersburg PA
CBHW060950120726
47910CB00002B/567